John de Caynoth

THE MANGO MYSTERY

by

John de Caynoth

The Mango Mystery

Published by Claire Lilley Enterprises Limited 2016
www.clairelilley.com

Edited by Claire Lilley

Copyright © 2016 John de Caynoth

All rights reserved.
This book is sold subject to the condition that it shall not, by way of trade or otherwise, be lent, resold, hired out, or otherwise circulated without the publisher's prior consent in any form of binding or cover other that that in which it is published and without a similar condition, including this condition, being imposed on the subsequent publisher.
The moral right of John de Caynoth has been asserted.

ISBN:
ISBN-13: 978-1530600977
ISBN-10: 1530600979

John de Caynoth

Dedication

This book dedicated to Mr. Benson, my English Teacher at Woodcote County Secondary Modern School, more years ago than I care to remember, whose wise words encouraged me to use written English to the best of my ability

Table of Contents

DEDICATION **1**
ACKNOWLEDGMENTS **5**
    Prologue 7
PART 1 .... **9**
LONDON - CHRISTMAS **9**
    CHAPTER 1. JOELLE 9
    2. THE WARNING 12
    CHAPTER 3. THE ENQUIRY 14
    CHAPTER 4. THE SECOND INTERVIEW 16
    CHAPTER 5. THE COMMISSIONER 19
    CHAPTER 6. CROSS EXAMINATION 22
    CHAPTER 7. LONDON 24
    CHAPTER 8. THE EVIDENCE 27
    CHAPTER 9. THE ROW 29
    CHAPTER 10. THE AMERICAN 31
    CHAPTER 11. RECONCILIATION 35

PART 2 .... **37**
AMSTERDAM - SOME MONTHS EARLIER **37**
    CHAPTER 12. DOUGLAS JAY 37
    CHAPTER 13. ARRESTED? 41
    CHAPTER 14. RELEASED 47
    CHAPTER 15. CONFRONTED 50
    CHAPTER 16. DAVID EVANS, SOLICITOR 53
    CHAPTER 17. FOLLOWED 57
    CHAPTER 18. GATWICK AIRPORT 62
    CHAPTER 19. BURGLED 68
    CHAPTER 20. KAETA 72
    CHAPTER 21. NEASDEN 76
    CHAPTER 22. THE MEETING 82

John de Caynoth

Chapter 23. D. S. Derek Passmore 90
Chapter 24. Knock Out 96
Chapter 25. The mobile phone 101
Chapter 26. The Picture 112
Chapter 27. The Prison...................................... 118
Chapter 28. The Confession.............................. 125
Chapter 29. DCI Barbara Green 132
Tuesday *134*
Chapter 30. Threatened 140
Chapter 31. The Private Detective 144
Chapter 32. The First Kiss 152
Chapter 33. Shot 157
Chapter 34. Confidential 162
Chapter 35. The Interview................................ 171
Chapter 36. Summoned to Amsterdam............. 178
Chapter 37. The Button 183
Chapter 38. Bermuda... 190
Chapter 39. The Morgue, Amsterdam.............. 196
Chapter 40. Amsterdam Police Headquarters 202
Chapter 41. Jamboree Club 210
Chapter 42. The Black BMW 216
Chapter 43. The Button 222
Sunday 223
Chapter 44. Monday Night 231
Joelle 231
Chapter 45. The Apartment 237
Chapter 46. The Hangover 244
Chapter 47. The Arrest Warrant 247
Chapter 48. The Russian Woman 251
Chapter 49. On Surveillance............................. 256
Chapter 50. Plan 'A' 263
Chapter 51. Bad Weekend................................. 267
Chapter 52. Identified 271
Chapter 53. The Strange House 279

CHAPTER 54. LONDON 284
CHAPTER 55. THE RESTAURANT INCIDENT 292
CHAPTER 56. TONY'S PHONE CALL 299
CHAPTER 57. DISAPPEARED 305
CHAPTER 58. THE PAPER TRAIL 310
CHAPTER 59. REVEALED 317
CHAPTER 60. THE CONFERENCE CALL 321
CHAPTER 61. THE COMMISSIONER 328
CHAPTER 62. KAETA 332
CHAPTER 63. THE INVESTIGATION 339
CHAPTER 64. STARTING WORK 343
CHAPTER 65. PROGRESS 346
CHAPTER 66. MOUSEY 353
CHAPTER 67. DEATH 356
CHAPTER 68. JASMINE 362
CHAPTER 69. THE ARREST 368
CHAPTER 70. FOUND 379
CHAPTER 71. SOMETHING IMPORTANT 384
CHAPTER 72. GONE 388

EPILOGUE 393
ABOUT THE AUTHOR 395

John de Caynoth

Acknowledgments

Thank you also to the readers of my first book, *The Coconut Affair*, whose kind words gave me sufficient encouragement to write the second, and still to come the third as well, of the turbulent and danger-ridden installments of the lives of Joelle and Douglas. I hope, dear reader, this story lives up to your expectations.

The Mango Mystery

This is a work of fiction, Names, characters, businesses, organisations, places, events and incidents either are the product of the author's imagination or are used fictitiously. Any resemblance to actual persons, living or dead, events or locales is entirely coincidental.

Prologue

The girl lay on the floor of the building. She noticed it smelt of animals, cows, she thought. Her name was Marika van Dam. She wriggled to get more comfortable but that did not work, as she was gagged and bound, hand and foot, and chained to a ring set in the concrete. She had been tortured once, but she was not very brave and had quickly told them everything she new, which, in reality, was not much. She smiled, remembering that she had really upset her captor when she had pulled a button of his jacket and swallowed it. She wondered what they would do with her now. The woman told the man with the black eyes to get rid of her. She doubted that the woman meant for her to be freed.

The Mango Mystery

PART 1

London - Christmas

Chapter 1. Joelle

It is the day after Christmas, Boxing Day, late morning I guess. I don't know because they have taken my watch away. My mind is in a jumble, a chaos of thoughts, making it difficult to understand what is going on. I need to think logically about how I got into this mess, and try to puzzle out what they have found, if I am to stand any chance of giving a coherent and believable explanation. But as I concentrate on one thing, another thought tumbles into my head, confusing any logical thinking.

Life had seemed to be going my way, that is until seven-o-clock this morning.

*

I had been promoted and was working on secondment to a Drug Investigation Unit based in Scotland Yard, London, before returning to the Caribbean island of Kaeta to take over from Bernie Strange when he retired.

Douglas, with whom I had an on-off relationship, came to see me on Christmas Eve and took me to a swanky London Club. I told him he could not drive home that night and offered to put him up on the couch in my flat, and, as neither of us had anything else to do over Christmas, we decided to spend the holiday together. I say holiday, but I had to work Christmas

The Mango Mystery

Day and Douglas offered to prepare a Christmas dinner for when I got home.

Douglas! My thoughts whizzed down another cul-de-sac. He is another problem. I am fond of Douglas, I enjoy his company and value him as a friend, but I can feel he wants more than just a friendship. But, don't get me wrong: if I was going to take a lover it would probably be Douglas, but all my previous relationships have ended with me being hurt and after the row and way we walked out on each other, well, I have be sure I can trust him before I make any commitment.

I pulled my mind back to my current situation.

We had been woken this morning by an insistent ringing of the doorbell. Douglas, who was nearest, had answered the intercom to the flat and I heard him shout 'Go away, we are still asleep!' Next thing I knew, he put his head round the bedroom door and told me I had better get up as a DCI Bob Cash was coming up to see me. I put on my dressing gown and went to meet Bob, my boss, who was standing in the living room with a detective sergeant who I recognised as George, together with a uniformed constable. I was aghast when George cautioned me and told me to get dressed.

They took me to Paddington Green police station, where, on arrival, I was processed like a common criminal and put in a cell. I was not there for long before I was escorted up to an interview room. By this time I was thinking that there must be some mistake: I was expecting an explanation and apology.

Bob and George walked into the interview room but they did not apologise - Bob started questioning me, aggressively. Now, I don't even remember what his questions were, all I can recall is George's closing remark, 'Why don't you just admit you are part of the drug gang and passing them information - it would be much better for you, and then we can all go home. You are going to be charged anyway, with perverting the course of justice and as an accessory to murder.'

2. The Warning

I sat on the cot in the cell and forced myself to think how this had all started. It had to be connected with that investigation, code named Coconut. That had ended up a fiasco, but life for me had returned to normal and I had been working happily in my old job as a Detective Sergeant on the Caribbean Island of Kaeta when one day I received a telephone call from Inspector Willam Ince.

'Joelle?'

'Yes it's me, Willam.'

'This is a private line and we are not being recorded?'

'Yes, it is my home phone line,' I confirmed, thinking this was all a bit cloak and dagger for a telephone conversation. I had spoken with Willam before when we were mopping up after the Coconut investigation collapsed, but he had never sounded this agitated.

'I am sorry about all this secrecy,' he started to tell me, 'but after all that has happened it is better to keep this conversation off the record to protect both of us. I wanted to warn you that there is to be an enquiry into the conduct of police officers during the Coconut investigation.'

'Oh!' I exclaimed, as Willam told me that he had been suspended and Inspector Jan van de Leuven was now running the drug squad in Amsterdam. What really concerned me was that Willam also told me that Tony Choizi, had made accusations of incompetence and possible criminal involvement against both the Dutch and Kaetian Police: it seemed that someone involved with the Coconut investigation had leaked information

John de Caynoth

about the undercover police woman, Marika van Dam, which had resulted in her murder.

The Mango Mystery

Chapter 3. The Enquiry

A month later I received a letter summoning me to Amsterdam: the Commissioner gave me two weeks' special leave to enable me to attend. On the way there, I stopped off to see Douglas. After the Coconut case collapsed, and he was cleared of any criminal involvement, we had become friends and I had not seen him for months since he left Kaeta.

Thinking of Douglas distracted me, but I pulled my line of thought back to the Enquiry and the interviews to see if I could find any clues to what was happening to me now.

The Enquiry was held in the plush wood-panelled conference room on the top floor of the police headquarters building in Amsterdam. On the panel, seated in a line at a table at the far end of the room, was Hoofdcommissaris Van den Peters, the chairman, together with Commissaris Gaelander and Commissaris Van Spaken. I never found out if Commissaris Gaelander disliked women in general, or whether it was just me, but he gave me a hard time in those interviews.

Hoofdcommissaris van den Peters opened my first interview, explaining that the job of this enquiry was to establish if there had been any failure to follow proper procedure, or negligence, on the part of the Dutch Police during the recent drug investigation, code-named Coconut. He noted that there was a separate and on-going investigation into the murder of a policewoman, which, while it may have been connected with the Coconut operation, was not part of this enquiry.

After the preliminaries, establishing who I was and that I had been involved with the Coconut investigation I was asked to explain, in my own words, the surveillance operation carried out on Kaeta last year. That first interview was fairly straight forward, I thought I did okay explaining my role. I sat in the cell racking my brains, wondering if I had said anything that could be construed as improper.

Gaelander had questioned me about delays in submitting reports and who was responsible for sending them to Miami. The only other thing that came to mind was that Van den Peters had expressed surprise that Willam had trusted me with confidential police information when we first met. While I explained why that was and that I had ensured the information was secure on Kaeta, the Panel, concerned about security, adjourned my interview when they decided to send someone to Kaeta to review our security arrangements.

I was told to remain in Amsterdam for a second interview.

Chapter 4. The Second Interview

The second interview took place four days later and it was over that period that the trip to Amsterdam went from bad to worse. The only bright spot was that Douglas, who had also been summoned to attend the enquiry, came to Amsterdam early to stay with me. But even that turned sour after Douglas was arrested for fighting with Tony Choizi, then we had a stupid argument and he walked out on me. At this thought, sitting on the lumpy cot, I lost it and started crying with self-pity, being locked in a police cell and remembering those four terrible days.

I don't know how long I sat in the cell feeling miserable, but eventually I chided myself, *Come on woman get yourself together, the clue you are looking for might be in the second interview.*

That interview was more of a cross examination and I was un-nerved from the beginning by Commissaris Gaelander who sat silently glaring at me.

Van den Peters opened the proceedings by explaining that it was important to identify the source of the leak, which had resulted in the death of Marika van Dam. He asked me again to confirm who I had told about the undercover operation. I repeated my earlier explanation, but Gaelander challenged me as he did not believe I was telling the whole truth. I still remember his words, 'I find it difficult to believe that a woman would not share this information with her lover during the course of pillowtalk. So, young lady, who else did you tell?'

That comment still makes me angry. Of course I denied it, but on reflection I think they must have believed that Douglas and I were in a more intimate relationship than was the case. Van den Peters told me they would be returning to my relationships with my lovers.

Again they went over the preparation and submission of reports and it was Gaelander who let slip that my explanations were in direct contravention of other evidence they had been given.

They accused my of obstructing Tony Choizi's investigation and enticing him to drink, making improper suggestions and trying to seduce him. Despite my denials I think they believed I was having an affair with Douglas all the time he was on Kaeta, and even, God forbid, having an affair with Tony Choizi at the same time.

After lunch, Gaelander had another go at me when I was explaining that I believed drugs had been planted in Douglas's hotel room. He had been making *hrumph* noises and shaking his head all the time I was speaking, and finally burst out, 'This story is a fairy tale and in direct contravention of evidence already presented by Detective Choizi. What qualification does a woman on a remote Caribbean Island have to contradict an experienced senior detective and to question the profile of a drug user?'

I was incensed at this comment, and probably made a mistake in trying to score a point telling them I had doctorate in criminal psychology, but perhaps Gaelander had let slip something important. He had said that my explanations contradicted the statement from Tony Choizi: suddenly a tremor of fear ran down my spine as I remembered what Tony whispered to me just before he tried to rape me.

I sat alone in the cell, feeling very cold, convincing myself that Tony Choizi must be behind all this, but what could I do about it, locked up in a police cell with the threat of being charged as an accessory to murder.

John de Caynoth

Chapter 5. The Commissioner

I lay on the cot in the cell pondering dark thoughts about the enquiry and about Tony Choizi, although I really didn't want to remember what he did to me, and so I went over the events that had brought me London only a month or so ago.

It was November and I remember that the weather was not good on Kaeta. It was windy, with heavy rain clouds blowing over the Island from the Atlantic. That morning we, Bernie and myself, had been called to a meeting in the Commissioner's office. Unlike our offices, which were just pale cream painted walls, with posters Sellotaped to them by way of decoration, his office was colonial in style, with wood-panelling, and a large ceiling fan, which created just enough movement of air to gently rustle the piles of paper sitting on the mahogany sideboard. The Commissioner, himself, sat behind an imposing desk, while in one corner was a beautifully polished oval mahogany table, with six matching carver chairs arranged round it. I smiled as I remembered this room: it was created by my father when he was Commissioner of Police on the Island and had the foresight to buy antique furniture and fittings just after Independence, when many of the old sugar plantations were broken up and contents auctioned off.

The Commissioner spoke in deep mellow tones, with just a hint of a Kaetian accent, which I was always certain he cultivated just to appeal to the electorate.

'Thank you for your time,' he smiled benignly at the pair of us. 'I expect you know that the Enquiry you attended will not be making its conclusions public but, I have been given, personally, a summary of those

The Mango Mystery

conclusions.' he paused for effect before passing round a short document for Bernie and I to read.

The Enquiry panel had reported that they had found no evidence that the Dutch police had failed to follow proper procedure, and although there was a mild criticism of Willam for sharing knowledge of the undercover operation without first clearing it with his senior officer, they commented that they accepted he had been put in a situation that required immediate action as he had been threatened with exposure of information that would have put his operation in jeopardy. I later learnt that Willam had been reinstated and transferred to a new job with the Amsterdam police.

The report went on to say that they were unable to offer the same assurances regarding the operations in Kaeta and Miami, as the police officers concerned had all presented conflicting information.

Bernie had handed the report back to the Commissioner who threw the paper aside, commenting it was rubbish and that he had full confidence in his officers. He looked reflectively at us telling us he had spoken to the Americans who were incensed by the criticism, intending to launch their own investigation. 'I have assured them that they will receive our full co-operation.' he stated, in conclusion.

My concern at this report was soon overtaken by excitement caused by his next proposal. He observed that Bernie would soon be retiring and that he considered that I needed more experience operating at an inspector level if I were to take over the role. He beamed at me as he explained that he had spoken to Chief Superintendent Passmore in London, who had a vacancy for an inspector in one of his serious crime

John de Caynoth

units and would be delighted to offer me the role of acting Detective Inspector on secondment to the Metropolitan Police.

I lay on the cot remembering how thrilled I had been and how my mother, Mary, had encouraged me to go and even Jasmine, my daughter, agreed I should take the role, but secretly did not want me to leave her, and had cried when I actually left for London a week later.

I was still daydreaming about how excited I had been at the opportunity, and how well things had initially gone for me, when I was abruptly returned to the present by the custody sergeant who came to escort me to the interview room.

The Mango Mystery

Chapter 6. Cross Examination

Waiting in the room was DCI Bob Cash and DS George, I never did find out about George, not even his surname. Bob Cash, however, was running the team to which I had been appointed. He was a young, dark haired graduate, who had joined the police on a fast-track promotion scheme and I had been placed in his team as one of two Detective Inspectors running a drug investigation. Ketamine tablets had recently been appearing on the black market in London and Bob thought he was really clever when he gave the investigation the code name *Mango*, as he had said, feeling pleased with himself, it follows on from your previous investigation, *Coconut*.

The two policemen sat silently, George staring at the floor and Bob reading a file. Bob asked me, 'Do you understand why you are here?'

'No,' I replied. Bob said he wanted to ask some questions about the Coconut surveillance and my role in it, and then proceeded to go over the same ground that the Amsterdam Enquiry had covered months previously. He fired questions at me for over three hours going over and over the same points until eventually I became so confused that I started contradicting myself. He openly accused me of passing information to drug smugglers. I denied this and pointed out that he absolutely no evidence on which to base such an accusation.

'Oh, but that is where you wrong, I have all the evidence I need.' He declared smugly.

'What evidence?' I asked.

Bob did not reply directly but told George to take me back to the cell to reflect upon my guilt. I asked

John de Caynoth

George as he escorted me back to the custody suit if I was under arrest.

'Not yet,' he replied and then added, 'Why spin things out like this, Bob will get you eventually, so why not just own up now.'

He handed me over to the custody sergeant who I asked, as he locked the cell door, if I could have something to drink. He paused and looked at me sharply, 'Have you had nothing to eat and drink all day?' he asked.

'Nothing', I told him and heard him mumble, 'bloody Cash!' as he shut the door.

A few minutes later a policewoman, a constable, unlocked the door and came in with a tray. She apologised, telling me that the cell catering was finished for the day but she had got me a ham sandwich and an egg roll with a cup of tea, and a bottle of water, from the canteen. She asked me if I needed anything else, I asked for another blanket.

I sat back down on the cot again and ate, even though I did not feel hungry, but I knew I had to eat to keep my mind alert.

As I ate, I started to think. *What other evidence has Bob cash got, and more to the point, how did he find it?*

The Mango Mystery

Chapter 7. London

He could not have picked up anything from the Coconut surveillance, I reasoned, or he would have charged me by now. Perhaps he has found something that had happened after I started the secondment and moved to London.

When I arrived in London, I firstly met Derek Passmore who introduced me to Bob Cash, on whose team I would be working. Derek told me to take a week off, find somewhere to live, get some transport and familiarise myself with London. Bob took me on an introductory tour of the station and had introduced me to Andrea, who was a short, slightly overweight, blonde, Londoner and she had been made up to an acting sergeant to work with me with me. She was married to Jim, a traffic constable, and knew London like the back of her hand.

Bob Cash explained that ketamine, known as cat valium, was now being sold the on the London black market and, in view of my previous work, I had been given the job of finding out who was supplying it.

I thought about Andrea and wondered if she could have grassed me up somehow, but I could not believe she would do that. She was a lovely lady, about my age, and we got on well together right from the start, becoming good friends. It was Andrea that found the flat in Clapham for me, through one of her many contacts. She said I would need a car but I told her I would rather have a motorbike and told her about the Triumph Thunderbird I rode back in Kaeta.

'Ah! A super-bike!' was all she said, 'I am on the case, I will let you know when I have found one.'

John de Caynoth

She had also invited me to her Docklands flat for a meal, and to meet Jim. *No*, I thought, *I can't believe Andrea would drop me in it, even she found something, she would have told me first.* I turned my mind to the investigation: *Mango*, what a stupid name, I thought.

We set up surveillance on a house in Shepherds Bush on Andrea's suggestion: the word on the street was that it was used for acid parties. We had put a team outside to watch the house for a week, before deciding to raid the building. Under the floor we found a tin containing ten pale cream tablets. 'I recognise those tablets,' I told Andrea, 'I think they are ketamine, but send them to be analysed and tell the lab I want to know who manufactured them and to check if the tin has any finger prints.'

Andrea looked at the tablets and asked, 'How do they use them, they are a bit big to swallow?'

'If they are what I think they are, a veterinary drug, an illegal user would crush them and use them in powder-form. In modest doses, they introduce a dream-like state and cause a lack of physical control: that's why they are used as a date-rape drug. In more heavy doses they cause a severe hallucinatory, out of body illusion, which they call they call the K-Hole.'

'Nasty.' said Andrea.

The four residents were told to dress, and were arrested, and taken to Paddington Green police station. Three of them were just kids, and their stories checked out, so we gave them a stern warning and sent them home. The forth man was older and already known to Andrea as a small time dealer, a nasty piece of work. He even admitted that he did buy drugs, explaining that he was always contacted by phone and never saw the supplier, but was told where to collect them and leave the money. He then denied the pills we found were his and, as we could not prove otherwise, we had to let him go. We also tried to get him on a rape charge as well. He had given the girl some ketamine before she was gang-raped by the three men, but she was so out of her mind at the time that we could not rely on her statement.

The analysis proved that the drugs were ketamine but any identifying marks on the pills had been scraped off. On a hunch, I told Andrea that I thought I knew where they had come from and told her to get a car, as I wanted to go to Crawley to visit VP Ltd, a veterinary drug manufacturing company, with whom I had previous dealings.

We were seen by Mr Herbert, the finance director, and he had confirmed that the pills we found were KetPil and made by his company, agreeing to give us access to his records so that we could identify who were the most prolific buyers of the drug. I left Andrea with his sales desk manager, Jack, to laboriously crawl through invoices while went back to the offices we were using to report to Bob Cash.

I remembered telling Bob that I hoped that Andrea's analysis would show us who had recently started buying drugs in large quantities and that might give us a lead. Bob told me that he required daily written briefings on his desk first thing in the morning and sent me away to write it all down. I also remembered I had spoken to Bernie in Kaeta, who had phoned me to see how I was getting on in London, and he was surprised how much progress I had already made. I must have dropped off to sleep at this point as I was startled awake by the cell door opening and George telling me to wake up.

John de Caynoth

Chapter 8. The Evidence

Bob Cash looked tired, but not as tired as I felt. I was still half-asleep and having trouble concentrating on what Bob was asking. We were back in the interview-room and Bob was asking why had I released the dealer who Andrea and I had arrested in the house raid. He was saying something along the lines of him being '*my dealer*,' and that was why I had let him go.

My brain was slowly coming back into focus, and I looked at Bob in amazement. I told him he had been fully briefed and knew exactly why we had let the dealer go. He moved on, asking me about a vet called Hans Gruber and accusing me of warning him that he was about to be arrested.

Andrea had identified a small animal veterinary practice in Neasden as being a large user of KetPil. This was suspicious as the drug was prescribed as a sedative and relaxant for large animals, rather than small ones, so Andrea and I took a trip over there.

The practice manager confirmed that a locum vet called Hans Gruber had recently joined and used KetPil in large quantities. When we asked to see Mr Gruber, we were told he had walked out a couple of days earlier and not returned and on checking his lodgings we discovered he had disappeared. Bob was telling me that I was the only one who knew in advance that we were to visit the Neasden practice and that I must, therefore, have warned Gruber that he was about to be arrested.

I could not think of an answer and just shook my head, denying the accusation. Bob Cash looked smug again and stood up saying he had other things to attend to, telling George to keep an eye on me as he left the room.

The Mango Mystery

As soon as he had gone George switched off the recorder and said, 'You are in deep trouble Joelle, admit it.' I shook my head and plaintively told George that all I had heard was circumstantial. George moved closer to me in a conspiratorial way and in a low voice said, 'Look Joelle, you are a copper and you know how it works, you don't want to end up in a foreign prison: admit you are passing intelligence to the drug gangs and get sent back to Kaeta for trial. If you don't the Americans and Dutch are after you for attempted murder and drug related crimes. You remember Bob went to Amsterdam before Christmas to attend an evidence review.'

'Yes,' I said, 'I prepared the reports for him to take.'

'Well, the Americans have evidence that the leak came from Kaeta and Tony Choizi says he can prove you were the source. Think about it.' George said as he too left the room.

I was dumfounded and just sat in stunned silence, looking at the motionless constable standing guard by the door.

I don't think I have every felt so lonely and homesick as I felt at that moment. Indeed, I think if Bob Cash had walked in at that moment I would have admitted to anything just to get back to Kaeta.

Chapter 9. The Row

I was too tired and confused to try and think anymore, I just sat miserably in that interview room with sad thoughts tumbling through my mind. One of them was that dam Enquiry. That had started all this, and had finished my relationship with Douglas as well. Oh! How desperately I wished he was with me now.

We had a stupid row. It was after my last Enquiry Panel interview. I had met Bernie in the hotel. He was also in Amsterdam giving evidence to the Enquiry, and on the evening before we were due to fly home I had arranged a dinner for the three of us, not realising that Douglas had planned a romantic dinner for two on the same evening. Douglas was miffed that we had not spent that last night in Amsterdam, just the two of us, was in a bad mood all through the dinner and when I accused him afterwards of spoiling the evening, he accused me of ignoring him and stringing him along. We were both stressed and irritable at the time and had a stupid row which ended up with Douglas telling me that if this was how I was going to treat him he did not know if he wanted to go on, and me replying that if that was how he felt I did not want to continue anyway, and flouncing out of the room.

I heard him to come to my bedroom door in the middle of the night and hoped desperately he would come in and hold me and we could make up, but he didn't, he went back to bed. I did leave him a letter telling him I was sorry and that I loved him, and as he was booked on the same flight as Bernie and myself, I even tried to catch him at Schiphol and Heathrow the next morning, but I think he was ignoring me.

The Mango Mystery

George returned to the interview room and asked me if I was ready to see Bob and make a statement.

'No, I don't believe you have any evidence and are just trying to stitch me up.' I sounded more confident than I felt. George just shrugged and left leaving me alone with the constable again.

I was thinking about George's comment that Tony Choizi said he had evidence, and wondering what Tony had found, when Bob Cash and George came into the room.

'George says you still will not make a statement admitting you were the source of the information the drug gang was receiving,' Cash confronted me. I remained silent.

'Take her back to the cells, we will start again in the morning.' Cash instructed George.

John de Caynoth

Chapter 10. The American

I fell into an unsettled sleep that night, peppered with bad dreams, my mind churning over and over with dark thoughts concerning Tony Choizi.

He had sworn to get even with me over the way I had cornered him over the Coconut investigation and thwarted his efforts to arrest Douglas, and, at first I thought even Tony would not go this far and get me arrested, but, now and after what he did to me in Amsterdam I was not so sure.

It happened on the Saturday evening between my two sessions with the Enquiry Panel. I was in the shower when I heard the phone ring. It was Tony, who said he needed to speak with me. I told him I would meet him in reception in half an hour but as I finished my shower, I heard a knock on the bedroom door. I put on a hotel dressing gown - it was too small for me and very tight across the back and barely decent when I wrapped it round. I vividly remember everything that happened next.

I opened the bedroom door and Tony Chiozi pushed me aside and barged into the room. He eyed me up and down and said, 'No need to dress for me, honey,' coming right up close to me and trying to flick the collar of dressing gown open.

'What do you want Tony?' I asked, pulling the dressing gown round me. I could see his eyes roving up and down my body and I wished I was fully clothed.

'Just renewing old friendships,' he said, 'and I want to know what you said about me in the enquiry.'

'What I said to the enquiry is my business, and I am certainly not discussing it with you. Please leave now, or I will call the porter and have you thrown out.'

The Mango Mystery

He smiled nastily at me, and stood so close I could feel his body pressing against me. He whispered in my ear. '*Revenge.*' I backed of as far as I could but I was trapped as I felt the bottom of the bed against my legs.

I was suddenly woken by someone shouting through the communication hatch in the door, 'Are you okay in there?'
'Just a bad dream,' I called back and the hatch slammed shut. I lay in a muck sweat, calming down after the nightmare remembering what had really happened.
Tony had me trapped against the bed and was saying, 'And how are you going to call for help then? You are stuck with me - I am not letting you go until you tell me what you told the enquiry.' he threatened.
I tried to move to one side but he was a big, fat man and easily blocked me. He stared at me, silently blocking my moves to step around him: the more I tried the more he enjoyed my frustration. I had seen that lustful expression on men's faces before and I was beginning to fear what he might do next.
He just stood in front of me with a wild, excited, look growing in his eyes. For ages he did not say anything, but just staring - looking me up and down as I tried to pull the dressing gown tighter round me. He was frightening me now and I pleaded, 'Please Tony, stand aside and let me go.'
That broke the spell and he growled at me, 'I really should teach you a lesson, bitch, after you stitched me up in Kaeta. You caused all my problems, you know.'

John de Caynoth

I was frozen to the spot, like a rabbit in caught in a car's headlights: suddenly he grabbed the lapels of the dressing gown and pulled it down over my elbows. The robe fell open and my arms were trapped at my sides by the collar pulling tight across my back. As I struggled to free my arms Tony started to undo his trouser-belt and unzip his fly. I could see he was aroused and I knew what he wanted. My fear turned to anger as pushed me backwards onto the bed and jumped heavily on top of me, knocking my breath away. I struggled but I was crushed under his weight. He must have been well over one hundred kilograms and I was unable to move as I lay there helplessly.

I felt him press himself against me as I made a huge effort to throw him off but I could not, and heard him say, 'Go on, struggle, its more fun like that.' I felt him pushing his knee between my legs trying to force them apart but now, though still angry, I felt icily calm as my training kicked in.

I remembered the retired policewoman who told us, if you find yourself being physically and sexually attacked, stay calm and go for the groin, sooner or later they all expose it.

So I waited until I could feel my right leg close to Tony's crotch as he forced his right knee further between my legs. He shifted his weight slightly to one side as he tried to force my legs further apart, and then I used all my strength to jerk my right leg up. I caught him in the groin with my thigh, not really very hard, but enough to make him yelp, throwing him off-balance, giving me a split second to push him to one side and scramble off the bed as he rolled on to the floor.

The Mango Mystery

I ran to the door, wrenching it open, and ran down the corridor hoping he would not follow me, but there was no around to help and I just sank to floor crying.

John de Caynoth

Chapter 11. Reconciliation

After re-living Tony's attempted rape I lay on my cot, shivering, missing Douglas, recalling how comforting it would be to be held in his arms right now, and wondering what was going to happen in the morning. I thought that if anything good emerges from this situation it at least has made me realise that Douglas does mean something to me.

After the row with Douglas in Amsterdam, I had gone back to Kaeta and we had lost touch. It was one of those situations where the longer you leave it before making contact the harder it gets to take the first step. Happily though when I moved to London, Douglas contacted me and suggested we meet.

He wrote me a very sweet letter, I still carry it round and can remember the exact words,

My Dear Joelle
I hope you will read this letter and not instantly tear it up, although, after the way I have behaved, I would not blame you if you did.
I am writing to you now because I realise what a stupid, self-pitying, fool I have been for the last three months. My behaviour that night in Amsterdam was crass and selfish and I am truly sorry for the way I treated you and that stupid and unnecessary row. You had the courage to apologise to me in you letter but in my haste to get to the airport and see you, I just put the letter in my bag and never opened it until now. So, all this time I have been nursing the thought that, as couple, we were finished. Your letter gives me hope that we may be able to find some way of getting together again, and I truly hope it is now not

The Mango Mystery

too late for me to say how sorry I am for the way I treated you, and ask for a second chance.
    Please, please accept my love,

Douglas

    I was not sure if it was a good idea to meet him: I was afraid of being hurt again and was uncertain about his motives, but Andrea persuaded me I should arrange to see him in a London Pub and take it from there. We started seeing each other again, with Douglas inviting me down to Wiltshire to spend Christmas with him, but as I had to work he had come up to London to see me. *I wonder what he is doing now?* I thought, as I drifted off to sleep again.

I was woken by the cell door clanging open as George marched in telling me to get up. I felt dirty and dishevelled as I followed him upstairs. 'Where are we going?' I asked.

'I have been told to take you the canteen for some thing to eat and then take you to the interview room.'

'What is happening?'

'I don't know.' George replied. 'Bob is reviewing the evidence with Chief Superintendent Passmore now, so I expect they will charge you.

Part 2

Amsterdam - some months earlier

Chapter 12. Douglas Jay

The morning after Joelle and I had the argument reception handed me a note from her, scribbled on the back of an envelope, telling me I had a seat booked on a flight leaving for Heathrow later that morning. I looked at the time and realised I could just make the flight if I rushed. I hoped I might catch Joelle, maybe even sit next to her on the plane, giving me the opportunity to apologise and make up. In the event, I was not sitting next her: I did see her at the back of the plane but she was not looking at me, and when we disembarked at Heathrow I got entangled with a queue of passengers arriving on a Jumbo jet, although I dawdled hoping so catch Joelle, I missed her and assumed she did not want to see me.

I thought about her a lot over the following weeks, I even considered contacting her, but what would I have said? She was the one who had actually walked out and I reasoned that if she had changed her mind she would contact me.

I was lonely and with Joelle out of my life I decided to contact Jean Handley with whom I had a brief holiday affair on Kaeta. That was a mistake, it just made realise how little I had in common with Jean and how much I missed Joelle. I even took Edith Meadows out to dinner once, but that was an even bigger mistake. Good neighbour she might be, but spending an evening

The Mango Mystery

listening to stories about her horse and village gossip was tedious to the extreme.

I was pleasantly surprised one morning to receive an email from Jasmine. Since I had left Kaeta, Jasmine and I had exchanged a few emails, mainly about Joelle's old Austin Princess, which Jasmine and I had started to restore, and I assumed this email was to do with that. But I was wrong and when I opened it I read,

Hi Douglas,

I know it is not my place to interfere, but I shall anyway because I love you both. Mum is in England now. She has been seconded to the Met. to work on another drug investigation and I would like you to keep an eye on her for me. She is living in London and the address is Flat 6, Park House, North Side, Clapham Common. Mum says that is the posh side of the common.

Love Jasmine

I liked Jasmine and we had become friends, and I smiled as I thought that she was a cunning little madam, she had put me in a position where I could hardly refuse to contact Joelle.

My dark mood had lightened. I had an excuse now. Since we broke up, I had thought a lot about the argument and now I could not even really remember what we rowed about. Thinking about things now I remembered the note Joelle had left me. In my rush to catch the flight I had slipped it into a pocket on my travel-case and forgotten it was there. I remembered the note was scribbled on the back of an/ envelope which I had never even opened.

I found the envelope exactly where I pushed it in my haste. I paused, looking at Joelle's writing and remembering her. I read the note about the flight and, on turning the envelope over, noticed she had addressed it to Douglas Jay, underlined. I hesitated before I opened it. I was expecting a note inside telling me she was returning to Kaeta and would not be seeing me again, and I was not sure I wanted to read that. Perhaps it would be better to reply to Jasmine that things were finished between Joelle and I, and that it was best for us all to just get on with our lives. That was not I really wanted to do though. Jasmine had been, still was, my friend, and I owed it to her to at least contact Joelle. I tore open the envelope and read the note inside:

Dear Douglas
Goodbye.

I am truly sorry we ended this way and even though you think I was pushing you away I was not really. To push you away is the last thing I would do. Your friendship, truthfully, is one of the best things that ever happened to me, and I had hoped that when this drug thing was behind us we could have built our friendship into something more permanent.

I wish you all the best for the future and perhaps one day you will come to Kaeta again, and well....I shall miss you.

Goodbye
All my love
Joelle

I read Joelle's letter, and then I read it again, carefully, and then I re-read it and studied those last three words for ages with my eyes filling with tears. What a fool I had been. Why had I not opened the note at the time? I could have caught her at Heathrow if I had really tried, instead of feeling sorry for myself. What would she be thinking, having left me that note and then getting no response: was it too late now?

I had to force myself away from this mental self-flagellation to think what to do. If I had her phone number I could telephone her. But what would I say; 'Hi Joelle, it's Douglas, would you like to meet me for a drink?' or 'Hi Joelle, it's Douglas. Shall we pick up again where we left off in Amsterdam?' No, that approach would not do at all.

Then I thought of Jasmine's email. She had given me the lead by only giving me Joelle's address. I would write her letter, apologise for my behaviour and ask her to meet me.

John de Caynoth

Chapter 13. Arrested?

Douglas

After my letter, Joelle did telephone me and we arranged to meet in a London pub. Since then we have kept in touch and met each other as often as possible. Joelle had to work on Christmas day so I came up to London on Christmas Eve to take her out and she invited me to stay in her flat and spend Christmas with her.

Today, I am sitting in the flat alone.

After I watched her leave with the police yesterday I sat in a state of shock wondering what to do. I did asked Bob Cash if they were arresting her and he told me they were not, she was just needed to help with enquiries at the moment.

I comforted myself that if she was just helping answer some questions she would be back by lunch time, so I just sat in the flat waiting for her, not worrying too much.

But by lunch time she had not returned and I phoned Andrea to tell her what had happened, and as she had invited both Joelle and I over for a dinner I warned her we might be late. I asked Andrea if she new what was going on and she answered that she had not got a clue but it was probably to do with the investigation she and Joelle were working on.

'Don't worry,' she said, 'something new will have come up which Joelle needs to deal with - perhaps they have arrested someone and she is tied up with an interview. She might be delayed, but I am sure she will phone you when she gets a chance. '

The Mango Mystery

By midnight I had still heard nothing and I was seriously worried that something had happened to her. Eventually I fell asleep on the couch and I woke in the early hours of this morning, stiff and cramped. I had a shower and changed my clothes and sat in the kitchen nursing a coffee, considering what I should do.

I decided first to phone the police station, but was told Joelle was not available. I asked where she was and was told that she was assisting with enquiries and, no, I could not speak to her. I asked for DCI Cash but was told he was not available either. So in desperation I asked to speak to someone who could tell me what was going on. Eventually I was connected with the Duty Officer at Paddington Green who would not tell me anything other than Miss deNouvelas was assisting with enquiries.

At this point, despite the early hour, I decided to ring Andrea again and ask she if she could help. She just said it sounded ominous and she would see what she could find out and ring me back. Ten minutes later she called back saying that she had not been able to speak to anyone concerned with Joelle, and that all she was told was that Joelle was helping with enquiries. I was getting nowhere and decided to get a taxi to Paddington Green Police Station.

I walked in and asked to see Joelle deNouvelas. The constable behind the desk shuffled nervously and went off to find his sergeant. He returned saying he nothing of Joelle deNouvelas.

'I know she is here somewhere and I am not leaving until I have seen her.' I said. All this did was summon a sergeant out from the back somewhere. 'Miss deNouvelas is helping with enquiries and you cannot see her.' he explained. 'I suggest you go home and wait there until the matter is sorted out.'

I hung around the Police Station for a while but I was pointedly ignored. I know what I will do I thought, I will phone Derek Passmore and see if he can help. He is in charge of this lot so he should know what is going on.

Joelle had told me that he had given her his telephone number and told her she could phone him anytime if she needed help. I headed back to flat to find the number. It was in her address book on the bedside table. I dialled his mobile hoping he would answer.

'Passmore,' I heard after a couple of rings.

'DS Passmore, we have not spoken before, and I am sorry to bother you so early in the morning, but I am Douglas Jay, a friend of Joelle de Nouvelas, and I am very worried about her. She left home very early yesterday morning with DCI Cash, a sergeant and two constables, she was cautioned and then taken to Paddington Green to answer some questions, and I have not heard from her since. All I am told is that she is helping with enquiries but no one will tell me what is going on. Can you help me?'

'Mr Jay, I know who you are and I am sorry, I can't help you. I know nothing at all about this but thank you for contacting me.'

'Would you be able to find out what is going on and let me know?' I asked.

'I will certainly find out what is going on and make sure someone gives you some explanation' He replied guardedly, and then said goodbye and hung up.

I next rang Andrea again to see if she had managed to find out any more. Once again I was stunned when she said, 'I went into the office after I spoke to you earlier to see if I could find out what was going on. When I got there nobody seemed to know anything, so I was making some calls when Bob Cash appeared and told me that serious allegations had been made regarding Joelle's conduct and, as I had worked with her, I was suspended pending investigations.'

I was now very worried. Joelle was obviously in some sort of trouble and I was desperately wondering what I could do. I told myself to calm down and start thinking. Had she said anything to me that might give me a clue to what was going on?

She had spoken about discrepancies between her recollection of events on Kaeta and what was on the US Drug Enforcement Agency files. Could this be something to do with the Kaeta investigation? I tried to phone Bernie Strange to see if he knew what was going on. I got his answerphone and left a message telling him Joelle had been detained for questioning and I needed to speak with him.

I was staring at my mobile phone, willing it to ring, and when it did and I nearly fell off the chair with surprise. It was Joelle and she sounded exhausted. 'Douglas,' she said 'I am sorry I could not ring you before but I have been sitting in a cell and interview room now for over twenty four hours trying to answer questions.'

'What is going on Joelle? Are you in trouble?' I asked.

'I just wanted to let you know where I was and that I am basically okay, but, yes, to your second question. I can not really talk now - I am in the restaurant and there are a lot of people around.'

'Have you been arrested for something?' I asked.
'No, not yet. I am voluntarily helping with enquiries.'

John de Caynoth

I detected a note of sarcasm in that answer. I next asked if I could do anything.

'Yes, when you get chance, go and find Mary and ask her for my file containing my diary and some notes, the one I gave her. She will know what you mean. I am sorry I must go now, and I don't know when I will be home,' and with that, she rang off.

I phoned Derek Passmore again. 'Mr Jay,' he answered 'I thought I might hear from you again soon.'

'Were you able to find out what is going on?' I asked him bluntly.

'Indeed I have,' he replied 'I am, at this very moment, sitting with DCI Cash discussing the problem.'

'Well, can you tell me what the problem is?

'Not specifically, I am afraid it is a confidential matter at the moment. What I can tell you is that Joelle has been very helpful and is free to leave at any time.'

I heard someone in the background exclaim that they could not let her go she might disappear, before the line went dead for a few seconds as the microphone was turned off. When Derek Passmore spoke again he said, 'Sorry about that. Joelle will be home soon. I am going to drive her myself. Is there anything more I can help you with?'

Yes, I thought there certainly is, and asked him, 'Can you recommend a good solicitor in case Joelle needs one sometime soon?'

To my surprise he immediately answered, 'Yes, I think that would be a very wise move. I can recommend you contact Mr David Evans from Benson, Dodd, Sugar. He is very experienced in handling this sort of matter.' And he gave me a phone number before he hung up.

The Mango Mystery

I was relieved Joelle was on her way home and I went to her bedroom and waited, looking out of the window. It took over an hour before I spotted a dark grey Audi crossing from the opposite carriageway to stop on the wrong side of the road in front of the flats. Joelle climb out and paused, speaking to the driver before she shut the passenger door and the Audi pulled out and accelerated away back across road. Joelle stood in the road watching the Audi drive away for a few moments before she walked slowly towards the pavement. It was at that moment I saw a black Range Rover accelerate hard across the road towards Joelle. I thought she jumped aside before I saw her fall on to the pavement. I ran out of the flat and down to her with the dreadful thought that she had been badly hurt.

John de Caynoth

Chapter 14. Released

Joelle

I was sitting in an unmarked grey Audi with Derek Passmore driving. There had been an accident south of the River Thames, just behind Waterloo Station, and as a result the traffic had tailed back on all the bridges in the area. It was impossible to get over Westminster Bridge so Derek had gone another way. Lambeth Bridge was similarly congested and Derek had weaved his way through side streets to get to Vauxhall Bridge. We were now sitting in traffic waiting to cross the river.

Derek was explaining the evidence, which appeared to implicate me in the illegal ketamine drug affair. 'I have had a look at Bob Cash's notes from the meeting in Amsterdam,' he was saying, 'and looking at what was said in yesterday's interview with you, and it appears to me that the evidence they are relying on is circumstantial.'

He turned his head and smiled at me, 'It is like a re-run of your investigation into Douglas Jay except you are in the frame this time. Jay is very worried about you, by the way.' He continued, 'I am sure you will understand that we have to be very through in a case like this so, I am afraid, I shall have to suspend you and hand all the evidence over to the Police Investigations Division to consider. I also have to ask that you stay in London during the suspension and be available to assist with further questions.'

After what I had been through over the last twenty-four hours I had expected to be arrested, so suspension was a bit of a relief. I least I would be in my

The Mango Mystery

own flat, but I was still very worried and homesick for Kaeta.

My mind turned to the last twenty-four hours and I tried to piece together the evidence of my guilt that Bob was relying upon.

He had been concerned with the drugs planted in Douglas's hotel safe and had accused me, 'From the evidence, it appears that you were the only one with access to that room and safe, and must have planted those drugs on you first visit to the room after Jay's accident, in order that you could find them later when you searched the room.'

I told him that was pure supposition and was untrue. He moved on and asked me to confirm that I was in a relationship with Douglas and then said,

'Detective Choizi believes you built a case against Douglas Jay in order to deflect attention away from your illegal activities. At some point you then became romantically involved with him and had to find a way to destroy the evidence you had earlier constructed against him, in order to prove his innocence. You were able to do that quite easily, because you knew who you were looking for and how the smuggling was carried out.'

He looked at me with a smug expression and again I was shocked at the way the evidence was twisted to fit but, at least, I knew that Tony Choizi was at the root of the accusations, and I remembered his threat.

In one of the later interviews he accused me of passing on details of a Dutch, undercover police operation to discover how ketamine was being smuggled on to the black market through Cordite Vets, stating that I was the only possible source of that information to the drug gang. But, looking back, I think the final straw was the disappearance of the vet Hans

John de Caynoth

Gruber, and Bob stated that only Andrea and I knew we were going to visit Neasden and it had to one of us who warned Gruber. He was not very pleased when I reminded him he also knew and had the incident in writing in one of the daily reports.

It was while I was sitting in the restaurant with George that Derek Passmore walked in, looking for me. I had asked George if I could borrow his phone as I wanted to tell Douglas where I was: I had just handed the phone back, and was sitting staring mindlessly into my second coffee when Derek Passmore approached. Here it comes, I had thought, he is going to charge me, but instead he said he had come to drive me home. 'Easier to talk in the car rather than here,' he explained.

I sat in the car listening to Derek as he explained I was to be suspended but it was warm, I was sleepy, and I nodded off only to awake suddenly when Derek pulled across the road and told me we were back at the flat. I opened the passenger door, still half asleep, and as got out I leaned back into the car and said to Derek,

'I am innocent of all this you know. I would never get involved with illegal drugs and betray colleagues.'

'I believe you,' Derek replied, 'but accusations have been made and we need to go through the correct processes now.'

I shut the car door and watched Derek drive off wondering what would happen next. As I started to walk towards the flat I heard a car engine roaring somewhere behind me and, acting on instinct, threw my self to the side of the road.

Chapter 15. Confronted

Douglas

When I saw Joelle sprawled across the pavement yesterday morning I had run out to the road, fearing that she had been hit by the Range Rover. When I reached her, Joelle was just picking her self up and looking a bit shaken and dazed. I rushed over to help her and asked if she was okay. Luckily she had managed to jump out of the way of the car and had only a few grazes on her hand and knee where she had tripped over the curbstone, landing on the pavement.

I had insisted on calling the police as, to me, it looked like a deliberate attempt to run Joelle down. A couple of uniformed constables presented themselves later on Sunday afternoon. They wanted a statement from Joelle, so I had to wake her as she had gone to bed more or less as soon as she got back to the flat. She told them she had heard a vehicle engine revving behind her and just jumped. She had not seen the driver or the vehicle. They were very sceptical about it being a deliberate attempt to run Joelle down, and said that it was probably a accidental incident and Joelle, being stressed at the time had over reacted. Of course, I had challenged this and told them I seen the whole thing and the Range Rover had clearly deliberately swung across the road and driven at her. Having looked out of the window, they disregarded saying that my vision was obscured by trees, and the perspective from the window would have distorted my view. 'Rubbish!' I exclaimed, as they turned their backs, pretending not to hear my exclamation as they left.

John de Caynoth

The day after the incident Joelle was very tired, so we did not do anything much, but I did persuaded her that we should take a walk across Clapham Common to the pub on the other side and have a Sunday lunch there.

We had just returned to the flat in the afternoon when Andrea and Jim called by to see Joelle. Andrea told Joelle that she had also been suspended and Joelle briefly explained to Andrea what had happened at Paddington Green and why, she assumed, she had been suspended. Andrea turned to Jim, 'Jim, tell Joelle what you heard.'

Jim started his story, 'The gossip is that Superintendent Passmore steamed into the station looking for DCI Cash. Well, he found him and took him into one of the offices. Those offices are not really soundproof and voices were raised. My mate told me that they could hear every word that was said. Anyway, Passmore was furious, and demanded to know why DCI Cash had acted without consulting him first. He told Cash he had acted improperly and failed to observe basic procedures. He should never have arrested you, he should have turned all the information he had over to Police Investigations, but first he should have consulted him, DS Passmore.

Cash tried to defend himself by saying he had not arrested you, and that you came in of your own free will. He had been told by the American Detective, Tony Choizi, that you were the drug-gang mole, and that, if you were brought in for questioning, you would collapse and admit guilt.

DS Passmore, was furious and asked Cash, 'Since when did the British Police take instructions from the Americans?' He called Cash a fool and asked him why

The Mango Mystery

he had cautioned you before asking any questions. 'That is tantamount to arrest,' he told Cash, and he said that a good solicitor would make mincemeat out of him. Passmore then told Cash he could be suspended as well if things got too hot. In the mean time Passmore instructed Cash to keep right away from you, Joelle, and everything to do with your suspension. And he then stormed out.'

'Ain't that good,' gloated Andrea, 'I never liked Cash anyway, he is just a jumped up university boy.'

Joelle looked a little more sanguine and said, 'Yes, but it does not help me, I am still suspended and under suspicion, and while I think I know why, I don't know what evidence they think they have found. I can't even try and help myself as I have been told to stay in London and they have taken my passport.'

This conversation brought us round to David Evans and I explained that I was trying to contact him and arrange a meeting and I was sure he would be able to advise us what to do.

'I have heard of him - he supposed to be very good.' Andrea assured Joelle.

John de Caynoth

Chapter 16. David Evans, Solicitor

Douglas

The next day I telephoned David Evans and asked him if he could advise us and, if necessary, act for Joelle. He asked me to briefly explain the situation and then suggested that we visit his offices that afternoon.

And, so it is now 2.00pm on Tuesday afternoon and Joelle and I are sitting in the reception area of the offices of Benson, Dodd, Sugar waiting to see David Evans.

I suppose I had expected to find Benson, Dodd, Sugar in an old Victorian building, reeking of dust and old manuscripts, with David Evans an elderly stooped gentleman in a faded black suit and wing collar. Nothing could be further from the truth. Their offices were on the eleventh floor of a new glass and steel, fifteen-storey building near Victoria Station. The reception was minimally, but tastefully, furnished with abstract art paintings on the wall facing a large glass window. Black leather armchairs were arranged around a coffee table with copies of the Financial Times displayed. On another wall a television was showing Sky news. A receptionist sat behind a modern black-ash counter and offered us coffee from an Expresso machine in the corner. She explained that normally they had two receptionists on duty but, as it was still the Christmas holidays, they only had a skeleton-staff working.

A young man approached us and introduced himself as Jason Manners, assistant to David Evans. He led us into meeting room 3, and offered tea or coffee

The Mango Mystery

and biscuits and said that Mr Evans would join us shortly.

When he entered the room, David Evans was one of those people who give a first impression of competence and confidence. A man in his early forties, I guessed, smartly dressed in a dark grey pinstripe suit and blue shirt. We sat down round the table and introduced ourselves. David Evans, 'Please call me David', shook our hands and got straight down to business by asking Joelle to explain in detail everything that had happened.

'Try to remember everything they asked you about, and what answers you gave.' he instructed Joelle.

It took Joelle about an hour to go through the recent events. David, himself, scribbled on his pad and I noticed that Jason was keeping detailed notes as well. David tapped his pen on his bottom lip and contemplated his pad thoughtfully before saying, 'This is all very irregular. If necessary, I am sure we could successfully argue that you were improperly arrested and that proper procedures were not followed: you were not allowed a phone call and were detained, without charge, for over twenty-four hours. We can then discount anything that was said in that interview. However, we will save that for when, and if, it is needed. From what you have said, they do not appear to have any real evidence and are working from circumstantial evidence and supposition. I will ask for sight of the evidence they have, even though I am sure they won't let me have it at this stage.'

He went on to say, 'As DS Passmore explained, I expect that what will happen now is that the accusation and evidence files will be passed to an independent police force for investigation. You will remain on suspension pending their conclusion. I doubt you will hear anything more for about three weeks. No one will do anything until after the New Year and then it will take them a week or two to go through the files. At that point, I expect you will be interviewed again. Let me know when, and I will attend with you. Refuse to answer any questions unless I am present,'

He paused for thought again, 'In any event, I think our strategy will be to say nothing until we know what evidence they have against you.'

The Mango Mystery

We more or less finished the meeting at that point and David gave us his personal card with a mobile number telling us to contact him any time, day or night. Before we left, I asked him about what I saw as a deliberate attempt to run Joelle down. His advice was to say nothing about it at the moment, as it could be misconstrued as a further indication of guilt. I had not thought of this but as David said, the only reason why someone would want to run Joelle over was because they believe she knows something and they want rid of her before she can tell.

'Well that is very likely to be true, given her involvement in earlier investigations,' I commented.

David replied, 'Yes, but it could be interpreted as she is a member of the drug gang and needs to be silenced.'

On the way back to the flat we went over the interview together. Joelle was feeling frustrated that there was nothing she could do help prove her innocence and, as she said, 'Tony Choizi is behind this and for what ever reason he is out to get me and there is nothing I can do because I am stuck here in London.'

'Yes,' I said, 'but I am not stuck in London and there is something I can do. You mentioned a file that Mary has. My starting point is to go to Kaeta and get that file and see where it leads.'

John de Caynoth

Chapter 17. Followed

Joelle

'Right,' Douglas looked at me, 'I am logging onto the computer to find a flight out to Keata. I will go and see Mary and get that file you say she has, and then we can see if it contains anything to helps us. I will also try and find out what Tony Choizi was up to when he was on the Island and perhaps we can piece together what evidence they think they have against you.'

Still watching me, Douglas asked, 'What are you thinking?'

'They are working on the assumption that it was me who was passing information to the drug gang. If we could find who it really was, that would go a long way to proving my innocence.' I continued, pensively, ' I never trusted Tony Choizi, but I never found any actual evidence that he was bent. He did once say to me, when you were under investigation last year, that it did not matter whether you were guilty or innocent, he just needed someone to arrest to take back to Miami to earn his gold star.'

'Do you really think he could be the informer?' Douglas questioned.

'I don't know. He was certainly knew most of what was going on, but the only thing is, he did not know about the undercover police officer working in the veterinary practice in Holland so it could not have been him who grassed her up.'

'Perhaps he found out somehow,' Douglas speculated.

'Maybe.' I replied doubtfully.

The Mango Mystery

I watched Douglas log on to Google and look for flights to Kaeta. British Airways and Virgin Atlantic operated flights to the Caribbean and Douglas hunted through their web sites, looking for a seat.

'The soonest I can get there is on a direct Virgin flight out of Gatwick next Sunday morning,' he said. 'There is a Premium Economy seat available going out and I can get a First Class seat on the return flight a week later. Shall I book it?' he asked me. 'Will you be okay on your own for a week?'

'Of course I will be okay on my own. Book it,' I replied.

He tapped away on the lap top for a few minutes and then, putting his credit card back in his wallet, turned and said, 'That's all organised then. What shall we do for the next few days?' and answering his own question, 'Let's go down to Wiltshire. The pub is organising a fancy dress party for New Years Eve. We could go to that; it will be much more fun that sitting here, brooding.'

I agreed but pointed out I had been told to stay in London.

'I am sure they will not mind you going to Wiltshire just as long as they know where to find you,' Douglas said confidently, 'I will contact Passmore and tell him.'

Meanwhile, I phoned Mary to tell her Douglas was coming. She was delighted and insisted that she would meet him at the airport and that he should stay with her and Jasmine. She was disappointed that I would not be with Douglas but I side stepped the explanation by telling her I had to work and Douglas would explain all when he arrived.

John de Caynoth

On Thursday morning, New Years Eve, I insisted we did not leave until the shops were open. I had remembered a florist shop on the way to the tube station, which sold a variety of different-coloured feathers, used in flower arranging, and I wanted to buy some to make a fancy dress costume. I was thinking of a "bird of paradise."

It was while I was in the shop that Douglas first noticed the man, and then saw him again after we had boarded the train. 'That's a coincidence,' Douglas said, as he pointed out
the man to me, 'I think that man walking up the carriage was behind us in Clapham, looking in a news agent's window while you were buying your feathers.' I looked carefully at the man but did not recognise him. He walked right through our carriage and into the next one.

We left the train at Chippenham and found a taxi to take us to Stratton Avonhead and Douglas's cottage. Edith had left the heating on, but the cottage smelt musty and while I opened the windows to let some air circulate, Douglas checked his answerphone messages. Most were mundane, wishing seasonal greetings. There was one from his ex-wife asking him to contact her urgently.

'I don't want to talk to her,' he muttered as he deleted the message.

There was also a message from Jean Handley. 'I am home from my travels,' the answerphone said, 'I thought I might come down to Wiltshire for a few days before going back to work in January. Ring me and we can arrange something.'

The Mango Mystery

I flashed my eyes at Douglas, 'That's the woman you met in Kaeta last year. I thought you said there was nothing between you!' I accused him.

'There isn't.'

'Well it doesn't sound like it to me. Why is she ringing you up and inviting herself down to stay with you in a very familiar way?'

'She is not inviting herself down. She asked me to ring her.'

'Why would she do that if there was nothing going on?'

'Honestly Joelle, I promise there is nothing on between me and Jean Handley and I have no intention of phoning her back.'

'Look, I am not stupid. She clearly thinks there is something between you or she would not leave a phone message like that. You had better tell me the truth or I am going back to London.'

He answered, 'After we split up in Amsterdam back in the summer I felt lonely and I met Jean on one occasion only. It was not a great success and we had very little in common. I swear I have made no effort to contact her again since.'

I looked into Douglas's eyes and hoped he was telling me the truth. I decided to give him the benefit of doubt when he put his arms round me and whispered,

'Joelle, its you I love and want to be with.'

******

The fancy dress party was okay, but I did not really enjoy it. For a start I did not know anybody and I was worrying about my suspension, but what really spoilt the evening was when the landlord took Douglas on one side and pointed out a stranger sitting alone in a corner of the bar watching us. He was dark-skinned, with jet-black hair, sporting stubble and very dark, brooding eyes. 'He was asking after you earlier wanting to know where you lived and he sounded foreign,' we were told.

He was the same man we had seen at Clapham, and then again on the train.

Chapter 18. Gatwick Airport

Douglas
  Joelle and I left home at 5am on Sunday morning. I wanted to be at the airport in good time, as I hate having to rush to catch a flight. We were using my BMW: Joelle was going to drive me to Gatwick Airport to catch the plane to Kaeta, and then drive back to her flat.

  We were just joining the M3 motorway when Joelle commented, 'I might be paranoid, but I think that car behind has been following us since we left the village. He's stayed right with us up the duel carriage way, speeding up when I went faster, and he slows down when I do'.

  I turned around to look, but as it was still dark all I could see were car headlights. As the traffic built up on the motorway, it became more difficult to see if we were being followed or not. As Joelle signalled to take the exit off the motorway towards Gatwick airport, so did the car behind, following us directly into the short-term car park. As we parked, the lighting was not good and I could not identify the driver.

  I took my wheelie bag out of the boot and Joelle locked the car. We made our way to the lifts and then through the connecting corridors into the departures area, continually looking round to see if we were being followed.

  'Why would anyone want to follow us?'

  It was a rhetorical question but Joelle answered, 'It must be something to do with this drug business and the leaking of information to the gang, but what they want, I don't know.'

'Perhaps it is the police following you to see if they can find something.'

'Unlikely,' Joelle considered, 'if it was the police they would be much more subtle in their technique but in any event I don't think an internal investigation would work that way.'

I thought of a far more alarming possibility. 'It could be the drug smugglers then, but why are they watching you? And don't forget, someone tried to run you down; it must be all connected somehow. Please be careful Joelle, it looks as if someone is out to get you.'

Joelle thought about this for a moment, 'It does not make sense. If someone is trying to hurt me or worse they have had plenty of opportunity since the incident outside my flat but nothing has happened except the appearance of this dark man.'

By this time we were in the departure area. I had already received my boarding card on-line, but I needed to check-in my bag for loading. I got to the front of the luggage check-in queue, looking round for anyone suspicious. Joelle spotted a person in a hoodie lurking by a pillar near the check-in area but he had moved on by the time I had turned around.

As we stood on the escalator, leading to the departure gate and security check. Joelle standing behind me, took one last look round the hall and then pulled my arm urgently, saying, 'Douglas, quickly, look there he is.'

A man, wearing a dark fleece with the hood partly up round his neck, was asking the check-in clerk something and pointing in our direction. Joelle had the quick presence of mind to pull out her phone and take a picture as we disappeared from view, onto the floor above.

'I think I got him,' she said looking at the screen, 'He has dark hair: he could be the man asking about us in Stratton Avonhead. I will get this picture cleaned up and hopefully it will be good enough to identify him and check if he is on any police files.'

We waited for fifteen minutes or so but he didn't come after us.

'I had better go through now,' I said to Joelle and we stood hugging each other, both worrying about each other's safety and telling each other to be careful. I kissed Joelle on the cheek and finally broke away, heading to the security check.

I thought a lot during the eight-hour flight about the current predicament and what I could do to help Joelle counter the accusations against her; I thought about the pair of us together. I also thought about Joelle's mother, Mary and her daughter Jasmine.

I mentally catalogued all that I knew about the drug smuggling and leakage of the investigation to the smugglers and came to the conclusion that it was not really much at all. Someone was worried about what Joelle knew, or what they thought she knew, in view of the attempt to run her down, and the dark man following us. I was inclined to agree with Joelle that it was not the police, which left the smuggling gang - here I was inclined to concur with David Evans' speculation - did she know something which could identify them, but what?

John de Caynoth

Joelle had told me that the USDEA reports covering the investigation on Kaeta were much-edited versions of the reports Joelle had submitted to Bernie. It might be a clue if I can find out who did that editing. I remembered Joelle had also told me that Bernie was the Drugs Enforcement Officer for Kaeta. I made a mental note to talk with him.

I also knew that Joelle thought that Tony Choizi was behind this whole business and he had told DCI Cash that he believed Joelle to be the drug gang mole. I needed to find the evidence he claims to have, I concluded.

My thoughts turned to rather more personal matters as I reflected upon my relationship with Joelle, Mary and Jasmine. I recognised that, for me, Joelle was becoming someone very special, but I was not sure of her feelings. Of late, she had certainly seemed to return my affection but I knew from experience that she could quickly change and become distant. Take things slowly, I thought. Lets get through the current problems and accusations first. As for Mary and Jasmine, I thought ruefully, but with some affection, that they were kindest people I had met for a long time and, since my close family had all passed away, the nearest thing to a family I have now. This led me to the thought that perhaps I should settle in Kaeta. With my redundancy and bonus payments and the money I had made from selling my shares in VP, I had more than enough money to buy a property on the Island, while retaining my cottage in England, and supporting myself without having to work. As a white man settling in a predominately black community the transition might be difficult but, if it did not work out, at least I would have somewhere in the UK to return to.

The Mango Mystery

I knew we were near Kaeta, the captain had announced that he had started our decent, but I was unable to see out of the window as I was sitting in the centre of the aircraft. We landed and, after a short wait, disembarked from the aircraft. I followed the passengers ahead of me across the tarmac into the arrivals building. The heat felt very intense, especially after the cold winter I had left behind, remembering the last time I was here, when I was detained by immigration and had met Joelle for the first time.

On this occasion I was passed quickly through the arrival hall. I fought my way through the noisy, crowded, baggage retrieval hall and found my bag amongst others, stacked in a corner. I cleared customs and made way into the sunlight. Outside it was even more crowded and confused with holidaymakers looking for their tour representatives, taxi drivers and porters jostling for business. At first I could not see Mary, but she saw me first and sailed through the crowd towards me. She gave me a big hug welcoming me to the Island and telling me how pleased she was to see me again. Jasmine, standing behind her, rather more shyly, also hugged me and asked how I was.

We drove back to 'Windrush', Mary's home, on St Martin's point with its views across St Martin's bay and the Caribbean Sea. It was a large five-bedroom villa built by Mary's late husband, just after the Island gained independence, and was set in an acre of gardens in what was now one of the most desirable and expensive parts of the Island.

As we drove Mary wanted to know all about Joelle and the trouble she was in. When I explained,

John de Caynoth

Mary was outraged and exclaimed that we had to do something to help her.

'That's why I am here,' was my response, 'you have a file that Joelle gave you for safe keeping. It may give us a clue to what is going on.'

'That's a coincidence,' Mary replied, 'only a couple of days ago Bernie Strange called into the bar to ask if I knew where Joelle had left her personal diary. Of course, I told him I did not know what he was talking about. Joelle told me not to tell anyone about her diary and notes and not to give it to anyone unless she was in trouble. I suppose I should ask her what do with it now.'

I assured Mary that Joelle had asked me to collect the file, but suggested that we ring Joelle and Mary talk to her if it would make her feel more comfortable about giving it to me.

We soon got that sorted out and I was sitting in the study at 'Windrush', reading Joelle's file, when Jasmine walked in.

'What is the matter, Jasmine?' I asked.

'Will mother go to prison?' she asked me, a worried look on her face.

'No, of course not,' I replied with rather more confidence than I actually had, 'we will find out what is going on and prove that she is innocent.'

Jasmine regarded me seriously for a moment and whispered, 'You will work it out won't you, Douglas?'

She left the room before I could say anymore.

The Mango Mystery

Chapter 19. Burgled

Joelle

After I left Douglas, the rest of Sunday was uneventful. I hung about at the airport for some time to see if I could spot the dark man and I also prowled around the car park looking for the car that had followed us in. I had noted that it was a red Peugeot 208 but not seen its registration number. After a frustrating hour spent looking, I found neither the man nor the car so decided it was time to head back to Clapham. I reached the flat, apparently without being followed and there was no sign of anyone hanging around the flat or immediate area.

I began to think I was imagining things and that I was not being followed at all, but such hopes were soon dispelled. Although I was suspended from duty, no one had said that I could not go into the Yard and, as I wanted to process the picture I had taken of the dark man, I decided to call into base to use their equipment and see if I could identify him.

It was an unpleasant, cold damp morning so I decided to take the tube to Westminster. Although I did not see the dark man following me from the flat, I did spot him on the platform at Clapham North just as the train pulled in. I also spotted him getting off the train after me at St James's Park and following me to the Scotland Yard. As I got nearer to the building, I was very tempted to accost him and ask him why he was following me. I turned and walked towards him but he ducked into Caxton Street and down an alley on to Victoria Street, disappearing into the crowd.

John de Caynoth

In the office, I grabbed one of the computers and downloaded the picture from my phone. I used the photo enhancement software to zoom into a close-up of the dark man's face. It was not brilliant but good enough to see his features. This had taken me about fifteen minutes and during that time no one had challenged me. In fact one of my colleagues, an enthusiastic biker himself, had come over and said 'hello', and asked what I was doing. I explained that I was processing a picture of a man I thought was following me. He raised his eyebrows and told me to be careful and returned to his own workstation. I was just sending the picture to the printer to make half dozen copies when I spotted George, marching across the room towards me looking very angry. He told me I was on suspension and not allowed anywhere near the office, and demanded I leave immediately. He then looked to see what I was doing on the computer: when I explained that I thought I was being followed, he looked sceptical but when I told him about the Range Rover incident, he became more interested and studied the picture properly.

'I think I should report this,' he told me, as he saved a copy of the picture I had just processed, and continued, 'You must leave now Joelle, and please don't come back until we have cleared this matter up.'

I collected my coat and bag and walked out past the printer, picking up my pictures as I left.

I stood in the street feeling rather uncomfortable at being thrown out, realising that I missed Douglas, wondering what he was doing, and trying to decide what I should do next. The idea of going back to the

The Mango Mystery

flat and sitting on my own did not appeal so I rang Andrea to see what she was doing.

'Nothing love' she said, 'come over for lunch and a chat.'

'This is the picture of the man who was following us,' I told Andrea as I pushed one of

the A4 size prints of his face across the table. Unfortunately I did not get time to look for a match on file before George caught me and threw me out.'

'Leave it with me, I'll give it to Jim and see if he can find a match.' Andrea offered.

I spent the rest of the day with Andrea. We speculated why someone would want to run me down and then follow me. Andrea thought there was something odd about that behaviour and speculated, 'If they tried to run you down about ten days ago, why have they not tried again, but just followed you instead? Let's assume they really intended to run over you to kill you and silence you because you know something that would lead to them. Perhaps they now think you have something they want, and they are following you, waiting for a chance to get it.'

'Well, that might explain why they are following me but I have not got anything they could possibly want.' I replied.

Andrea asked about Douglas, which led to Andrea asking, 'You are really quite fond of him aren't you?' I agreed and told her about our few days in Wiltshire over the New Year.

I was getting ready to go back to the flat by late afternoon when Andrea asked me what I was doing tomorrow.

John de Caynoth

'Nothing really,' I replied.

'I have an idea that might help us find out who had tipped Gruber off,' she said, excitedly.

'Go on.' I was curious.

'Lets go and see the vet in Neasden and ask if they know how Gruber was warned about us visiting. I will come over to you and we can use your car. We only have one vehicle, and Jim is using it tomorrow.'

I walked back across the edge of Clapham Common feeling positive. At least I had something to do that might help. I reached the flat and went to unlock the street door but I did not need to, as someone had broken the lock. It was a fairly flimsy lock anyway and it had obviously been forced, splitting the frame. There was a note on the wall beside the door saying it had been reported to the landlord. Someone had lost their key, I assumed. I went up to my flat. Funny, I thought, as the door swung open to my touch, I could have sworn I locked it this morning. I walked through the lobby and pushed open the door to the living area. I stood in the open door way and gasped with horror. I was speechless. The room had been ransacked. The furniture was all over the place, cushions ripped open, everything had been pulled out of the cupboards and thrown on the floor. Even the carpet had been pulled up in one place. I looked into the bedroom - it had been similarly torn apart. Even the bathroom had been searched and wrecked. I was distraught and just sat on the floor crying not knowing where to start. I heard footsteps in the hall outside the door to my flat and froze.

The Mango Mystery

Chapter 20. Kaeta

Douglas
My plan for today was to read Joelle's diary detailing the earlier investigation on Kaeta, which had resulted in my arrest and subsequent release. I planned to ring Bernie and ask him if would see me. I wanted, if possible, to talk with Merv and any others who been involved with the drug smuggling investigation last year. I wanted to see what I could find out about this apparent difference between the USDEA evidence files and the Kaetian police files. If possible I wanted to know what Jeff Conway and Tony Choizi had been doing on the Island, but first I intended to read Joelle's private diary. Years of experience had taught me always to make a working copy of important documents, and this was no exception. I was in the study at 'Windrush' and I used Mary's printer to make a copy of the diary and put the original in a desk drawer and settled down to read the copy.

The diary started with a sort of pre-amble in which Joelle had summarised the incidents seen during the surveillance, how she had initially interpreted them. I realised how, unwittingly, my actions at the time had mislead Joelle into thinking I was involved with drug smuggling.

She had noted in great detail how Tony had attempted to seduce her during that investigation. At one point she had concluded that his behaviour was designed to goad me into actions to confirm my guilt: I was rather less charitable about his motives. However, apart from his rather dubious police methods there was no real evidence of Tony's involvement in anything criminal in those diaries, but it was clear from what Joelle had written that she disliked Tony and thought he was involved in something illegal. I could see why she wanted to keep the diaries secret - some of her comments could get her into trouble.

On reading the diaries I realised how much she had done for me, and the professional risks she had taken to prove my innocence. I had not appreciated it at the time, and the realisation now not only made me feel guilty, but confirmed my feelings for Joelle.

The final entries in the diary were made after the Joelle returned from the Enquiry in Amsterdam and she had recorded her worries about what Tony Choizi had said about her, the way he had distorted, even lied, in the evidence he had presented, and that she had been accused of having affairs with both Tony and myself.

At one point I went for a walk in Mary's garden to clear my mind, and I came to the realisation that I wanted to live on Kaeta and, if Joelle would have me, spend the rest of my life with her.

When I finished reading, I sat back and stared at the diary wondering what to do next. The clock in the study chimed - it was late in the afternoon and I had not yet phoned Bernie to arrange to see him. I made the call, but he did not really want to talk to me, saying he said he could not tell me anything so there was no point in meeting me. He even suggested I would be better off at home looking after Joelle rather than running round the world on a fool's errand. However I insisted I wanted to see him and, eventually, when I implied that he did not want to help Joelle, he relented and agreed to talk to me the next day.

The Mango Mystery

With my brain a jumble of information from the diaries I decided I would go down to the Glass Bar, the restaurant Mary ran, for a drink and to clear my head.

'Mary,' I exclaimed, when I got the bar, 'It's all changed, it looks completely different.'

The decking terrace area at the front of the building which had stretched out towards the sea had gone and the building had been extended out to one side to create a new outside bar, opening out to a dining area under the coconut and date palms at the top of the beach. The old bar and dining area were still there but had been completely redecorated.

'What has happened?' I asked Mary.

'We had a storm last autumn which washed away the old outdoor patio and damaged the front extension on the old bar. It was Jasmine's idea to move away from the old cafe appearance and move up market with open-air dining tables and a posh restaurant. That's what tourists expect now, Jasmine assures me.'

'Well it looks very good,' I told Mary as I sat down at her new bar and ordered a cocktail.

I asked her for a paper and pencil and started to note down what I learnt from reading Joelle's diary.

Who edited the USDEA evidence files?

Who had tampered with my motorcycle and who had planted drugs in my room?

Who knew about the undercover policewoman working in the Dutch veterinary practice?

and as an afterthought I added,

John de Caynoth

and who knew Joelle and Andrea had traced the veterinary practice in London where Gruber was working?

Who gave the instruction not to arrest Zach?

What else do I know, I thought and added some more items to the list:

Who is the dark man and why is he following Joelle?

What is the new evidence that Tony Choizi has found which has directed attention towards Joelle?

And finally, Joelle is obviously suspicious of Tony Choizi. Could he be the informer?

I need to find out more about Tony Choizi and I was not looking forward to meeting him again but, if I could find the answer to these questions, my suspicions could be confirmed.

The Mango Mystery

Chapter 21. Neasden

Joelle

When Andrea knocked on the door at 10.30 this morning I had completely forgotten that she was meeting me today. I pulled away the chair that I had used to keep the door shut to let her in.

'Oh my God' she exclaimed as she surveyed the devastation in the flat, 'Did I miss a wild party last night?'

'No, I have been burgled.'

'What have they taken?' Andrea asked.

'That's the thing; nothing as far as I can see but it is such a mess I can't tell.' I replied.

'You had better tell me all about it,' Andrea pulled a chair upright and sat down.

'I was told not to move anything until the SOCO people come round this morning.'

'Tough,' said Andrea 'we are not standing up all morning waiting for them.'

I started to tell Andrea what had happened.

'I came home yesterday to this,' I spread my arms round to demonstrate. 'While I was taking it all in my neighbour from upstairs came down, frightening me to death. I thought it was the burglar returned, but had heard a noise around lunchtime and thought I was having a fight with someone. Anyway, he says he saw me come home so came down to ask if everything was okay. He called the police for me and waited until they arrived.'

John de Caynoth

'And what did they do? Andrea asked with a note of cynicism in her voice.

'Not a lot really. Two constables took statements and asked if I knew who was responsible, saying that they would report it and get the crime-scene people round as soon as possible. They told me not to touch anything until after they had been.'

Shortly after Andrea arrived, a detective constable with a couple of SOCO officers turned up.

The SOCO people busied them selves dusting for fingerprints, muttering that it looked a professional job and they would be surprised to find anything helpful. The DC asked me if I had any idea who had turned over the flat, and why. I explained who I was, the case I was working on, and that I had been suspended. I believed the break-in was associated with an attempt on my life and that I was being followed.

Andrea interrupted, 'Yes, and here is a picture of the culprit.'

The DC took it and beginning to look completely out of his depth said, nervously, 'I think this may be more serious than a simple break-in and I had better report this to your senior officer.'

'Yes, you better had, ' Andrea said, squaring up all of her five-foot, four-inch frame in front of the six-foot tall DC,' and do it now. The man you want is Detective Superintendent Derek Passmore at Scotland Yard.'

The DC made his excuses and hurried out, to be followed shortly after by the two SOCO officers who told us we could clear up now as they had finished.

'Got any bin bags?' Andrea asked.

The Mango Mystery

'Only these.' I held up some little white swing bin bags.

'They're no good. I will go and get some proper black rubbish bags.'

She was back in five minutes. 'I spoke to a mate - he's a locksmith and on his way right now to fix the doors. I will straighten up the furniture. You'd better go through all the stuff on the floor, I don't know what you want to keep and what can be thrown away.'

Actually, the flat looked worse than it really was and it took us only a couple of hours before it was looking habitable, and even tidy. While we were clearing up, the locksmith arrived. He surveyed the damage.

'Amateur job, very untidy,' he said, as he examined the door frame and then set to and repaired the broken frames, both downstairs and on my flat door, and replaced the lock on my door.

'They won't break through that lock again.' He smiled as he demonstrated the new lock he had put on the front door.

'How much do I owe you?' I asked.

The locksmith looked at Andrea as he packed up his tools, 'Nothing love, favour for a friend.'

'Nice geezer, Barry the Burglar' Andrea informed me after he had gone.

'What,' I exclaimed, 'he is a burglar?'

'Course he is, or was. What better person would there be to fix your locks properly. Mind you, I have never seen him not be able to pick a lock yet, but don't worry, he is as honest as the day's long and he is straight now. He does actually work as a locksmith.'

John de Caynoth

I was not sure whether I was confident or not, but let it pass.

'Okay,' said Andrea, looking in the fridge, 'What have got for lunch? Then we will go and sort out this vet in Neasden.'

I looked round the room and asked Andrea if she had found my iPad while she was clearing up. She said she had not, and I had not found it either.

'I think they must have taken it - I know I left it on my bedside table but it seems to have gone now.'

'What was on it?' Andrea asked.

'Nothing really, I had only just bought it,' I answered.

We took Douglas's car and I drove over to Neasden. We asked to see the practice manager first. She remembered us but could not tell us anything more than we had learnt on our first visit. I showed her a picture of the dark man but she said she had never seen him before. Andrea asked her if it could be Gruber, perhaps trying to disguise himself. She told us it did not look at all like Gruber. Andrea then asked her about the phone call Gruber had received just before he disappeared.

'The call would have come through the main switchboard,' she told us ' it is operated by the receptionists.'

She took us out to the reception area and we asked if either of the receptionists remembered answering a call and putting it through to Hans Gruber.

The Mango Mystery

'Yes,' replied the younger of the two ladies, 'I remember it. The person phoning sounded very agitated, and insisted on speaking to Hans in person. I told them he was consulting with a patient and I could take a message, but they insisted it was urgent, said they were calling from overseas and had to speak to him now. I had to interrupt him to ask him to take the call.'

'Do you remember anything more about the caller,' I asked.

'Not really' the receptionist replied, 'That's all he said to me.'

'It was a man then,' Andrea asked her to confirm. 'He told you called from overseas. Did he tell you where?'

'No, he just said overseas.'

'Did he have an accent of any sort, European or South African perhaps?' I asked.

'No, not European and I don't think South African or Australian. Might have been American, but he had a sort of lilting, sing song, drawn out accent. He had a deep voice as well.'

Andrea and I looked at each other wondering who had a drawn out, sing song, American accent. Andrea said she could not think of anyone, but I thought it could be Choizi, trying to disguise his voice. I did not tell Andrea.

When we got back to the car, we checked our phones and I saw I had a message to ring one of the civilian administrators at Scotland Yard. 'I wonder what that is all about?' I said to Andrea as I called the number.

John de Caynoth

It was answered quickly. 'DS Passmore wants to see you,' I was told, 'It's too late this afternoon - he is in another meeting right now - but can you come in at nine tomorrow?'

I agreed I could and looked nervously at Andrea. 'I wonder what he wants?'

'I will come with you,' Andrea declared firmly.

Chapter 22. The Meeting

Douglas

Mary gave me the keys to Joelle's car, a Toyota, and told me to use it while I was on the Island.

'I don't want you a riding around on a motorcycle again. She stalked off muttering about dangerous machines. I smiled, and drove into Kaeta town to see Bernie.

I had had unhappy experiences in that police station, and I hoped Bernie would not take me into the interview room, which held memories I would rather forget. He came down in person to meet me at the public reception counter and I was relieved that took me up to his office.

'Coffee?' he asked pointing to a chair, indicating that I should sit down. 'How can I help you, Douglas?'

I quickly explained Joelle's situation, and that I thought that if I could find out who was actually was passing information to this drug gang, Joelle would be cleared of any suspicion. Bernie regarded me with a very serious expression.

'And exactly how do expect to do that, when the combined recourses of three police forces across the world have failed so far?'

I had not exactly looked at the situation that way before and I began to realise what a daunting task I had set myself. However optimistically I pointed out to Bernie that those police forces had a lot of evidence and, presumably from that evidence had concluded that Joelle was involved with some sort of illegal drug related activities.

'If I could be permitted to look at that evidence, a fresh pair of eyes may spot where they had been misled into suspecting Joelle, and that might then lead to the real culprit.'

Bernie grunted: I added, 'Naturally, I want to work openly with the police.'

Bernie replied, 'I think you are going to find you are on your own. The police do not share information with, or work with, the public on investigations.'

Bad start, I thought and changed the subject. 'Joelle told me you were the Drug Liaison officer for Kaeta. What does that involve?'

'It is only a title really. All drug related issues are passed to me, but I get all crime reports anyway, it is just what I do.'

'But you have travel to drug control meetings, mainly in the USA, I believe.'

Bernie looked surprised. 'How do you know that?'

'I think Joelle mentioned it.'

Bernie was non-committal, but did say that he occasionally had to travel as part of the job. I asked him about the difference between the USDEA crime files and the local Kaeta police crime reports covering the period while I was being watched. He shrugged and said he could not explain the differences but added that he thought the enquiry had made too big a thing out of it.

'If the Americans were preparing a case to prosecute, of course they would summarise the evidence.' Bernie commented.

The Mango Mystery

I moved the conversation on to Zach, the small-time dealer who had admitted to involvement with the drug smuggling gang when they were actively using Kaeta as a base last year. I asked Bernie what had happened to Zach.

'He got a twelve month prison sentence for dealing in illegal drugs and stealing a motor boat. He is currently being entertained in the Island prison.'

I asked Bernie if he knew who had given the instruction that Zach should be watched, but not arrested, when it was discovered where he was hiding.

'Can't really remember now, it might have come from America, or it might have been Joelle.' Bernie replied unhelpfully.

I let it pass, and asked Bernie if I could see Zach. He confirmed Zach was allowed visitors and surprised me by helpfully offering to arrange an appointment for me to visit the prison and interview Zach.

The conversation carried on a bit longer, with me trying to get Bernie to talk about the investigation and what information he had. Bernie stuck to generalities and gave very little away. We finished the meeting with Bernie telling me he would let me know when he had arranged my prison visit. As I left the office Bernie called me back, 'Douglas, by the way,' he asked, 'I think Joelle kept a diary, there might be something in that, if you know where it is?'

I was surprised that Bernie knew of Joelle's diary. She had been very careful to stress to me that she had kept it secret and told no one. If I tell Bernie I have it, I thought, he will probably want me to hand it over as evidence, so I replied with a shake of my head and said, 'No idea, sorry.'

I sat in the car thinking about the session with Bernie. It was disappointing - I had not really learnt anything I did not already know, but on the other hand, I realised I was going to have to change my tactics, as clearly the police were not going to cooperate with me.

I had the car windows open and looked round as I sensed someone standing next the car. It was Merv. He apologised for following me out, and asked how Joelle was. He had heard that Joelle was in trouble and shook his head, saying that she was the last person who would get involved with drugs. I asked Merv if I could talk to him, 'I want to find out what Tony Choizi and his colleague, Jeff Conway, were doing on the Island.'

Merv scanned the car park nervously. 'We have all been told not to talk to you, but I want to help Joelle. You know Glass Bar, I will meet you there this evening.' He hurried off.

I drove off reflecting on what Merv had just said and that, obviously, I was not going to get much help, officially, from the police. I had another four days on the Island and I wondered what else I could do. I planned to speak to David Rail, the attorney who had represented me last year in the extradition hearing. I was not sure what I wanted to ask him yet, but I figured I could not lose anything by talking to him. Apart from anything else, he could probably advise me on moving to live on the Island.

I had no idea what time Merv might meet me so I went over the bar in the afternoon and gave Mary a hand preparing for the evening meals.

The Mango Mystery

'Now you have gone 'up market', have you changed the menus as well?' I asked her.

She smiled, 'Yes, we have changed the words on the menu but not the food. The Caribbean Bass Delicacy, flavoured with local spices and served with home grown local vegetables, is still the catch of the day served with what I got from the market this morning.'

I smiled back, her food was delicious before, and I was pleased she had not changed it.

She continued, 'That storm did me a favour really, though it did not feel like it at the time. We got some insurance money, and Joelle helped out. It has made life a lot easier because we have fewer tables, and the income is the same as we have put the prices up.'

We talked and gossiped together like old friend while we worked in the kitchen. One thing Mary told me was that Zach had hidden at his sister's place on the other side of the Island before he was arrested. I made a mental note to go and find Zach's sister and see if she could tell me anything.

By seven I began to wonder if Merv was going to come at all. By seven thirty I had given up, and was sitting at the bar nursing a drink when Merv arrived and suggested we sit in the old bar where no one would hear us.

I started by telling Merv what had happened in England - that Joelle had been questioned and then suspended, someone had tried to run her down, and that we thought she was being followed. Merv was quite upset. I then asked him what Jeff Conway, and then Tony Choizi, had done when they visited the Island at the end of last year. Merv told me that Jeff Conway had just gone through the surveillance investigation in which I had been the suspect.

He explained, 'Jeff Conway was interested in the drugs found in your room, who had found them, who had access to the room and safe, that sort of thing. He wanted to know who had sabotaged your motor-bike, and who had given the instruction not to arrest Zach when we found him. I know Joelle had her suspicions about who was responsible but we never found out, or proved anything. Jeff Conway wrote everything down and left.'

'Then, what did Tony Choizi do when he was here?' I asked Merv.

'He picked up on all those points. He was also interested in who had submitted the evidence files to his department.'

'Picked up how?' I prompted Merv.

'I told him that we all wrote our individual reports and Joelle used to go through them, correcting the spelling and that sort of thing, and then gave them to Bernie. Tony challenged that saying Joelle changed the reports. I told him she did not change the facts, but he pushed and pushed, insisting that I confirm Joelle had changed the evidence.'

'What else was he interested in?' I prompted again.

'The drugs in your room. He wanted me to confirm that Joelle was the only one who had access to your room prior to the drugs being found. And then there was your motor-bike. He suggested that Joelle had organised the sabotage of the brakes in the hope that

The Mango Mystery

you would have an accident and kill your self right at the start or the investigation. Of course, we said that was nonsense, in the hotel garden we had found the hack saw that had been used to cut the brake cable, but Tony claimed that we had no evidence as to when the bike was sabotaged and that it must have been done in the workshop before you even collected the machine.'

I sat looking a Merv for a few minutes wondering if I could find out how Choizi had reported all this to the meeting in Amsterdam before Christmas. I decided I needed to talk to Willam Ince. I turned back to Merv.

'What did Choizi say about Zach's arrest?' I asked him.

'Just that he had never given an instruction not to arrest Zach, so it must have come from someone on the Island. I told him it could not have been Joelle because she was in England at the time, but he dismissed that saying he knew she had been in telephone contact while she was away and could easily have given the instruction. I told him she might have said something, but that would have been after we started the surveillance. I have to say, Douglas, I was very uncomfortable with the way he was twisting the facts to make it look like Joelle was up to something,'

I agreed, and Merv continued, 'I did my best to stop him, but, well, I think he wrote down just what he wanted to hear.' Merv looked round nervously as someone came into the room and said he did not want to be seen with me and was leaving. 'One last thing' he said to me as he stood up, 'Tony insisted that you and Joelle were having an affair and that was why she suddenly switched from proving you were involved with the drug ring to proving you were innocent. You weren't, were you?'

'I wish we had been, but no, we never had an affair, even after I was released and staying with the family in Mary's home.' I assured Merv as he left.

When he had gone, I said good bye to Mary and went back to 'Windrush'. The answer- phone was blinking, announcing a new message. I was not sure if I should answer it, being a guest in the house, but I did anyway. The message was for me from Joelle, saying she needed to speak to me, asking that I phone her back as soon as possible.

The Mango Mystery

Chapter 23. D. S. Derek Passmore

Joelle

I arranged to meet Andrea at a little coffee bar near Westminster Underground Station first thing in the morning and when I got there she had already bought two coffees and was half way through drinking one of them. I took a couple of gulps but that was all as I was anxious to get the meeting with DS Passmore over with. We walked together across Parliament Square and a short way up Victoria Street to Scotland Yard.

'Wonder what he wants?' Andrea speculated.

'Bound to be something to do with my suspension,' I replied.

'Perhaps he is going to re-instate you.'

'Or arrest me.' I replied miserably.

'Don't be so negative.' Andrea chided.

When we arrived at the Yard we were immediately escorted up to Derek Passmore's office where he was sitting waiting for us.

'I had not expected you, Mrs Spooner, but no matter, I needed to talk with you anyway after I have spoken to Joelle.'

I told Derek I had asked Andrea to come with me, and that I would like her to stay with me through any interviews. Derek had no objections and then explained why he wanted to see me.

'A report concerning a break-in and burglary at your flat has been passed to me by the Clapham police. It has been referred to us, as it contains statements concerning certain more worrying incidents, and I would like you to tell me in your own words what is going on.'

I confirmed that the reported break-in was true, but Derek interrupted me before I could say more. 'But, apparently, nothing, was taken. Furthermore, the Clapham police report that you claim there was an attempt to run you over and that you are being followed.'

I told Derek that I thought my iPad had been taken, and as he made a note on the file, I gave him a detailed account of the attempt to run me down, and how Douglas and I had been followed down to Wiltshire, then to the airport.

'Are you still being followed?' Derek asked as he pulled the picture of the dark man out of the file and pushed it across to me, asking if this was the man who had followed me. I confirmed that it was, but told Derek that I had not seen him for the last couple of days. He asked me if I knew the man in the picture. Andrea chipped in and said we were trying to find out.

Derek looked uncomfortable. 'I have to ask you again, Joelle. Do you have any connection with this man - have you ever seen him before? Please answer truthfully - if it turns out there was some previous link, things could be very serious for you.'

I confirmed I had no idea who the man was and that I had never seen him before. Derek then asked me why I thought that I was being followed and targeted. I speculated that who ever had broken into my flat must have been looking for something but I had no idea what. Derek looked at me skeptically, but asked me if I had any idea why there had been an attempt to run me

The Mango Mystery

down and asked if the same people were now following me. I told him I had I had no idea and he rubbed his chin in thought, before he spoke again.

'Let us assume that it is the same people, and it may be that, initially, there was an attempt on you life to ensure your silence. Later, however, they discovered that the knowledge, they believed you possessed, had been written down, and they followed you in an attempt to find it. That would explain the events leading up to the break in and the loss of your iPad. Was anything on it that fits with this hypothesis?'

'No nothing like you are describing. I bought it when I arrived in London and all that was on it were some emails to home, some pictures I have taken of London and Wiltshire, and some music - all personal stuff.'

Derek then asked me if I had any idea what they might be looking for. I did not want to say anything about my secret file and diary just yet. I knew I would have to disclose it eventually, but Douglas had just gone to get it and I wanted to make sure I had not written down something that might further incriminate me before I told anyone about it.

Derek continued with his hypothesis, 'You say you have not been followed since the break in. I think we have to wait and see what happens next, but in the mean time, you must be on your guard and if anything at all happens, let me know.' He finished the interview by telling me he would pass a copy of the file to the investigating officers and dismissed me, but asked Andrea to remain for a few minutes.

I waited outside Derek's office for Andrea and it was not long before she came out beckoning me to follow her out of the building. When we got outside she said, 'Lets go and have a coffee and I will tell you what he said.'

I ordered a cappuccino, Andrea ordered a straight Americano and explained that she was on a diet, that was until she saw a plate of muffins and decided she was hungry.

'I thought you were on a diet.'

'I am, but I did not have any breakfast this morning,' she explained, as she looked jealously at me, 'I wish I was tall and slim like you.'

'If you did not gorge on fattening buns you could at least be slim' I said, unsympathetically, as we sat down. 'Now tell me what Derek wanted.'

'To begin with,' she started telling me, 'they are going to reinstate me. Derek even told me that I should never have been suspended in the first place as there was never any evidence against me.'

'I am really pleased for you. When does this take effect?' I asked.

'Ah! Well, that's the even more interesting news. Bob Cash has gone back into uniform and been accepted for a job as Chief Inspector in the British Transport Police, and he has already gone.'

'Could not have happened to a nicer person.' I commented sourly, but Andrea ignored me and continued, 'His replacement is DCI Barbara Green. She was a DI working in the drug squad here a few years ago, and then she took a secondment and went to America, Washington DC, in some sort of liaison role, as far as I remember. Anyway, she was okay, looked after her team but would not tolerate any fools or slackers.'

'When is she starting?' I asked.

'In a few days time. She is on leave at the moment, but as soon as she gets back she is going to contact me. Until then I am no longer on suspension and Derek told me to enjoy a bit of time off.'

I was pleased for Andrea: she never deserved to be suspended, but then neither did I. I thought, perhaps there being no evidence against her might help me somehow. I was also pleased that Bob Cash had moved on. I had never felt particularly comfortable working with him, but I supposed I ought to feel sorry for him, as a uniform role in the BTP did not sound like a promotion.

I turned to Andrea saying, 'Just to change the subject, that dark man who was following me, do you think Derek Passmore knew who he was, and that was why he said it would be serious for me if I had a prior connection with him?'

Andrea looked concerned before she replied, 'I don't know. It's possible, the first thing he would do is to run the picture through the file and see if there is a match. I will ask Jim if he has found anything and, if not, I can go into the station now and look for myself.'

I was in the middle of telling Andrea to be careful and not to get into trouble when my phone rang. It was Douglas. He said he was returning my call and asked what had happened.

I told him about the break in at the flat and loss of the iPad and he asked if I was okay.

John de Caynoth

'They must be looking for your diary.' he said, jumping to the conclusion immediately. He confirmed he had found the diary and had read it. 'I did not know how much you did for me during that drug smuggling business' he told me, saying how grateful he was before turning to practicalities again.

'You wrote some pretty strong stuff about Tony Choizi and implied you thought he was involved in illegal activities; perhaps that is what they are after. It could be read as incriminating if Choizi is a bent cop.' This thought silenced us both for a few seconds while its implications sunk in.

Douglas spoke first. 'I have seen Bernie, and he was not very helpful, but last night I spoke privately with Merv. Apparently, Tony Choizi, when he was in Kaeta interviewing them, had tried to twist what was said to put you in a bad light.' I asked Douglas what he meant, and he went through what Merv had told him. He then told me he would be back at the end of the week, but was planning to go to Miami next to see what he could find out about Tony Choizi. Before we finished the conversation I asked after Mary and Jasmine, and Douglas was in the middle of telling me how much he liked the new Glass Bar, when something happened.

'Hang on a minute, there is someone downstairs,' he said. He must have carried his mobile phone down with him because I could hear his footsteps and the old stairs creaking as he descended. Then the phone went dead.

The Mango Mystery

Chapter 24. Knock Out

Douglas

I was lying, face down, on the stone floor of the hall in "Windrush". I was not in any pain, but my brain was not really working. I felt something wet and warm on my cheek and wiped it away with the back of my hand and then rather stupidly looked at the red stuff on my hand wondering where it had come from. It was probably only milliseconds before my nose started to feel thick and heavy and a huge throbbing sensation started to pound away at the back of my neck. As the pain kicked in my dazed state receded, and my mind began to focus. At that point a jumble of thoughts filled my head, all at the same time. I had come downstairs because I had heard someone moving about the house, I had been on the phone to Joelle at the time - where is my mobile phone? I must have a nosebleed, and, finally someone had hit me on the back of the head.

I moved slowly into a sitting position and tested my body for other injuries. Apart from the nosebleed, which was now almost stopped, and a very tender area at the base of my skull, throbbing furiously, the rest of me seemed to be in good working order. I looked around and spotted my mobile phone lying at the base of the stairs. I crawled over to it and peered at the screen. The call to Joelle had cleared, but some instinct prompted me to check the time of the call - twenty minutes ago - and I had been talking to her for about ten minutes, so I had been unconscious for about ten minutes. I sat there debating whether I should stand up or lie down again, deciding to get moving to find out what the visitor had been doing and why he needed to bash me on the head.

The hallway was intact, but then there was not much in the hall to damage, only an antique mahogany dresser, a chair in the corner and pictures on the wall. The study door was open and as I walked in I could see it had been ransacked, and not very carefully. All the books and papers on the shelves had been pulled down, the rugs on floor had been thrown aside, the desk drawers pulled out and their contents thrown on the floor. By now my mind was firing on all cylinders and I recalled I had just had a conversation with Joelle, and we had speculated her flat had been broken into to search for her diary. I scrabbled through all the papers on the floor but the diary, which I had left in the desk drawer, was missing. I ran upstairs to my room and breathed a sigh of relief, the copy was still there, on the dressing table where I had left it; not a very clever place to leave secret papers, but at the time I had not expected anyone to be serious about finding them.

I quickly checked round the rest of the house, but no other rooms had been disturbed. I called the police, and when I explained who I was, and told them that "Windrush", Joelle deNouvelas's home, had been burgled I was promised immediate attention.

I decided I ought to call Mary and tell her what had happened. She and Jasmine had gone to the market to buy food for the restaurant and were then going over to Glass Bar to tidy up and supervise the cleaner. Mary answered the phone, cutting me off before I had finished speaking, in her anxiety to drive over.

Mary, Bernie and Merv all arrived at about the same time. Mary was fussing round me, more

The Mango Mystery

concerned about me than the house. While I was telling Bernie what had happened, he spotted, lying in corner, a heavy antique wood carving which had stood on the dresser in the hall. 'I reacon that is what they hit you with,' he said as he picked it up carefully and dropped it into a large evidence bag.

Meanwhile Merv had moved into the study and surveyed the scene and concluded that whoever broke in had been searching for something in particular. 'We will check for finger-prints but I don't expect to find much,' he said.

Bernie asked Mary what was missing. She looked round the study and said that until she had cleared up she would not be able to say for sure. I was not asked, and kept quite about the diary.

Mary was getting agitated by this time and told the two policeman she had to take me to hospital for a check up. After the last time I had hit my head and had nearly died from complications I was getting a bit anxious myself, and was not sorry when Mary bundled me into the car and drove me to the hospital.

Meanwhile, Bernie had decided there was nothing more for him to do so he had taken the police car back to the station after instructing Merv to check around outside and see if he could find any clues. It was obvious that the intruders had left a car by the back door, which had not been locked, had come in that way and left the same way in a hurry, as they had sprayed gravel all over the flower bed by the door as they drove off. Merv also found a couple of footprints in the flowerbed under the kitchen window.

'They must have looked through the window to check the room was empty,' he speculated as he placed a seed tray over the footprints so a plaster impression could be taken later. He asked me if I had heard or seen a car at all.

'Yes, I think I might have heard a car while I was on the phone but I took no notice of it.' I told Merv.

He thought about this and calculated that they could only have been in the house for about ten minutes before he delivered his final conclusion. 'They must have started in the study and you disturbed them, so they ran off before they could take anything. You should make sure the house is securely locked at all times in case they come back.' He looked perplexed, clearly wondering how he was going to get back into town, but he solved his dilemma by asking Mary if she could give him a lift back to the police station on her way to the hospital. He told me he would come to find me later, as he needed a statement from me.

When we got to the hospital, Mary explained what had happened and the duty doctor concluded I was suffering a mild concussion, but when he read my notes he decided to X-ray my injury and admit me overnight, just to make sure no complications developed. By this time I had the mother-of-all headaches, was feeling queasy, and did not mind at all being bundled into a bed and given painkillers. The last thing I remembered before dropping off the sleep was Mary saying goodbye and that she would come by in the morning to see how I was.

I woke up during the afternoon. I wanted to ring Joelle and tell her what had happened but I did not have her phone number with me, so I settled down to watch television. There was an American detective

The Mango Mystery

programme showing, about a private detective who was conducting a one-man vendetta against a corrupt marshal in a small American town. It was not particularly good, but it did give me some ideas. It had just finished when Merv turned up. I seemed to be his best buddy these days as he greeted me warmly and spent quite a long time sitting with me, talking about Island life, where best to go house hunting, and reminiscing about Joelle and how he could not believe she was involved with illegal drugs. I agreed with him and told him I was planning to go and see Zach.

'He is unreliable as a witness,' Merv told me, 'he admitted in court that he told Tony Choizi and Joelle what he thought they wanted to hear just so he might get a lighter sentence. He did tell me that as far as he knew you were never involved in the drug smuggling.'

I was pleased about that, and asked Merv if he knew who had given the instruction not to arrest Zach when he was first found.

'You know, I don't really remember: Joelle spoke to me on the phone and I think she mentioned that Zach was not to be approached, only watched. That's what I told Jeff Conway anyway.'

Eventually, Merv got round to taking a statement from me and I told him more or less what I had already told Bernie earlier. As he finished writing it down he commented, 'You know, a funny thing, I thought Bernie said he was going back to the police station after he left 'Windrush' this morning, but when I got back he was not there. He turned up just before I left to come over here. I asked him where he had been but he just said, 'personal business.'

John de Caynoth

Chapter 25. The mobile phone

Douglas
I had a good nights sleep and was woken, with a cup of tea, by the nurse early this morning. She asked me how I was feeling as she took my breakfast order and, as I was hungry, I asked for scrambled eggs, sausage and toast. She commented that I must be better and told me the doctor would be round to see me shortly.

I had nearly finished breakfast when the doctor appeared. He asked me how I was feeling, checked me over, confirmed that the X-ray had shown no damage, and discharged me, warning me that I had some heavy bruising to the back of my head and that I would have a stiff neck for a few days, but nothing to worry about.

While I waited for Mary I went for a walk round the gardens, which were quite spectacular, laid out with many varied tropical plants and trees with manicured paths weaving round and strategically placed seats where recuperating patients could sit and enjoy the garden and warm climate. The hospital had been built by, and was run by, an American medical corporation. Its main business was medical care and plastic surgery for rich American clients, but as a condition of allowing the hospital to be developed, the Kaetian authorities had insisted that a general medical and accident facility be provided to care for the local Island population.

I positioned myself in a seat with view of the entrance drive and car park and thought through yesterday's events as I waited for Mary.

The Mango Mystery

Obviously, whoever had broken in was looking for Joelle's diary, which they now had. I wondered what it was that was made them want the diaries so badly and thought again of Tony Choizi. I wanted desperately to find out what it was that had lead to the conclusion that Joelle was involved so I could look for ways of disproving it. Thank goodness I made a copy, I thought, and wondered how best to use it. No one, not even Joelle, knew I had made a copy, and for the time being I decided I would keep it that way, and keep the copy with me all the time.

I saw Mary's car rolling slowly up the drive and walked over to the car park to meet it. The vehicle had hardly stopped before Jasmine jumped out of the car and ran over to hug me, asking how I was feeling. She was followed my Mary who asked the same question.

'I am absolutely okay.' I told them, 'I have been discharged and free to go.'

We went straight back to "Windrush". The study was still a mess and Mary explained, with some exasperation, that she was still waiting for the police to finish looking for clues. I asked if she had seen my mobile phone and she told me that it had been taken by the police as evidence.

'Evidence for what?' I asked,

'I have no idea,' Mary replied, 'Bernie took it yesterday.'

I asked Mary if I could use the house phone as I wanted to let Joelle know what had happened and that I was okay.

'You can't phone her yet, it's only six in the morning in the UK,' Mary protested, but I phoned Joelle anyway.

She picked up the call almost immediately and sounded relieved when she heard my voice. She explained that after the phone went dead yesterday she repeatedly tried phoning my mobile, which was dead, the 'Windrush' house phone and Mary's mobile but got no answer from anyone. Eventually, she explained, she had phoned my mobile again and Bernie had answered it, telling her that there had been a break in at 'Windrush' and that I had been injured and was in hospital again.

'I have been going out of my mind with worry,' she told me anxiously.

I explained what had happened and that I was perfectly okay, and had only been in hospital overnight as a precaution and she started to calm down. 'They took you diary notes' I told her, finally.

She fell silent for a moment, and then said, 'Who, I wonder?'

'It has to be the smuggling gang, but its not as bad as it might have been,' I replied, looking round to check I was alone and not being overheard, 'I made a copy of the diary which no one but you and I know about. I will bring it back with me on Saturday.' We talked for a little longer basically telling each other to be careful, but Mary had come into the room, hovering wanting to talk to Joelle, so I said good-bye and handed the receiver over.

I went up to my bedroom and the first thing I did was to check the diary copy was still in its hiding place, under my mattress. It was, and after considering if there was anywhere safer to keep it, I decided to leave it where it was while I went into the en-suite to take a shower. I walked back into the bedroom drying myself with a bath towel. I got quite a shock as I entered the room and saw Jasmine standing in front of the wardrobe looking at me and blushing. I hurriedly pulled the towel round so I was decent, and asked Jasmine what she was doing. She looked as if she was going to cry and started apologising saying 'I brought you a clean shirt, I have just washed it and ironed it for you; I was just hanging it in the wardrobe. I heard you in the shower, and I thought I would be gone before you came out. I am sorry Douglas.'

I smiled and assured there was no need to be sorry, I had not expected anyone to be in the room and was surprised, that was all.

She saw the back of my neck and the large bruise that was beginning to come up and walked across the room towards me. She touched my neck, very gently, but I flinched anyway and she asked if hurt.

'Only when I laugh' I joked. She was standing very close to me now, and I realised she was tall certainly as tall as he mother and very nearly as tall as me and also very pretty if a little skinny. I stepped away from her as she said, 'Please be careful Douglas.'

I moved across the room to the wardrobe explaining that she must leave as I needed to get dressed, and as I dressed I reflected how quickly Jasmine was growing up.

That afternoon I drove into town. I still had an appointment with David Rail and I intended to go into the police station and see if I could get my phone back.

John de Caynoth

I parked the car and went into the Police Station and asked for Bernie. When he came down I asked him if I could have my mobile phone back. He looked doubtful and repeated that it had been retained as evidence.

'Evidence of what?' I asked.

'The intruders might have handled it, and it might have their finger prints.' Bernie explained.

'Well, have you looked and did you find any?' I asked, and rather grudgingly Bernie admitted the only prints on the phone were mine.

'So can I have it back now then?' I looked at Bernie, who stared back at me for a few seconds seeming reluctant to release the mobile, before he shrugged and went off to get the phone.

As I walked over to David Rails office I was puzzled. I could not see any reason why Bernie was reluctant to return my phone. I checked the display, suspicious that my call-logs and messages had been accessed. All I could tell was that the last call from Joelle had been answered, but I knew that anyway because Joelle had told me Bernie answered my phone, so I shrugged, and put it in my pocket - I had nothing to hide.

Next stop was David Rail's office, and he seemed please to see me, greeting me warmly and offered me a cold beer, which I gratefully accepted. I had not been in his offices before and I looked round with interest. He had the top floor of one of the older Edwardian houses in what is now the commercial quarter of Kaeta Town. Despite that, the offices themselves looked very modern and David explained that the top floor of the building had originally been the servants' quarters and were always very plain, without the gothic-style wood panelling that graced the rest of the building. When he and his partner had taken over the top floor suite, they had knocked out some walls to create larger open plan areas, redecorated with plain white walls, sanded floors and simple white painted doors. 'A very cheap refurb-job,' he laughed.

We went into his office and he asked me what he could do for me. I explained that Joelle was suspended, and under suspicion of passing police information to a criminal drug gang.

'I know,' said David, 'And I can't think of anyone less likely to indulge in a criminal act. I have worked with Joelle on more than one occasion and, as well as being a very nice person, I always thought she was one of the most moral and honest people I have met on the Island. She is one of the few, who, when she spot-fines the tourists, does not add on her 'expenses'! He paused and looked reflective, 'but, you never know; in my experience, some of the most unpleasant criminals have superficially appeared to be upright pillars of society. Anyway, how can I help?'

I explained one of the accusations appeared to be that Joelle had passed information about the existence of the undercover policewoman, working at a veterinary practice in Holland, and who subsequently had been murdered, and I was trying to find out who else knew about this.

'As I recall,' David paused for a moments thought, 'that information was presented at the extradition hearing when the American DEA were trying to get you back to the States, and it was heard in-camera, with the judge ordering that none of the information was to be disclosed outside his chambers, and that associated documents be securely locked away.'

'That's my understanding.' I agreed. David left the room for a few moments returning with a file that he started to thumb through before he spoke again.

'Here it is, Bernie Strange, Joelle, myself and Justin Cramp were present in the Judge's Chambers when that evidence was heard. I think we can assume that Bernie and Joelle did not tell anyone, I did not either, so that leaves Justin Cramp and I doubt he told anyone, but he might have been under pressure to explain to his client why they lost the case. By the way, how do you know about it all?'

I explained that Joelle had kept a secret diary, which I recently recovered and read.

'Did she!' David exclaimed, 'Are you sure it was kept a secret?'

'Yes, certain,' I replied with more conviction than I could actually justify.

David let that pass and suggested that he phone Justin Cramp to ask him if he had told anyone. 'He won't admit it outright, but if he wriggles and gives a weasely-worded answer we will know.' He smiled cunningly as he dialled a number on his phone. He asked to be put through to Justin Cramp.

'I don't care if he is busy, this is urgent and I need to speak now.'

'He always says he is busy,' David whispered to me.

'Tell him I will subpoena him if he does not speak to me right now!'

The Mango Mystery

Justin Cramp answered the phone, but I could only hear one side of the conversation. After the polite pleasantries were over, David asked him if he remembered the extradition case, and than asked him who he had told about the undercover policewoman. I could hear a lot of blustering going on but could not make out what was being said. Eventually David hung up and told me.

'Well, that was interesting. Their client, represented by Detective Tony Choizi, insisted on a post case conference and wanted to know why their case had failed. He refused to accept that he should not be told of all the evidence that had been presented. Apparently he was incandescent with anger. Anyway, at that moment it seems that Justin Cramp had to leave the room suddenly and in his haste left all the case files on the table. As he said, it was not his fault if Choizi read the files.'

'So I can assume that Choizi knew about the undercover policewoman shortly after the extradition hearing,' I surmised, David agreed.

We spent a few more minutes talking through the events of last year but David really knew no more than I did and could not add anything more to help me. As we concluded the meeting I asked David about foreign nationals wanting to settle permanently on Kaeta and he explained the regulations.

'You can get a six-month visitors permit, but you have to leave after six months and cannot return again for another six months. You can also get a twelve-month student's permit but you have to be accredited to a recognised place of study on the Island. You can get a resident's permit but you need to prove that you will not be a burden on the Island's social fund, which basically means that you need quarter of a million US Dollars lodged in cash accounts on the Island, or prove that you are the first line descendent of a native Kaetian and have some means of supporting yourself. Once you have a resident's permit you can get a work permit provided you have job arranged, and can prove that you are not taking the job of a Kaetian. Or, of course, the other to get on the Island is to marry a Kaetian national.'

I left David's office, feeling quite pleased. David had given me a transcript of his conversation with Justin Cramp, and, as for moving to live on the Island, I had money from my redundancy, bonus payments and sale of my shares in VP Ltd. I easily had enough capital to meet the financial requirements for a residents permit, and buy somewhere to live on the Island and support my self and have money left over.

On my way back to the car I passed a Land Agent's offices and went in to enquire what properties might be available on the Island. Naturally, they were delighted to see me and quickly spread out details of all the properties that they had for sale and rental. I explained that I was not looking to rent so they went through their for sale portfolio. Most of the properties they had to offer were apartments or bungalows on managed estates with communal shared facilities and prices ranging from under $100,000 to over $500,000. I explained that I did not want to live on one of the managed estates and asked if they had any other properties. There were two or three set in some of the more exclusive developments on the Island, one on the headland where Mary and Joelle lived. These were all larger houses set in their own ground with private pools, tennis courts - one even had a nine-hole golf course - all priced at upwards of a million dollars which was way out of my price range, I explained. Rather sorrowfully, they explained that the sort of property I was looking for very rarely came on the market as those properties tended to be owned by Kaetian families and usually passed on from generation to generation. I gave them my contact address and they promised to email me details of any new properties that came up for sale.

On my way home I called in to the Glass Bar. I chided myself to start calling it by its new name, 'The Crystal House Restaurant'. But all the local still called it Glass Bar with regulars still congregating after work for a drink in the old bar area. I nodded to the drinkers that I recognised and ordered a beer and sat at the bar, telling Jasmine about my day. Mary had finally decided that now Jasmine was sixteen she was old enough to stand behind the bar. I had a couple of beers before Mary appeared and told Jasmine she could go home if she wanted to, as they were not busy that evening. This prompted me to finish my beer and offer Jasmine a lift home.

When we got back to 'Windrush' I plugged my phone in to re-charge; the battery had died that afternoon. I left the phone turned on and before long a stream of missed calls and texts came through. There were messages from Joelle asking me call her, but they were all sent before I spoke with her earlier today.

There was also a text and couple of messages from Edith Meadows, who looked after my house in Wiltshire when I was away. She had tried to phone me all afternoon and then sent me a text message saying

John de Caynoth

that there had been a break-in at my house and asking me to contact her urgently. I tried to phone but there was no answer.

The Mango Mystery

Chapter 26. The Picture

Joelle

I do not think I am getting paranoid, just being very careful these days, but when I am in the flat I keep looking out of the windows periodically to see if I can spot anyone acting suspiciously. When I am out of the flat, I keep looking behind me, doubling back just to check if I am being followed. This morning, I looked through the bedroom window and across Clapham Common as usual, and saw a black Range Rover, still parked in the residents bay next door. There was nothing suspicious in this, except that I had never seen this vehicle before until yesterday. It had darkened windows so it was difficult to see if there was anyone in the vehicle, but I thought I could see a shadow. I told myself not to be paranoid - it was probably nothing at all - but I would keep an eye on it anyway.

I was bored, with nothing to do but mooch around the flat, waiting impatiently for Sunday morning when I was due to go and meet Douglas, when Andrea rang to tell me she had been into the Yard that morning and had some interesting stuff to tell me. 'I am on my way home now, so come round and have some lunch with me.' She instructed.

Half an hour later I was ready to leave. It was a mild, dry morning, so I decided to take the bike and ride over the Andrea's. I went out to the small courtyard behind the block of flats, where I had left the bike, and looked around checking if I was alone. I mounted the bike, switched on the Sat-Nav, plugged my helmet sound system in, switched on the ignition and hit the starter, expecting the bike to roar into life.

John de Caynoth

Nothing - the engine did not even turn over. I tried again with the same result. I turned the lights on and they seemed good so I concluded it was not a flat battery. I dismounted, checked I had fuel and looked round to see if there were any loose wires hanging down, but I could not see any reason why the bike would not start. I concluded there was something more seriously wrong with the bike than I would be able to fix, so I went back up to the flat to change and phone Andrea and tell her I would be late.

Fifteen minutes later I left the flat again, by the front door this time. I walked slowly past the Range Rover, checking its number plate, and casually glanced through the window and saw two people sitting inside. I walked on, deciding this was definitely suspicious - if it was a residents car they would not be sitting in the vehicle unless they were about to drive off and the Range Rover showed no sign of moving.

When I reached the tube-station, I waited on the southbound platform by the exit, which also connected across to the northbound platform. Three people followed me on to the southbound platform, a woman with a small child and a coloured man wearing a hoodie, which hid his face from view. A northbound train pulled in on the opposite platform, and at the last minute I sprinted across the platform and jumped into the train as the doors slid shut. The man with the hoodie was taken by surprise and tried to follow me but was not quick enough, and the train pulled out leaving him on the platform.

I got to Andrea's flat without further incident and immediately told her that I was sure I was still being watched and followed. Andrea sensibly handed me the

The Mango Mystery

phone and told me to ring Derek Passmore. He sounded concerned, and asked me if I had seen anyone I recognised. I told him I had not, but I gave him the registration number of the Range Rover so he could run checks on it, and to get an officer to question the occupants. He assured me he would also organise a regular patrol past my flat.

While I had the phone in my hand, I asked Andrea for the phone number of the bike shop in Hackney who had sold the Triumph. She rummaged through a drawer and came up with the number I rang the shop and explained that I could not get the bike started and asked them if they could have a look at it. They asked me where the bike was so they could send the van over to collect it.

'Good,' Andrea announced, 'that's the phone calls all done, so now come into the kitchen and have some lunch.'

She had made a pasta and tomato dish, topped with melted cheese, accompanied by a bottle of Italian Pino Grigio.

'Delicious,' I congratulated her as I took a mouthful.

'Actually, I cheated,' Andrea confessed, 'the tomato sauce is out of a bottle and I just add some extra herbs and chopped chorizo to give it a bit of a zing.'

'Well, it's still very good. What is this important news you want to tell me about?'

Andrea explained that she had taken the picture of the dark man into the office and run it through the computer. 'No match against any known British criminals so I ran it against an international data base, and guess what; I got a match, not a hundred percent match, as the picture on the Interpol file was of a much younger man, but apparently he is Xavier Zedanski, known simply as Zed. He is said to be of Eastern European origin with a German passport and no fixed address. He has only one conviction, a suspended sentence for drug- dealing some time ago.'

We mulled over this information but could not come to any conclusion that helped us. As I said to Andrea, there may be a drug connection somewhere but without more information it was tenuous at the very least. Andrea suggested that I ring Willam Ince, but I was reluctant while I was under suspicion to involve him especially **as he was no longer connected with the investigation.**

Andrea then said, 'there is something else that happened today. You remember Jack, the sales desk manager at VP Ltd? Well, he phoned me this morning and asked if I was still interested in vet practices ordering unusually large quantities of KetPil. He told me they had just had an order from a practice in the Midlands, near Coventry. He said that historically they have ordered the drug regularly but in small quantities, but their last order was for over a years supply at their previous rate of usage.'

'Could be Gruber, working from a new practice?' I thought out loud.

'Worth a look to see,' Andrea responded, 'but how do we organise that? You are suspended and I am not supposed to be working until the new DCI moves in.'

The Mango Mystery

'I suppose you ought to tell Derek Passmore, but don't tell him you have told me, I am not supposed to be involved.'

'I guess you are right, but it seems a pity we can't follow it up, we might have actually caught him this time. I will phone the DCS this afternoon, in fact I will do it now,' Andrea said pulling out her mobile, telling me as she did, 'By the way, the word in the Yard is that Derek Passmore has been promoted.'

I waited patiently while she spoke to Derek Passmore. When she had finished the call I asked her what he had said. 'He wanted to know if I had told anyone else; you heard me say no. He wanted to know if there was a picture and description of Gruber on file and I told him the only one was the picture you had of him from the CCTV cameras at Gatwick last year. He said he would get someone to send it up to the local Midland force with a request to check it out.'

'That will blow things' I said, 'if Gruber gets the slightest whiff of police interest he will just disappear again' Andrea agreed but as she said, it is out of our hands now and there is nothing we can do about it.

Shortly after that I left Andreas and headed home. By the time I got to Clapham North station, it was after four in the afternoon and beginning to get dark. Out of habit now, I hung around in front of the shops, checked my mobile and watched to see if I was being followed, but I saw no one suspicious. I did have two messages on my phone. One was from George, the sergeant in the drug squad telling me he had been told to check out the Range Rover. The other message was from Bernie.

John de Caynoth

When I got back to flat I decided to phone George first. He was following up the reports I had made to Derek Passmore. He told me the black Range Rover was registered to a gentleman in Yorkshire. 'We are checking it out, but my guess is that we will find the number plates have been copied. Also, by the time the officers arrived at your flat, the Range Rover had gone. However, the good news is that the vehicle is probably stolen, and certainly suspicious, and appears to have you under surveillance. I have put out an alert for it and I expect we will soon find it.'

As for the man following me he had found nothing, and I had only the vaguest description of a coloured man in a dark hoodie and jeans. The final thing George told me was that Barbara Green was starting on the following Monday and had asked that I be available to see her early next week.

When I had finished talking to George I tried to ring Bernie. He was not answering his mobile phone so I rang the police station in Kaeta. They told me that Bernie had been called out to the Island Prison where there had been a major incident. I asked what was wrong but I was told there was no further information at the moment. I knew Douglas was planning to visit the prison today and I worried wondering what trouble he had got himself into now.

The Mango Mystery

Chapter 27. The Prison

Douglas

I woke Friday morning with a stiff neck, but a shower somewhat relieved that. I dressed and went downstairs to find some breakfast. Jasmine was in the kitchen picking at a bowl of fruit. She made a plate up for me, to which I added some toast. She declined my offer of toast so I said to her 'You have hardly eaten anything, Jasmine. Next time I come to Kaeta I will bring you some Marmite, it's very good on toast.' She pulled a face and said 'Uggh! Sounds disgusting!' when I told her what it was.

While we ate our fruit, Jasmine said to me, 'Have you seen that man, the one who has been hanging around at the bottom of the drive for the last couple of days?'

'What man?' I queried.

'I don't know, I have seen him in the road outside two or three times and I have also seen him at Glass Bar. I think he is down there now. Do you think he is anything to do with the break in?'

I thought it quite possible, but I did not want to worry Jasmine so I told her it was unlikely, 'He is probably some back-packer looking for somewhere to find a cheap bed. I will go and have a look after breakfast.'

As discreetly as possible, I went for a walk in the garden and moved round to the front of the house, trying not to look too obvious. Indeed, there was a man sitting on a rock on the opposite side of the road looking out to sea who looked familiar from the back, but it was only when he turned to look up the drive that I saw he had a pair of binoculars, and, as he put them down, I recognised the dark man. I don't think he saw me, as I was shielded by some bushes. Using a circular route around the garden, I made my way back to the house.

It seemed that I was being watched as well as Joelle, but what should I do about it? I decided to phone Bernie and tell him. He was not in the office, so I was put through to Merv. I explained that this man was following Joelle and I in the UK, and I thought he might have something to do with the break in here earlier this week. Merv promised to come out and have a word with the gentleman.

I was a bit rattled by the appearance of the dark man on the Island and, it occurred to me, perhaps I was not as safe here as I had previously felt. However, apart from being vigilant, there was not a lot I could do about it, but I did decide that carrying the only copy of Joelle's diary around with me was not such a good idea. I collected it from under the mattress and took it into the study where I used Mary's all-in-one printer to make a second copy, which I wrapped in a plastic sheet and cardboard and addressed, with a covering letter, to David Evans at Benson, Dod, Sugar. My plan was to go via the Post Office and post the package, express delivery, to the UK on my way to the Island Prison to visit Zach this morning.

Before I left to drive to the prison, I remembered the message from Edith Meadows and telephoned her. When she answered the phone she was in a bit of a flap and told me that my cottage had been burgled, and was a total mess, with all the contents of the draws and

The Mango Mystery

cupboards thrown all over the floor. 'I have reported it to the police and done my best to tidy up, but I don't know if anything is missing: the police want to see you as soon as you return,' she explained. I established that she had made the house secure and told her not to worry and that I would come to Wiltshire next week and sort things out. That calmed Edith down, but I felt very uncomfortable, not really understanding what was happening.

There was some sort of flap on when I got to the prison, the whole building was locked down and initially I could not even get to the visitor reception. I joined a crowd of people outside the prison all wanting to know what was going on and eventually a warder came out and told everyone there had been a incident in the prison overnight and there would be no visiting that day. I caught him as he was about to go back inside and told him I had appointment to interview Zachariah Farthing. He looked at me and I repeated the name and added, 'known as Zach'.

'You had better come with me Sir.' He said and showed me into a small room in the visitor reception and asked me to wait. Shortly, a smartly dressed man in a blue shirt with epaulets and grey slacks came into the room and introduced himself as the Assistant Governor.

'Are you related to Mr Farthing?' he asked me, and then asked what was my business with Mr Farthing.

I thought I might get further if I could give my self some functional legitimacy, so I told him I was working with Benson, Dodd, Sugar, a London firm of lawyers collecting background evidence in a drug-related investigation. He regarded me seriously for a few moments before he spoke.

'I am afraid it will not be possible for you to see Mr Farthing now.'

I asked if it would be possible to visit him next morning as I was due to return to the UK tomorrow evening.

'No,' he replied, 'you don't understand. It is not possible for you see him at all. He died last night.'

It was my turn to stare for a few moments before I stammered, 'How, why?'

'One of the prisoners smuggled a kitchen knife into the prisoners' leisure hall yesterday evening. A fight broke out, but the only person injured was Zach who was stabbed and died later from the injuries. It looked like he was deliberately targeted.'

He went on to ask me a few questions - how I knew Zach, did I know if he had any enemies or why would someone would attack him. I told him all I knew, which was not much. He thanked me anyway and showed me out: I stood outside the prison wondering what to do.

I recalled that Mary had told me Zach had been hiding at his sister's house on the other side of the Island. I knew roughly where it was and reasoned I had nothing to loose by driving over to find his sister and see what she could tell me. There was a risk that she might just throw me out, especially as her brother had just been murdered.

As I drove across the Island I thought about Zach's death. Was it an unfortunate coincident that he died only hours before I was due to interview him, or

The Mango Mystery

was someone trying to stop me from talking to him and, if the latter, why? The most likely reason was that he had information that might be helpful in identifying the drug gang. Perhaps his sister would know something.

I found her easily enough by asking around the neighbourhood. She lived in a small, but colourful, wood and corrugated-iron house, and was preparing a stew in a large pot on a small stove, in a lean-to at the back of the house. I started by asking her if she was Zach's sister.

She replied, 'I know about Zach already - the police were here early this morning and told me had been knifed and had died last night. Can't say I am sorry, he was a sponger and waster. He stole money from me and even tried to sell drugs to my children.'

I was not sure if this was a good start or not for a conversation with her, but I pressed on, and using my newly found cover with Benson, Dodd, Sugar, told her I was interested in the period when Zach had hidden in her house just before he was arrested.

She could not tell me much, but she did explain that he been very frightened, and not just of the local police, she said, but from the drug gang he was involved with. She told me he had stupidly stolen some drugs, and thought that the gang was after him. She went on to tell me, 'But what really frightened him, he told me after he had been drinking one night, was that he knew one of the gang leaders on the Island. He told me he had hidden by one of the dead drops the gang used, and he had seen who collected the money there.'

I was excited now and interrupted her, asking whom he had identified.

John de Caynoth

'He would not tell me - just said he recognised the person immediately, and it was some one you would never even think of being involved with drugs.'

That was all she could tell me, so I thanked her for her help and left. As I drove back to "Windrush", I thought carefully about what she told me, especially that Zach knew who the contact was and it was someone you would not suspect.

I went through a mental list of people I knew on the Island. Unfortunately Joelle sprang to mind immediately, but I dismissed that thought as ridiculous. However, Zach might have seen someone else in the police, or perhaps in an official position, or could it be a regular visitor to the Island and not a resident? The dark man sprang to mind - perhaps Zach knew him. Clearly, this line of thought was not helping; with Zach dead it would be impossible to compile a list of individuals. I was stumped, and decided to talk it through with Joelle when I got back to the UK.

I spent the rest of the day at 'Windrush'. I wrote notes, summarising what I had learnt that week, before I went down to Glass Bar for the evening and sat alone with a glass of beer, trying to think clearly about the mass of information in my head and sort out the facts, deciding what I needed to do the next day.

Mary dropped me off at the Airport well before my flight was due, as she had to get back to the Glass Bar to open up for the evening. As usual, the airport was crowded and hot as I checked my bag in and collected my boarding card, making my through emigration control and the security check. As I went through the body scanner, the operator asked me to step to one side as they put my travel bag through the

The Mango Mystery

system again. The bag was taken to an empty table and searched: I was patted down. The security assistant pulled the copy of Joelle's diary out of the pile of belongs they had stacked on the table and asked me explain what it was. She then took it into an office to one side of the security area. She returned after a few moments, and told me they were confiscating the diary as it contained police evidential reports, and apologised for the inconvenience, telling me I was free to go. I tried pointing out that the diaries were personal papers, but it was clear there was no point in arguing so I quickly loaded everything back into my travel bag and went through to the departure hall before someone thought to arrest me as well.

Sitting in my seat on the plane, I pulled out my notebook to re-read my notes. Was it just coincidence that Zach had been killed only hours before I was due to see him and that I had been stopped and searched and the copy of Joelle's diary confiscated? If they were related incidents, this drug gang had good information, and a long and powerful reach. I also speculated on the evidence emerging from investigations into the drug-smuggling affair last year, and while a lot of it was circumstantial, recent events were leading me to the uncomfortable conclusion that Joelle could be involved. On the other hand, I reasoned, Tony Choizi was putting his spin on the facts and embroidering his reporting to incriminate Joelle.

But the seed of doubt was planted and I was beginning to fear where this was going to end.

John de Caynoth

Chapter 28. The Confession

Joelle

Saturday was one of those days when I just could not settle to anything. I put the television on, but quickly got fed up with cookery programmes. I tried to read a book, but decided to go shopping and stock up with ingredients for a nice meal for Douglas's return tomorrow. I habitually checked if I was being watched but I had seen nothing suspicious so far. Nevertheless, I was careful as I left the flat and deliberately set off in the wrong direction so I could check if anyone was following me, but thankfully there was no one else on the pavement. As I walked to the local supermarket I did see a man wearing a hoodie behind me at one point but he then disappeared. In the supermarket there was a black man wearing a hoodie pulled over his head. He did not seem interested in me though, and I had to tell myself to stop imagining that everyone with a hoodie was spying on me.

It was nearly lunchtime when I got back to the flat: I decided to phone Bernie, even though it would still be early morning in Kaeta. I felt quite homesick as he told me it was a beautiful sunny morning and a pleasant twenty-degree temperature in Kaeta. It was cold and drizzly in London!

Bernie asked me how the investigation was going and if I was still suspended, and then commiserated when I said I was bored and still waiting to hear. I asked after all my old colleagues in Kaeta and how they were keeping and if Bernie he was busy. He apologised for missing me yesterday when I had phoned, and explained be had to spend the day at the prison as an

The Mango Mystery

inmate had been knifed in a fight and subsequently died.

'Anyone I know?' I asked.

'Actually, yes,' Bernie replied,' you remember Zachariah Farthing - he was the unfortunate one, wrong place at the wrong time.'

I commiserated, the significance not dawning on me at the time, and then I asked if Bernie had seen Douglas. He said he had not, and did not know what he was doing. I asked if there was any news on the break in at 'Windrush', but again Bernie told me they had no leads and had put it down to an opportunistic burglary, which went wrong when Douglas disturbed them. We talked a little longer until Bernie announced that his wife wanted him and he had go, but before he said good bye, he asked, 'By the way, did you ever find your diaries you were telling me about?'

I replied, 'Yes and no, They were at 'Windrush', but it seems they disappeared in the break-in, but it is okay as Douglas made a copy, which he says he will bring back with him later today.'

'He never mentioned that at the 'Windrush' burglary,' Bernie commented, and I replied that he probably did not realise they had gone until later, and we finished the phone call at that point.

After lunch I decided to go for a walk across the common and this time I did suspect I was being followed. I had noticed a red Peugeot parked next door, near where the Range Rover had been, but what drew my attention was that as I started walking across the common a man wearing a hoodie, whose features I could not see, got out of the car and started walking

John de Caynoth

across the common as well. While he was not obviously following me, I noticed he always kept me in sight. I got bored playing a game of hide and seek with him and ducked into a newsagent's, buying a film on DVD to watch later. As I walked back to the flat the hoodie-man had gone, as had the red Peugeot.

That evening I watched my film with a glass of wine and went to bed early as I was getting up at four the following morning to meet Douglas.

Five-o-clock on Sunday morning found me standing anxiously at the arrival point at Gatwick airport watching travellers, as they emerged, trying to guess where they had come from. It seemed ages since I last seen Douglas, much longer the than the week he had been away and when he eventually appeared I ran up to him, and we hugged and kissed.

I drove back into London as I thought Douglas would be tired after an overnight flight, but he said he had managed to sleep and was feeling quite awake. I told him how the flat had been broken into and my iPad stolen, that Andrea had been reinstated, Bob Cash had been transferred, and a new DCI, Barbara Green, was taking the team over. Finally I mentioned that I was still being watched and followed, but by a different person - a black man wearing a hoodie. I told Douglas that Andrea had identified the dark man as Xavier Zedanski, known as Zed, but all we knew about him was that he had a German passport and that we had not seen him over the last week.

Douglas replied, 'I know, I spotted him in Kaeta watching me. They have the diaries now, so why they are still watching you?' Neither of us had an answer to

The Mango Mystery

this, so Douglas started to tell me what he had been doing in Kaeta.

'I saw Bernie first but it was very clear I was not going to get any official help from the police, he was very non committal with me. Merv, however, was a lot more help, but unofficially. I told you on the telephone about how Tony Choizi had taken statements from everyone and how Merv thought he had slanted what he wrote down to put you in the worst light possible. Fortunately, in your diaries, you refer to a lot of the same incidents but put a quite different spin on how they happened. Which reminds me, you know 'Windrush' was broken into and you diary taken.'

I interrupted Douglas by asking about the copy he had made. 'I will come to that in a minute,' he replied, 'but first, one thing I did discover was that Tony Choizi knew, very shortly after my extradition hearing, about the undercover police woman working at the veterinary practice in Eindhoven.'

'How?' I asked.

'Justin Cramp more or less admitted he left the file open, and Tony was alone with it in the office.'

'So he could have told the drug gang about the undercover police woman,' I thought out loud, 'but would he have known about Gruber, who was clearly tipped off to disappear when we found him in Neasden.'

Douglas thought about this and reminded me, 'Did you not tell me that Bob Cash asked you for daily reports and that he was sending reports on in advance of the meeting in Amsterdam before Christmas. Tony could have found out about Gruber that way, couldn't he?'

I agreed, but Douglas continued, 'There is something else I found out. You know Zach was killed before I was able to speak with him, but I did talk to his sister, and she told me he was very frightened when he went into hiding before his arrest. She thinks he recognised the person who was involved with the drug smuggling on Kaeta.' Again I interrupted and asked who it was.

'Zach did not tell his sister, all he told her was that it was someone who would never be suspected.'

I noticed Douglas was watching me intently as he told me this, and then continued to stare at me quizzically. Eventually, to break the silence I said, 'Well, it could be anyone then - is that all he said?'

Douglas did not answer my question, but picked up the conversation again, saying simply, 'I was searched at the airport as I left and the copy I made of you diary was confiscated.'

I looked at Douglas in surprise and asked, 'how do you mean, confiscated?'

'I was the only passenger stopped by the security check: they went straight for my bag, emptied the contents and went straight for the document. I think they knew exactly what they were looking for and I am left wondering if Zach's death and the loss of the copy of your diary is just coincidence, or whether there is more to it.'

Again as he said that, I saw him watching me carefully before he continued, 'Anyway, it's not the end of the world - I had a second copy which I posted to

The Mango Mystery

David Evans, the solicitor we spoke to, he should get it early next week.'

'That was clever,' I congratulated Douglas and thought that I would not have considered of doing that. We were nearly back to the flat by this time and we had exhausted our conversation and finished the journey in silence.

When we got back to the flat I prepared breakfast while Douglas unpacked his bags. Over breakfast Douglas told me that he would have to go down to Wiltshire to sort out his cottage following the break in there. He asked me to go with him but I told him I should stay in London as I was expecting the new DCI, Barbara Green to contact me. We had a discussion about the break-ins and agreed it was pretty obvious that someone, and it had to be the drug gang, were after the diaries, and that I must have put something in those diaries that would lead the police to them. As Douglas said, the only thing he could think of was that my diaries contradicted Tony Choizi's version of events when he, Douglas, was under surveillance, or alternatively, they think there may be something incriminating in the diaries.

After breakfast we mooched around the flat and I could see there was something on Douglas's mind. Eventually, I could stand it no longer and I had to ask him what was bothering him.

'Nothing,' was his first answer so I pressed him further.

'I am thinking about the break in at the cottage,' was his next reply.

'Is that all?' I questioned him and after a pause he said, 'Well, no not really. Some of the things I have turned up, combined with the way Tony Choizi appears to have reported certain events.' He paused here and I could see he was looking for the right words. 'I mean, well, they could be interpreted in a way which puts you in very bad light.'

'What exactly are you trying to say?' I asked, fearful of the way his mind was working.

'I suppose I am looking for an assurance that it was not you that Zach recognised as being the drug contact, or organiser, on Kaeta.'

Suddenly it hit me: if Douglas was thinking I might be guilty, how many others believed I was the police informer? With an edge of panic in my voice I accused Douglas, 'So you believe I am the mole, the informer working within the police and giving information to the drug gang.'

'Of course I don't believe it.' he said, but then qualified his conviction by asking, 'but I want you tell me its not true.'

I knew I had to convince Douglas, and so I put my arms around him and whispered to him, 'Of course it is not true, surely you know me by now and know that I would never be like that.'

Douglas hugged me back whispering, 'I am sorry. It is all such a mystery at the moment, I just needed you to tell me.'

But, secretly, I was very worried now. If Douglas could think like that I could soon be in very deep trouble, and I was not sure what I could do about it.

Chapter 29. DCI Barbara Green

Joelle, Monday

Douglas left the flat this morning saying he had to go back to his cottage and sort out the break-in there. He asked me again if I wanted to go with him, but I declined partly because felt I should stay in London and partly because there had been an atmosphere between us all Sunday and it was still there this morning. Douglas was barely speaking to me and I asked him again, today, if there was something troubling him and if he still thought I was a police informer.

'No.' He said, 'If you tell me you are not, I will believe you.' I pushed and asked what was bothering him then, and he told me he was worrying that we were getting involved over our heads. There had been too many coincidences, we were obviously being watched all the time, and, he told me, 'Don't forget, there has already been one attempt to run you down.'

'This is just part of my job,' I reminded him, 'but you do not have to be involved, in fact as a civilian, you probably ought not to be. It should all be over when this enquiry finally reports.'

'You don't believe that any more than I do,' Douglas frowned. 'It won't be over until this drug gang is found and arrested. Anyway, I am involved now, and we have to find evidence to show you are not trading police secrets.' I could see what he was thinking before he told me, 'I plan to go to Florida as soon as I have finished sorting out the cottage.'

John de Caynoth

I had to protest at his going to the States, but secretly I was pleased he was not going to desert me, but I was very worried what he might get involved in. 'Please be careful and watch out for Tony Choizi,' I told him.

'Don't worry,' he smiled, 'I have a plan, but there is something I would like you to do this morning; phone Bernie and see if he knows anything about me being searched and the copy of your diary being confiscated.'

He left shortly after this conversation, promising to phone me that evening.

Later in the morning I did phone Bernie. It was a brief conversation with me asking him if he knew why Douglas had been stopped on his way through the airport on Saturday and the copy of my diary confiscated.

Bernie's had no idea why Douglas had been stopped, but most likely they could not identify something in his baggage. He added that if security found official documents being taken out of the country without authorisation, it was routine to confiscate and destroy them. I told him I had never heard of that before, and that my diary was not an official document.

'Probably just a mistake if looked like a police evidence report, there's nothing suspicious to worry about,' Bernie assured me, and than added, 'but I suppose this means that you have lost all the copies of that diary of yours.'

'Well, no fortunately, Douglas had the foresight to make another copy before he left Kaeta.'

The Mango Mystery

'That's lucky' Bernie commented as he said goodbye, terminating the call.

Tuesday

I was having breakfast this morning when my phone rang. It was Barbara Green inviting me, in no uncertain terms, to come to a meeting in her office at 2.00pm this afternoon. 'I can't see you earlier as I am in meeting the team to get up to speed with the investigation. I know you are on suspension, but you are still a member of the team and I want to know what you are up to.' She rang off, leaving me feeling a bit nervous.

I did not want to be late for my appointment with the new DCI, and so I was very early, nearly two hours in fact. I went to the coffee bar thinking I could perhaps meet Andrea there and have some lunch and girl-talk to calm me down, so I phoned her to see if she was free.

'I'm sorry love, I would love to meet you but I am on duty. The new DCI says I can work on my own until you return to duty: she has got me doing odd jobs and follow-ups until then. In fact you will be interested in what I am doing right now. I am driving up to the vet in Warwickshire, you know, the one I told you about that had just made a big order for KetPil. Apparently the local plods went in on Saturday and asked if they had a locum vet called Gruber. There was a locum working, but he was South African and his name was Dirk Shnaps, so they just reported back that Gruber was not there. Unbelievable! Barbara has sent me up to check it out properly. Must go, see you soon.'

John de Caynoth

I drank a coffee cheered up by the comment that the new DCI expected me to return. I decided to phone the bike shop and see if my Triumph had been repaired yet. I spoke the owner, the guy with the long white beard.

'It's all ready for you.' He explained, 'We have road tested it and its now running fine, but I'll tell you, you were bloody lucky it would not start. If you had ridden it in that condition you would probably be toast by now.'

I asked him what he meant.

'One of the injectors was cracked and would have sprayed petrol out all over the exhaust, so you were sitting on a potential fire bomb. I have never seen anything like it before. It would not start because the sensor feed to the control unit had come off, so the management system thought it had no injectors and refused to start the machine. Bloody lucky really.'

I asked if he new how the damage had occurred and if he thought it was deliberate.

'Hard to say, luv: we were not looking to see if it had been tampered with so I really can't say. We have still got the old injector and were going to put it in our museum but you can take it if you like.'

I thanked him, arranging to collect the bike tomorrow, and settled down to waste an hour having lunch. I tried to call Douglas, but his phone went to the answering service.

At five to two, I was in the office we used, near Scotland Yard, waiting to meet the new Detective Chief Inspector.

The Mango Mystery

DCI Barbara Green walked confidently up to me and shook my hand warmly as she introduced herself, telling me she was pleased to meet me. She was a striking woman in her late forties, I guessed. She was about my height and looked very fit. I later discovered she went to the gym in her lunch breaks whenever possible. She had very dark hair, flecked with strands of grey, wore a pair of tinted glasses and was smartly dressed in a tailored brown knee-length skirt, teamed with a cream-coloured, roll-neck jersey, worn beneath a tweed jacket. When we reached her office she wasted no time with pleasantries and told me to tell her, in my own words, what was going on.

'Start right at the beginning, when you went to the airport on Kaeta to interview Douglas Jay, suspected drug smuggling,' she instructed me.

It took me over an hour to go over the whole story. She questioned me on the details and made her own notes. I finally brought her up to date, telling her that I thought I was still being followed by a black man, wearing a dark-coloured hoodie, which caught her interest. I also mentioned that my Triumph might have been tampered with.

'We picked up the Black Range Rover yesterday evening on the M25,' she revealed, 'the driver was a Caribbean gentleman, who we detained for questioning. I hope he is still at Paddington Green. He said he found the car, which had been hot-wired with a broken steering lock in a car park in Sutton, and he has admitted to stealing it. Derek Passmore discovered it had false number plates, and we are trying to trace the owner at the moment, but it matches a vehicle reported as stolen in Kensington before Christmas. The interesting thing is that there was a dark blue hoodie on the passenger seat when the vehicle was stopped.'

I stated the obvious conclusion that the driver could be the man who had followed me.

Barbara agreed, but changed the subject by telling me, 'I have seen the minutes of the meeting in Amsterdam: your explanation of the whole story is rather different to what was discussed, which resulted in your suspension. The facts are more or less the same, but the interpretation is quite different. I don't suppose you have any way of justifying your version of the story?'

'Bernie and Merv, who were involved with the original surveillance would surely describe the events as I have,' I told her.

'Well,' Barbara said, 'That's the thing, Tony Choizi's record of his interviews with the officers on Kaeta implies support for the Amsterdam version of events.'

I decided it was time to come clean about my diaries, even though I had not had chance to re-read them, so I explained to Barbara, 'When I became concerned at the way the investigation into Douglas was being handled, I started to keep my own private diary and contemporaneous notes, because I did not like the way Tony Choizi was relying on flimsy evidence and conjecture to construct guilt. My original notes, which were hidden on Kaeta, were stolen and a copy Douglas made has been confiscated. He went out to Kaeta last week to recover the diaries for me.'

Barbara looked at me sharply, clearly not very pleased. 'Why have you not mentioned these notes before now?' she asked angrily.

'I am sorry, they were very personal notes not just of what was going on, but of how I was feeling and my unsupported suspicions. I just did not think they were relevant.'

'They are very relevant,' Barbara said crossly, ' I wonder if we can retrieve the confiscated copy?'

'I don't think you need to,' I explained, 'Douglas made a second copy which he mailed to my solicitor, David Evans.'

Thankfully, Barbara's anger subsided and she smiled saying she would get the notes from David and read them and if she thought they were relevant she would submit them to the Enquiry. I must have been looking very miserable at this point, as I explained that she might find I had written rather uncharitably about Tony Choizi, his behaviour and methods.

Barbara responded, 'Cheer up Joelle, it all helps: Tony Choizi has said some very nasty comments about your behaviour, but I am inclined to believe you. I have spoken to your Commissioner on Kaeta and he speaks very highly of you. In fact he told me you were the best officer he has, and he wants you back. He says he liked your father and has known you since you were a young girl, and he does not believe a word of the accusations against you.' She paused before continuing, 'I also know Tony Choizi - I came across him when I was in Washington. He gets results, but his methods are rather suspect some times. I believe you when you say he came on to you: he has a reputation as a womaniser and he made a pass at me when I met him once in

John de Caynoth

Washington.' I saw her shudder at the memory before she continued, 'Now, tell me, is there anything else you have been up to which I should know about?'

I then told Barbara what Douglas and I had discovered over the last week or so while I was suspended. I told her everything, except that Andrea had told me about the Warwickshire vet, as I did not want to get Andrea into trouble. Barbara solved that problem for me as she, herself, told me that they might have a lead on Gruber at a veterinary practice in the Midlands.

We were more less at the end of the interview now, and Barbara complimented me again, telling me that I got more results in the period before Christmas, than the rest of the team had done since KetPils started appearing in London back last summer.

'I want you back on the team as soon as possible, but in the meantime I don't want you or your man-friend thrashing around in an uncontrolled manner. Keep me informed of exactly what you are up to, and what Douglas is doing as well, and tell him to stop playing the amateur policeman, or he will get himself into trouble.'

I left, feeling happier than I had done for weeks. I liked DCI Barbara Green and knew I could work with her. It was good to feel that she, at least, had confidence in me. I just hoped that faith would continue when she read my diary notes.

The Mango Mystery

Chapter 30. Threatened

Douglas

Thursday morning and I am sitting in the new Terminal 5 at Heathrow airport waiting for my flight to Miami International Airport.

I have hardly seen Joelle since last Monday when I left her to go down to Wiltshire to sort out my cottage and we were not on particularly good terms when we parted. My fault, I know. Flying back from Kaeta, I had sat on the plane thinking about what I knew of this drug smuggling affair. The evidence could be interpreted in a way that implied Joelle's guilt, and once that thought was fixed in my mind it niggled away, so eventually I had to say something to Joelle, even though I could not believe that she was involved with drug smuggling. Of course, she assured me she was not involved, but I could see she was distressed that I had even suggested such a thing. **I guessed that she was worrying about her forthcoming meeting with Barbara Green,** and the atmosphere between us lasted through to my departure to Wiltshire.

When I got back to the flat yesterday afternoon she was in a much more cheerful mood, more like the Joelle I know, but I sensed there was still something on her mind. She explained that she had a good meeting with her new DCI and had enthusiastically told me all about it. I think I was as pleased as Joelle that Barbara Green appeared to believe that the whole case against her was a mistake. I was less impressed on hearing Barbara's advice that I was not to play the amateur detective and to leave police work alone. Nevertheless, I still wanted to follow up my suspicions about Tony

John de Caynoth

Choizi as I had already booked and paid for a non-refundable ticket to Miami. I was concerned that Choizi's investigation had been biased against Joelle and no one seemed to be questioning this. Joelle implored me to be careful, so I explained that my plan was to hire a private detective as I had no intention of getting involved myself.

Yesterday, David Evans had phoned Joelle to tell her he had received a package containing a copy of the notes and diaries she had written, suggesting that she go to his office to go through the papers together. He also told her that he had been summoned to pass the papers over to a DCI Barbaras Green and did Joelle want him to challenge that? She confirmed that she had agreed to Barbara having a copy.

This morning, Joelle had accompanied me to Heathrow. 'As,' she said, 'I have nothing better to do and it's the only chance I get to spend time with you before you go jetting off round the world again.'

We caught the tube to Paddington for the Heathrow Express connection to the airport. It was a cold, but bright sunny day and, as Joelle looked out of the window, she wistfully wished that she could go back to Kaeta, even just for a couple of days. 'I want to feel warm, bury my toes in wet sand, see Jasmine and Mary, and sit outside Glass Bar with you, watching the sunset. Do you remember when we did that before?' I felt a rush of affection and said to her, squeezing her hand, 'When this is over we can take a week off and we will do just that.'

I woke from my day dreaming with a start at the announcement, asking the remaining passengers for the Miami flight to go to the gate where the aircraft was

The Mango Mystery

now boarding. I grabbed my bag and rushed to the departure gate: I had only got cabin luggage this time as I did not intend to stay in Miami any longer than necessary. As I stood in the queue to board the aircraft I saw, to my horror, the dark man, who I now knew was known as Zed, standing four people back in the queue and smiling evilly at me, making no attempt to look inconspicuous. There was nothing I could do and I reasoned he was not going to try anything on the plane. I had a horrible thought that he might be sitting next to me, but to my relief he was sitting some distance further to the rear of the cabin from me. I planned to lose him at the airport, reasoning that, if I shook him off then, he would have difficulty finding me once I was in Miami. I was wrong, though, about him leaving me alone during the flight, on three occasions he deliberately walked up the aircraft and stood staring at me.

When the plane landed, I waited impatiently for the seat belt light to flash off. As soon as it did, I jumped up, retrieving my bag, and moved as far as I could up the line of people waiting for the aircraft to dock. The door opened and as the passengers started to disembark, I heard a commotion going on at the back of the aircraft, as Zed tried to push his way past the waiting passengers towards me. Fortunately, one of the stewards stopped him and I left the aircraft well ahead of him, but I was under no illusion, and expected that he would soon catch me up. Glancing over my shoulder, I saw him rapidly walking past the passengers behind me. I spotted a toilet a short distance ahead, and ducked in, feeling pretty sure that Zed would see me. Instead of going into the gents', I nipped into the ladies' waiting there until I heard someone, Zed, I assumed, enter the men's toilet. He would waste time in there looking for me, so I shot out amongst the travellers for cover. Luckily, the immigration hall was very crowded and I saw no further sign of Zed.

My visas were all in order and I passed through immigration quickly making my way to the Metrorail Orange Line to get the train to Downtown Miami, eight miles away. When I got into town I found a taxi to take me to the Miami Biscayne Bay Hotel where I booked a room for three nights, and as I got into the room, breathing a sigh of relief that I had not seen any more of Zed. I wondered why he had changed his tactics. Up until now he had been quite covert while following, but now he was openly pursuing me in a very threatening way. If he was trying to frighten me, then he was certainly succeeding.

Chapter 31. The Private Detective

Douglas

I felt calmer this morning: I had seen no more of Zed yesterday evening and he had not been evident at breakfast. I hoped I had, indeed, lost him.

Before I left Wiltshire, I had looked on the Internet and found some private detective agencies in Miami. As soon as I had finished breakfast I took a taxi to the first one on the list. I was not quite sure how to approach such an organisation and wondered, too late, if I should have made an appointment. This particular agency had a large foyer with an equally large reception desk and two pretty receptionist ladies. I introduced myself, one of the ladies said she would get someone to see me. In no time at all, I was directed to a lift, told to go up to the nineteenth floor where I was greeted by a smartly dressed lady, who introduced herself as an Investigational Assistant. I explained that I was representing a London firm of lawyers and was investigating the background of a detective, Tony Choizi. She stopped me there, informing me that her firm specialised in divorce cases and did not take on work involving the police. She apologised for not being able to help me and sent me on my way.

I got exactly the same reaction from the second agency that I visited. However, at the third agency I met one of the Senior Investigators and he was slightly more helpful, as he told me I was wasting my time going round the big organisations as none of them would touch investigations involving police procedure, but I could try one of the smaller guys. He gave me a

John de Caynoth

name and address and told me to contact them, as he knew they were not too fussy what work they took on.

I took a taxi to the Miami Historic District to find the offices of Joshua Worthington Inc. The taxi driver assumed I was a tourist as he proudly pointed out Palm Cottage, built in 1897 and the Jesu Church from 1896. He explained these were the oldest buildings in town and that most of the real estate in the Historic District dated from the 1920s and 1930s. I was not really listening to him - the only thing that really struck me was that the buildings were not as tall as the skyscrapers in the Commercial Quarter, which I had just left.

He dropped me outside a building, which I assumed housed the offices of Joshua Worthington Inc. I entered, looking around the gloomy hall leading to the stairs. On one wall was a set of engraved brass plates announcing the names of the occupants. Beside each plate was a buzzer switch. I pressed the one beside Joshua Worthington Inc. and a disembodied, tinny voice asked me who I was, and what I wanted. I was invited to walk up to the third floor, turn right and knock on the door third on the left. I did as I was bid and I heard the lock slide back. The door was opened by an imposing, black gentleman, who introduced himself as Mr. Josh Worthington. He must have stood over six-foot tall, with broad shoulders and massive hands, one of which nearly crushed my puny paw as he shook hands. He had a shaved head, which made it difficult to guess how old he was. Not a man I would like as an enemy, I quickly decided.

I looked round the large, untidy room I had just entered. A big desk, on which stood a personal computer, was covered with piles of paper. There were

The Mango Mystery

bookcases, filing cabinets, a large couch, and a wooden chair. None of the furnishings matched each other. I later learnt that Josh Worthington worked on his own and this room was his only office: I also suspected he probably slept on the couch but never really found out.

I began to wonder what I was getting into, if I had made a mistake, and whether this investigator could really help me, but, before I could change my mind, he invited me to sit down **on the couch, while he perched on the rickety chair,** and tell him what I wanted. I stuck to my story that I was assisting a London firm of lawyers to collect background information on individuals thought to be involved in a drug smuggling racket and had been asked to look at Detective Tony Choizi's role in the matter and said I needed his assistance.

'That's not enough information for me to decide.' he said staring out of the window. He stood up to get a better view of the street saying, 'For starters, who are these London Lawyers?'

I answered his question, **but had concerns about him contacting Benson, Dodd, Sugar, as I suspected they would not approve of my self-appointed status.** However, he just grunted and said he had never heard of them and invited me to go on with the story. I thought how much I wanted to tell him **before saying,** 'The lawyers are defending a woman who has been accused of passing secret information to a gang of drug dealers.'

His next question was obvious, I realised afterwards, but it took me by surprise, 'If this woman is accused in London, why are you interested in an American detective?'

John de Caynoth

He was staring out of the window again and before I could think of a reply he turned back to me and said, 'Have you had lunch yet?'

'No.'

'Neither have I, and I am hungry. Lets go out and get some food.'

He seemed to take a very convoluted route, even appearing to double back at one point before we reached a little restaurant on one of the back streets.

'Real Southern food here, the best in town,' he announced, as he was greeted by the chef, who clearly knew Josh, and showed us to a cubical at the back. Josh ordered the house stew for both of us and told me it was crocodile, laughing at the shocked expression on my face. He smiled and told me it was okay, it was really beef, and laughed again at his prank.

He started to tell me about himself, that he had lived in Florida all his life, his father was dead but his mother still lived out near the Keys and he had a brother and a sister. He explained that he had once been in the police force but had experienced resentment against negroes, so he decided to quit. He explained that most of his clients were black and usually in some sort of trouble.

The food arrived and conversation paused while we ate. When Josh had finished he spoke, 'Right Mr Jay. If you want my help you had better start telling me truth - I want the whole story, and you can start by telling me why that man in the corner over there is following you. I turned to look, and Zed was sitting in the corner apparently absorbed in a newspaper. I was very glad I had Josh with me.

The Mango Mystery

I took a deep breath, and started to tell Josh about the whole business, starting in Kaeta two years ago when I had been suspected of drug smuggling. I told him about Joelle and that she was currently suspended, suspected of passing police information to the drug gang, and that I was trying to collect evidence to prove her innocence. I told him about Tony Choizi and that it was he who had initiated the accusations against Joelle and we suspected he might have done this to divert suspicion from the real culprit. Josh said nothing until I had finished.

I could see him turning my account over in his mind and eventually he said, more to himself than me, 'I know Detective Choizi, I have come across him in the past and it won't be easy to get under his skin. He is a vindictive bastard; I will have to be very careful if I take this on.' He was silent again before he turned to me and said, 'this will be an expensive job.'

I nodded in acceptance.

'I will charge you $300 per day plus expenses, and there will be a lot of expenses, as I will have to pay for information. I will need a big payment up front, lets say $2000 for starters, non refundable.' He was serious now.

I swallowed, I had anticipates that this was going to be expensive, but $2000 up front before I even got any results was a lot more than I had imagined. However I could not see I had any alternative if I was going to help Joelle.

'Okay,' I confirmed, 'I would like you to take the job on.'

John de Caynoth

'Good,' Josh replied, 'lets go back to the office and sort out a contract.'

As we returned to his office, Josh doubled back a couple of times to lose our tail. Clearing a space on his desk, Josh asked how soon I could get the advance to him as we signed a simple contract. I had my lap top with me but was unable to get an internet connection, so Josh gave me his bank account numbers and I promised to transfer the money as soon as I got back to the hotel. He asked if I had any documentation I could let him have to read, but all I had were the notes I had taken last week on Kaeta and Joelle's diary which I promised to send him as soon a possible. When we had finished our business, we shook hands and Josh asked me what I was going to do next.

'There is really nothing you can do here.' he told me, ' It would be best to leave it to me for a few days and see what I can come up with. You would best to go back to the UK before you get in trouble here with that tail of yours. I will keep in touch every few days by phone and send you written progress reports.' He promised, we exchanged phone numbers and email addresses, then he phoned for a taxi for me.

I got back to the Marriott and went up to me room. I was alarmed to see the door was open, I was sure I had locked it, and timidly entered the room. The first thing I saw was that my belongings had been searched and thrown all over the room. I was thankful to find there was no one in the room or the bathroom. I breathed a sigh of relief and locked the door. I collected my clothes to put them back in my overnight case and noticed that the lining had been ripped out. I swore and sat on the bed feeling very uncomfortable, wondering what to do. I rang Josh and his advice was to get the next flight back to the UK. I was to lock myself into the hotel room until it was time to leave, and, 'get a taxi from outside the hotel to the airport, don't book one in advance.'

I asked him if should report the break-in to the police. If nothing valuable was taken, he advised me not to bother, as they would not do anything. His last words were, 'Anyway, we can guess who did it can't we?'

I used my laptop, connected to the Hotel network, to contact my bank and transfer the money to Josh's account. Then I went on the airline websites and booked a return flight to Heathrow departing the following morning and finally phoned Joelle, but my mobile rang with an incoming call before I got through to her.

It was Josh again and he said, 'I have had a thought. Don't use the hotel network to make arrangements. Its not secure and they sometimes monitor messages to make sure nothing illegal is going on. If your tail is any good, he will have found a way to check your messages.'

'Too late,' I said, 'I have already done it.'

'Probably be okay,' was his reply, 'that account I gave you was just a clearing account I use. No money is ever left in it and you will be safe at the airport and on the plane. Good luck,' and he hung up.

I did then phone Joelle and told her I would back tomorrow, Saturday evening.

'Oh,' She said, ' Andrea has invited me over for dinner, I will put her off.'

John de Caynoth

I told her not to do that, as I did not expect to be back to the flat until around 9pm. I was only slightly disappointed when she agreed and said she would see me back at the flat tomorrow evening.

I lay on the bed worrying what I had got into and waiting for morning when I could leave to go home.

Chapter 32. The First Kiss

Joelle

Last Wednesday I dressed in my bike leathers, and carrying my boots and helmet, went to collect the Triumph from the repair shop. I think I was tailed by a pimply looking youth but I was amused as I wondered how he was going to follow me back. The bike was running well, so I took it for a long ride, just for the fun of it, but also to see if anyone came after me. A blue Nissan seemed to be behind me as I rode down the A23 out of London, but once I got to Coulsdon and the M23 I was able to open the bike up on the quite stretch of motorway before the M25 junction and leave the Nissan behind: I did not see him again that day. I headed into Brighton and stopped at a bike accessory store and bought a waterproof cover for the Triumph. It was not much in the way of security, but I found a way of padlocking it round the bike so I could tell if there had been any interference.

Next day, I reported to Barbara Green and gave her the faulty injector asking if she could get it checked for deliberate damage. I told her Douglas was in Miami and planning to hire a private detective. She swore and told me to keep her informed if the detective found anything. I also told her I thought I was still being followed whenever I went out. She frowned at this, promising she would assign a team to keep me under surveillance for a few days. If a tail was spotted, he would be brought in for a chat. She also told me that they had questioned the hoodie-man caught in the Range Rover but he stuck to his story, so all they could do was to charge him with vehicle theft and let him go on bail. 'I have a funny feeling we will never see him again,' concluded Barbara.

On Saturday, I had cleaned the flat ready for Douglas's return, and then, late afternoon rode the Triumph over to Andrea's for dinner with her and Jim. I took the Triumph as I wanted to be back at the flat for 9.00pm, when Douglas expected to return; I wanted be there when he did.

Andrea cooked a tasty roast chicken and Jim opened a bottle of chardonnay to go with it, but the disadvantage of taking the bike was that I could only drink one small glass. We had a good evening and Jim was on form, regaling us with his stories of bad driving on the motorways. The time flew by and it was after eight thirty when I gave my apologies and left.

The streets were fairly quite and I made good time and was approaching Clapham Common just before nine. On a whim I diverted slightly to return past Clapham North underground station and then rode slowly along the route I knew Douglas would use to walk back to the flat. I had not really expected to see him and was therefore nicely surprised when in the distance I spotted his unmistakable silhouette trudging along pulling a wheelie bag. I let the bike tick over and slowly caught up with him, but before I reached him, I stopped suddenly.

I had spotted another person behind Douglas, walking along but sticking to the shadows and I was ninety-nine percent sure I recognised him as the dark man, Zed. I dropped back and lost sight of Douglas but watched Zed as he followed Douglas. Douglas went into the flat and Zed crossed the road and stood in the shadow of a tree watching. I pulled the bike between

The Mango Mystery

two parked cars switched off the engine and lights, and sat with Zed in my sights.

He waited for about half-an-hour before he moved off again, this time crossing the road and making for the cars parked outside the neighbouring flat. He got into the red Peugeot and I watched while he drove slowly out of the car park and headed south across the Common. I let him get well ahead, started the Triumph and followed him. Even though the orange streetlights distorted the night colours, I knew he was in the red Peugeot as it had been parked in the same place for the last four days. He headed for the A23 and, with the slightly heavier traffic on the main road, I was able to close the gap between us and followed him easily. At Streatham, he turned off and headed towards Lewisham but the roads, being less busy, made it much harder to track him without being spotted. At one point I thought I had lost him, but luckily he got delayed turning towards Dulwich and I rode past him, doubling back to follow him. He was driving faster now, which made it easier for me to keep up without looking suspicious. He headed for Dulwich Village and the posh expensive houses. He signalled left, pulling off the road into a private estate, and again I road past, noticing that the estate was security guarded. I waited a few moments before re-tracing my tracks, pulling into the drive and stopping by the security cabin. As I expected, the guard shouted through the window that this was private land and what did I want. I took my helmet off and explained I was lost and wanted to get to Purley: I remembered the place from my ride down to Brighton. The guard, realising I was a woman, came out of his cabin and started chatting me up as he gave me directions, which gave me sufficient time to notice that the red Peugeot was parked in the space outside the fifth house along on the right had side and note that the estate was called, rather unimaginatively, Green Lane Mews. The security man rather obligingly told me that there were thirty terrace houses in five blocks arranged in a crescent, overlooking a grassed area behind the houses.

'The houses are built with the front looking out over the green and the back facing the road way,' he told me.

'That must make the numbering rather difficult,' I said.

'Not at all,' and pointing to the right he said, 'those are all even numbers and,' he said, indicating to the left, 'those are all odd ones.'

'So, that means, for example, that Peugeot along there is actually parked behind house number ten.'

'You got it,' he happily told me, 'that's where Mrs Lecarrow lives, although I think it's rented out at the moment.'

I declined the invitation to join him in his cabin and get warm, thanked him for the directions and set off to the flat feeling very pleased with myself.

When I got back, Douglas was waiting for me and asked if I had a good evening. I sat on the couch next to him and told him how I found Zed's lair. He congratulated me and told me how Zed had followed him to Miami and then he started to tell me about his trip. As we spoke we leant towards each other and I felt Douglas, very tentatively, put his arm behind me along the back of the couch. To my surprise, I did not mind and when I felt his hand on my shoulder I leant

The Mango Mystery

towards him knowing that he wanted to kiss me. Our first kiss led to another and as we slumped back on the couch I felt his hand start to caress my breasts. His kisses and caresses became more urgent as I felt him become aroused. 'No, Douglas, not yet.' I pleaded.

He backed off and with just a hint of frustration, and disappointment, asked me what was wrong. I told him I was sorry but I was not ready yet and before I could give myself, this time, I had to sure.

I was relieved when he gave me one last quick kiss and said, 'Okay, we will take it day by day, but I can't wait for ever.'

John de Caynoth

Chapter 33. Shot

Joelle, Monday

I tried to contact Barbara Green on Sunday to tell her I thought I had found where Zed was living but I was told she was not available. I phoned Andrea on her mobile and told her, but, while she was quite excited to hear my news, she did advise me to speak to Barbara in person, so first thing on Monday, I phoned Barbara.

She congratulated me for good work and then deflated me by reminding me I was still suspended and was supposed to distancing myself from any active investigations. However, she then went on to discuss with me what we should do.

'After all,' she mused, 'we don't really know who he is or why he is following you, it is supposition that he is connected with a drug gang.'

I pointed out that he had been involved with drugs in the past and, in any event, he was clearly following and threatening Douglas, and me, so should we not bring him in for questioning?

Barbara considered this and agreed, but added, 'If he is connected to this drug gang, they are pretty ruthless and I doubt he would admit to anything. I think we will do this by the book, I will get a search warrant and we go in, search the house and hopefully find something useful, catching him off guard. I will also find out who this Mrs Lecarrow is and if we have anything on her.'

Barbara then moved to another matter, 'Now, Joelle, I need to tell you that I read through that diary of your last week: it does put a very different interpretation on the circumstantial evidence that resulted in your suspension. You have possibly overdone your suspicions regarding Tony Choizi, but no doubt that will get followed up in due course. I was interviewed, at my request, by the Enquiry Board team last Friday and I have given them the diary. I told them quite bluntly that in my opinion this accusation, concerning your alleged involvement with a drug smuggling gang, was made on the flimsiest of evidence, without the proper checks being made to substantiate the facts. I was horrified when they told me they had not spoken with the Commissioner of Police on Kaeta, but had relied on character assessments provided by the USDEA. Finally, I told them that you are one of the best officers on my team and I want you back.'

Barbara then explained, 'I probably should not have told you what I discussed with the Enquiry Panel, but I have just received a message that the Panel wish to interview you at 10.30 tomorrow morning. When you attend, be confident in yourself - not looking miserably guilty as you did when you first met me. Oh - and by the way, you will have to go to Birmingham. Can you manage that?'

When I got home, I told Douglas about my forthcoming interview. I explained that Barbara had spoken up for me, which cheered me up no end, and I hoped perhaps this suspension would be lifted tomorrow. I told Douglas, in my excitement, that I was going to phone Bernie and tell him the good news, but Douglas told me to calm down, and said he doubted that the Enquiry would reinstate me, 'I expect they will just issue a report and it will up to your senior officer what the do. I also think that you ought to contact

John de Caynoth

David Evans and let him know you are to be interviewed by the enquiry panel.'

I made some phone calls, firstly to David Evans who said he would accompany me to the interview, arranging to meet me at Euston Station in the morning to take the train to Birmingham. I phoned Bernie anyway, and told him that I was to be interviewed by the Enquiry Panel and that I was hopeful this business would be finished soon. The other person I wanted to tell was Andrea, but it was late afternoon before I got hold of her.

'I don't know what you said to Barbara this morning,' she said, 'but she pulled the whole team in after you spoke to her and she has had us jumping around all afternoon, organising a house search and trying to find information about a Mrs Lecarrow. I have to go in at four o'clock tomorrow morning as we have an early morning raid. I will say this for Barbara, when she moves she goes quickly.'

Tuesday

Douglas decided to come to Euston with me, to wish me luck. He offered to come to Birmingham as well but I told him it was probably best not to as David Evans wanted to use the train journey to talk through the evidence and discuss managing the Enquiry Panel.

As we left the flat to walk to the Underground Station I pointed to the neighbour's parking area, 'Look Douglas, the red Peugeot is back.'

'Are you sure it's the same one? There are lots of red Peugeots about,' he answered.

The Mango Mystery

'I think it is but I can't be sure - I never got the registration of the one Zed was driving on Saturday.'

At that moment my mobile phone rang. It was Andrea calling.

'Can't talk for long love, in fact I should not be talking to you at all, but I have just slipped out for a smoke and I thought you would want an update on the raid this morning. When we got there, both the car and the resident were absent and the house was empty. We went in anyway and searched the place and took photos. Clearly, a man is living there, his clothes were spread all round the bedroom, and there was food in the kitchen. There was nothing to indicate who he is, and all we found was a small envelope of hash. I spoke to the security guard who told me he did not know his name, but confirmed he had arrived just before Christmas and gave me a description that sounded very much like Zed. Anyway, the DI leading the raid has left a couple of DCs there to wait for his return. Sorry got to go now, see you soon,' and she disconnected.

While I was talking to Andrea, Douglas walked over towards the car to take a closer look, and wrote down the registration number saying, as he returned to me, 'There's no one in it - if we were being tailed surely there would be someone in it, watching the flat.'

I told Douglas about the raid. We kept an eye out for a tail as we walked to the Underground Station. The train we boarded was so crowded that it was impossible to spot anyone following us. When we got to Euston, Douglas waited with me until David Evans appeared. He shook David's hand and kissed me goodbye wishing me luck. 'Ring me and let me know how it goes,' he said as he walked away. I felt a pang of loss as I watched him disappear into the crowd realising how much I had come to rely on him and how much support he gave me. I had horrible sense that I might never see him again.

David looked at me curiously and asked if I was okay. I shook the feelings of foreboding aside and smiling, said, 'Yes, I'm fine. Lets go and get on the train.'

The platform was heaving with people as we walked up to the front of the train. David had bought first class tickets explaining it would be quieter there, and easier to talk. About half way along the platform we heard a commotion behind us. I looked at the train, thinking that someone might have tripped getting into a carriage, but David had a clear view down the platform. Suddenly David pulled me sharply over behind a pillar: I think heard a pop as we both stumbled and fell, with David landing heavily on top of me. I was winded for a moment, but when I got my breath I asked David what on earth was going on. As he stood up, he pointed to the broken window of a train on the opposite platform and said, 'Did you not see the man with a gun? He looked at me in horror and gasped, 'You're covered in blood - looks like you've been shot!'

The Mango Mystery

Chapter 34. Confidential

Douglas

After I left Joelle and David Evans, I headed straight to the Underground and got the train back to Clapham North. As I was walking back to the flat, my mobile phone rang. I paused to answer it and it was my voicemail callback. I recognised Joelle's voice and, from her tone, knew immediately that something was wrong.

'Douglas, it's Joelle. There's been an incident: the Police have taken charge and called for ambulances, insisting that David and I go to the hospital. I will call you again when I know more.' I tried to call her back but got no answer, so I left a message saying that I was returning to Euston and asking her to ring me as soon as possible.

There was pandemonium at Euston. I was stopped by a member of the station staff as I tried to get into the main station and advised to make alternative travel arrangements. I told him I was meeting someone and pushed past him.

The station concourse was packed with people, commuters arriving late for work trying to push their way to the exit and travellers, pushing their way in, trying to find a train going to their destination. As I fought my way through the crowds, I saw a couple of police officers keeping the access to one of the platforms clear so I pushed my way through to them. They were preventing anyone from leaving, or walking onto, the platform but eventually I got near enough to explain that I was meeting one of the passengers, who was supposed to join the Birmingham train. He just

John de Caynoth

shrugged and apologised, saying there way no way he could let me through, and walked off. I tried to slide past the other officer to get to the platform, but to no avail. As he stopped me, blocking my way with his outstretched arm, I told him I was the fiancé of one of the injured passengers, which got his attention and he asked me which passenger. I gave him Joelle's name: after thinking for a few moments, he called someone on his radio explaining that he was with a man claiming to be the fiancé of the injured woman. The voice on the other end told him to let me onto the platform and find Sergeant Kahn.

Again, it was a matter of pushing through the crowd who were by now getting very irritated at being prevented from leaving. However, once I had pushed beyond, them the platform became much clearer and I saw a group of policeman standing with a knot of passengers round them. I asked for Sergeant Kahn and was directed to an officer holding a megaphone. I introduced myself to him and he asked me to wait a moment, while he dealt with the people on the platform. He proceeded to address the crowd trying to leave, bellowing through his megaphone, asking if anyone saw what had happened to please leave their name and address with one of the officers. Only two people stepped forward. At that point he told the two constables at the exit to allow people to go on their way, turning his attention to me.

I explained who I was, and that I was looking for Joelle. He told me there had been an incident in which a gun had been discharged, and that a lady and gentleman had been injured and taken to hospital, confirming two people to be Joelle, and David Evans. I asked him if they were seriously injured. He informed me that the woman appeared to have been hit by the bullet, but her injury did not seem to be serious and that they had been taken to St Thomas' hospital, near Waterloo Station.

I fought my way back across the station concourse, making for the Underground, but changed my mind when I saw the crowds around the entrance, deciding to take a taxi instead. The immediate area outside the entrance was almost as crowded as inside: the press had turned up, as had the TV cameras, but the atmosphere was quite different. People were gathering to see what was going on and the mood, if not exactly festive, was certainly curious as people exchanged stories and theories. There was not a taxi in sight, and after standing looking round in some despair I came up with Plan C - to walk along Euston Road in the direction of Warren Street Underground Station and, if the Northern Line was disrupted, which I thought it might be, I could continue to Baker Street where I could pick up the Bakerloo Line, which would take me directly to Waterloo.

Eventually, I reached St Thomas's and was directed to Accident and Emergency where I explained that I was looking for the two people who had been involved in the Euston Station incident. I used the fiancé excuse again when asked if I was a relative, and I was to wait until a member of staff was available to talk to me. It was not long before a nurse told me that both Joelle and David were fine, but a bit shocked, and were having a cup of tea and a sit down while they recovered. She took me through to a wide corridor with seats down one side where I found Joelle and David. Joelle and I hugged, but then I remembered she had been injured so I stepped back in case I hurt her.

John de Caynoth

I asked, 'What happened, where are you injured?'

'I'm not,' Joelle replied, 'I just had a nose-bleed and it had dripped on to my clothes'.

'It must have been quite a nose-bleed,' I commented as looked at the front of her shirt.

David joined in the conversation, 'It was, it looked quite serious as she lay on the ground trying to get her breath back. I tripped and I must have hit her on the nose and winded her as I fell.'

Joelle winced as she touched her nose, 'It is a bit sore, but at least its not broken. We have both been checked over and are free to go when we have finished our tea.'

I asked what had happened about the interview with the Enquiry Panel.

'I have spoken to them and rearranged the interview for tomorrow' David answered and then explained, 'As soon as we are finished here we have to report to the British Transport Police offices in Whitfield Street, and make our statement of events.'

I asked if they knew who had done the shooting and again David replied, 'No, Joelle was looking the other way so did not see anything, and all I saw was the muzzle of a gun pointing directly at us. I was vaguely aware of a human being behind the gun but the whole event was over in milliseconds and my attention was entirely on the gun.'

He had finished his tea by now and put his cup down asking us to excuse him, 'I am going along to Whitfield Street now to make my statement and then back to the office. I will see you in the morning, Joelle, and we will try to get Birmingham again.'

The Mango Mystery

Joelle said she needed to go back to the flat to change her clothes before she did anything else.

When we got back to flat Joelle had a shower and walked into the living room wearing a dressing gown, towelling her hair dry.

'Do you think you should telephone Barbara Green and let her know what has happened?' I suggested, speculating that Zed was involved, 'after all, his empty car was parked outside the flat, so I bet he was around somewhere watching for us. I don't think it was by chance that someone took a pot shot at you - it's got to be because of your interview.'

Joelle replied, 'I have been thinking the same, except we don't actually know that was Zed's car, but what puzzles me is why would he change tactics now, and in such a public place?'

'Well, I think that is obvious, who ever it is, they don't want you to talk to the Enquiry Panel. Incidentally the red Peugeot has gone,' I commented as I looked out of the window.

'Yes, I suppose so. Anyway, I will phone Barbara Green as soon as I have dressed.' she replied as she moved to her bedroom to find fresh clothes to wear.

I sat quietly in the living room as Joelle phoned Barbara Green and tried to listen but Joelle had shut the door so I had to wait until she ended her call and came and joined me in the living room.

'What did she say?' I asked

'She was cross, very cross.'

'Not with you surely.' I queried.

John de Caynoth

'No, with the **British Transport Police.** Of course she knew there had been an incident and I told them who I was. Apparently, Chief Inspector Cash was running the investigation and did not feel it necessary to inform Barbara. She's not at all happy! She said she is going to arrange for twenty four hour protection for me, and has told me to stay in the flat until she can get that organised.'

'I thought you were supposed to go and make a statement,' I said.

'Barbara says she will send someone round. She agreed that it is most likely Zed behind this and she is circulating his description. She thinks he will probably try and leave the country, but that's no comfort to us, as she also thinks someone else will take over from him.'

I looked out of the bedroom window, the common and everything out there seemed so normal, but I felt fearful, not just for Joelle, but for myself as well.

About two hours later, Barbara Green arrived in person. She nodded politely to me and asked Joelle if there was somewhere they could talk in private. I took the hint and went into the bedroom with my laptop, settling down to read my emails.

I had fifty-three of them in my inbox and forty-nine of them were rubbish, which I deleted without reading. Of the remaining four, there was one from Edith Meadows telling me all was normal in the village, and one from a management consultancy organisation offering me a temporary job, but I declined feeling I could not take on any work until the current mess was sorted out. There was another one from the Land Agents in Kaeta offering me a list of properties for sale.

The Mango Mystery

The details of one house in particular caught my eye, and I made a note to go and look at it next time I was in Kaeta, if it was still for sale. The final email was from Josh Worthington with his report on his initial investigations. It was read as follows:

> *CONFIDENTIAL*
>
> *Using a reliable source, (not disclosed) I have conducted initial enquiries about Detective Tony Choizi.*
>
> *He is a senior detective assigned to drug related investigations within the US Drug Enforcement Agency. He rents a house on the outskirts of Miami currently occupied by his wife, from who he is now estranged. It is understood that he pays her an allowance and she covers the rent on this property. He rents an apartment in central Miami in which he lives. He drives a new European car (BMW).*
>
> *(As far as I could establish at this stage, he only has his police income but appears to have an expensive life style. I have not yet had the opportunity to investigate his finances.)*
>
> *He is tolerated, rather than liked, by his colleagues and is recognised as an officer who 'gets the results', but he does not always work to the book and his methods are sometimes questionable and have, in the past, resulted in abortive prosecutions. He is considered ruthless and can be vindictive towards those who cross him. His colleagues consider him to be a bully and a womaniser.*
>
> *That is a summary of what I have got so far. I can dig deeper and see if I come up with anything else if you wish me to continue. Costs so far are two days of my time and expenses of $500.*

John de Caynoth

I replied asking Josh to dig a little further and then printed the email for Joelle to read, not thinking that the printer was in the other room and would produce the document under the noses of Joelle and Barbara.

Barbara was with Joelle for about an hour. When she left, Joelle came into the bedroom to tell me what they had discussed but first she thanked me for the copy of the email. 'Barbara read it with great interested and said she could have told us all that, but she did say to let her know if his finances turned up anything interesting.'

Joelle then explained that she had made a formal statement which Barbara took down for her to sign, but as she did not see anything was not really able to say much except her suspicion that Zed was behind the shooting.

'Barbara then told me that the witness descriptions of the man with the gun are vague but the majority describe him as wearing a plain hoodie, possibly grey, pulled right up hiding his face and wearing baggy, black training trousers with a red stripe down the side of each leg. They say he pulled the gun out of a pouch on the front of his hoodie, and after he had fired the shot, calmly replaced the gun and walked off down the platform.'

'So he could not be identified as Zed,' I mused, 'But also it could actually be him.'

'Yes,' Joelle continued, 'but there is more. Just after the shooting, an attendant found the hoodie and trousers in the gent's toilet, so it looks very much like a professional hit. Barbara is pretty sure Zed is behind it. I gave her the registration number of the Peugeot when

The Mango Mystery

I spoke to her earlier and she has already traced the owners. It was stolen from the long-term car park at Gatwick airport and reported by an elderly couple when they returned from holiday. But, get this, they say they left for the Canary Islands just before Christmas for a three-week holiday, staying in the Gatwick Runway Hotel the night before they left, booking a parking place through the hotel. After they had checked-in, a porter came up to them and asked for the keys to the car so he could take it to the car park. He told them it would be outside the hotel on their return and to ask at reception for the keys. They described the man as having a foreign, European accent, with dark swarthy features.

'Zed!' I exclaimed and Joelle continued, 'The hotel confirmed that they had no one like that working as a porter, and anyway they would never ask for a guest's car keys to take the car to the long term car park. So, yes, we can pretty sure that it was Zed.'

John de Caynoth

Chapter 35. The Interview

Joelle

At just after seven, the morning after the shooting incident, the doorbell rang. Luckily both Douglas and I were up, getting ready to go to Birmingham. Douglas went to the door and using the intercom, asking who was calling.

'Police - for DI de Nouvelas,' was the answer, to which Douglas replied, 'Yes, but who are you and what do you want?' He asked, wary of the last occasion the police had called early in the morning.

'My name is John, I am from the firearm squad and I have been sent to assist DI deNouvelas.'

'Okay, come up.' Douglas said opening the downstairs door.

John was a burly six-foot rugby playing type, wearing a woolly hat and loose-fitting fleece coat. I did not ask to see his gun, assuming it was under his coat somewhere. He introduced himself and told me he and his colleague Winston would be with me during the daytime.

'I came early this morning as I understand you have to go Birmingham. I will accompany you.' He looked around and asked if he could check over the flat. He said it looked pretty secure and reckoned we would be safe enough locked inside. He did not have the man power for twenty-four hour coverage so either he, or Winston, would be on duty during the day. 'You will find one of us sitting in the grey Honda, parked outside, when you are in the flat. Let us know if you are going out and we will accompany you wherever you go. You

The Mango Mystery

won't necessarily see us, but we will be with you all the time.' He then gave a phone number telling me, 'That's for emergencies - if you feel threatened at night, call that number and someone will be here in ten minutes, max.' He gave us a cheery smile and said, 'Oh, and by the way, don't go out on your motorbike, we won't be able to keep up: if you need to get somewhere ask us, and we will take you in the Honda,' and with that, he disappeared.

Douglas said he was going to come to Birmingham with me today. I told him I would be perfectly okay, as I had a protector now, but he said he would still come - he would feel safer that way!

Today, the journey was uneventful. We met David Evans at Euston Station, which this morning had returned to normal, and we caught the train to Birmingham. John appeared as we sat down and moved us to seats where he could position himself in a gangway seat opposite us and he settled down with his head apparently buried in a newspaper.

David and I presented ourselves at the Police Headquarters in Birmingham. John appeared just behind us and showed his warrant card to the duty sergeant. There appeared to be a dispute over the gun but John clearly won the argument, whispering to us, as he walked past, that he would be waiting in the staff canteen. He gave me a mobile number, instructing me to phone him when we finished. Meanwhile, the duty sergeant was eyeing me very suspiciously, and I commented to David that he probably thought I was some sort of arch- villain that John was guarding.

I was getting nervous now as we were escorted into a meeting room. There were three uniformed

John de Caynoth

officers sitting round the table, together with a Superintendent and two Chief Inspectors, one of whom was an Asian lady. David informed the panel that he was my solicitor and he would be attending the interview. He had decided the best tactic was to let them talk so we could try and find out what evidence they had against me.

In the event that was quite easy: the Superintendent informed me that they would be reviewing information they had been given, and would be seeking my comments. They cautioned me, before asking if I accepted that I had been acting suspiciously, during the surveillance of Mr Jay on Kaeta. I was about to deny this, but David jumped in and objected to the question, telling them be specific in their accusations.

The superintendent consulted his notes, 'It is alleged that you caused Mr Jay to have a nearly fatal motor cycle accident, planted drugs in his room to incriminate him, and edited the reports sent to the US investigating detective in order to implicated the said Mr Jay in a drug smuggling racket, and that this was done to divert attention from your alleged involvement.'

David responded, 'My client does not wish to comment at this point.'

The superintendent continued, 'It is further alleged that you then had an affair with Mr Jay and, having become infatuated, had to find a way of undoing the trail of evidence you had built up against him. This was easy for you to do, as you already knew how the operation worked. Subsequently, you travelled to London and Amsterdam, in a private capacity, in order to divert attention from the operation in Kaeta.'

David repeated his previous response.

The Mango Mystery

The superintendent continued again, 'You were one of a small number of people who knew of a police undercover officer who was subsequently murdered. It is alleged that, **having discovered the identity of this person,** you informed the gang leaders.'

I was seething by now. David put his hand on my arm to silence me, making no comment himself, so after a silent pause the lady inspector asked, 'Is it true that you tried to seduce Detective Choizi when he visited the Island to distract him from his investigation?'

This process of firing these accusations continued until I could stand it no longer, and I whispered to David that this was all wrong, and I wanted to deny everything. He interrupted one of the Inspectors and said, 'Miss deNouvelas denies all these accusations and would remind you that, while the underlying events to which you refer did indeed take place, the interpretation of those events, as presented to you, is, at best, unsupported supposition, and in some cases downright lies. In her defence, my client has presented her contemporaneous notes and diaries, which are a true record of the events, to her senior officer and these throw a completely different light on what has occurred, exonerating my client.'

The superintendent smiled, confirming that Barbara Green had made a copy of these notes, which were available to them.

David continued, 'Furthermore, my client denies that she was one of only a handful of people who knew of the undercover officer. The USDEA Detective involved was made a party to this information, which would then have become widely known in the Miami police offices.' He then gave them a copy of Douglas's notes, made while he was in Kaeta earlier this month, as proof.

David then finished by saying, 'Miss deNouvelas is a first class policewoman - a highly respected and competent officer - who has the full support from her superiors on Kaeta, which of course, you will have confirmed with the Commissioner of Police on Kaeta.'

There was some mumbling amongst the panel members before the superintendent said they had one last point we would like to clarify.

'We understand that you and DS Spooner traced a veterinary practitioner, believed to be involved in obtaining KetPil and selling them illegally, but that this person was warned of your interest and disappeared before he could be detained. You and Mrs Spooner were the only people aware of this, and in a position to warn the suspect.'

Before David could silence me I said, 'That is not true, I was making daily reports to DCI Bob Cash and informed him that it was our intention to interview the vet and I understood that he was forwarding those reports to Amsterdam and America.'

Again there was more whispering by the panel members, before the Superintendent informed us that the interview was finished and we were free to leave. He confirmed that the panel would be finalising their conclusions within the next few days, and would be sending their report to my senior officer for him to take the appropriate action.

As we left, I phoned John and he met us in the reception area and I arranged for us to meet Douglas, who was in a coffee bar around the corner. John sat at a

The Mango Mystery

separate table, and after ordering our drinks, Douglas asked how the interview went. I told him I found it difficult and stressful, sitting through a string of accusations based in erroneous supposition and lies. Douglas commented that he could probably guess the source of most of the accusations. I agreed, and we both mouthed 'Choizi!' in unison. David Evans, however, was quite cheerful, saying he thought it had gone well, 'We now know the weight of evidence they have against you: we have enough ourselves to cast doubts on much of it, if not actually discount it. I am confident that if this proceeded to a prosecution, we could get the case dismissed, but I very much doubt it will ever get that far.'

I was still tense when we got back to the flat, and, while Douglas went into the kitchen to find something to eat, saying he was hungry, I decided to phone Bernie to tell him about the enquiry. He was not answering his mobile. On phoning the Police Station in Kaeta, Merv told me that Bernie was having a few days off in preparation for his retirement, and said he was going to visit some of the other Caribbean Islands. 'He is thinking of leaving Kaeta, as too many people know him as a policeman.'

That shocked me: Bernie had always been such a rock. I had not really taken on board his retirement yet, let alone the fact that he might leave the Island for this next phase in his life. At that point Douglas came out of the kitchen, grumbling that there was no food and nothing to do in the flat. I answered, rather tetchily, 'That's not my fault, go out and do some shopping if you're bored.'

John de Caynoth

'Oh yes, and how am I supposed to that with a policeman sitting outside telling us not to leave the flat?' Douglas threw back at me.

'Don't be so stupid,' I responded, 'he is only doing his job. Order some food online, to be delivered, if you don't want to go out.'

I am afraid we had both lost control at that point. Douglas shouted, 'How dare you accuse me of being stupid - you are just selfish and self-centred.'

I retorted, 'How dare you speak to me like that after all I have done for you!'

We exchanged more insults and eventually I just walked out of the living room, telling Douglas he could do what he liked. I did not want to talk to him anymore and, as I slammed the bedroom door, I heard him say, 'Fine, if that what you want. I am going down to Wiltshire for the weekend - I'll see you next week when you have calmed down.'

Inwardly seething, I cursed men in general, particularly Douglas and Bernie, for deserting me when I needed them. I busied myself with cleaning the flat, dragging the Hoover around after me. Good riddance!

The Mango Mystery

Chapter 36. Summoned to Amsterdam

Joelle

Douglas came back to the flat on Sunday evening, presenting me with a large bunch of flowers and a tea mug he had bought that said '*Sorry Love*' on the side. It also said on the bottom '*I have a headache*', but he explained he had not seen this when he bought it. I was sorry as well, but had nothing to give him in return, but as he said, when you really love someone it does not matter. I still felt cross with him for starting such a stupid row as we lounged on the sofa together, listening to music. Douglas told me how he had spent the weekend tidying up the cottage, and asked me what my reaction would be if he moved out to live on Kaeta. I was surprised at this - I had not even thought he was considering moving, but I had been mulling over returning to live in England with him, when this business was over. Eventually, we exhausted our conversation and, feeling the effects of a second bottle of wine, slumped into a warm, cosy embrace. Douglas fell asleep and lay there with me holding him, wondering how much I was prepared to give up for this man.

When we arose on Monday morning, Douglas looked out of the window, noticing that Winston was on duty today. He made a cup of tea and took one out for him, sitting in the car while Winston drank it. When he returned, he reported that Winston told him there had been no sign of anyone else watching the flat, and that he and John had been reported, by the neighbours, to the local nick as being suspicious characters lurking outside the building.

John de Caynoth

Later that morning I received a call on my mobile from Barbara Green, asking me if I could come into to see her that afternoon, as she had something urgent to discuss with me. Of course I could!

As I walked into her office she jumped straight to the point.

'I have told DS Passmore I want this suspension business finished and you back on active service - now. I have told him that, in my opinion, all these accusations against you are mischievous, to which he agrees. Anyway, he has spoken with the Enquiry Board, who are going to report that the accusations against you are open to question, and that any prosecution is unlikely to succeed. Derek has agreed that you should be reinstated, with immediate effect, to be reviewed when the Enquiry Board submits its final report. Inspector van den Leuven, who is now running the drug investigation unit in Amsterdam, wants you to go out there. He believes that you may be able to assist them with their investigations. They have another dead body, which they are hoping you can identify.'

I was lost for words: having been bored and isolated for days, I now appeared to back in the middle of events again. I did not hesitate to say yes, but thanked Barbara, telling her I would do what ever was necessary. She told me to spend some time in the incident room, to get up to speed with the investigation, before travelling to Amsterdam.

I went back to the flat full of expectation at being involved again, but slightly fearful of telling Douglas, concerned about his reaction.

Of course, Douglas was pleased that the suspension was ended but pointed out to me that it

The Mango Mystery

appeared they had not exonerated me, but had just said a prosecution was unlikely to succeed. In my excitement, that had not occurred to me. He also asked what was going to happen about my two police protection officers and whether their surveillance would continue, 'After all, being back at work does nothing to reduce the threat to you,' he commented. I thought he may be right, but on the other hand, it was certainly going to make working difficult if I had an armed constable following me around. I resolved to talk to Barbara in the morning.

Meanwhile Douglas had fired up his PC and was looking through his emails. He shouted across to me, telling me he had another one from Josh Worthington. I went over and read it over his shoulder. This mail was short and to the point. Josh had written that he had further information, but would prefer to meet Douglas to tell him in person what he had found, as it was not the sort of thing he wanted to put in writing. If Douglas wished him to proceed, he would meet him in the Caribbean, concluding by asking Douglas to confirm that he had received this email.

I looked at Douglas puzzled and he returned my gaze and raised his eyebrows in question. 'What is that all about?' I asked, 'I can guess he is referring to Tony Choizi, but why meet you in Kaeta?'

'No, I don't think he is talking about Kaeta,' Douglas said thoughtfully.

The penny dropped, and I remembered that Tony had once told me he had a luxury apartment in Bermuda and had suggested I should visit it with him.

Douglas continued talking, 'Your guess is as good as mine, but I'd better do as he says and confirm I got the mail,' and he sent the reply as instructed. A few seconds later, his mobile phone rang. He picked up the call and whispered to me that it was Josh, but almost immediately, the call ended. I was confused: Douglas shook his head and told me that all Josh had said was that he would phone again in ten minutes. 'I have no idea what is going on, but I guess I am about to find out.' he said.

It was a little over than ten minutes before his phone rang again and this time the conversation was longer. I was dying to hear what was going on but Josh did most of the talking.

They ended the call. 'Well, that was interesting,' Douglas said to me, 'he apologised for all the cloak-and-dagger stuff, explaining that he has been tipped off. Tony Choizi has discovered he was digging around, so he has set up a monitor on his phone and email box. He was using a pay-as-you go phone for this call. Anyway, he says he has dug out more about Mr Choizi who, apparently, has a secret life, which he wants to talk through with me. He is not sure how this information will help, so he wants to discuss how we move forward. He has also spoken to Tony's estranged wife who apparently called him an odious creature: she wants a divorce but Choizi is being difficult. She did tell Josh that he has bought an apartment in Bermuda. She only found out about it as he took a loan to purchase it - the company sent the confirmation to her address, so she opened the letter. When she challenged Choizi about it, he told her he needed an off-shore base where he could keep his private stuff. Josh thinks it is worth visiting Bermuda to see what else he can dig out. I said I would meet him there as soon as I could get a flight.'

The Mango Mystery

This is getting serious and dangerous, I thought to myself. I really was worried now, wondering what Douglas was getting mixed up with.

I told him, 'Do think this is wise? Perhaps you should leave it to the proper authorities to sort this out. After all, Barbara has already warned you not to get involved and to stop playing the amateur detective. I think you should tell Josh Worthington to finish his investigation right now and give what ever he has found to the police to deal with.'

Douglas looked at me and pointed out that we were mixed up in this affair whether we liked it or not, 'Anyway,' he said, 'even if I do call Josh off, I need to meet him and settle up, and finish things off properly. I will be out of harm's way in Bermuda - no one needs to know where I have gone, so I will be quite safe. I will listen to what Josh has to say and, if it looks at all risky, I will tell him we don't want to go any further.'

Douglas was obviously going to go to meet Josh, whatever I thought about it, so I made him promise not to get personally involved or take any unnecessary risks.

As we went to bed he said, optimistically, 'You know, I think we might be able to crack this soon. With you back working at this end, with a bit of luck, you will nail the European contingent of the smuggling gang and it might be that Josh has enough to close in on the Caribbean end, and put Choizi away.'

John de Caynoth

Chapter 37. The Button

Joelle

I was up early this morning, before my bodyguard for the day turned up. I asked Douglas to tell him I had gone to my office near Scotland Yard.

I was pleased to see that my name was still on the door of my small office. There was no one else in yet as went into the incident room to catch up with progress.

I struck me that there had not been a lot of progress while I had been away. The team seemed to have spent most of the time visiting bars and nightclubs, with little to show except the arrest of a few small time dealers.

They had noted that Zed had been identified, and advised Interpol that he had been seen in London, but then done nothing more. They highlighted the raid on the **house he was using in London,** and that a small quantity of drugs had been found, presumably for personal use. They had taken photographs of all the rooms, and then watched the property for two days waiting for him to return. He never reappeared. It was also mentioned that he was suspected of being involved with the Euston shooting, but as he had not been seen since that incident, it was assumed he had left the country. I was pleased that they had picked up that the shooting had involved a Drugs Squad Officer and that this team had taken over the investigation from the BTP officers. There was a picture of the hoodie and the jeans, worn by the suspect, with a note that the legs of the jeans had been roughly cut to shorten them. The sleeves of the top had also been chopped off short and

The Mango Mystery

were wrinkled where they had been rolled up. Also one witness had said that the man's clothes looked too big for him.

There was a report from Andrea from her visit to the vet outside Coventry, where large quantities of KetPil had been purchased recently. She had confirmed that the locum vet, Dirk Shnaps, had ordered the drug. Coming in to work on the Monday morning, after the local police had visited the surgery, he had been told that the police were enquiring about a German vet called Gruber. That occasion was the last time anyone saw Herr Shnaps, who subsequently disappeared.

The team had also been trying to build a profile of Mrs Lecarrow, the owner of the house in Dulwich. They had discovered that she had a correspondence address in Switzerland and that the Swiss Police had been contacted. They were able to confirm Mrs Lecarrow was Swiss and had frequently been seen with a Mrs Vidnova, of Russian extration and the estranged wife of an American millionaire, she now lived in Switzerland but also owned a house in the Bahamas. Apparently, the Swiss did a background check on Mrs Vidnova when she moved to Switzerland, but felt that neither she, nor Mrs Lecarrow, were of any particular interest.

By now, the General Office and Incident room had started filling up as people came in to work. Some had said they were pleased to see me, others gave me the cold shoulder, looking at me suspiciously. The other Inspector on the team was one of my more friendly colleagues. He was pleased to see me back, telling me they had been buggering about getting nowhere since my suspension. Barbara Green arrived, shouting across

John de Caynoth

the room, 'Daily briefing at nine, don't be late!' She disappeared into her office.

We all gathered promptly at nine and Barbara started the briefing. Andrea rushed in at the back looking hot and bothered, just in time to avoid a withering comment from Barbara. I was aware that the atmosphere in the room was quite different to when Bob Cash had held briefings. He had never held them on a regular basis, and when he had called them, officers were frequently absent and usually chatted and giggled through the proceedings. Barbara, I gathered, insisted on daily briefings, and on everyone being present. The atmosphere was pensive: everyone was quiet, listening intently to Barbara said as she went over progress. Firstly, she welcomed me back and pointedly said to everyone that the investigation about me had concluded that there was no real evidence indicating that I illegally passed on information, or had been involved in any illegal activities. As far she, Barbara, was concerned that was the end of the matter and she had full confidence in me. She glared round the room defying anyone to contradict her. Following that, she looked at Andrea and told her she would now be working with me again. She then asked for an update on the enquiries concerning the pubs and clubs.

'Same old story,' answered one of the constables, 'all we picked up was a small time dealer who collects their Ketpils from a prearrange drop, never seeing the contact. The only new thing, is that the supply of Ketpils had dried up again.'

Barbara commented on the hoodie that the gunman had worn saying that forensics had found a white hair in the hood, and there was no known DNA

185

match. I chipped in and pointed out that a witness had thought the clothes were too big for the man, and that the arms and legs of the garments had been roughly cut down, 'Possibly the shooter purchased those garments from a charity shop especially for this hit.' I speculated.

'Good observation,' Barbara congratulated me, and told a couple of the DCs to start going round the charity shops to see if any one recognised the garments and who had purchased them. There was a groan and someone commented there were hundreds of charity shops in London. Again I spoke up and said, 'Start in the Dulwich area and work your way in towards Clapham.'

Barbara finished the briefing and, as she walked past me to her office she said, 'A word Joelle.' I followed her into the office. She welcomed me back and showed me the fuel injector from the Triumph. 'See that mark there,' she pointed, 'forensics say that was probably made by something like a large screwdriver being hit hard with a heavy hammer, and that would probably be sufficient to cause a split in the alloy case, so it looks like you bike was deliberately tampered with.'

There was not much to say - we both realised that someone was trying to injure me, or worse, but I still asked Barbara about my police guard pointing out that it could get very difficult if I was being followed everywhere by armed police officers.

'Yes,' she answered, 'I have already spoken with the Superintendent about that and we have sorted it out. Constable John MacDuff is temporarily seconded to the drug squad and will be working with you and Andrea. Effectively, he will be your driver and he is waiting outside for you at the moment. Don't go off early to work again on you own without telling him.'

She then asked if I made any arrangements to go to Amsterdam. I told her I had booked a plane ticket.

'Cancel it,' Barbara instructed, 'John will drive you over. He is organising things today, and you leave tomorrow. Take Andrea with you: the experience will do her good. I have cleared this with Inspector van den Leuven, who is expecting you to report to him on Wednesday afternoon when you arrive. Phone me every day and let me know what you are up to.'

I left Barbara, thinking that she moves fast, and went to find Andrea to tell her the news. She was in the canteen having breakfast, so I joined her for coffee and said to her, 'Guess what Andrea, you are coming to Holland with me tomorrow.'

'What for, and anyway I don't speak Dutch?' she said.

'For the experience, and I don't know what we will be doing or how long we will be there, we will find out tomorrow.'

She was quite excited at the thought and immediately phoned Jim to tell him.

'Do you think I need to wear my uniform?' she asked me. I told her that plain, but warm, clothes were needed. 'Now,' I said to her, 'finish your breakfast. I want you to show me those photos taken when Zed's house was raided.'

While she went to fetch the photos, I phoned Bernie to tell him the suspension had been lifted. He sounded surprised to hear form me and said, 'I thought you had and an accident and were injured?'

The Mango Mystery

'No, how did know about that?' I asked.

He blustered for a few seconds before he said, 'I heard you had been shot and thought you had been hurt.'

'Well,' I replied, 'I was shot at and missed, so I am actually perfectly well and back on duty. I fact I am going to Amsterdam tomorrow; apparently they need my assistance.'

'What for? Flying over just for the day?' Bernie asked me.

'They have found a body they think I might be able to identify and we are driving over, so I don't know how long I will be there.'

Andrea returned with the pictures and I told Bernie I had to go. He said he was glad I was okay and to be careful and look after myself before he hung up.

I looked through the photos and paused at one taken in the bedroom Zed had been using. 'Tidy for a man wasn't he,' I commented, indicating to Andrea to pass me a magnifying glass. I looked carefully at an old flannel sports jacket hung over a chair. I gave the glass the to Andrea and told her to look carefully at the jacket. 'What do you notice?' I asked.

She studied it for a few moments, 'Nothing, should I notice something?'

'Yes, look at the buttons.'

'Yes, there are two buttons.' she told me as she examined the jacket again.

'Precisely,' I replied 'but there are three button holes.'

'So the lower button is missing, so what?' Andrea looked puzzled.

'I don't know,' I answered, 'I just wondered how he had lost a button. It seems curious for a man, who obviously looks after his clothes, not to replace a missing button. Do we still have a search warrant for the Dulwich house - do you know if the house has been cleared?' I asked.

'I expect we still have the warrant and no, we have not cleared the house, I don't know if anyone else has.'

'Good,' I said, collect the warrant and meet me downstairs in the car park. I would like to look round that house for myself.'

The Mango Mystery

Chapter 38. Bermuda

Douglas, Wednesday

Joelle and I rose in the dark again this morning - Joelle because John MacDuff was picking her up at seven to drive her to Amsterdam and me because I was going to Heathrow Airport again, to get a flight to Bermuda. I looked out of the front window and watched Joelle walk across the pavement to a new, black Mercedes S Class saloon, parked immediately opposite the flats. She handed her travel bag to John, who put it in the boot and opened the front passenger door for her. My first thought was that she had gone up in the world, a Mercedes no less, and my second thought was they had gone the wrong way. I watched for a few more minutes to see if anyone was following them and then noticed that John had turned around and was now heading east toward Dover.

My journey to Heathrow was uneventful and, thankfully, I did not think I was being followed. John had given me some tips to use when checking for tails, like stopping suddenly and doubling back, noticing if anyone acts suspiciously. 'My favourite though,' he told me, 'is to get on a bus, and then, when everyone else has boarded, suddenly jump off again. That way you either loose the tail, or he reveals himself jumping off after you.'

However, I was using the underground and that trick is even easier from a tube train. I tried it just before the doors closed and no one got off behind me.

As we flew into Bermuda, it struck me that the Island was much more developed than Kaeta. We

John de Caynoth

landed at LF Wade International Airport, somewhat isolated out on St Davids Island, and as I left the plane I was once more struck by the contrast in weather. Just under seven hours earlier I had left a cold damp England and here the sun was shining and the temperature warmed my skin.

Josh had told me to take a taxi to Hamilton and stay at the Royal George Hotel, waiting there until he contacted me. The hotel building was an old colonial mansion with all the public rooms furnished in the same colonial style but the bedrooms were large, modern and luxurious. The building was set in large, well laid out, tropical gardens with a large swimming pool. A bar and tennis courts were set in an area between the original house and a new extension, housing further accommodation.

I can definitely spend a few days here I thought, but I did wish Joelle was with me.

Friday

In the event, I only had a couple of days to myself to enjoy the hotel before Josh contacted me. He left a note for me at the hotel reception, telling me he would meet in the hotel Library Bar at 6.00 pm. on Friday evening.

The Library Bar was, indeed, the old library and still contained what appeared to be its original collection of books lining two walls. The front wall of the room contained a large window, which was open looking out over the gardens in the front of the hotel, while at the back of the room a bar had been discretely added in one corner. The room was furnished with an eclectic selection of armchairs, sofas and coffee tables.

The Mango Mystery

A large fan was suspended from the ceiling and hummed quietly, doing its best to keep the room cool.

The Library Bar was not well used in the early evenings, as most guests preferred happy hour in the cocktail bar at the back of the hotel, and so, on this evening at six o'clock, I found Josh sitting alone in a corner with a small glass of beer.

'Hi, thanks for coming.' he greeted me as I joined him. The waiter came over and we ordered a couple of beers. 'I chose this bar because it's quite and we can talk in here,' he said apologetically.

After we exchanged pleasantries, we got down to business and Josh explained what had happened since he sent me his first report.

'When you gave me the go ahead, I started going round some of my contacts on the streets to see what I could pick up about the target. Everyone I spoke to agreed that he was a nasty piece of work and warned me to stay away from him. I was told one his favourite ways of getting rid of people who cross him was to raid their homes, find a large quantity of some drug, and then sending them down for possession and dealing. I was told Choizi had found out I was asking after him: the next thing I knew, my phone calls were being intercepted and recorded, and my email box was being hacked. Fortunately, since the first report I emailed to you, I had not said or written anything about the man that he could have recorded, so he is probably guessing why I am asking about him.' Josh paused here and took a mouthful of beer before he continued.

'Anyway, he must have put the word out because suddenly no one would talk to me, even when I offered money. The only person who would say anything at all was his estranged wife and that was only because she hates him like poison. She told me he hangs out around the clubs, picking up women - the younger the better - and taking them back to his apartment. If they won't have sex with him willingly, he drugs them and does it that way.'

'Ketamine! One of its illegal uses is as a date rape drug.' I commented.

'Quite likely that's what he uses,' Josh replied, 'but I have been told that the ketamine supply on the illegal market is very short at the moment.'

'That's probably because the supply chain has been interrupted at the European end,' and I told Josh about the animal drug, KetPil, how it was acquired for illegal distribution and how the supply chain had been disrupted last year when the Kaeta operation was discovered.

Josh just nodded and returned to his story, ' Mrs Choizi told me he is not just kinky, he is a sadist, and some of the things he wanted her to do were disgusting.'

We both stopped at this point, with disturbing thoughts going through our minds about Tony Choizi and his predilections.

'Do you think we could find one of these girls and get her to make a statement, which we could use against Choizi?' I asked Josh.

'Possibly,' he answered, 'but let me finish telling you about his wife. She told me she thought he had some sort of deal going with the clubs - that's how he was able to get into the premises and pick up these women. I told you she found out that he had bought an apartment on this Island? That is where, she thinks, he keeps all his stuff, and she told me that, if I wanted to find out what he was up to, I needed to come out here and look. She reckons he must be getting money from somewhere, in addition to his police salary, to support his life style, and, she says, we will probably find the evidence here. She thinks he has a bank account in Bermuda. Talking of money, by the way, I need another advance, the first one is all but gone.'

'I thought you might, so I drew some cash out before I left the UK.' I handed him $1000 in large denomination bills and told him if he needed more, I would need to pay it by bank transfer.

Josh nodded, thanked me and continued, 'Since I have been here, I have put a bit of your money about and discovered that Choizi's influence is not as strong out here as it is in Miami. I am told he is not particularly popular with the local police either: they don't like the way he throws his weight about. Apparently, he likes to hang around the clubs here and pick up women - there is one here in Hamilton, the Jamboree Club, that he particularly favours: we might find what we want there.'

I thought through what Josh had told me, 'So we know he is not a nice man, he rapes women and he has the Miami underworld running scared. His wife wants to sink him, he has another, as yet unknown, source of income, and it sounds like he is trying to set up some sort of scam in Bermuda. But we have no real evidence of what he up to, and we have nothing that points directly to him being involved with drug smuggling.'

'That's about the size of it so far,' Josh agreed.

'What do we do now?' I asked him.

John de Caynoth

'Well, assuming you want me to carry on, now I have more funds, I will go to this Jamboree Club and see what I can find out, and then, I reckon I have to get into his apartment and search it.'

'H'mm,' I mumbled, 'Isn't that a bit risky?'

Josh stood up to leave, 'Man', he said with exasperation, 'Of course it is risky, but do you want to find out about Choizi or not?' I shrugged, unsure of the answer. Josh walked out, saying he would meet me back here at the same time tomorrow, Saturday, evening.

Chapter 39. The Morgue, Amsterdam

Joelle

Yesterday was uneventful. John MacDuff drove us to Dover, where we boarded a ferry to Calais, continuing on to Amsterdam. He explained we had to use the ferry as it was cheaper than the channel tunnel, and he was on a budget.

We duly admired the car as we travelled - John explained it was a Guard Model S Class Mercedes Benz with a V12 Bi Turbo engine. Andrea asked him how fast it went and what was a Guard Model anyway?

'I don't know how fast it goes: if we need to go Germany we will find out on the Autobahns, but it does 0-60mph in about five seconds.' I shuddered and hoped we would not need to go to Germany, as John then explained that the Guard Model was a hand-built armour-plated car with a bullet proof, and blast resistant, passenger cabin.

'Good God!' Andrea exclaimed, 'we are not in that much danger are we?'

'No, not at all. They have given me this car to use because it's brand new and a trip like this is a good way to shake it down, finding out what it can do, before it goes into service. It's normal job will be transporting heads of state, politicians, VIPs and the like,' John explained.

We reached Amsterdam in the late afternoon and drove straight to the Police Headquarters to meet Inspector, Meneer Jan van den Leuven, who was another tall, over six -foot, middle-aged Dutchman, with iron grey hair, wearing dark blue chinos and a dogtooth checked sports jacket. He was very formal and polite, bowing his head slightly as he greeted us, shaking hands in strict order of seniority, starting with me. He thanked us for coming to Amsterdam and explained that he wanted to take us to the morgue, where there were a couple of bodies he hoped I could identify.

'Is that all?' I queried feeling slightly disappointed that I was not going to be more involved.

'We will visit the morgue first and see where that leads,' van den Leuven replied, 'I will send someone to pick you up at your hotel in the morning.'

John spoke up, informing him that we would be using our own vehicle. Van den Leuven was about to object, but John produced some sort of identification and explained to the Inspector that he was a Close Protection Officer: there had been two attempts on my life, and he did not want a third. I think van den Leuven was only too happy for us to use our own car after that, especially when he discovered that John carried a Glock17, 9mm hand gun in a shoulder holster, and that the boot of the car was fitted with a gun-safe in which was a rifle, a Heckler and Koch G36 long barrel, with telescopic and night sites, a second Glock17, an X26 Tazer, and ammunition for all the weapons. Also in the boot, were four bulletproof vests. John assured him he had clearance to bring the weapons into Holland. Van den Leuven shrugged saying, 'Its nothing to do with me, I just hope you don't have use them.'

'So do I,' John replied.

We were staying at the Crown Hotel, near Rembrandt Square, the hotel I had used last summer when I was in Amsterdam giving evidence to the Dutch Enquiry Board. That seemed a lifetime ago, I mused, sitting in reception this morning, waiting for Andrea to come down. John was sitting in the car right outside the front door, much to the annoyance of the head porter who wanted him to park round the corner. Andrea appeared and we went out and quickly got in the car. The doors locked automatically.

I asked John if he knew where the morgue was. 'No problem,' he smiled tapping the built in SatNav in to which he had already planned a route.

At the morgue, John drove slowly round the car park twice, before stopping right outside the door to let us out, moving off to stop in the middle of the car park where there were no other vehicles. John said he would stay in the car, and Andrea came with me, saying as we walked into the reception, 'He made a meal of that didn't he, why not just park the car like everyone else.'

I told her I did not think he was parking the car, he was checking there was no one interested in us.' I think the seriousness of the situation was beginning to dawn on Andrea.

Jan van den Leuven was waiting for us inside: he was a little more relaxed today, asking if he could call us Joelle and Andrea, and invited us to call him Jan. We were given robes and masks and taken through to a chilled room, with banks of large draws facing each other along opposite walls. There were two steel tables set over drainage troughs in the centre of the room. I felt Andrea shudder with discomfort as we were led across the room to a particular drawer, which the attendant pulled open. I felt slightly queasy, as I looked at a middle-aged man with a bullet hole in the exact centre of his forehead. The attendant happily told me that this was his pretty side: the back of his skull had been blown out by the bullet, together with most of his brains. I stared at the man, but Andrea was very pale and looking anywhere else but at the drawer.

Jan explained that they had fished him out a canal a few days ago and that he had obviously been executed with a dumdum bullet. 'We have identified him from dental records as Jan den Ould, a forty nine year old resident of Eindhoven,' he told us.

I looked at the body and said, 'I think I know him. I never actually met him, but I have been carrying his picture round for a year or so. I think he is the man who, over a year ago, carried drugs into Heathrow to be smuggled onwards to Kaeta. We now know him in the UK as a vet using the identities of Hans Gruber, a German national, and Dirk Shnaps, a South African.'

Jan thanked me and a voice behind me said, 'We believe he was a veterinary surgeon and a partner in the Cordite Veterinary Group in Eindhoven. That practice closed down shortly after this gentleman disappeared. All the ex-employees we have spoken are unsure of this man's identity, but hopefully, with your confirmation, we can clarify this.'

I turned round to see Willam Ince standing there, apologising for being late. I gasped with surprise and asked, 'I thought you were no longer involved with the drug squad?'

'I am not,' he replied, 'but I am involved with murders in Amsterdam: at the moment we are trying to find out why this man was in Amsterdam and **with whom he met.** But let's leave that one for a moment, as I have another murdered body I would like you to look at. We know nothing at all about this man, except that he also was executed and dumped in a canal like Herr den Ould. I am working on a hunch, and its a very long shot that you will be able to identify him. I am asking you because he is wearing clothes that can only be purchased from an English mail order company.'

The attendant walked across the room and pulled open another drawer. Andrea had recovered by this time and she and I peered into the drawer together. William informed us that the man lying there also had a neat round bullet hole in his forehead. I told the attendant we did not need a graphic description of his injuries this time. I guessed that this man, like me, was of Caribbean origin but he had a darker skin than me.

But before I had chance to speak, Andrea exclaimed, 'I know him - he is the Range Rover driver that we arrested and questioned in the UK. Eventually we charged him with car theft and drug possession and he was on bail awaiting trial.'

'Do you know his name?' Willam asked.

'No, I don't remember as I was not involved in his arrest, but if you contact DCI Barbara Green in Scotland Yard, she will be able to give you all the information we have.'

'I also know him,' I said, 'I recognise him as the man in the hoodie and he was one of the individuals that's been following me in London over the last few days.'

Willam and Jan looked at each other and Jan asked me if I thought he was somehow involved with the drug gang.

'Yes, almost certainly I think. I am afraid I don't know why he was following me or why I am being targeted, but the most likely explanation is that the drug gang believes I know something that could lead us to their organisers. I have racked my brain, and I just wish I knew what it was.'

Jan then spoke, 'I agree with Joelle, it does seems likely these two men were connected somehow and were involved with this drug gang, who executed them, but why? My guess is that because Joelle, and the UK Police, were on to them, the gang wanted them both silenced before they were caught.'

Willam nodded in agreement and Jan then said, 'I don't like this place. Lets go back to Headquarters and talk: we might come up with something if we pool our ideas'.

Jan apologised and said he had other things he had to do today, but suggested we have a conference tomorrow. Jan and Willam drove off in their separate cars, and as Andrea and I got into the Mercedes to drive back to the hotel, I thought, nastily, last time they all got together and pooled ideas it got me into trouble.

The Mango Mystery

Chapter 40. Amsterdam Police Headquarters

Joelle

We met in Jan van den Leuven's office - Jan, Willam, Andrea and myself. John asked if he could join us so he could pick up the background to the investigation. We each described how we had been involved, beginning right from the start of the investigation when I had put Douglas under surveillance on Kaeta, where he was suspected of smuggling ketamine.

When Jan mentioned the two latest murders, John interrupted, 'Do I understand that you believe this drug gang has now committed three murders, those two and the undercover police woman, and has made two, thankfully unsuccessful attempts, on Joelle's life?'

Willam joined the conversation saying, 'I am not sure about the two alleged attempts on Joelle's life, but the drug gang do seem to shoot their victims.'

Jan reminded him that they tortured the undercover policewoman first.

Willam agreed, but pointed out that they shot her in the head to kill her and then said, 'Clearly the railway station shooting was a direct attempt on Joelle's life, but the alleged first attempt, involving a vehicle, could just have been accidental.'

I interrupted to tell him that Douglas had seen the vehicle and believed it was the same stolen black Range Rover that the hooded man had been arrested in. I continued, 'Anyway, I am not sure that there have not been four murders. Zach, the go between on Kaeta was killed a few days ago in prison on Kaeta. Bernie and the prison authorities put it down to an accidental stabbing during a prison fight, but it was a bit of a coincidence that he was killed the night before Douglas was going to visit him.'

John spoke again, 'So there probably have been four murders and two attempts on Joelle's life. It seems to me that this gang is covering their tracks now. They are finishing off anyone who might give us a lead to them, which puts a very different complexion on my role here. It appears to me the threat to Joelle is very real and much greater than first thought.' He turned to me, 'By the way, I also think that your partner Douglas is at risk as well. He has been crashing around in the undergrowth, digging stuff up and you can bet that the drug gang will be on to him.' He then turned to the other two detectives in the room, 'And you gentlemen might like to consider your own security as well.' John sat back quietly and we all looked at him seriously as we took on board his warnings.

After a while I spoke again, 'There is another thing I have just remembered. When Douglas was on Kaeta earlier this month, he spoke to Zach's sister. She told him that Zach had once gone to one of the dead-drops, **earlier than arranged, to collect instructions, and see who else turned up there.** He would not tell his sister who it was, but said he recognised someone important and that she would never guess who.'

The two Dutchman looked at me and Jan shrugged, saying that he was not sure that helped us move forward. 'After all,' he said, 'we know there had to be at least one organiser on Kaeta, or at least visiting it, and with this Zach dead we have no way of identifying that person.'

The Mango Mystery

A girl from the outer office knocked and put her head round the door. 'I have a message for DI deNouvelas,' she said, 'Barbara Green is trying to contact you - could you phone her when it is convenient?'

I thanked her and said I would as soon as we finished our conference.

Andrea spoke next, 'I believe we still have a lead we should follow. We know that the house that Zedanski was living in is owned by a Swiss lady - Mrs Lecarrow. Zedanski has disappeared for the moment, but as far as we know, he is the last one connected with the drug ring who might still be alive. If we can find Mrs Lecarrow, she might lead us to him.'

'Good point,' Jan congratulated her, 'but the trouble is, the Swiss can be secretive and not always helpful to fact-finding investigations concerning their residents.'

'Well,' said Andrea, in her typical practical way, 'they don't have to know. John wants to try out his new car on the Autobahns and what better way than to take it on a run through Germany to Switzerland for a weekend break.' She looked to John for confirmation and I groaned, guessing what was coming.

John beamed, 'What a good idea, the car needs running in anyway.'

Jan looked worried and said that he did not want to know anything about such a holiday. 'Its your business where you go, but let me know if you come across Mrs Lecarrow.'

John de Caynoth

I stood and said, 'I need to phone my DCI but before I do, would it be possible for me to look at the evidence and file on the murdered police woman?'

'Yes, I guess so,' said Jan, 'but that investigation is now in the hands of the police in Eindhoven. I can clear it with them but you would probably need to go there. What are you looking for?'

'It might be nothing, just a long shot, that's all.' I thanked him and went to find a phone on which I could call Barbara.

I asked if I could use an empty office and settled in to talk to Barbara. She answered after a couple of rings. 'Joelle - thanks for calling. How are you getting on?'

I told Barbara about the two cadavers we had identified and how we had spent the rest of the day going over everything we knew.

'Your hooded man,' she interrupted me, 'I guessed he would never turn up to the trial.'

I continued, 'It's pretty clear that this drug gang is totally ruthless, systematically killing off anyone we have identified who might give us a lead. The only remaining possibility appears to be Zedanski but he has disappeared and could quite possibly be dead as well, I guess.'

'Ah, Yes Zedanski - that is why I am phoning you. Your proposal to try the charity shops and to see if they had sold the hoodie and baggy trousers has paid off. As you suggested, we started in Dulwich and moved back towards Clapham. We found the shop in Streatham and the assistant remembered selling the garments. She said that they turn over a lot of stuff, so it was unlikely she would remember, but she did recall the man who bought those garments asking for a pair scissors and cutting the garments down in the shop. She described him as white, with black hair and a dark complexion: when we showed her your picture of Zedanski she identified him immediately, so I think we know *who* our gunman is but we don't know *where* he is.'

'That makes sense, it had to be Zed and he must have followed me from the flat, realising that once we were on the train, he might not get another chance to shoot me. **Once we were outside London it would be much more risky for him, as he would have had no car and would depend on public transport so his chances of getting away would be much reduced.**'

I then explained to Barbara that I was worried about Douglas and thought he might be in danger as well, as he knew as much about this drug gang as anyone else. I heard Barbara take a long breath, but this time she did not tell me off, but said, 'Yes, I think you are right, I will see what I can do. Where is he anyway at the moment?'

'Bermuda.' I answered.

'What the hell is he doing there?' she asked.

I explained he was meeting a private detective who he had hired to check out Tony Choizi. I heard Barbara take another long breath and pause before answering. 'That man is going to get you into trouble if he carries on like this. I can call the Bermudan police and see what they can do, but they will probably just arrest him and put him on a plane back to London. In fact, I might arrest him for his own good.'

John de Caynoth

'No,' I pleaded, 'please don't do that. He should be quite safe in Bermuda. No one knows he's there and he is with Josh, who seems quite capable.'

'Okay,' Barbara replied after a few moments thought, but you tell me when he returns to London. I am going to bring him in and put the fear of God up him.'

We returned to the subject of Zedanski. Barbara agreed with me about the shooting, but not that he might be dead. She speculated, 'I think he has gone to ground somewhere in the world and we won't be seeing him again, unless of course he is the drug gang's hit man. I guess we will find out eventually.'

She changed the subject and asked what our plans were. I told her we were going to Eindhoven as there was something I wanted to check out, and then driving down to Switzerland.

'Switzerland!' She exclaimed, 'What ever for?'

'A sort of working holiday,' I answered and asked her if she had any more information on Mrs Lecarrow.

'I see,' she replied 'I don't want to know about your weekend plans, but please be careful - if you run into Zed again I suspect he won't miss a second time. And no, we have no more on Mrs Lecarrow.'

I told her I would indeed be careful, but reminded her I had John MacDuff, the one- man-army, looking after me now.

Barbara finished the call, 'Better go now. Look after Andrea and, oh, bye the way, this will amuse you. Our mutual friend Tony Choizi rang me a couple of days ago and congratulated me on my new role and said

207

how much he was looking forward to working with me again.' I could feel Barbara shuddering down the phone.

'He also asked after you, and if there was a trial date set yet. He said he might take some holiday and come over and watch the trial.' It was my turn to shiver.

'Anyway,' Barbara continued, 'I told him the evidence against you did not hold up and you were back on duty, helping the Dutch Police in Amsterdam.'

'What did he say to that?' I asked.

'Nothing.' Barbara replied, 'It was rather disappointing, I thought he would explode but he said absolutely nothing.'

His reaction seemed strange to me, but I also thought that he was up to something, reminding myself that it was not just the drug gang that I needed to be careful of. But then, I thought, perhaps Choizi and the drug gang are one and the same. I hoped Douglas and Josh would find something.

We finished at the Amsterdam Headquarters and John brought the Mercedes round to the back door to pick up Andrea and me. Half way back to the hotel John said, 'Don't look round, but we are being followed by a black BMW. We picked him as we left the Police Headquarters and he has been on our tail all the way, so far.'

'Are you sure he is following us?' Andrea asked.

'Yes, I have done a couple of detours and backtracks and he has been behind us the whole time. What would you like me to do, lose him?'

'No,' I said thinking, 'can you contact Jan van den Leuven on that radio and tell him we are being followed, suggesting he sends a couple of cars to pick up the driver.' John actually used the car phone and called Jan who immediately agreed to the plan. John listened on the phone for a few minutes and then just said, 'Understood,' explaining as he hung up, 'Jan has got a couple of traffic cars after us. He told me to just keep driving round, and has given me their frequency so I can tell them where we are. After a few minutes, a voice came through requesting a call sign. John replied and stated our position and where we were heading. After a couple of minutes, two police cars with sirens blaring came down the road towards us. They passed us and did a U-turn in the road, and I watched as the cars overtook the stream of traffic behind us with one car pushing in behind the black BMW, and the other trying to get in front of it. The BMW braked sharply and I saw the police car behind him hit the back of it, with the car behind them colliding with the back of the police car. The BMW then swerved sharply left and disappeared down a side street.

John just said, 'We are out of here!' He put his foot down and shot along the centre of the road at high speed, scattering the oncoming cars into the gutter, causing much horn-blowing. When he judged us to be safely away, he slowed down and said, 'That was a right balls-up, we won't try that again.'

I replied, 'More worryingly though, how did they know where to find us?'

Andrea replied, 'Obvious, the mole is still active and at large and he is after you. It puts you in the clear anyway. There's no way you could have organised that.'

The Mango Mystery

Chapter 41. Jamboree Club

Douglas

When I woke up this morning, I decided I would ring Joelle: I was missing her and felt the need to hear her voice. When she picked up, she answered rather formally, 'DI de Nouvelas.' I guessed she was on duty somewhere. I replied, trying to sound more cheerful than I felt, 'Hi Joelle, it's Douglas. How are you?'

'Oh, Douglas, hold on, my phone is connected through the car's hands-free and everyone can hear you.'

I asked her if she was in the Mercedes and she replied, 'Yes, we are on our way to Eindhoven, via Belgium. Hold on, I am taking my phone off the bluetooth. I will call you back if I loose the connection.'

After a few moments she came back, 'Hello, are you still there?'

I said I was and Joelle continued, 'Yes, it is a long way to Eindhoven via Belgium, but we had a little problem leaving Amsterdam. I will tell you about it when we see each other again. From Eindhoven we are going to drive down to Switzerland to see what we can find.' She paused then asked, 'How are you getting on?'

I told her that I was fine and had met Josh yesterday. I brought her up to date with what he had told me.

'Douglas,' she replied 'Please be careful, Tony Choizi is a very dangerous man, and if we are right and it is him passing information to the drug gang, he, and they, won't think twice about silencing you.' She went on to tell me what she had been doing in Amsterdam

John de Caynoth

but before she had got into the story she paused, telling me to hold on again as John was saying something, then she warned me, 'John has just told me that we should not be talking on an open mobile connection in case someone is listening in.'

John, of course, was right but it did leave us with little to say to each other and so we discussed the weather in our respective locations and I told Joelle I was thinking of going on the Kaeta for a couple of days when we had finished in Bermuda.

'What are you doing there?' she asked and told her I was just going to visit Mary.

When Joelle was back in London, she told me, she thought she would try and get some time off to go home to Kaeta for a few days. 'Its months since I have seen Jasmine and Mary,' she concluded, rather sadly, I thought.

As I hung up, I wondered whether I should tell Joelle that I was looking at a house on Kaeta with the intention of buying. The agent had sent me the details of a property that looked just right for me. It was an old sugar plantation house, located on the Atlantic side of the Island, over-looking the sea. Apparently, the current owner wanted to sell up quickly as his wife had a terminal illness, and they wanted to move nearer to her family on one of the other Caribbean Islands. 'It is priced to sell and I think they will take an offer,' the agent had informed me.

With that in mind, I rang Mary to tell her I was planning to visit Kaeta again shortly and asked if I could stay at 'Windrush'. She was delighted, 'You are welcome any time,' she assured me. Will Joelle be with you?'

The Mango Mystery

'No I am afraid I am on my own again. Joelle is in Holland, and then going to Switzerland for a few days, but she says that, when she gets back to London, she hopes to take a few days leave to come home to see you and Jasmine.'

Mary said she would look forward to that and then excitedly told me that she and Jasmine had been invited to a grand civic dinner later that evening. 'Its hosted by the Commissioner of Police and every one of importance on the Island will be there. We only get invited because Paul, my husband, was Commissioner before he died. Bernie has kindly said he will give Jasmine and me a lift. He is a nice man, always stopping by and asking how Joelle is getting on and what she is doing.'

I stopped Mary there and said I had to go as I had things to do. Actually, I did not have much to do at all but, from experience, I knew that once Mary started rambling on she never stopped.

I spent the rest of day waiting for 6.00pm when I was meeting Josh again.

As usual, the Library Bar was deserted and this time I was there before Josh. I sat in the same corner to wait for him: when he arrived we got straight down to business.

'I went to the Jamboree Club yesterday and spent the evening there making friends with both the barman and the doorman. I had to spend some more of your funds, but we have made progress. The doorman told me that Tony Choizi is trying to set up a protection racket on the Island. Apparently, he approached one of the local Police officers and showed him how much money he was making in Miami out of a similar scheme, and then tried to recruit him for his scam. Anyway, he chose the wrong person as he was told to get lost. The officer told him that, if they were going to run a protection racket, **they could do it without his help.** I guess that is why the Bermudian Police don't like him. The other scam he is trying to get going, I was told, is to supply the club with black-market drugs. He told the doorman he had a source in Miami and could supply what ever they wanted. They told him they would let him know, once they had seen the stuff he had. Anyway, apparently he has not produced anything to date.'

'That's interesting,' I said, 'this could be the connection we need. It could be that he is offering to supply ketamine, but, until a new supply chain is set up, he can't get hold of any. Did he tell them what drugs he was offering?'

'No,' Josh confirmed, 'he wasn't specific about what he could supply.'

'We need to find more to prove the link, then we've got him.' I said, excitedly.

'Yes, I will come to that, but firstly I need to tell you what the barman said. Again, I had to spend more money, but he confirmed that he had also been offered drugs by Choizi, who had shown him a couple of pills in an envelope. He told the barman that these were a great way to enhance his sex-life. He said he only had his personal stash with him but could bring a supply the next time he came to Bermuda. The barman thought he was talking about Viagra so told him that he was doing all right without pills, and that he did not want any illegal drugs. Tony then said he would show him how they worked. He pointed to a hostess, said he fancied her, and asked for a drink to be taken over to her. According to the barman, Choizi spiked it with half of one of his pills, and that within ten minutes of drinking it, the girl looked completely drunk and spaced out, leaving with Choizi. She was back in the club a few nights later but never told the barman what had happened. I got her name and address and went to find her this morning.'

'It must be ketamine he is dealing in,' I said 'there must be some way we can prove a link, or catch Tony out. Did the girl tell you anything?'

'Eventually, after I offered her money. She told me she remembered feeling very funny - light-headed, like being unconscious, but still awake. She remembered getting in a taxi with Choizi, and being told he was taking her home but, she says, he started touching her in the back of the cab. She does not know where he took her: it was a strange apartment, she said. She says she can't really recall exactly what happened, it was like having a nightmare you could not wake up from. Well, without going into the details, it seems Choizi raped her.'

'Why did she not go to the police?' I asked.

'She said she was found lying on a beach, half-dressed and half-conscious. Someone called an ambulance and they then called the police. They assumed she was drunk and took her home to sleep it off.'

Josh then said, 'there was more.' I told him I did not think I could take more of Choizi's cruelty.

Josh said, 'No it's not like that. If we are going to nail him we need evidence, not hearsay, so I think I need to get into his apartment and search it. I went out there this afternoon and spoke to the security man. I informed him I was interested in buying an apartment, the one belonging to Mr Choizi, who was currently in Miami. He was a bit doubtful at first about letting me in, but I gave him $20, which persuaded him to allow me access. I only had a quick look, but I did manage to get hold of the key and I will have copy made as soon as I can.'

'Didn't security miss the key?' I asked.

Josh produced a small tin and grinned, 'Give me some credit. I made a wax impression, and then dropped the key by the door for him to find. I should be able to get the key cut on Monday by my contact and then, if you agree, I will go back and have a proper look round.'

Joelle's warnings, and my promise were ringing in my ears, but I thought this could be the opportunity to find conclusive evidence to get Joelle off the hook, and I owe her that, I considered.'

'Josh, can I come with you?' I asked.

The Mango Mystery

Chapter 42. The Black BMW

Joelle

We got back to the Crown Hotel in Rembrandt Square yesterday, late afternoon. John dropped us at the front door and went to park the car. Andrea and I collected out keys and the receptionist gave me an envelope. There was nothing written on it except DI deNouvelas. I studied it curiously, but there was no clue regarding the sender, so I asked the receptionist. She told me a man had left it earlier in the day before she came on duty. I opened the envelope and it was empty, nothing at all inside. I showed it to Andrea who just shrugged and said who ever sent it obviously forgot to put the note inside. 'Don't worry, they will soon realise and chase it up.'

But I was not sure, and when John arrived I showed him the envelope. He took it more seriously and said, 'I think they have found out where we are staying. This is an old trick. You take an envelope round all the likely hotels and ask to leave it for the person you are looking for. When you hit the right hotel they obligingly take the envelope and tell you they will pass it on as soon as possible. Simple, really!'

'What should we do, John?' I asked.

'We stay in our rooms tonight, and first thing tomorrow we leave without checking out.'

'We should pay our bills.' Andrea said.

With a withering look, John replied, 'and then they know we moved on! No, we will tell van den Leuven to sort it out next week.'

John de Caynoth

This morning, we crept down stairs very early. We had left our cases in our rooms and only carried the minimum of luggage. We skipped breakfast and followed John to the car, driving quietly away before the Saturday traffic built up in the city.

We got on to the Amsterdam ring road, the traffic was still light as John turned off down a slip road.

'John,' I said, 'You have gone the wrong way. This is the A4 to Den Hagg and Rotterdam. The junction with the A2 to Eindhoven is a couple of junctions further round.'

'We are not going that way,' he replied, and carried on down the A4. I don't know if we are being followed yet, but I am taking no chances. There is a silver VW Golf behind us - I first noticed him when we got on the ring road and, if he is following, I want him to think we are going back to the UK.'

John told me there was a rear view mirror on the passenger side of the car fitted discretely beside the sun visor. I thought it was a vanity mirror but John corrected me. 'It is so who ever is riding shot gun can see what is going behind us,' he said. I adjusted it and, sure enough, there was a silver Golf behind us.

The drive to Rotterdam was interesting with our tail behind us all the way. John had slowed right down, speeded up, and even detoured round the A44 to Den Hagg, then back on to the Rotterdam motorway and the Golf just kept on following us. When we got on to the Rotterdam ring road John decided, 'We will lose them just outside Antwerp and then double back to Eindhoven.'

217

The Mango Mystery

We were on the A1/E19 now, passing Dordrecht a few kilometres back. Just past the motorway services, situated after the junction with the A17, John said, 'Hang on girls, I think we have trouble coming,'

Andrea and I looked round behind, but could not see anything at first, and so I looked questioningly at John. 'A black BMW pulled out of the Service Area just as we went past and I think it is the same one that followed us yesterday,' he told me. John carried on driving at a steady 80KPH down the inside lane. The traffic that had built up round the junction was clearing now and, sure enough, I could see this car in the fast lane catching up with us.

'Maybe he needed a pee and is getting in front of us again,' Andrea suggested hopefully.

'Maybe.' John said unconvinced 'or maybe he is in contact with the Golf and keeping track of us. We will just carry on steadily and see what happens.'

The BMW was still gaining on us, but the silver Golf had dropped back. I checked again a moment later but the BMW had slowed down. He was still in the fast lane but was holding his position, at the same speed as us, a couple of vehicle lengths behind. The road ahead had cleared and suddenly it all kicked off.

John said, 'I don't like this,' slamming the brakes on as the BMW came alongside, nearly overshooting us, but also braking sharply. The Mercedes jumped forward as John gunned the engine and for a second the two cars were side by side. The driver of the BMW realised the Mercedes was accelerating and tried to match its speed. The Mercedes, being an English car, was a right hand drive model while the BMW was a left hand drive. The passenger in the BMW and I were staring at each

John de Caynoth

other, no more than a meter apart. He was pointing a gun through the open window, straight at me. He fired two shots. The window-glass chipped but did not break and I remembered, gratefully, that the Mercedes was armour-plated and bullet proof.

By the time the gunman had fired, the Mercedes had gained a good half a car-length on the BMW. John swerved across to the left, hitting the front of the BMW, with the extra weight of the Mercedes pushing the BMW onto the central reservation. As it hit the barrier, John pulled back into the middle of the carriageway, continuing to accelerate down the motorway. I looked back and saw the BMW's driver had lost control of the car, which was spinning across the road on to the verge.

John was swearing now because of the damage to the car but was also happily saying, 'I am impressed with this car - after all that, it still feels normal and handles well.' He reduced the speed back to 80kph and phoned 101 for the Belgian police. 'I am on the A1 just approaching the junction with the A59 and I have just seen a black BMW hit the central reservation and crash, I think the driver is drunk.' and he hung up before they could question him. 'That should slow them up - hopefully they will find the gun,' he said.

As we approached the outskirts of Antwerp, John checked the mirror, 'Time to part company with our friend here,' he muttered to himself, as he accelerated away, soon losing the Golf which was no match for the Mercedes speed. We joined the Antwerp ring road, and John slowed up a bit, but still kept up a good speed, assuring Andrea that our tail would have trouble catching up with us now, especially with all the traffic.

The Mango Mystery

I looked at Andrea, who was very pale, 'This has got very serious and dangerous now,' I told her, 'that was third attempt and I don't think they will stop until this whole business is finished. I think you should go home before you get hurt.'

She tried to protest, but John agreed with me and told her we would take her to Brussels airport, where she should be able to get a flight back to London. 'That will be good for us too,' John commented, 'We can check if we are still being followed before heading on to Eindhoven.'

We got to the airport and all three of us went in with Andrea. John hung back, watching as I went up to the BA sales desk to buy Andrea a ticket with my credit card. She had three hours to wait for her flight but said she preferred to go through to Departures as she felt safer there, so we parted at the security check. 'Look after yourself, Joelle,' Andrea said, as we hugged and kissed goodbye, and she fought back her tears as she hurried through.

Meanwhile, John had bought a hat and dark glasses, giving them to me along with his coat. 'Hide your hair - put these on - go and have a coffee, and in half an hour walk out to the pick up area where I will be waiting for you.'

'What are going to do?' I asked, puzzled.

'Drive off without you, as a precaution, just in case anyone is watching. If there is, they will see me drive off without you and assume you left by plane.'

I joined him half an hour later and I noticed the door was looking a bit crumpled and scratched. 'Shame about the dent,' I said as got in the car.

John de Caynoth

'Don't worry' John replied, 'Its not the only damage it will pick up: the body-shop will soon fix it when we get home.'

We drove on to the ringroad, heading nort-east on the A2 towards Maastricht and Eindhoven. As we drove, I thought about home, missing my mother and Jasmine. **I was frightened that after three attempts to finish me off, I might never see them again.**

John was still being cautious, so instead of heading into Eindhoven, he turned off beforehand, to Geldrop, where we found a small motel. 'This will be good until Monday when, after you've been to the police in Eindhoven, we can drive down to Switzerland.'

We had adjacent rooms at the front of the building on the first floor, overlooking the car park and road. The rooms were en-suite, but small and sparsely furnished with a double bed, a wardrobe, desk unit and collapsible suitcase-stand. As I lay on the bed, exhausted after the drive, I heard a scraping and thumping in the corridor and then banging on John's door. Shortly after that, there was a lot of noise in John's room, which suddenly went silent. I tentatively crept out of my room, checking there was no one in the corridor, before I knocked on Johns door calling out, 'Are you okay John?' There was no answer.

The Mango Mystery

Chapter 43. The Button

Joelle, Saturday evening

On Saturday evening I lay on the bed worrying that something had happened to John and trying to decide what I should do about it, but I drifted off to sleep and was woken by someone knocking on my door. John was standing there looking very cool.

'What happened John, are you all right?' I asked him.

'I am fine,' he replied 'what are you talking about?'

'I heard a lot of banging and noise from you room earlier and, when I knocked on your door to see of you were okay, there was no answer.'

'Oh that! I asked for a chair and you heard it being dragged along the corridor, and then I had to move the furniture in bedroom round to fit it in by the window.'

'What did you want a chair for?' I asked, puzzled.

'I wanted to sit by the window for a couple of hours and watch for anyone acting suspiciously, and the reason why I did not answer your knock was because I went out to move the car to where I could see it better.'

'And did anyone appear?' I asked.

'No, I think we have lost our tails for the moment and that's good, because I was going to suggest we go out for supper. The hotel only does bed and breakfast but there is a restaurant a short walk down the road, if you would care to join me.'

I enjoyed that evening. We had a good meal, and off duty, John relaxed and was good company, actually very amusing. We ate well and had just a bit too much to drink, and with me feeling less stressed, we walked back to the hotel joking and laughing together. When we got up to the room John stood just a bit too close to me for a few seconds and it surprised me that I did not mind, and was finding him attractive. I thought he was going to kiss me, but he just touched my wrist, said good night, and went to his room.

As I closed my bedroom door behind me, I noticed my mobile phone blinking, telling me I had received a call. Douglas had phoned while I was out and he had left the message, 'Nothing important, I am missing you and just rang to talk too you. I will ring again sometime.'

'Shit!' I said to my self, angrily. **I was feeling cross with Douglas remembering our last row and thinking he was being a bit wimpish and, I realised, a teeny bit revengeful, as I knew I would have returned John's kiss if he tried.**

Sunday

John and I did not breakfast together. He ate early and then sat by his window, on watch for a couple of hours, while I had breakfast in my room, lounging in bed most of the morning, wondering whether to phone Douglas. In the end I decided not to bother, as I was not sure what I wanted to say to him, and did not want a silly argument over the phone. Whatever I said was bound to be taken the wrong way.

Just before lunch, I heard voices in the car park and saw John and the hotel owner doing something to the Mercedes. They were at the back of the car doing

The Mango Mystery

something with the rear light. Not long after, John knocked on my door and asked if I would be okay on my own for an hour or so as he was going into Eindhoven to get a tin of paint and a light to replace one that broke yesterday.

'Will they be open on a Sunday?' I asked.

'The guy who owns the hotel knows someone who runs an auto shop and they have what I need, but I have to collect them.'

While John was out, I walked along the road to a little supermarket. I wanted to by some food so I could eat alone in my room. I did not trust myself to eat dinner, spending time with John again - I might enjoy being with him just a bit too much. The supermarket was closed, so I walked back to the hotel thinking that missing dinner would not kill me! However, when I got back to the hotel the owner's wife, clearing the breakfast bar and vacuuming the carpets, kindly let me take some ham, cheeses and a couple of rolls.

John did invite me to go for dinner with him on Sunday evening and looked disappointed when I said 'No, I am waiting for a call from Douglas.'

Douglas did ring me later that evening. He sounded very sorry for himself, and said he was missing me, wishing I was with him. I thought he was still being rather pathetic, but I did not say anything. He told me he and Josh were planning to visit Tony Choizi's apartment, and remembering John's advice, I stopped him telling me more. It was a fairly short phone call and Douglas did most of the talking, which was good as I was still unsettled by Saturday night's experience, and not at all sure what I wanted to say to him. He finished the call by telling me to be careful and that he was glad

John de Caynoth

I had John to look after me. Love you, Joelle.' he said as he hung up and that made me feel even more guilty and uncertain about my feelings for him.

I sat on the bed thinking, with some emotion, *oh dear, what am I getting into now? Here I am travelling round Europe with this attractive man, who I know fancies me, and now Douglas is telling me he loves me and I am just getting cross with him.* To blank out my confusion I turned the television on, putting men right to the back of my mind.

Monday

I did eat breakfast this morning with John and we settled our hotel account before John drove me into Eindhoven to the Police Station. I was relieved to see he was very business-like this morning and made no reference to Saturday night. I noticed the rear wing did not look so damaged and the back of the car looked back to normal. 'Had to do something,' he explained, 'it is illegal to use the car with a broken light and the German police are hot on things like that.'

He dropped me right by the Police Station door and went off to park the car. I walked in explaining to the duty Sergeant who I was and what I had come for. He directed me into a waiting area while he found one of the detectives involved with the murder case. A young man came to find me: he did not introduce himself, just told me that he had been instructed to let me see all the evidence, as he took me into an interview room where everything was laid out. I asked him to show me the reports and findings from the post mortem, so he directed me to a report and a small box of personal items that had been found on the victim. I

The Mango Mystery

looked into the box of personal items and saw a button. Then I read the postmortem report, finding the proof I needed. I was pleased, my hunch was right and I asked the detective if I could use the phone.

'Willam,' I said as he answered, 'I know who killed your undercover police woman.'

To say Willam was surprised would be an understatement and he stammered, 'How, who, where are you?' He collected his wits and said, 'No, don't tell me on the phone, stay where you are and I will come and see you.'

Willam and Jan van den Leuven arrived later that morning and explained they had been driven down at high speed in a police car, wanting me to go through exactly what I had found from the beginning.

'I was working on a hunch, but this report confirms my suspicions. I retrieved this from the boot of the Mercedes,' I produced Zed's flannel sports jacket. 'When I saw the pictures of the house, where Xavier Zedanski had been living when he was in the UK, I noticed this jacket had lost a button.' I then showed them the post-mortem report and the paragraph that referred to the button, which the unfortunate policewoman had swallowed.

Jan looked puzzled and said, 'We never found a match for that button. She must have swallowed it to give us clue as to the killer.'

'I think that's exactly what she did,' I agreed. Pointing out a small hole and ripped material, I took the loose button that had been recovered in the post mortem, comparing it with the ones on the jacket.

John de Caynoth

My God, it is an exact match,' exclaimed Jan, ' are you sure this jacket belongs to Zedanski?'

'Without actually asking him to confirm it is his, yes, I am pretty sure; it was found with his clothes in the house he was living in.'

Jan joined the conversation, 'We can probably prove he wore it by getting a DNA sample off it, if we could link the jacket to the dead woman, we have our murderer.' Jan took the jacket and button away to show the Inspector, now in charge of the case, to get things moving.

They both appeared a few minutes later, congratulating me. All we needed to do now was to find Xavier Zedanski.

'Don't worry, he will show up soon, dead or alive.' I reminded them.

There was some discussion about where Zedanski might now be. He had not been seen since the shooting incident on Euston Station and, although Barbara Green had circulated his description, no one had reported any sightings. 'Now we have a suspect, we can intensify our search, so hopefully that might turn something up,' said the Inspector. The three Dutch detectives went into a detailed discussion about how they might set up a search for Zed.

It was time for me to leave. I used the excuse that I had a long journey ahead of me and needed to get moving, as I walked off to find John.

We had an address for Mrs Lecarrow in Lausanne near Lake Geneva and I asked John how long he thought it would take to get there.

The Mango Mystery

'If we head East towards Essen and Dusseldorf, we pick up the E35 and follow that road south for most of the way. Should take ten to twelve hours I reckon.'

It was well past lunchtime when we got on the road and I asked John if he was planning to do the whole drive in one go. 'Up to you,' he said 'You are the boss.'

I replied, 'I don't fancy arriving at Lausanne at 2.00am and having to sleep in the car. We will see how we go, but I think we will stop and find a hotel for the night somewhere.'

For the first couple of hours John was on his guard, watching the rear view mirror carefully, slowing down and speeding up, and pulling into service areas, studying the cars following us in. Eventually he declared we were clear, and he could not see anyone tailing us. I could see him relaxing and when we hit a clear stretch of road he grinned at me, 'Lets see what she can do,' and put his foot down. We hit a hundred and sixty miles an hour: I was terrified - we were passing everything so quickly. 'That's enough John!' I screeched at him, 'there are enough people trying to kill me without you having a go as well.' Thankfully he slowed down and set the cruise control to 90mph.

John sat back in the driving seat and relaxed, I looked out of the window and we motored on in silence for quite a long time. Eventually, John turned to me and asked me what it was like working on Kaeta.

'Pretty mundane most of the time,' I explained, 'a lot of the work is looking after tourists: most of the crime is low level stuff, pick pockets, small time drug dealers, and so on, preying on the visitors. It is a pretty safe island - I can't remember the last murder we had.'

John de Caynoth

'Sounds like a good existence to me,' John commented, 'being a Close Protection Officer can be exciting, and fortunately I very rarely get shot at, but it often involves a lot of boring waiting around. This is one of the more interesting jobs, lots of excitement and working with a pretty lady,' he smiled at me expectantly, but I said nothing, so he continued, ' but the real problem with being a CPO is that it destroys you home life. Duty shifts can be very unpredictable and if you are assigned someone who travels a lot you can be away from home for long periods, sometimes. My wife finds it very difficult.' He paused here before telling me, 'We are having a trial period of separation at the moment, just to see how it works out.'

I said I was sorry to hear that, but registered with a flash of disappointment that he was married.

John changed the subject by asking me what was the most interesting case I had covered on Kaeta. I thought before answering but told him, 'Year before last, you know, the one we discussed in Jan's office. We were notified that a drug smuggling gang was using the Island as a staging post and asked to set up surveillance on the suspected smuggler. He was actually an innocent tourist, but the international ramifications of the investigation became a farce and it was suspected that there was a mole inside the police somewhere, feeding information to the gang. That is how I became involved in all this now.'

'I see,' John said, 'and would that innocent tourist happen to have been Douglas Jay?'

'That's right.'

'So what is your relationship with Douglas Jay. Are you close, is he your partner?'

The Mango Mystery

That question made me think: *Yes, I believe we are close and I know that is what Douglas wants*, but it was a long time before I answered. It occurred to me that I was not at all sure what relationship I had with Douglas. 'I don't know,' I replied.

John de Caynoth

Chapter 44. Monday Night

Joelle

It was getting towards the end of the afternoon and we had driven a few more kilometres southwards down the E35.

Since John had asked me about my relationship with Douglas, I had been thinking about that question and why I had answered John the way I did. I thought I loved Douglas, so why did I not say so? I was feeling tense and worried having just been shot at again, on top of which I am worrying about Douglas getting himself into trouble. The phone calls over the weekend unsettled me: Douglas was in a strange mood, feeling sorry for himself, completely disregarding my problems which made me cross, sounding so pathetic when I am worrying for my life. But then, I realised with a jolt that Douglas knew nothing of the trip from Amsterdam to Belgium: I had not told him, and perhaps I was being a bit unfair towards him.

But, as I remembered how John had nearly kissed me, what really was bothering me was that I am attracted to John - does that mean my love for Douglas is fading?

I was feeling guilty as it was my fault Andrea had been put in a dangerous situation, and I was worrying for her as well. I needed to talk to her. She has a knack of straightening out my emotions when I get them in a tangle.

Perhaps I should telephone Douglas and apologise for being tetchy and, to hell with John and his security, tell Douglas what was going on and talk like we always had done....

John interrupted my thoughts. 'Sorry John,' I apologised, 'what did you say?'

'I was thinking about you and Douglas and I asked if you were living together?'

I should have told him it was none of his business, but I did not, instead I said, 'No, he has his own place in Wiltshire, he was just staying at the flat to help me out while I was suspended.'

John thought about this answer and said, 'I would not have thought he was much help, in fact a liability you don't need really, playing the amateur detective - crashing around the evidence like he has been.'

'Where did you get that idea from?' I asked him sharply.

'Oh! Just the gossip around the office,' he replied off-handedly, 'I think I get the picture.'

Before I could challenge him again he said, 'Look, the turning for Baden-Baden is coming up now, so if it suits you, I suggest look for somewhere to stay for the night. It is a spa town and tourist resort so we are bound to find a hotel here.'

John drove into the town centre and found the tourist office, which luckily was still open. 'You stay in the car and lock the doors while I go and check out the hotels,' he advised.

I read the notice board, next to the parking space. It informed me that Baden-Baden goes back to Roman times, when it was called it Aurelia Aquensis, and that the ruins of the old Roman vapour-baths could still be found. John returned while I was reading that the present town gained in popularity in the early 19th century, when the Prussian Queen started to visit it to enjoy the spa waters.

'I have booked us into a hotel - it is a bit expensive, but it is a sport hotel with a swimming pool and gym, plus an excellent restaurant, and as I suspect this is the last chance we get to relax, I thought we would treat ourselves. Unfortunately I could not get adjacent rooms, but they are both on the same corridor so it should be safe enough.'

It certainly was a luxury hotel and the porter looked askance at our motley luggage as he showed us to our rooms. John took the double room immediately next to the lifts, while my room was a twin about three doors further along the corridor.

John told me he had booked a table for us in the restaurant at 8.00pm and he would meet me in the bar at 7.45pm. I had thought to eat in my room again, but John saw me hesitate and said, 'Please Joelle, don't make me eat alone again, it is a first class restaurant and I would really like to take you dinner. My treat, please.'

I relented and agreed.

The first thing I did when I got to my room was to phone Douglas - I was disappointed when he did not answer, leaving a message asking him to phone me. I decided to go swimming and try again later. I bought a costume in the hotel shop and went to find the pool. I looked in at the gym and saw John in there pounding away on a running machine. He waved to me, so I went over and told him I was going swimming.

It was while I was swimming lengths that I remembered Douglas had said he and Josh were going

The Mango Mystery

to search Tony's Choizi's apartment. My first reaction was anger, he had promised me he would not do anything dangerous: breaking into Tony's apartment would get him arrested, or even worse. He could be hurt if he was caught, and then it would be me who would have to bail him out again. I seethed angrily as I stormed up and down the pool, noticing, once I had calmed down to a leisurely breaststroke, that John had joined me. We started chasing each other round the pool splashing, trying to push each other under as we played together. Eventually John saw the time and said we should go and change for dinner or we would be late. When I got back to the room, I tried to phone Douglas again but still got no answer. That rekindled my anger but I calmed down after telling myself that he might phone me later, so I took my phone down to dinner with me.

I went down to the bar and ordered a gin and tonic, before spotting John sitting in a corner. He had ordered a bottle of Champagne and insisted we should drink it, 'to get into the right mood before we go into eat,' with the result that I was already feeling very slightly light headed as we went into the restaurant.

The food was good - John ordered roasted wild boar for his main course but I opted for a rare fillet steak. We both chose smoked salmon as an appetiser and John ordered a white wine to drink with it, followed by a full bodied red wine for the main meal. I enjoyed the meal and John's conversation as he told me about his time in the army, and then stories about some of the police work he had been involved with. I lost track of how much I had drunk and by the time we had finished my head was starting to spin. As we walked to the lift to go back to our rooms I stumbled and John

John de Caynoth

put his arm out to catch me. 'As your CPO I have to look after you and I certainly can't let you fall over,' he joked holding me close, with his arm around my waist, as we got into the lift and travelled up to our floor. We reached his bedroom door and he was still holding me as he put the key in the lock and pushed the door open.

I said, 'You can let me go now John, I will be okay - it's only three doors along to my room.' But he did not let me go, he held me closer and turned towards me. Something at the back of mind told me I should not be doing this, but as John kissed me I realised I did want it. He half carried me into his room and kicking the door shut we embraced and carried on kissing. He stepped back and undid the zip on my leather jacked and took the jacket off, and then pulled off his sweater and shirt, and stepping behind me, put his arms round me again and started to kiss my neck as he unbuttoned my blouse and unhooked my bra. He moved his hands and as he cupped my breasts, he pulled me closer and I felt his erection hard and demanding pressing against me.

I put thoughts of Douglas to the back of my mind.

I don't really know how long I was in John's room as I lay in the bed beside him. I was fully aware of what I had done, my head thumping a bit, having had too much to drink. I mulled over in my mind if I regretted sleeping with him or not. He was quite fit, and some might see him as a bit of a catch. Did I feel disloyal to Douglas?

John was snoring gently as he slept still. I was now stone-cold sober and crept out of bed, not wanting to wake him. Gathering my clothes, I slipped my leather

The Mango Mystery

jacket on, and let myself out of his room, hoping there would be no one in the corridor as I ran back to my own. I stood in the shower for ages trying to wash away any feelings of guilt before I went to bed.

I was woken in the morning by knocking on my door. It was John, asking if I was okay and was I coming down to breakfast. 'No,' I groaned, 'I have a headache.' He shouted through the door that we needed to get moving and he would see me in the car in forty-five minutes.

I dragged myself out of bed and got dressed and made a coffee in the room. I went to pay my bill but the receptionist winked at me and said it had already been settled, and that my partner was sitting in the car outside the hotel door waiting for me. As I got into the passenger seat, and John commented that I looked tired.

'I have a hangover, please don't talk to me,' I replied. I felt tired, I did have a hangover and not just from overdoing the wine. I pretended to sleep while John drove but I was still trying to rationalise last night and what effect this would have on Douglas. At least sleeping with John had tested my feelings for Douglas. I acknowledged the sickness of guilt in my stomach, regret creeping into my consciousness. I checked my phone, and realised with a pang of anxiety that Douglas had not phoned me. Yesterday's anger gave way to worry now. Had he been into Tony's apartment already - had something happened to him?

John de Caynoth

Chapter 45. The Apartment

Douglas

I felt that the phone conversations with Joelle over last weekend had not been a great success. She had sounded very abrupt and short when she had spoken with me, and I wondered if I had done, or said, something to upset her. I did not want to believe the other possible explanation - that the working relationship between her and John MacDuff had developed into something more. After all, I reasoned, she is not that sort of person and just would not do that to me but I was not sure if phoning her again was a good idea. If I had upset her it might just make things worse, so perhaps it would be better to wait until we were back together and could talk properly.

This was all turning over in my mind as I sat trying to read a newspaper, when Josh walked into the hotel to find me.

'I have got the key to Choizi's apartment,' he said, 'Are you still wanting to come with me?'

I said I did.

'I will pick you up just after lunch. I have been watching the estate and it seems to be fairly deserted through the middle of the afternoon, so I think that is the best time to go.'

'Would it not be better go at night when there is no one about?' I queried.

'No,' Josh replied firmly, 'someone might spot a light and that would look more suspicious than being seen walking round during the day.'

The Mango Mystery

I mooched about the hotel for the rest of the morning, alternately worrying about Joelle and then feeling apprehensive at the thought of breaking into Choizi's flat.

I ate a very light lunch and then went to my room to get ready to meet Josh. He told me to look like a tourist, and if we were challenged, the story was that Tony Choizi gave him the key because he was thinking of buying the apartment, and that I was a friend he was showing around for a second opinion. I saw my phone on the bedside table blinking, telling me I had a message. I listened and it was a rather cross instruction from Joelle to phone her. I decided to do this later, as Josh was waiting for me.

We got to the apartment complex and Josh waved to the security guard, driving straight in, explaining that he and the security man were 'brothers' now as they had been drinking together.

'Isn't that a bit risky - he could identify you couldn't he? I asked Josh.

'Not really,' he replied, 'He thinks my name is Charlie Keys and anyway, he doesn't like Tony Choizi. He also told me that he has offered him drugs and brings women back to the apartment.'

We parked out of sight round the back of the block, checked no one was about and entered the block by the fire door, taking the stairs rather then using the lift. Josh's key turned smoothly in the lock and we walked into the apartment.

'Search carefully,' Josh instructed, 'we have plenty of time so go through everything, but try and put every item back exactly as you found it. Best if Choizi does not realise the place has been searched.'

'What happens if he comes back unexpectedly?' I asked, feeling nervous again.

Josh assured me that was very unlikely, as the next plane from Florida did not land until the evening, in three hours time.

Somewhat reassured, I started searching.

There was a small entrance hall giving access to a bathroom, a second bedroom and, directly ahead, a large open-plan living room leading to a balcony, which overlooked the sea. There was a small kitchen at one end of the open-plan room and a door to the side, which led to a large bedroom with an en-suite wet room and toilet. The living room was sparsely furnished with a large sofa and reclining chair, a television and music-centre and an old- fashioned pedestal, and kneehole, desk in one corner. A nondescript picture hung on the longest wall. Josh quickly checked the picture but found nothing, so he headed for the desk and started methodically going through the drawers and their contents.

'He has an expensive lifestyle,' Josh commented as he went through a pile of credit card statements, photographing them with a small digital camera he had brought with him.

I searched the sparsely furnished bedroom. The king-size bed was not made up, there was a chair, a chest of draws, with a dressing stand and mirror on top. I looked round and under the bed, lifting the mattress, revealing nothing of interest, so I went over to the chest. The bottom drawer was full of bed linen, and the

The Mango Mystery

other drawers were all empty, except one, which contained a collection of handcuffs and silk scarves. I called Josh to take a picture of the drawer contents. I checked round the room again, and in the en-suite, but drew a blank, so I went back into the living area and across to the kitchen. The fridge was empty, and the cupboard under the sink and worktop only contained bottles of detergent, and a dustpan and brush. I checked the wall-units - two were empty but the third contained tinned food at the back of which I spotted a small, brown envelope. I called Josh over as I opened it shaking out three pills into the palm of my hand. 'These are KetPil tablets - ketamine,' I told Josh.

'Are you sure?' Josh asked picking up one of the tablets.

'Yes, I used to work for the company that make them, and he has to have come by these dishonestly, as they are only legally sold as a veterinary drug.'

Josh took a photograph of the pills and replaced them in the envelope, which I put back in the cupboard.

I walked back to the desk with Josh, 'Found anything?' I asked Josh as stood in front of the desk looking puzzled.

'Not sure,' he answered, 'nothing particularly interesting in the desk drawers, just bills, shopping lists, addresses - mainly of clubs, that sort of thing - but look at this,' he pulled a draw out from each side of the desk placing them side by side on the top. The right-hand drawer was six inches shorter than the left one.

We pulled all the right-hand drawers out and peered into the space, but all we could see was the back

John de Caynoth

of the desk pedestal. Josh felt around but found nothing. We pulled the desk away from the wall and it moved very easily as, unusually this type of desk, it was on wheels. 'Strange,' Josh commented thoughtfully, as he peered at the back of the pedestal which appeared to be solid, giving a resounding 'clunk' as he knocked it with his fist. I looked around for a hidden switch and I noticed the kick strip round the bottom of the pedestal appeared to be loose. I pulled it and it slid back, releasing a catch. The wooden panel at back swung open.

Inside was a book, a folder containing bank statements, a paying in book, a debit card and a large envelope. Josh opened the columnar accounts book and we looked at it together. On the pages at the front of the book, one set of entries per page, were details of clubs and bars, including the name of the establishment, the name of a manager or owner and the address. Other details included the number of members, average attendance, monthly income, and, at the bottom of each page, was an amount of money in US dollars.

At the back of the book was a list of names, with amounts of money against each one. I looked at Josh, puzzled, but he just shrugged - the names meant nothing to us. In the centre of the book was a section of pages set with columns, each dated month by month, with the clubs and bars listed by name down the side of the page. In the columns were amounts of money against the club names and at the bottom of each column was a total. I checked the totals against the bank statements, and each total matched a credit entry on the statement.

The Mango Mystery

'These establishments are all in Miami - my guess is that he is operating a protection racket,' Josh declared, seeming pleased with himself. He proceeded to photograph each page of the book.

I picked up the envelope and looked at the contents, photographs, all of which were pornographic. They were of women, mostly naked, some of who were tied to the bed in the other room. Josh photographed a selection of the pictures, before we put everything back where we had found it.

Josh said, 'I think we have got what we wanted, but we had better check - just in case we have missed something.' We found nothing else, so on checking there was no-one about, we quickly left the apartment.

As we drove back to Hamilton, Josh was very quite and thoughtful. I asked him what was wrong.

'I am not sure we have got enough to nail Detective Choizi,' He told me.

'Well,' I offered, 'we have no direct proof that he is a member of the smuggling gang and a police informer, but he is obviously running an illegal racket and probably kidnapping and drugging the women he picks up before he rapes them, plus he has those KetPils, the smuggling of which started all this.'

'Yes, maybe,' Josh replied, but that accounts book on its own does not prove anything illegal - it might just be a rent book - there is nothing written in it to show it is protection money, or even Choizi's book. As for the pictures, while they are pornographic, unless we can find the women, and they are prepared to give evidence that they were abducted, held against their will, and raped, it will be difficult to prove anything against him on the strength of just the photographs. Anyway, Choizi could always deny the pictures are of his activities.'

I pointed out to Josh that the sums of money, apparently collected from the clubs, agreed with the amounts paid into the bank account. Josh agreed that could be helpful, but pointed out that Choizi was not named on the account. He concluded that he needed to look at all the pictures he had taken, and make a plan for what to do next.

'I will come over and meet you in the Library Bar again tomorrow evening,' he told me, as he dropped me off at my hotel.

The Mango Mystery

Chapter 46. The Hangover

Joelle

I had been fast asleep, but I jolted awake as I realised that the Mercedes was no longer moving and John had disappeared - I was alone, and, as I tried the door handle, found I was locked in the car. I wondered where we were, a car park of some sort, I realised, but I had no idea where we were or even what time it was. I looked at my watch - 1.00pm! I must have been asleep for three or four hours. That was hardly surprising, I said to myself, as I had not slept much last night.

Last Night! The thought clanged in my head as I the details came back to me. Guilt at betraying Douglas was overcoming me again. The voice in my head was nagging loudly, telling me I was an unworthy fool, and asking how I ever thought I could live with what I had done and make it right again with him. 'Shut up, please.' I said out loud to the voice, but it continued to niggle away only fading away when I started to think about what I should do about my current predicament, locked alone in the car.

Fortunately, I did not have make any decisions because John came back with a carrier bag containing some sandwiches, a carton of orange juice and two coffees.

'I thought you might need a drink and some food,' he said to me.

I was very thirsty and drank the orange juice. John told me that we were at a service area just north of Basel and probably had another hour or two's driving to Lausanne. 'I need a break from driving and to stretch

John de Caynoth

my legs for a bit before we continue. I think we are quite safe here: there is no sign of anyone trailing us if you want to use the ladies room and freshen up.'

I thanked him and agreed I would, so he walked with me across the car park and gave me the car keys. 'Lock your self back in the car - I am just going to jog round for a few minutes before we set off again.'

Though the traffic got heavier as we approached Basel, John decided we would stay on the motorways and take the route via Berne. In places the traffic was extremely slow and we eventually reached Lausanne at around four in the afternoon. John had entered the address we had for Mrs Lecarrow into the sat-nav, so we went straight there, driving slowly past the house. It was a semi-detached property in a quite residential street, east of the town centre. John turned the car around, retracing out tracks, stopping just up the road with a good view of the house. The street was very quite, with just a few cars parked in front of the houses but no people around, and, John pointed out, no car in front of Mrs Lecarrow's house.

'We can't stay here for too long - we stick out like a sore thumb, sitting in a black Mercedes with a dented door,' I said to John. We watched the house for a few more minutes before John agreed with me and said we should move on. We drove off slowly and I said, 'I think we should hire a small discrete van, and watch the house and hopefully get some pictures of Mrs Lecarrow. Also I will see if I can get a name and address for this widow person she has been seen with.' I looked at my watch, 'It is getting late now: I think we will have to organise a van first thing in the morning.

The Mango Mystery

Let's go and find somewhere to stay for a couple of nights.'

I phoned Andrea from the car, asking her to find out the name and address of the widow. We drove back towards the centre of Lausanne and found a hotel overlooking the lake. John carried the bags in with me following him. He walked up to the reception desk and asked if they had a double room available.

'Yes Sir, for how many nights?' John was asked.

'I think three,' he replied, but I interrupted.

'No, we require two single rooms.' I told the receptionist, who looked at John for confirmation. He shrugged his shoulders as I repeated firmly, 'two single rooms, please.'

The receptionist consulted her screen and handed over two sets of keys. Once we were out of earshot, I turned angrily to John.

'What do think you are doing, just assuming I am going to share a room and fall into bed with you!'

'I am sorry,' he muttered, 'After you said you were not with Jay, and after last night, I just assumed...' He trailed off as I interrupted him again.

'How dare you assume,' I accused him, 'Douglas is more than a friend to me, he is not a liability, and I am with him. Last night was a mistake after drinking too much, and you can be very sure it won't happen again.' I stalked off to my room and left him standing.

John de Caynoth

Chapter 47. The Arrest Warrant

Douglas

Wednesday was a frustrating day: I was just wandering around the hotel, looking for something to do while I waited for the next meeting with Josh. I went for a walk and thought a lot about Joelle. She had phoned twice and left a message for me to phone her but she had sounded very cross: I was not sure speaking on the phone was a good idea. However, by lunchtime, I did decide to phone her. I wished I had not bothered, as the conversation was brief and left me feeling more worried than before. She had answered her mobile very quickly and although she did not sound cross with me she was speaking with her police voice.

'Douglas,' she said 'Thanks for phoning me back, but I am not alone and I am tied up at the moment and it's difficult to talk, hold on a moment.' The phone went quiet and I could hear background noises and voices. She must have gone out to the street because suddenly I could hear traffic passing. 'Douglas, are you still there?'

I told her I was.

'I am sorry I can't talk for long they are waiting for me inside. Are you okay? I was worried when you said you were going to search Tony's apartment.'

I replied, 'Yes, I'm fine. We searched Tony's place yesterday and it looks as if he is running a protection racket, but we didn't find any obvious connection with the drug smuggling. How are you and what are you doing?'

'I am good, but I wish you were here with me. At the moment John and I are organising a stake-out, so it looks like a boring day ahead waiting for something to happen. Douglas, I must go now, but there are things I need to tell you - not over the phone.' And with that she hung up, leaving me worrying about what she wanted to tell me and whatever it was that had upset her.

I went for another long walk in the afternoon and got back to the hotel just in time to meet Josh. I was waiting in the usual place, in the Library Bar, when he arrived looking very nervous and worried.

'What's up?' I asked him.

'I phoned a friend in Miami just now,' he told me, 'Apparently, Choizi has searched my office and put an arrest warrant out for me. At this moment he is running around Miami and is very cross that he can't find me. It won't be long before he guesses I am in Bermuda.'

'Josh, I am sorry, I got you into this - I did not think Choizi would go this far.'

He reminded me that Choizi had tried to stitch-up Joelle, and that was how this had all started. 'Anyway,' Josh started to look happier, 'it's all part of the game. I did not have to take the job, and I will just disappear until it all blows over.' He then said, 'Douglas, I want you to look at this and tell me what you think.'

He showed me four A4-sized copies of the bank statements he had photographed, and pointed out that it was a numbered account with a box-number address. 'Of course, he will probably claim that the monies are nothing to do with him and that he is just providing an accommodation address,' Josh commented, ticking off all the credits that agreed with amounts collected, according to the cash sheets. The only exceptions were the occasional, large deposit. Also, there were irregular large withdrawals. Each month, there were four regular payments of different amounts, but the same amount every month went to the same person. They were paid by standing order and the reference was given as names - Mickey Mouse, Donald Duck. Popeye, Homer.

I looked at Josh and said, 'Well, I think we can be pretty sure that this is Tony Choizi, and the bank must have details of who opened the account, and who is a signatory. I guess either he is being blackmailed or he has associates in a protection racket, and pays them each month. What do think the irregular amounts are for?'

'Don't know,' Josh puzzled, but nodded in agreement, 'I don't see Choizi standing for blackmail, so my bet is on associates. I am guessing they are in the Miami Police, which gives us a problem.'

'How so?' I asked, 'Don't we just send them what we have found and let them investigate? Choizi will be arrested and all the drug smuggling business will come out.'

'And how do we know who to send this stuff to? Look here,' he said, pointing at a name, 'Popeye get a much bigger payment than the others. so my assumption is that he is probably a senior officer. If he gets this stuff first he will bury it deep, along with you and me.'

'Ah, I get the point,' I said, 'what do we do, then?'

Josh produced five envelopes, which contained copies of the more explicit and damming photographs, a statement of our suspicions, and a CD onto which

The Mango Mystery

Josh had copied all the pictures he had taken in Choizi's apartment.

He explained, 'One is for me, and one I will give to the local police here in Bermuda with a note tipping them off that he is dealing in drugs on the Island, and that they will find evidence of this in his apartment. We know the local Police don't like him so hopefully that will get him detained. The other three envelopes are for you. One is for you to keep, the second you should give to the British Police and the third is to be sent to that solicitor of yours, with a letter telling him to open it in the event of something happening to you,' concernedly adding, 'or me.'

I wondered why we should not send a copy to the Miami Police because as I said, 'they can hardly bury this if there are five other copies around.' but Josh was not happy. 'If we do that, Choizi gets warned, and if he clears that apartment before it get officially searched our evidence is worthless.'

'Okay,' I said 'I will go with that, what do we do after we have sent the copies?'

Josh looked grim, 'I am going to drop one into the local police now and then I am disappearing. I advise you to do the same before the shit hits the fan.'

And with that he left, telling me he would be in touch when the dust had settled.

It was strange seeing Josh walk away - suddenly I felt very vulnerable.

John de Caynoth

Chapter 48. The Russian Woman

Joelle

I was up early on Wednesday morning and feeling much more cheerful. At least the incident over the rooms yesterday had cleared my head and made me realise how I felt for Douglas. I felt guilty though and now desperately needed to tell Douglas what I had done, hoping he would forgive me.

I was first down to breakfast, drinking coffee, when John came into the room. He walked rather sheepishly across to me and apologised for his behaviour the night before, saying that he had just got the wrong end of the stick, and it would not happen again.

I was not going to let him off lightly so I said, 'Yes, you did get it completely wrong and you took advantage of me when I was feeling vulnerable. However, we still have to work together so let's be professional and get on with it.' John started to apologise all over again. 'Let it go John, you have said you are sorry, so get some breakfast and come and join me so we can plan what we do today,' I sighed.

We discussed how we could set up surveillance of Mrs Lecarrow's house. The Mercedes was too obvious to use, and anyway, if Mrs Lecarrow was connected to the drug gang, they would recognise it straight away. 'We need a van, preferably one with blacked-out windows, so we can sit inside it without being seen,' I concluded.

John was not particularly happy about leaving behind the Mercedes with its safety features and

The Mango Mystery

pointed out that, if were shot at, we would have no protection. While I agreed with him, I did make the point that it was more important that we were not recognisable to the gang.

John looked critically at me, 'You know, if we hid your hair and you wore one of my old fleeces we could make you look like a man.'

'Thanks for the compliment!' I retorted.

John continued, 'No, I mean that two men in a van look a lot less suspicious than one man and an attractive woman.'

'Okay, John, that's enough of that,' I said, ending the conversation abruptly. We finished breakfast and John went off to locate a suitable van.

Half an hour later, having removed all my make-up and pulling my hair back off my face, I was waiting for John in reception and trying, probably unsuccessfully, to look more masculine. John surprised me by walking in through the street door carrying a plastic bag.

'What have you got there?' I asked.

'Rations for the day, and disguises,' he said producing a flat cap for me and baseball hat for himself, 'There is a tourist gift-shop just around the corner,' he explained, 'and I have found a van-hire company just out of town - on the Geneva road.'

The hire company offered us a choice of three Fiat vans - a Punto, a Fiorino Combi, or a Scudo, apologising that all their biggest vans, Ducatos, were out on hire.

John de Caynoth

We went out to inspect the vehicles and chose the Fiorino Combi, which had darkened rear windows. It was also sign-written with the name of the hire company but John said that was good as a disguise, as a lot of companies would hire a van if their in-house fleet was short for any reason.

We went in to complete the paper work: I was about to sign the contract and pay the deposit on my credit card, when my mobile rang. It was Douglas - he could not have phoned at a more difficult time. The girl handling the hire had a couple of other people waiting for her attention and was hurrying us to finish, nevertheless, I told them I had to take this call and went outside to talk to Douglas. It was good to hear his voice but it was a very short call and I wanted desperately to tell Douglas about the other night, but this was not the right time or place. I did tell him I had something to talk to him about, but then guiltily realising that this would have worried him, I wanted to eat my words.

We completed the hire-contract and payment, and John asked if he could leave the Mercedes in their yard, out of sight.

John drove the Fiat as we headed for Mrs Lecarrow's address. We were approaching an area of small houses and apartment blocks when, suddenly, I told John to stop. He slammed the brakes on, nearly tipping me onto the floor.

'What on earth is the matter?' John asked, puzzled.

'That sign back there - I want it,' I explained as I got out of the van.

The Mango Mystery

It was a 'MEN AT WORK' sign, next to a couple of red-and-white cones and an orange plastic barrier. John took the barrier and I picked up the sign and the cones and we threw them into the back of the van. 'Inspector deNouvelas,' John chided me as we drove off, 'this is theft.'

'No its not,' I replied, 'we are only borrowing them - we will put them back when we have finished. Anyway, they were just left on the pavement and did not seem to be there for any reason.'

'Actually, they were marking some loose paving,' John observed.

We parked the van up the street, in a position from where we could watch Mrs Lecarrow's house. I put the sign and barriers up behind the van and John got his camera out, fitting a zoom lens, ready to take pictures.

'That's a nice bit of kit,' I complimented him. He had a Canon EOS 7D with a 75-300mm zoom lens. 'Thanks,' he replied and explained, 'we always carry a camera in the car but I prefer this one to the standard police-issue. It is faster and lighter and will shoot ten frames a second. Useful on a stake-out.'

We sat in the back of the van, taking turns to watch the house. We positioned ourselves at the rear of van trying to look busy behind the plastic barrier. Breaking our boredom, an elderly gentleman knocked on the van door, asking us what we doing. I answered in French, informing him that we were surveying the routing of service pipes under the pavement. He was trying to peer into the van so I quickly shut the door, pointing out that we had a lot of sensitive equipment inside. He asked how we located the pipes and was

John de Caynoth

obviously going to linger over the conversation. 'Radar,' I retorted as I got back into the cab. He shuffled off.

Just after lunch, I had a text message from Andrea, with a name and address for the widow. She was Russian and her name was Maria Vidnova, with an address in Geneva.

By late afternoon, John concluded there was no-one in the house and said he was going to have a look around. He was gone for about twenty minutes before he returned, looking very pleased with himself.

'It hardly looks lived in,' he explained. 'While I was walking around the rear of the property the neighbour appeared, asking what I was doing and if she could help me. I told her I was a friend from the UK and thought I would look up Mrs Lecarrow while I was in the area. Apparently, she lives with her partner and only comes back occasionally to check the house.'

'And I bet her partner is Maria Vidnova,' I said showing John the text from Andrea.

We agreed that there was no point in continuing to sit outside Mrs Lecarrow's house: tomorrow we would take a drive into Geneva and find Maria Vidnova.

The Mango Mystery

Chapter 49. On Surveillance

Joelle

I dined in my bedroom again last night as I was keeping out of John's way and did not want him getting any more ideas. However, I did come down this morning, joining him for breakfast so we could plan today's surveillance.

'More or less the same format as yesterday,' I said. 'We drive out in the van and park where we can watch the Vidnova residence and see what transpires.'

John produced a map of Geneva and pointed out where Marina Vidnova lived. It was on the west side of the lake, just over a kilometre out of Geneva itself: he reckoned it should be a fairly easy drive.

We arrived about an hour later, with me map reading, and John bemoaning the loss of the Mercedes sat-nav. The surveillance here was going to be much harder than yesterday as this house was well out of sight, behind a high brick wall, with heavy wrought-iron gates which appeared to work on some kind of remote-control opening system. Beyond the gate the drive, bordered by shrubs - which screened our view of the house itself - swept around to the right. All we could see was the roof with a couple of dormer windows, which we guessed had been converted into some sort of room.

'You would need money to live here,' John commented, as I looked up and down the road wondering where the best place to park the Fiat might be. He scanned the roof with his binoculars which, unlike the camera he informed me, were police issue,

John de Caynoth

standard equipment for the Mercedes. 'Those windows in the roof look pretty new, and they are positioned to give a pretty good view of the road.' He turned the binoculars on to the gates, 'and the security system they have at the front looks state of the art.'

'If we park just up the road - under the corner of the wall - we should be just out of view of anyone looking out of those windows,' I said to John, pointing.

'Yes,' he replied 'but we can't see the gate from there, or anyone standing behind it, and if anyone leaves the house we would only be able to get a picture of them if they turn in this direction.'

In the end, we compromised and parked just up the street - on the opposite side - where we could see through the gates. If anyone asked what we were doing there, we would use yesterday's excuse that we were surveying the underground service systems and we decided it would look less suspicious if we moved up the street from time to time.

We set up the sign and barrier: John laid a black bin bag on the road behind the barrier and trailed a length of flex from under it, still with the desk-lamp attached, in through the back door of the van.

'Where did you get that from?' I asked eyeing the desk-lamp suspiciously.

'Borrowed it from my room and got the bin bag from the porter,' he told me, 'I thought your excuse, that we were surveying, was good but we needed some props to be more convincing.'

'So what are you going to do - walk up and down the road pointing the lamp at the ground?' I asked, sarcastically.

The Mango Mystery

'Actually,' he replied 'that's quite a good idea, it gives me an excuse for wandering about, taking pictures.' I shrugged, not entirely convinced, unable to envisage how on earth he expected anyone to believe he was surveying for underground service pipes by waving a table lamp around.

We had not been settled in our van for long, when a post-van turned up and stopped outside the gate. The postman rang an intercom and bent towards it speaking. John got his camera ready. After a minute or so someone came to the gate, opened it and took a package and the letters from the postman. John clicked away. The van drove off and the man who had come to the gate looked up and down the road, pausing when he saw our vehicle and staring at us for a moment before going back into the grounds.

John checked his camera, confirming he had some clear pictures. It was obvious that the man had noted our presence. I suggested that we needed to move up the road a few metres in order to look more convincing. John nodded, retrieving the plastic bag and placing his camera in his black camera bag, which he slung round his neck and rested on his chest. He took the desk-lamp, detached the base and inserted the flexible lamp arm into the bag. He wandered off up the pavement, pointing the lamp holder at the ground, using it as though it was a pipe-detector. It looked almost realistic as he walked slowly up the road, but I could not help laughing. At the end of his walk he paused, put the lamp into the bag, removed the camera and walked slowly back to the van, taking pictures of the road, house gate and wall. He climbed into the van, grinning, as he extracted the lamp from the bag, waving it around, telling me, 'well I think that looked convincing enough. Let's move further up the road.' He moved the van about three metres, moving the signs, barrier and props before we settled down to watch the gates.

It was not long before the same man as before appeared at the gate, walking out into the street and closing the gates behind him with a remote control. He came straight over to the van, knocking on the passenger window and asking, 'Que faites-vous?' John climbed into the passenger seat and opened the window just enough to say through the gap, with a cockney accent, 'You will have to speak English, mate.' The man asked his question again, 'What are you doing?'

John, avoiding a direct answer, replied, 'Bloody hire-vans! It's a hell of a job setting up the equipment in here but, like, my own van is off the road. Who wants to know what we are doing?'

The man just repeated, 'Que faites-vous?' obviously getting impatient.

John replied, 'I would not stand too close if I were you mate, we are using high power microwaves, which will scramble your brain if you get to close - that's why we are in the back of the van - shields us, you see.' He shouted to me, 'turn the emitter off for a moment while I talk to this bloke.' He turned back to the man. 'Yeah, we are plotting the ground services, like, they have to know where they are before they start digging up the road.'

The man then said, suspiciously, I thought, 'Pourquoi les Anglais le faire?'

'Sorry mate, no idea what you are talking about,' John replied, with a note of condescension in his voice.

The Mango Mystery

The man repeated in his broken English, 'Why the English this do?'

John, paused, looked at the gates, and again avoiding a direct answer informed the man that we were Irish, not English before asking, 'you live in that big place over there, right. Have you got a swimming pool? I have always wanted on of those but living in a terrace, well like, I could not afford it anyway. Your place is it?'

The man, obviously not understanding John, looked confused as he asked, 'Pour qui travailles-tu?'

John started rambling again deliberately misunderstanding the question, 'Oh! You are the gardener are you?' The man frowned but before he could say anything John continued, 'That shower I work for, they can't even keep their vans running - mine would never have made the drive over here. Hell of a job, like, without the van, getting all our gear out here - cost us a fortune in extra baggage. Should finish this road today or tomorrow. Got a tight schedule, see. Better get on, now.'

He went to shut the window, but the man started to walk round the back of the van so John leaned out, his hand on the window-winder, and warned him, 'Don't go round the back mate, the emitter is on again, see.' The man paused, John added, 'Rayonnement, dangerous.' Indicating the danger by slicing his forefinger across his throat.

The man muttered something, shrugged and walked back opening the gates he approached them.

'Gardner, my eye,' John said as he climbed back over the seat, 'his hands are too soft and he was tooled

John de Caynoth

up. We have hit on something here - this place is secured like Fort Knox and they have at least one armed handyman wandering around.'

I agreed, and complemented him on his diversionary tactics, but John said, 'well I hope I have confused him and put his of the scent for a bit, but I fear we have probably not seen the last of him.

We sat in silence again, watching. Just before lunchtime, the gates opened and a red Ferrari pulled into the gateway, pausing to check if the road was clear. John whipped the camera out and started taking pictures, using the automatic shutter-release. The Ferrari pulled out, accelerating past us, disappearing down the road. It had only taken a few seconds - hardly enough time for us to register who was in the car - until we looked at John's pictures. He had shot just over thirty frames, missing the first few moments where the car had stopped to check if the road was clear, but had got it pulling out and driving towards us. As the car had approached the van, he had three clear pictures of two women sitting in the car. The driver was a middle-aged woman with short hair and a sever face, with a slightly younger-looking attractive blond in the passenger seat.

'I guess that might be Mrs Lecarrow and Maria Vidnova,' John said.

'I hope so,' I replied.

John went through his performance with the desk lamp again and we moved the van opposite the gate. It was not long before the 'gardener' came out and indicated we should move on as we were blocking the access. John told him we would only be a few minutes longer, but he stood behind the gates watching us.

The Mango Mystery

'Dam!' John said. 'We can't move while he's there, he will spot the bin bag and flex plug which will give the game away.' Still the man just stood, staring at us.

'I'll go over and distract him and you recover the emitter,' he snorted, smiling, and got out of the van and walked over. They looked as if they were arguing and eventually John shrugged and walked over to the gatepost and started to urinate. This was sufficient distraction for me to hop out of the back of the van to retrieve the bag and flex. John returned and we moved the van further up the road. Unfortunately, from this new position, we had only a restricted view of the gate. Shortly after, the Ferrari returned and while John tried to take more pictures, the only clear one he got was a side view of the older lady as she drove through the gates.

The gardener reappeared and stood behind the gate again, watching us.

'Time to go, I think,' John said, 'He is getting too suspicious.'

I agreed, and we drove off back to the hotel. We had reached the outskirts of Lausanne, John was driving slowly letting traffic pass us, when he said that he thought we were being followed. 'There is a dark blue Citroen which has been behind us since just after we left the Vidnova house and, whoever it is, seems content to just sit on our tail.'

John de Caynoth

Chapter 50. Plan 'A'

Joelle

Following John's announcement that we were being followed as we drove back to Lausanne we had a brief discussion. He insisted that it was time to leave, saying, 'we have done all we can here: they are suspicious but not sure who we are, so I get the feeling they are checking us out at the moment. There is only one person in that Citroen and it's not the 'gardener' chap, so we know there are at least two of guards, the one following us now and the one I spoke to earlier and they are not carrying guns for fun. If they identify us they will use the guns.'

I said to John, 'if only we could be certain the two women we saw were Lecarrow and Vidnova.'

He interrupted me and was even more insistent, 'we are as sure as we can be. To do anything further we need armed backup and a search warrant and don't forget that we are operating here without even informing the Swiss Police. If we do end up using guns, there will be hell to pay and you and I will be so deep in the 'soft and sticky' we will probably never emerge. No, sorry, but we get out now while we can.'

He was right, of course, and I had to agree with him.

He went silent and pensive, and I knew he was thinking up a plan and he spoke out loud. 'We used our real names at the hotel. We can't risk them finding out where we are staying, and we need to get the Mercedes without them seeing us or it: if they do, the game is up. It's too risky to try to lose this Citroen that is following

The Mango Mystery

us. They could be using two cars, and anyway I am not sure of the capabilities of this van, it's not the fastest thing in Switzerland.'

I suggested I could drive the van and drop him off somewhere and he could then get the Mercedes and take it to the hotel.

'No,' John said, 'that won't work - I should draw them off rather than risk you getting caught, anyway, what would you do with the van? But it's not a bad idea, and it might work if I drop you off, and without being seen you go and get the Mercedes, taking it back to the hotel where I will meet you.' He made his mind up, 'Yes, that should work.'

We drove into the centre of Lausanne and John gave me instructions. 'Plan A! we will park somewhere quiet, near the shops hoping the Citroen stops near me. I will leave the van and wander off, letting our friend follow me on-foot. You will then check that the Citroen is empty and, when no other vehicles are in sight, leave the van, walk around a bit, check you are not being followed, and take a taxi to the van-hire yard.'

'That sounds a bit hit and miss,' I commented 'What is Plan B?'

'Don't know yet, I will worry about it if Plan A does not work.' John grinned.

Actually, the plan went like clockwork. We stopped in a quite side street. I hid in the back of the van, while John got out, walking up the road and round the corner. The Citroen pulled up right behind us, and the driver leapt out, hurrying off after John. I waited a couple of minutes, listening. One car drove past but did not stop. **I peered out of the back window** - the road was empty, and there was no one else in the Citroen so I left John's coat and the cap behind and walked off calmly, in the opposite direction to him, towards some shops. I bought a hat, a coat and dark glasses and, deciding I looked suitably feminine again, strolled around window-shopping for a while. No one was taking any interest in me so I hailed a taxi to take me to the van-hire yard.

The taxi dropped me outside. I walked in and waved at the girl in the office, a porter-cabin by the yard gate, walked up to the Mercedes, unlocked it, got in it, started it up and drove away without anyone challenging me.

Once I got used to the power of the engine, I rather enjoyed driving the Mercedes and even thought that I might buy one for myself one day, when I am too old for my beloved motorbike.

I got to the hotel without incident. As I had learnt from John I drove past it, turning around and driving back to see if I had been followed, but thankfully I could see nothing suspicious. I chose to park in the hotel's underground car park, pondering whether I should park in a dark corner or with the other cars near the lift to the hotel lobby. I chose the latter place as I reasoned the best place to hide a car was with a lot of other cars, and went up to the hotel lobby to wait for John.

He eventually arrived a couple of hours later, explaining that he had found a hardware shop. 'I was worried that I might bump into you, but I guessed you would walk off in the opposite direction. The Citroen chap followed me all the way and even watched while I bought a screwdriver.' **He laughed and explained that he**

The Mango Mystery

had returned to the van. 'I drove off in the opposite direction to this hotel and found a Holiday Inn. The Citroen followed me into the car park behind the hotel. The driver sat in his car watching me as I walked into the hotel through the back door. I walked straight through the building, out of the front door and hurried off down the road to get out of sight. Luckily no one followed me - only problem was I had to walk a couple of miles back into the centre of town before I could get taxi.'

We decided we had shaken our tail off for the time being and hoped that, by letting them follow John back to the Holiday Inn, they would think that we were genuine, 'unless they went in to check,' John reminded me, prompting a decision to get out of Switzerland as soon as possible. We agreed to get a few hours sleep and then meet at four next morning, driving back to Amsterdam in one day.

John de Caynoth

Chapter 51. Bad Weekend

Douglas
There was not much more I could on Wednesday evening after Josh left me, but in the morning I went into Hamilton and posted the envelope to David Evans as Josh had suggested. After that, I went to the tourist office to ask about getting a flight to Kaeta. They told me there was a daily flight run by Island Hopper that did a circular flight each morning, calling at four of the smaller East Caribbean islands, including Kaeta, before returning to Bermuda. Unfortunately, I had missed the Thursday flight but the girl in the tourist office helpfully phoned the operators of the Hopper to book me a seat. Unfortunately, the Friday flight was fully booked as was the flight on the following Monday and Tuesday. She said she could get me on the Wednesday flight, but I told her that was too late and asked if there was some other way I could get to the Kaeta.

'I will tell you what to do, Sir,' she said trying to be helpful, 'go to the airport and talk to the girls in the ticket office and tell them you need to get to Kaeta urgently. They will put you on the stand-by list and you may pick up tomorrow's flight.'

I did go to the airport, and did get on the stand-by list, and Friday morning found me, and my wheelie bag, waiting by the Island Hopper ticket office to see if I would be able to fly. Unfortunately, there were three people on the list ahead of me and only two seats came available. The girls in the ticket office were sympathetic and offered to put me first on the list for Monday.

The Mango Mystery

I did not bother to go back into Hamilton but booked into a hotel near the airport. It was a modern, functional hotel and I could have been anywhere in the world. Josh's concern for his, and my, safety concerned me; I wanted desperately to leave Bermuda behind.

I spent one of the most miserable weekends that I can remember. What upset me most of all was worrying what it was Joelle had to tell me, and the more I worried the more convinced I became that she must be having an affair with John and was going to dump me. I tried to ring her on the Saturday and on the Sunday but on both attempts got a message, 'Please try again later'. Did that mean she did not want to talk to me, or had something happened to her?

Monday morning, I arrived at the airport early, even though I would not know if I was on the flight until just before the gate closed. Today I was lucky, I did get on the flight and, as we took off, I breathed a sigh of relief and my depressed mood began to recede. The plane was an elderly turbo-prop Fokker Fellowship and carried around fifty passengers and it operated just like a bus. Kaeta was the third island it landed on - at each island some passengers left the plane while others joined it.

I was sitting in a gangway seat so I could not really see out of the windows as we landed on Kaeta, but as we walked across the apron to the arrivals building I could feel the anticipation of returning to a place I was increasingly thinking of as home. The immigration procedures were much laxer for inter-island arrivals than for the international tourist flights. There was one bored official at the immigration desk, who did a couple of perfunctory spot checks before

John de Caynoth

waving all ten of us passengers through. I collected my wheelie-bag and, as there was no-one manning the customs desk, just walked straight through and into a waiting taxi.

I had phoned Mary over the weekend to let her know I was coming to Katea again, but I did not know when. Without question, she expected to me stay at "Windrush" and told me to go straight there. 'You know since the break-in we lock up now,' she said, 'and if there is no one about just let yourself in.' She told me where the key was hidden.

As the taxi took me out to 'Windrush' I thought that, even if my relationship with Joelle was over, maybe I would still come and live out here. Just because Joelle and I were not together did not mean I could not still be friends with Mary, and anyway I was beginning to like the relaxed lifestyle of the Island.

I walked into the house with mixed feelings. For now, I was pleased to be on the Island and I proposed going to look at the house the agent had sent details of. I was still worrying about what Joelle wanted to tell me, and I felt sad, convincing myself that our relationship was probably over. There and then I tried to phone her, but I just got the same automated message that she was unavailable.

I phoned the land agent's office to arrange to visit the house I wanted to look round. He got back to me about an hour later, making an appointment with me for tomorrow afternoon. He explained that there was one room in the house he would not be able to show me as it was set up as a nursing room for the owners wife, who was ill. I told him that would not be a

The Mango Mystery

problem and arranged to meet him in at his office in Kaeta town.

Chapter 52. Identified

Joelle

In the event, we did not leave Lausanne until after five in the morning as both John and I overslept, but we did do the journey back to Amsterdam in one day with us both taking turns at driving. The trip was trouble free except for one incident. I could not find my mobile phone.

'Have you seen my phone?' I asked John, with panic in my voice, as I hunted round the car, feeling under the seat. I could not find it. I told John I thought I should phone Amsterdam and speak to Jan van Leuven, the detective now running the drug investigation unit, tell him what we had discovered and were on our way back.

'Use the car phone,' was John's solution. I made my call, but van den Leuven was not available. I really wanted my mobile to phone Douglas: I was worried about him and wanted to speak to him, so I made John pull off the autobahn at the next service area so I could search the car properly.

I still could not find the phone and with John prompting me I remembered I last used it in the hotel bedroom when I tried to phone Douglas.

'I must have left it in the hotel room,' I told John, annoyed with myself.

'The hotel will be able to trace you as we used our real names and addresses to register.' John stated thoughtfully, 'should not matter though, nobody knows which hotel we stayed in.'

The Mango Mystery

'In that case then, it will do no harm if I phone the hotel and ask if they found the phone.' I replied.

After some hesitation John agreed and handed me the car phone. The hotel had got my mobile, and agreed to post it back to London for me, charging the postage to my credit card. However, they explained, that it was hotel policy to remove and destroy sim-cards to prevent unauthorised use of the phone.

'That's a nuisance,' I said to John.

'Look on the bright side,' he replied, 'at least you get your expensive iPhone back and, if you wait till you get back to the UK, your phone operator will be able to give you a new sim- card.' John paused and frowned, 'actually, it is a good idea to avoid using your mobile anyway as anyone who has the number could trace the whereabouts of the phone.' He paused before adding, 'the same goes for Douglas Jay, he should turn his phone off as well. It would be better if you and he avoided phone contact for the time being.'

I just nodded, I wanted to contact Douglas and just talk with him: I knew he would be trying to get hold of me, but if his phone could be traced such contact would put us both in danger.

Despite driving non-stop, it still took us over twelve hours to get to Amsterdam, not arriving at the hotel until after seven on the Friday evening. As we had never checked out and left most of our luggage, the hotel had kept the rooms for us, which I thought was fortunate. John was concerned that, of course, we had been charged for the rooms, and that we would never be able to reclaim all these expenses. I told him not to worry: I would get his expenses cleared.

John de Caynoth

Using the hotel telephone, I tried to ring both Inspector Jan van den Leuven and Detective Willam Ince on Saturday morning, but was told they were both not available until Monday.

John suggested that, as we apparently now had a weekend off, we should go out together somewhere on the Sunday. I remembered how, last summer, I had done just that with Douglas and I wondered what he was doing this weekend. I told John I did not think that it was a good idea for us to go out together, he just shrugged and walked away.

Mid morning on Sunday, John knocked on my door asking me if I was okay. He told me he thought the hotel was being watched and invited me into his room to have a look. My room was at the back of the hotel, his was opposite, overlooking the front. I fleetingly wondered if this was a ploy to get me into his room for other reasons, but dismissed the thought and followed him.

'Look, over there.' John pointed to an individual, leaning on a lamppost, smoking. The person was huddled in an oversized, padded coat with a hood and I could make out long mousy-coloured hair spilling out, shielding their face, but could not see if the person was a man or a woman. John continued, 'That person was standing in the square most of yesterday afternoon and was back again there this morning.'

John detected the angst in my voice as I whispered, 'Who is it that follows me and is trying to kill me?'

It was not really a question but John answered anyway, 'I think we can be sure it is the drug smuggling outfit. For some reason they are getting desperate to

The Mango Mystery

silence you. I am guessing that they lost track of us when we went to Switzerland and they have someone watching the hotel to see when we return. I have checked with the hotel and a smartly dressed man has been to reception twice while we have been away, enquiring if you were in.'

'Do you think they know we are back?' I asked.

'I don't know, I did not notice anything on Friday when we arrived, but then it was dark and raining. They might know we are back but can't do anything while we are in the hotel and so they are watching, waiting for us to make a move.'

'Oh well,' I said, trying to remain calm, 'I was not planning to go anywhere this weekend anyway.'

On Monday morning first thing I phoned Jan van den Leuven and told him we needed to see him and brief him on what we had found in Switzerland. He told us to come to his office straight away.

John decided we would not take the Mercedes but would get a taxi to pick us up from the back of the hotel, 'I have not seen anyone there so hopefully they will not see us leaving.'

We were escorted straight up to Jan van den Leuven's office where he was waiting with Willam Ince. Jan explained Willam was involved because of the two murders in Amsterdam. Willam started by explaining that they suspected that Zedanski was the murderer and the Dutch police had launched a world wide search for him through Interpol, but so far nothing had turned up. Willam summed up saying, 'He has just disappeared and basically we have made no progress since we last met.'

John de Caynoth

I summarised what we had done in Switzerland.

'We were told Mrs Lecarrow is living with her partner, who we believe to be Maria Vidnova. The Vidnova house is well fortified and guarded. We know there are at least two men - the one who move us on, he appears to be guarding the front gate, and a second man who was driving a Citroen. We could not really get that near the house, and they became very suspicious as we watched the house from a van parked in the road. The Citroen followed us as we returned to Lausanne but I don't think they recognised us. We gave them the slip, but they are sure to be on their guard now.'

Jan rubbed his chin thoughtfully and said, 'it certainly sounds suspicious but there could be any number of legitimate reasons for them to be security-conscious and nothing you saw links them to our drug gang.'

'There is more.' I said, and asked John to show them the pictures he had taken. He asked to use the computer and explained he had downloaded the pictures to a CD using a hotel guest-computer.

The first pictures were of the man at the front gate, who we called 'the gardener.' Neither Jan or Willam recognised him, but asked if they could get copies so they could run him through their files and see if anything came up. John moved on through the pictures. Jan asked at one point what were doing with a bin bag on the pavement and where had we got the road signs. John explained, and Jan said he was not surprised they got suspicious.

We got to the pictures of the Ferrari. The first were a little blurred when viewed on the lap top screen and the faces of the occupants were not clear. However,

The Mango Mystery

the pictures taken as the car approached the van were good and the faces of the occupants could clearly be seen.

'We think that they must be Maria Vidnova driving and Mrs Lecarrow in the passenger seat, but we could not confirm that and I don't recognise either of the ladies,' I said.

'I do,' Willam announced. 'I interviewed the younger one, who you believe to be Mrs Lecarrow, over a year ago after our undercover policewoman was murdered. She was a French vet then, and called herself Miss le Corde and she was a senior partner in the Cordite Veterinary Group, where Jan den Ould, alias Dirk Snaps, or Hans Gruber, he used a number of different names, worked and was the origin of the original ketamine smuggling operation.'

No one said anything for a few moments while we all pondered on this discovery. Eventually Jan spoke and congratulated John and I for moving the investigation forward. 'I have a feeling we are getting to the centre of the rat's nest now,' Jan said, 'only trouble is we have to work out how to use this information. Unfortunately, you two were in Switzerland without the permission of the Swiss authorities, or even their knowledge, and we now need their co-operation, not an international squabble.'

Having let that sink in, Jan spoke again, turning to John and me, 'This is my problem now, and I don't think there is any more you two can do here now. What are you plans?'

John spoke before I could say anything, 'We should return to England. I suspect the drug gang are watching for us here, and I think it is too risky for us to stay - I don't want any more incidents.' Both Jan and Willam looked relieved and told us that was an excellent plan.

John then said, 'There is a problem. The hotel is under surveillance and our car is there - we have not checked out yet and all our luggage is still in our rooms. It would be better if we did not return to the hotel but left immediately from here.' He looked at the two Dutch Police officers expectantly.

Willam took the hint and said, 'I will get your luggage and the car collected and sent over here for you.' And looking at Jan said, 'Okay to get the hotel to send the bill for your attention as it is your investigation.' Jan grumbled but agreed and John and I went off to the canteen to wait.

A couple of hours later Willam came to fetch us, 'Your car and luggage are waiting for you downstairs.' He turned to John saying, 'That's quite a car you have there, I can see it is armour-plated and obviously fast.' He paused and looked quizzically at us, 'I notice it has some body damage and a bullet mark on the passenger window. That would not be anything to do with a crashed black BMW the Belgian police found on the motorway to Antwerp following an anonymous call about the time you left to drive to Eindhoven, would it?'

John and I looked at each other and just shrugged.

Jan continued,' The car was stolen in Amsterdam a month ago and unfortunately the occupants got away before the police arrived.'

The Mango Mystery

Both John and I shook Willam's hand and thanked him for his help and made ready to leave. As we did, John turned back to Willam hinting, 'You might look out for a Silver VW Golf', giving him the registration number written on a slip of paper, 'I saw it following the BMW down the motorway.' Jan said he would let us know if he found it.

John de Caynoth

Chapter 53. The Strange House

Douglas

On my first full day back at 'Windrush' I sat in the garden alone trying to control my feelings of panic, due partly to Josh's warnings and advice to disappear, which had unsettled me, but also because I was miserably thinking about the last telephone conversation with Joelle. She said she had something important to tell me, and I was expecting the worst while getting more and more anxious at not being able to contact her.

I spent all day in the garden, alternately trying to read a book and walking aimlessly around, hoping Jasmine would come home. She did not, which didn't worry me, but I rather selfishly wanted her company to take my mind of things. In the end I decided I needed to do something, so I phoned the land agent to make an appointment to view some properties, but disappointingly he said he could not see me until the next day.

Mary eventually got home about midnight, after she had finished work, and we had a cup of tea together. I asked her where Jasmine was.

'Staying with a friend tonight,' Mary told me, 'She is quite the young lady now, getting more and more independent by the minute. She is on a diet at the moment, telling me she is too fat - such nonsense!'

Mary was in her stride now and went on, 'She likes you, you know, and worries about her mother when she is away, but she is pleased you are together again. It is sort of like having a father she says.'

The Mango Mystery

I asked Mary if she had heard from Joelle, but she said she had not. 'That girl is hopeless: she gets caught up in her work and forgets everything else. You are more likely to hear from her than I am.'

I explained that I had tried to phone her but her but was getting no answer. 'I should not worry,' Mary assured me, 'I expect the battery on her phone has gone flat and she has lost her charger - she has done that before.'

We did not talk for much longer as we were both tired and retired to our respective beds.

In the morning, I tried to ring Joelle again but just got the same automated 'unavailable' message.

At lunchtime, I borrowed Joelle's car to go into town to meet the Land Agents. When I reached their office, I was invited to sit down and they explained that they needed to ring Mrs Strange to inform her that we were on our way. The office manager gave me details of some other properties available for sale on the Island to look at while we waited. Most were apartments in walled estates, but there were a couple of individual houses - in particular an interesting-looking timber beach house - at the southern end of the island. If I had time later, I decided, I might drive there and take a look.

A young lady introduced herself as April and said she would take me to view the property, so we set off in the agent's official car. The house was an old plantation property on a hill on the east side of the Island, set in about an acre of gardens, with a fantastic view of the Atlantic Ocean. I imagine the gardens were once magnificent, but were now overgrown with only a small area in front of the property being maintained to keep the access clear. April explained that the owner was retiring and selling up in order to move to where his wife was born and brought up.

'She is not a well woman,' April explained, 'and she wishes to spend her final years on her native island.'

I did not like to ask what was wrong with her. 'While you look around the house, she is going to stay in the nursing room and has asked that we do not disturb her.'

I told April that was fine with me.

We entered the house: it was not as big as I had expected. The front door opened into a large room furnished with a dining table and chairs. A door to one side led into a living room, opposite was a room at the front of the house being used as a study. Another room at the back of the property connected to a downstairs bathroom, both of which were now used by Mrs Strange the invalid. Upstairs were four bedrooms and a bathroom. At the back of the house were three much smaller rooms which had been converted into a kitchen and utility area, and which April indicated, would originally have been sparsely furnished and used by the domestic servants.

As we explored, April explained that the owners had already purchased another house and were anxious to sell this one and were therefore prepared to accept an offer. I considered that the house was nice enough, and would certainly need some decoration, but if the owners would take an offer it could be well within my budget. I had originally envisaged that I could be living there with Joelle, but as I now was uncertain how things stood between us I was feeling the house and grounds might be just too big for me alone.

The Mango Mystery

As we were about to leave I told April I would like a quick look around the study. It was a reasonably sized room and would catch the morning sun. It was furnished as an office with filing cabinets, bookcases and a large desk placed under the window. On looking out of the window, my eye wandering over the papers spread out on the desk. I blinked, surprised, and looked again at a pile pushed to one side of the desk, half covering what looked like the original copy of Joelle's diary. I pulled it out - it was the diary. At first I thought that the owner of this house must be the thief and very likely one of the drug smuggling gang, but then the penny dropped.

April was standing behind me and I turned to her to ask her if the owners of the property were Mr and Mrs Strange, 'Would that be Inspector Bernard Strange - the policeman?'

April confirmed that I was correct, seeming pleased that I knew Bernie. It occurred to me that that the Police must have found the burglar and recovered the stolen documents: Bernie was looking after the diary to return it to Joelle in due course.

We left the property and April drove me back into Kaeta Town to collect my car. On the way back, she asked me if I was interested in the property, stressing that Mr and Mrs Strange were very anxious to sell and were sure to accept an offer. I was non-committal, and told April I needed time to think about it. We got back to the agent's office and she said goodbye, telling me to let her know if I wished to make a second visit.

I decided to have another look at the Strange's house on my own, exploring the area in which it was located, before driving down to the southern end of the Island to look at the other properties.

I parked on the road outside the front gate, reflecting that it was in a magnificent setting with a fantastic view, partially sheltered from the Atlantic winds by the hills around it. Looking at the house, I got thinking. If the police had found the burglar and questioned him, he might provide the evidence to link Tony Choizi to the drug smuggling gang and even, perhaps, prove Choizi to be the informer.

I completed my drive round the Island, looking at the other properties, arriving back at 'Windrush' well after dark. By this time I was quite excited by the thought that I might be about to find the link which would remove any lingering suspicions about Joelle and finish this whole drug smuggling business. I resolved to go and see Bernie first thing in the morning.

The Mango Mystery

Chapter 54. London

Joelle

The drive back to the UK was uneventful. We got a late ferry from Calais on Monday evening, arriving back in Clapham in the early hours of Tuesday morning. John made me wait in the car while he checked around the flat, making sure that there were no nasty little surprises waiting for me, before escorting me in through the door. I took pity on him when he told me he had another two-hour drive back to his home and told him he could sleep on the sofa if he wanted.

Yesterday, I slept in and woke up to the smell of coffee and croissants and found John was up, having already been to the shops to restock my fridge, and busy in the kitchen preparing breakfast.

After we had eaten, John asked if he could use the bedroom for a bit as he wanted to check something and I guessed he was looking for anyone watching the flat. It occurred to me that I should ring Barbara Green to let her know we back in the country: I expected her to tell me to come into the office straight away to fill her in on what we had been doing, but she told me to take the rest of the day off.

While I was on the phone, John had been down to the car to fetch his camera and had disappeared back into the bedroom, which was a nuisance as I was still wandering round in my dressing gown and wanted to get dressed. Eventually John reappeared, showing me a picture of a person in a long, padded coat with the hood up. John asked if I recognised them, but he or she was so huddled up that I could see their features at all.

John de Caynoth

'I think the flat is being watched. This person is walking up and down outside: they sit on a seat for a few minutes and then walk up and down again. They were there when I went shopping and I have been watching now and they are always careful to stay within site of this flat block and street door.'

John asked me what I was going to do for the rest of the day. I intended to stay in, rest, clean the flat, order a new SIM card, and sort out the mail that had stacked up downstairs while I was away. John thought I would be safe enough if I stayed in the flat, and asked me if I minded if he went home.

Next morning, John was back at 8.00am to pick me up to take me into work. He still had the Mercedes and explained that he would drop me at the office near Scotland Yard before reporting back to his own base so they could inspect the damage to the car. 'They won't be very pleased when they see what I have done to it,' he told me ruefully.

Barbara Green caught me as I entered the office-suite, wanting to hear every detail of what I had done. In the privacy of her own office, she told me I had overstepped my authority by going to Switzerland without permission from the Swiss authorities, but agreed that the trip had been worthwhile as it had moved the investigation forward. 'I wonder how Jan van den Leuven will get round that one,' she said to me.

I showed her the pictures we had taken, but she just shrugged and said she did not recognise anyone. She then briefed me on the UK investigation, telling me that they had made very little, if any progress. 'Zedanski is still our prime suspect for the shooting at Euston Station, but he has disappeared and there have been no reports of him having been seen anywhere. I am pretty sure he's not in the country anymore, so that investigation has stalled. As for the drugs, that has also ground to a halt. We have been round all the clubs now and turned up nothing, and there have been no more ketamine tablets turning up since Gruber, or what ever his name was, disappeared. It seems to me that the focus of that investigation has moved abroad now, so I have stood down the team working on that one.'

Barbara turned to me, asking what I thought I should to do now. I said that I would like a few more days on the ketamine investigation, as I wanted to see if I could find out anymore about Marina Vidnova.

'I thought you would,' Barbara said, 'I have assigned the team to other cases, all except Andrea, so you can both carry on with Operation Mango, liaising with both the Dutch and American police.' As an aside she snorted, "Operation Mango! What a daft name - who thought that one up? Detective Choizi keeps ringing me and asking for an update and I am fed up with him. Can you deal with that?' Barbara noticed the look on horror on my face but she did not react, showing no emotion whatsoever.

I just shrugged, resignedly, and said, 'Okay.'

She then asked me if I still needed a CPO. I told her that John thought my flat was still under surveillance. 'Oh for goodness sake,' she sounded exasperated, 'Mc Duff had better stay with you until this business is finished - the budget is shot to pieces anyway!'

As I left her office she told me to do my expense forms and to let her have them that day. 'Derek Passmore wants to see me about finances at my earliest

John de Caynoth

convenience, and I guess your costs are going to make another big hole in the funds.'

I left Barbara and went to look for Andrea to tell her we were still assigned to the case. She was sitting in front of her computer reading something on the screen.

'Oh great!' she said when I told her, 'I have decided working with you is a high risk job, but I am glad we are still together.'

She told me she had been trying to find out more about Marina Vidnova. 'Basically I have drawn a blank. Apart from her name and address and that she is a widowed Swiss resident, which I managed to get out of the Swiss Police, there seems to be nothing else on file: she appears to be squeakily clean.'

I showed her the photos John had taken of the two women in the Ferrari and explained that Mrs Lecarrow used to be Miss Maria deCorde. She took the picture and said she would see if there was anything on Maria deCorde.

I went off to do my expenses but got fed up after an hour, wondering how much I could get away with, so I called across to Andrea asking if she fancied an early lunch.

'Sure do, love,' she said, grabbing her jacket from the back of her chair on the way out.

We went to the little coffee shop near Westminster, just around the corner: as we were early there were plenty of empty tables. We started with the usual, 'How are you and what have you been doing?' small talk before moving on to the more difficult stuff. Andrea became very serious, which was unusual for her, and said to me, 'Joelle I am really sorry I let you

The Mango Mystery

down in Holland and came home. I have never been shot at before and when John started driving at that car and pushing it off the road - well, I was so frightened I nearly wet myself. I would have stayed with you but I thought of Jim and what he would do I was injured or killed and, you know, I just did not know how to cope.'

I never expected Andrea to be frightened - she always seemed so brash and confident. I assured her, 'you did not let me down, it is me who should be apologising for getting you into dangerous situations - anyway, I sent you home, you didn't walk out on me: and I was scared shitless as well.'

Andrea simply said, 'I won't let you down again, Joelle.'

We were both quite for a few moments to let that discussion pass.

Andrea was first to speak, and asked me about Douglas and what was he doing.

'I don't know,' I admitted, 'I have not spoken to him since last Wednesday because I lost my phone, which reminds me - I need to get new Sim card.'

'That's tough,' said Andrea, 'Jim and I talk every day on the phone when one of us is away. Would you like to borrow my phone and ring him now?'

'Oh! Andrea could I?' I thanked her as she handed her mobile over and I dialled Douglas's number. I let it ring but the call switched to voice mail. I left a message, asking Douglas to call me as soon as possible.

I explained to Andrea, 'I don't even know where he is, he was in Bermuda but I think he was going to go on to Kaeta - I am really worried about him. I don't think he has any idea what dangerous stuff he has got involved. He suspects that Tony Choizi is involved in something illegal and has hired a private detective to find out: the last thing he told me was that he's running around with this guy, breaking into apartments to collect evidence.'

Andrea looked horrified, 'He is mad,' she said, 'why on earth is doing that? He should let the proper authorities handle it.'

'I know,' I replied, 'he is trying to help me by proving I am not a drug smuggler or passing on information about the investigation.'

'But surely that is all in the past,' Andrea looked puzzled, 'I thought the enquiry cleared you?'

I replied, 'Not really, they just said the evidence was not strong enough to secure a conviction. Barbara supported me and got the suspension lifted.'

Andrea looked exasperated. 'That's ridiculous, I have not known you long, but I know you are the last person to get involved in that sort of thing. No wonder you are worried about Douglas.' As an afterthought she added, 'still, he must be very fond of you to go round the world like that to help you.'

Without thinking, I blurted out, 'Yes, but that is not the worst. I slept with John McDuff while we were driving down to Switzerland.'

'What on earth did you do that for?' she asked, surprised.

'I think I was still upset after the shooting and the car incident. I was cross with Douglas because he was being pathetic on the phone, feeling sorry for himself and telling me how he missed me - not concerned how

The Mango Mystery

I was at all. I had too much to drink, and.....' I paused not wanting to admit, 'I think I was attracted to John at the time. Anyway I have been regretting it ever since.'

Andrea became her usual practical self, 'he is an attractive bloke, I must admit, and I can understand you falling for him. I suppose you saw him as a protector, saving you from danger. I guess it is a bit like when kidnap victims imagining they are in love with their kidnapper.'

'I guess you might be right, but it gets worse.'

'Oh no!' Andrea exclaimed, 'Tell me, what else have you done?'

'That last phone call to Douglas. I nearly told him what I had done, but instead I said there was something I needed to tell him but could not talk about it on the phone. I realised afterwards that he would misinterpret that and imagine all sorts of things.'

'Well, if I was him, under the circumstances, I would think that comment meant you were going to dump me,' said Andrea unsympathetically, 'so what are going to do now?'

'I don't know,' I said miserably.

'Well you could drop everything and go and find him,' she said. 'You could write him a letter, or at the very least text him and tell him you love him.'

She handed me her phone and I wrote a short text, '*Love you and need to see you, please phone me on this number so we can talk.*'

'Is that it?' Andrea said, reading the text I had just sent.

'I hate texting, its too impersonal!' I replied.

John de Caynoth

'I suppose it's better than nothing: I hope he understands.' and that was Andrea's final word on the matter.

Barbara Green caught us sneaking back late into the general office. 'Where have you two been?' she asked. Turning to me she said, 'You must be telepathic to miss being here when Tony Choizi calls. I told him you would ring him back but he said he would phone you tomorrow, same time, as he out for the rest of the day.'

Andrea went to start looking through files to see if we had anything on Maria deCorde while I finished my expenses and started reading the reports of last weeks enquiries round the clubs, but I was not really concentrating, I was thinking about Douglas and wondering what I was going to say to Tony Choizi tomorrow. I was not looking forward to that conversation.

The Mango Mystery

Chapter 55. The Restaurant Incident

Douglas

I thought I heard my phone ring while I was in the shower this morning. I quickly dried myself, slinging the towel around my waist, and moved back to the bedroom to check. I had a missed call: it was a number I did not recognize. I checked the message, which simply said 'Call me when you get chance.' Normally, I would have returned the call to see who it was but, heeding Josh's warnings about not picking up unknown callers, I left it.

I dressed quickly, anxious to get into Kaeta town and talk to Bernie. I found him in his office drinking coffee.

'Douglas,' he sounded surprised, 'I didn't know you were on the Island - we have been looking for you. What are doing here?' His manner turned from surprised to suspicious as he asked the question.

I put that down to natural police reaction and said, 'I have come to look at property - I am thinking of buying something on the Island, but why have you been looking for me? What can I do for you?'

Bernie shuffled round in his seat and gave me a rather evasive answer, 'Nothing really, I just like keep track of who's on the Island, that's all. Have you found somewhere?'

I explained, 'I have seen one property that might be suitable, and by chance it happened to be your old house on the Island. It is a beautiful building and in a wonderful position,' and, not prematurely wanting to

John de Caynoth

raise Bernie's hopes of a sale, I added, 'but I have not made my mind up yet, I want to go and look at some other properties before I decide.'

At the mention of his house, his manner turned from suspicious to worried. No wonder, I thought, with his wife obviously very ill. I did not want to pry, so I simply told him that I was sorry to hear his wife was poorly, and, after a suitable silence to confirm my condolence, I asked him when he was retiring and moving as I understood he already had found another house.

'Oh, no firm date yet, I shall go when this drug business is finished. The Commissioner has asked me to stay on until he appoints my successor.' I did not say anything to Bernie, but I did think that Joelle had been promised the job. Probably that was what he meant.

I moved the conversation on to the real reason I had wanted to see Bernie, 'I gather you have caught the individuals who burgled 'Windrush' and I wondered if they had said anything about this mysterious drug gang on the Island.'

Bernie's demeanour moved from worry to shock before he recovered his composure and asked, 'Who told you that? Where did you get that information? We have not arrested anyone and do not even have any suspects.'

It was my turn to look surprised as I answered, 'I am sorry, I saw Joelle's original diary yesterday on you desk at your house. I thought you must have caught the burglars and found Joelle's diary and was keeping it, waiting to return it to her.'

The Mango Mystery

'You are mistaken, Douglas,' Bernie said recovering his usual confidence, 'what you probably saw was my diary. I have always kept a diary and notes of all the cases I have investigated. I am thinking I might start writing detective stories when I retire.'

I apologised, 'Sorry, must be my mistake.' But I was certain it had been Joelle's diary.

Bernie was very clearly anxious to finish the conversation, leaving me feeling confused and puzzled as I took my leave.

My mind was on the possibility of moving to Kaeta and, as I stood on the pavement outside the police station, thinking that, actually, it was not such a bad idea to look at some different properties - perhaps I was being too narrow in my search and should look at some of the estate-managed apartments which would be much easier to maintain if I were to split my time between Wiltshire and Kaeta. I might even be able to rent it out when I was not on the Island, which would help pay running costs. I set off for the land agent, to discuss my latest ideas.

While I was walking, I checked my mobile phone and saw that I had a text message. The number looked like the one from the call I had missed this morning. I read the message and frowned. I guessed it was one of those calls from an Eastern European Country, supposedly from a pretty young girl hooking lonely men for money. I deleted it without giving it too much thought, but as I walked on I pondered on who might have sent it. Could it have been from Joelle on a borrowed phone? But, I thought, she does not like texting and anyway she would have signed the message.

John de Caynoth

I reached the Land Agent's office and went in to speak to the manager. He agreed with my thinking that an apartment would be very suitable for my purposes, and had some properties on his books, on one of the more exclusive developments, that might suit me. He hurried off to fetch a selection of properties for me to look at. There were a lot to go through, but in the end I found four properties I wanted to visit. One bungalow was set in its own small plot of land on a private road. A town house in a new development in Old Town on the Atlantic coast appealed to me, as did two apartments around the Grumble inlet, both of which were in developments with their own private moorings. The last two properties were recommended by the manager, saying there was a good demand for short term lets from visiting yacht-owners, 'half the time they do not even use the apartment, they just want the mooring.'

April was sent off to arrange the four visits, which the Manager assured me would not be a problem as three were empty and they had the keys there in the office. I asked him if he could arrange for me to have another quick look at Bernie's house. I did not particularly want to see the house again, but I wanted another look at the diary.

'Ah, I was going to mention that to you,' he told me 'There is a bit of a problem there. The vendor has just telephoned me to say he wants the property taken off the market immediately. I did tell him that we have a very good prospective buyer, but he was adamant. I am sorry.'

That's very odd I thought, Bernie had not said anything to me when I was with him, but at that

The Mango Mystery

moment April reappeared and invited me to come with her in the land agent's little car. It took us most of the rest of the day to look at the four properties. The bungalow was beyond my budget and I did not like it anyway, the town house in Old Town was not bad but I was not sure I wanted to live in that area. The best was one of the apartments at Grumble which had good views across the inlet, as opposed to the alternative apartment there, which was cheaper as it was at the back of the block and had no views, It was for sale or rent, fully furnished.

It was early evening before we got back to Kaeta town and I left April, promising to be in touch and to let the agent know what I wanted to do. I walked back to my car, which I had left near the police station, and drove off. I decided to go to Mary's bar and restaurant this evening as I fancied a beer and would probably eat there.

Mary was pleased to see me, but was quite busy and did not have much time to talk to me. Jasmine nearly always used to be at the bar in the evenings, but not today. When I asked Mary where she was, she told me with some exasperation, 'Jasmine is in her stroppy teenage phase at the moment and says she does not like coming to the bar anymore and prefers to go home and do her homework in peace. She's working hard for her exams at the moment so I suppose that is a good thing, really.'

She excused herself and went into the kitchen. She came out a few minutes later, 'I forgot to tell you Douglas, but there was man in here earlier looking for you: I told him you were not here and he said he would wait. Funny thing was, when you arrived he got up and

John de Caynoth

walked out without saying anything. Strange man - I did not like the look of him at all.'

I thanked Mary and said I had no idea who it was, but made a mental note to be careful to check if anyone was following me in future.

By the time I had eaten, night had fallen. I took my leave of Mary and walked to the car parked outside. I had arrived while it was still light but now the car was in a dark corner under the trees and I fumbled with the key, dropping it, as I tried to unlock the door. As I bent down to pick it up, I heard a pop and a thump as something hit the door just above my head. Instinctively I dropped to the ground and heard a car door slam, and glanced around to see a car race out of the car park at speed. For a few moments I lay by the car a bit dazed wondering what had happened, before I realised someone had tried to shoot me. I was shaking like a leaf by the time I had driven back to 'Windrush' with all Josh's warnings running through my head.

All the doors of the house were locked, which was strange as I could see that Jasmine's light was on, so I banged on the front door. From behind the door I heard Jasmine ask who it was. I told her, and she unlocked the door, letting me in.

'What on earth is going on?' I asked.

'I was frightened. You know that man I told you about when you were on the on the Island last time, the creepy looking white man with the black stubble?'

'Yes,' I answered, a picture of Zach in my mind.

'He is back, and was prowling round the garden when I got home. I asked him what he wanted, but he just disappeared without saying anything. Later I saw

The Mango Mystery

him prowling around again, but this time I saw he saw he had a gun, so I locked the doors and rang the police.'

'What happened then?' I asked.

'Nothing really,' Jasmine replied.

'Bernie came up and said he could not see anything and said I must be imaging the gun. He asked if you were here but I said no, so he told me keep the doors locked, just in case.'

I was deeply concerned. Zach was on the Island and I was obviously the target now, but by being here I was putting Mary and Jasmine in danger, and I had no idea what to do.

John de Caynoth

Chapter 56. Tony's Phone Call

Joelle

'Inspector de Nouvelas - a call for you,' the switchboard operator said as, with some trepidation, I put the hand-piece of my desk phone to my ear. I had been on tenterhooks all morning waiting for this call, rehearsing what I would say, while hoping he would not bother to ring.

'Joelle' I recognised the voice immediately, 'Tony Choizi here, you remember me. How're ya doin?'

'Tony, I will never forget you,' I said sarcastically, 'what do want?'

'Sorry to hear you've been in trouble.'

I could feel him gloating down the phone as I replied, 'Yes, and no thanks to you.'

'Only acting on information received,' he answered innocently.

'Oh yes, and what information was that?' I asked.

'One of my underworld informers told me that the leak was out of Kaeta,' He told me, maintaining his air of innocence, 'anyway, it was not me that dropped you in it, it was your Dutch friends on that Enquiry who set us both up to cover their own arses.'

I replied, 'that's rubbish, there was no leak in Kaeta and, if there was, it was probably coming from your department.' This conversation was going nowhere, so I asked, 'Look Tony, you did not ring me to apologise, so what do you want?'

The Mango Mystery

'No, you are right, but actually I am sorry, and I do need help now.'

That surprised me - I never thought I would hear Tony sounding sincere. I was not going to let him off the hook and forgive him for anything, though.

He continued, 'someone is on my tail: I don't know who it is, but there is a private investigator sniffing around after me.' His customary bullishness emerged, 'anyhow, they will have to get up early to pin something on old Tony, I have the boys on it, and then we will fix them - good and proper.'

Oh no! I thought, what has Douglas got into now? My concern for him ratcheted up a few more degrees. Keeping my voice calm I said, 'I can't help you with that Tony.'

'No, I know you can't,' Tony now sounded serious, 'but I am still trying to track down the organisers of the ketamine drug smuggling gang at the United States' end of the chain. There are still small quantities of the drug here on the black market - the Dutch tell me that there is none coming out of Europe at the moment, so there must still be some ketamine over here in America that is being released slowly onto the market, and I want to find it.'

'I am still not sure I can help you Tony, I have no information about the destination of the ketamine.'

'No, but the Dutch tell me you have traced some possible gang boss suspects to Switzerland, and they asked me to talk to you first to get the full story before bringing the Swiss Authorities on board.'

John de Caynoth

I guessed that Jan van den Leuven was behind this, but I could not see how Tony could influence the Swiss so I asked him how this would help.

'Ah well' he answered, 'everyone knows we Americans get information from all sorts of sources, no questions asked.'

I let that point go, explaining to Tony how I had found Mrs Lecarrow and how John and I, unofficially, had gone to Switzerland to track her down and had found her with Marina Vidnova.'

As I finished my story he interjected and exclaimed, 'Vidnova, I know that name, let me think.'

He must have put the phone down and I heard him shout, 'the Vidnova scandal - when was that?' I could not hear the answer, but Tony soon spoke to me again.

'Vidnova, that's it. There was a big scandal over here about three years ago. Marina Vidnova, of Russian decent, left Switzerland and married a small time, but rich American business man who was in the import/export business. Now, the unusual thing was that he took her name. Apparently, she still had contacts in the old countries who they used as trading partners, and within a few years they'd become millionaires. Anyway, she left him to go back to Switzerland, this was about three years ago, and she took all the key people from his company with her. As far as I know, the court case over who owns the company is still going on, but - and get this - the headline story was that she left him for another woman.'

The Mango Mystery

This could be the lead we are looking for, I thought, and asked, 'Tony, can you remember the name of the company?'

'They changed the name to some Russian name after they married, but I remember the company originally took the husband's name prior to the marriage - Simeon Trading Enterprises - something like that.'

I thanked Tony for the information.

'No problem,' he said 'pleased to be of service. I will get on to the Swiss now, and don't worry - I won't mention you.'

I walked out of the office to find Andrea, as I needed to talk to her. She was in the police restaurant with John, eating lunch. I asked her to come to my office as soon as she finished - I grabbed a sandwich and went back up stairs.

Andrea soon appeared and I told her about the conversation with Tony Choizi.

'We will split this stuff between us,' I told her. 'Let's stop going through the picture galleries, as that's getting us nowhere. You see what you can find on Mr Vidnova, or Simeon, what ever name he is using now and I will concentrate on the company to see what I can dig up.'

We both felt good about this. We now had another angle on Vidnova, which with a bit of luck, would pay off.

My new sim-card and phone number had arrived this morning and I decided to ring Douglas, but I still could not get through and now his phone was off. I was seriously worrying about what had happened to him. I decided to ring Mary to ask her if she had seen him.

I got no answer and, on checking the time, realised that she would be taking Jasmine to school.

I dialled Bernie's number instead. 'Bernie,' I said when he answered, 'I need your help.'

He told me he was driving to work and asked me to hang on while he pulled over.

'What do want Joelle?' he asked

'Have you seen Douglas? I am worried about him - he is not answering his phone. The last I heard from him, he was in Bermuda but planning to go on Kaeta, and I wondered if you had seen him.'

Bernie replied, 'Bermuda - so that's where he's been. No sorry, Joelle I have not seen him.'

I asked, 'could you check with immigration and see if he has arrived in Kaeta?'

'I could,' Bernie replied, 'but if he arrived on an inter-island flight, immigration might not have checked passports.'

I knew Bernie was right but asked him to find out anyway.

Half an hour later, I rang Mary again. This time she answered and I asked her if she had seen Douglas.

She replied, 'Yes, he arrived four days ago and was staying with us, but this morning he left early.'

'Is he all right? Where did he go?' I asked.

Mary replied, 'Well, I think he's okay but he's definitely worried about something. He left very early this morning before we were awake - he just left a note

The Mango Mystery

saying something urgent had come up and he had to go.'

'Did he say where he was going?'

'No, I have no idea where he is going, he did not say anything about having to leave, just the note.'

I had hit a dead end - I did not know what else to do, and was seriously concerned about what he had got himself into.

John de Caynoth

Chapter 57. Disappeared

Douglas

After worrying for a couple of hours yesterday evening I decided to phone Josh. He had given me a number in case of emergencies and I reckoned this was now an emergency.

He answered abruptly, 'What is the problem?'

I told him and wasting no words he said, 'Disappear, don't go through the airport or dock. Don't tell anyone where you are going. Be very careful you are not followed and if possible lay a false trail. Don't use your mobile again - it can be traced - and turn it off so it is not broadcasting where you are,' and he rang off.

I got up very early and used the house phone to call a taxi, asking them to wait for me at the end of the drive. I left a note for Mary and crept out of the house to wait for the taxi as arranged. All the time I was checking around to see if there was anyone about, but luckily I saw nothing suspicious and even more luckily no one tried to shoot me.

The taxi arrived. I peered anxiously out of the window as we made our way to the airport: on the way into Kaeta Town I spotted a motorcycle following behind us, but going out of town on the airport road the traffic got heavier and it became difficult to tell if I was being followed. I reached the airport and made way into the Departures building, which consisted of a small waiting room, housing the aircraft operators' desks, and a screen showing the times and gates of the flights. I was followed in by a guy wearing a tee-shirt and shorts. He had no luggage at all, not even hand baggage. I

The Mango Mystery

asked one of the aircraft operators if she could tell me what arrivals were expected this morning. Apparently there was an inter-island flight landing in about forty minutes, but no international flights until this evening. The local flight will have to do, I decided, and went over to a bench to wait for it to arrive. I looked carefully for anyone behaving suspiciously, and saw the guy who had followed me in sitting on a bench, reading an old newspaper.

Before the forty minutes was up, I heard an aircraft come in to land so I casually made my way out of the departure waiting area and ran across to the arrivals building. When I got there, I ducked into a toilet and changed my clothes, put on dark glasses and a straw hat and walked out of the airport and across to the taxis with the arriving passengers. I took a taxi into Kaeta Town where I needed to sort things out before I disappeared. Luckily I saw no sign of the guy in the tee-shirt.

Firstly, I went to the local bank. When I was on the Island last year, I had made arrangements with them to act on behalf of my UK bank so I could access my account, and I hoped that agreement was still operational as I was running short of cash. Luckily, I was able to get some money, and so next on my to-do list was to visit the local mobile phone shop where I bought a secondhand pay-as-you-go phone. I asked the young man in the shop if he could download my address book from the old phone to the new one. He wanted to know why I was swapping a rather good iPhone for a cheap second-hand model, but I gave no explanation and declined his offer to buy the iPhone from me.

John de Caynoth

Next was a visit to the Land Agents. I told them I wanted to experience living in the development at Grumble before I decided to buy and asked if I could rent, for a month or so, the apartment I had seen yesterday. Naturally, they were delighted to set this up but were surprised when I said I wanted to move in now - today. The manager shrugged and asked if I could wait for half and hour while he prepared a rental agreement. I said I would come back shortly, as I had something else to do, and left for the Hertz car hire office, which I had noticed just down the road. I hired a Suzuki Swift for a month and, while I did not anticipate using it much, I did not want to be without the means to move quickly if that should prove necessary. Last on the list was a visit to the market stalls and supermarket where I bought some bed linen, other essentials and some food. All the time I had been looking behind me to see if anyone was watching me but as far as I could see, all was clear.

I collected my purchases and put them in the hired Suzuki and went back to the Land Agents office, signing the rental agreement and collecting the keys to the apartment.

I drove to Grumble taking the long way round the Island, via Nelson's dock and the mountain road. I stopped at the top of the mountain road from where I could look back, for over a mile, and I saw no cars behind me in the distance. Reassured that I had not been followed, I made my way to Grumble and the development, parked the Suzuki amongst the other cars and let myself into the apartment, breathing a sigh of relief. No one knew where I was, except the land agent, and I had not told anyone about going house-hunting. I

The Mango Mystery

reckoned I should be safe for a month and by then, hopefully, whoever was after me would have given up.

I picked up my new phone and turned it on, cursing as I realised I had no charger for it. However, there were some urgent phone calls I needed to make and Joelle was first on the list. The drive to Grumble had reminded me that, over a year ago, Joelle had taken me on a tour round the Island: driving the same roads had made me feel rather lonely. I wondered what she was doing and hoped nothing had happened to her. I desperately wanted to talk to her and I dialled her number again, but all I got was a recorded message saying that the number was no longer available. In desperation I rang the only other number I had, Derek Passmore's, and I did get an answer, I was told Derek was in a meeting and advised to ring back later.

I had to wait until early evening before I made the next call. I dialled the number for 'Windrush' hoping that I would get Jasmine and not Mary. Mary would be too inquisitive and would want to know too much, whereas Jasmine would not ask too many questions. Jasmine did answer, and I explained that I had some urgent business to attend to and warned her to be careful of the man she had seen with the gun - if he came looking for me again, I asked her to say I had gone home.

'He has already been asking for you,' Jasmine told me, 'he came round this morning. I did not see him - he spoke to Mary - and she told him you had gone. Mary said he wanted to know where, but she said she did not know. He was a bit pushy, but eventually he went away.'

I told Jasmine that, if he reappeared, she was to phone Bernie.

John de Caynoth

Next, I rang Derek Passmore. I managed to speak to him this time and explained I was not able to get in touch with Joelle and asked him if he knew where she was.

'Yes,' he replied, 'she is back from Holland and still working on the drug smuggling case and, as far as I know, she is fine.'

I asked him if he could give her a message to phone me and then realised I did not know the number of this phone. Before I could explain, he interrupted me, saying he needed to go as another call had come through which he needed to take. He cut me off.

At least I knew nothing had happened to her, but reminded my self, sadly, that if she was dumping me it was really none of my business anymore. Maybe we could remain friends, I hoped.

The Mango Mystery

Chapter 58. The Paper Trail

Joelle

John was still acting as my CPO, which meant that he escorted me everywhere. This was getting rather tiresome, I suspected more for him than me, but although there had been no further direct attempts on me, the flat was still being watched: yesterday we had been followed to work and back, so I was glad I still had his protection. The Mercedes had gone for repair and John was now driving the grey Honda again.

However, there was a problem developing. As John had a long drive from his home to Clapham and back, I had allowed him to stay at the flat, sleeping on the sofa. That was okay for a couple of nights, but he had now acquired a camp bed from somewhere, which he had erected in my living room, which was now taking on the appearance of a second bedroom. Last evening, he had observed that the room was really too small be a bed-sit, and suggested that perhaps he should move into my bedroom. I had warned him to be careful, and reminded him that lodging in my flat was a strictly professional arrangement: nevertheless, when we were off duty he was getting rather too familiar. I was finding it really tiresome fending him off all the time, plus he was using my washing machine and hanging his underwear all around my kitchen to dry!

My other worry was Douglas - he seemed to have vanished - I did not know where he was or what he was doing, but I had a horrible feeling he was in trouble. He had left a message with Derek Passmore for me, and I was told had phoned to speak to me yesterday morning,

John de Caynoth

but when I tried to phone him his mobile was always off, as was the alternative number Derek had given me.

Between interruptions and being pulled away for other tasks Andrea had spent a frustrating day yesterday hunting for information, anything, on Mr. Vidnova/Simeon and Simeon Trading Enterprises, but had found nothing. I had not even started looking, as I had spent the morning on a conference call with Inspector van den Leuven, and others, which had just gone over old ground again. Yesterday afternoon, as I was the only Inspector in the office, Barbara had asked me to interview a suspected drug dealer, that the uniform lot had arrested outside a school that morning. By Friday evening we had not made much progress, and so I agreed with Andrea that we would come in today, on a Saturday, and hopefully get a quite day to do some research.

John drove me this morning and asked if I would be working all day, as he needed to go home to get some fresh clothes and see to chores. I told him I did not think I would need him until Monday morning, as I was planning to spend tomorrow in the flat, and I could get a tube home this afternoon. 'Yes,' I assured him, before he had to ask, 'I will be very careful and make sure I am not followed.'

Good, I thought, I need some time on my own, then I thought, no, I need some time with Douglas - I hope he is all right.

'I have been thinking,' Andrea said, as we sat sipping our first coffee of the morning discussing how to start, 'we are wasting our time looking through old police reports and pictures. We should widen our search on-line: if the Vidnovas' separation caused a

The Mango Mystery

scandal, it would be reported in the newspapers.' However, Andrea had second thoughts when she discovered there were nearly 1,400 newspapers published in the United States.

'No,' I encouraged Andrea, 'it's a good idea - they were millionaires and Tony said there was a big scandal when they separated, so it should be covered in the big national papers. I will take the Wall Street Journal and you look through the New York Times. The Vidnovas split up three years ago, so we will start then.'

I went through the whole year, looking for something on Simeon Trading enterprises or Vidnova, finding nothing, but Andrea had more luck. After about an hour, she found a short paragraph in the business section announcing that the millionaire Vidnova couple, who jointly ran Hyluk Trading Corporation, were to separate and the future of the company was uncertain.

I went back to the Wall Street Journal, this time looking for the Hyluk Trading Corporation and, as I had an approximate date, the search was much quicker. I found a report of an interview with Mrs Vidnova, in which she denied that she and her husband were separating. She went on the say that they had decided to split the business and relocate to Europe, where much of their trading was now based. She would be moving there to run the new European operation while her husband would remain in the United States and run the American side.

'That's interesting,' I said to Andrea, 'from reading this, it sounds as though she is not a widow and that her husband is still alive and kicking.'

John de Caynoth

'He might have died later,' Andrea commented. 'Let's continue working our way forward through the papers. There might be something more.'

Before long, she shouted across to me that she had found something else. 'It's in the social column of USA Today,' she said, as she summarised the article for me. 'It says that Mrs Vidnova's move to Europe may not be as amicable as she would have us believe. A reliable scource says that Mr Vidnova found out his wife was having an affair with another woman and threw her out, so she left him to go and live her in Europe, taking most of the key staff, and the greater part of the business, with her.'

She read on and after a few moments said, 'this bit is interesting. It says her husband is reported to be changing his name back to Simeon and moving to Florida.'

Andrea switched her search to the Miami Herald while I finished looking through the Wall Street Journal. I found nothing further in that paper and so I switched to the Washington Post where, around the same date as the other reports, I found a piece on Marina Vidnova, where she confirmed that she would be based permanently in Switzerland, and was starting a new company, which would be called Hyluk (Europe), assuming responsibility for the European business of the Hyluk Trading Corporation. She was confident that the new company would be successful and confirmed that a number of the key staff from the old business were relocating with her. I got excited here, because the next paragraph was a quote from the Hyluk's security manager in which he said that the staff were happy to follow Mrs Vidnova to Europe, as most were of

The Mango Mystery

Eastern European extraction and were looking forward to returning. The security manager's name was Xavier Zedanski.

I was buzzing, as I told Andrea what I had found. 'This has got to be the link,' I told her, 'Zed works for Marina Vidnova, allegedly as a security manager, but in reality we know he is an enforcer.'

'Here,' said Andrea, 'hold on a moment - I think I have found something as well.'

I hovered impatiently while she rolled down through screens of newspaper pages.

'Here it is. I found a notice that Daniel Vidnova has applied to change his name to Daniel Simeon and now I have a story in the Miami Herald that Dan Simeon, who recently changed his name, has now changed the name of his company, The Hyluk Trading Corporation, to AK Transport. The company, now based in Miami, will continue to run its transport and shipping operations in the Caribbean, and - get this - the letters AK stand for American Kaetian.'

We both sat back and looked at each other in amazement. 'I need a cup of tea,' Andrea announced, and so we went down the staff canteen.

Over our drinks, I said, 'Do you think we might have cracked this? Marina Vidnova and Mrs Lecarrow, or what ever her name was, set up the European end of the racket, recruiting Gruber as the expendable front man. They arranged to smuggle drugs into Kaeta from where Dan Simeon used his transport operation to get the drugs into America where they were then sold, presumably at an enormous profit.'

'Sounds a plausible theory to me,' Andrea replied.

John de Caynoth

'We need to write this up,' I said, 'and on Monday I need to see Barbara Green. I feel an urgent conference call coming on.'

By this time, it was late in the afternoon and we decided to call it a day. I told Andrea not to worry, I would write up all we had found out tomorrow.

'How are you going to do that?' she asked as we left, 'I thought your PC had been stolen?'

I told her I had bought another one to replace it.

I was pleased with our day's work and pretty sure we had worked out how the whole operation was running. I walked towards Westminster Tube station and on the way stopped at the small supermarket to restock my fridge and buy a bottle of wine. At Westminster I took a Jubilee Line train to Waterloo, where I was going to change to the Northern Line and back to Clapham.

I was still pleased with my self, thinking about Douglas and hoping we could soon wrap up this drug investigation and life would return to normal. I walked along the underground corridors from the Jubilee line platform to the Northern Line. At one point, I was alone in the passage, and still day-dreaming when a woman, walking round a corner towards me, suddenly shouted, 'Look out, behind you!' Fortunately, training and instinct saved me as I turned in time to see a person running towards me, holding a knife. At the last minute, I stepped to one side and grabbed his arm, twisting it backwards as he lunged past me. The knife dropped and person continued running, disappearing round the corner. It all happened in a split second - the woman came up to me and put her hand on my arm as I started to tremble with shock. I could have kicked

The Mango Mystery

myself at being so wrapped up in my own thoughts - I had not been vigilant and did not notice I was being followed.

'Are you all right dear?' The elderly lady looked at me, concernedly. 'It's so dangerous these days in London, what with muggings and so on - not a bit like the old days. You should report that to the police you know.'

I assured I would and she kindly stayed with me until I calmed down a little, offering to walk to my train with me. I thanked her, and said I was feeling much better and would be fine on my own. My assailant seemed to have disappeared, so I picked up the knife and made way cautiously onto the deserted Northern Line platform. He was standing there, alone, waiting for me.

John de Caynoth

Chapter 59. Revealed

Douglas

I had been sitting in this apartment since Thursday. I did turn on the mobile phone last Friday morning and try to ring Joelle, using her London office number, but was told she was not available. I saw the battery on the phone was nearly exhausted and I turned it off to conserve its power. Apart from that, I had had plenty of time to think.

Bernie taking his house off the market had struck me being as a little odd. The logical explanation was that his wife is too ill to move. I was certain that I had seen the original copy of Joelle's diary on his desk - I knew Joelle's handwriting, and had handled the diary myself. Yet he told me that they had not caught the burglars? Of course, it was possible that the diary was just found dumped somewhere and passed to Bernie, but then, why would he tell me it was *his* diary? Perhaps I was mistaken after all? These thoughts just kept going round and round in my head.

There was another thing bothering me. Zach's sister had reported that Zach had told her he recognised the drug gang organiser, and that it was *someone you would never think of*. Until now, I had been working on the assumption that Tony Choizi was the police informer, but, it was very unlikely that Zach would have recognised him. I got the impression that Zach had made his identification some time ago. As far as I knew, Zach had lived on Kaeta all his life, whereas I did not think Tony had ever visited the Island before my arrest, twelve months ago. So if Zach had recognised the gang member, it could not have been

The Mango Mystery

Tony Choizi. Despite searching, Josh and I had never found anything directly linking him to the drug smugglers. If Tony Choizi was not involved, then who could it be?

I decided to make a list of unlikely people Zach might know. I started with shady characters he might know from the underworld, but not knowing who they might be I dismissed them as not likely enough. I also dismissed Zach's family on the grounds that he would have known them well enough to know what they were up to.

Assuming that the drug gang member on the Island would also be the informer, it meant it had to be someone who had access to the police investigation or knowledge of what the police were doing. This narrowed the possibilities down significantly, as the drug gang had been getting information all the time, not just during the time when I was under surveillance, which was how Gruber had known when to disappear.

Why was Zach trying to kill Joelle and now me? Most likely because the gang, or more specifically the Island members of the gang, feared that Joelle and I had enough information to identify them and were trying to silence us before we worked it out.

My blood was running very cold as I came to the conclusion that the only people who fitted the scenario I had just created were the Kaetian Police, either an individual or a group of them.

Had I been wrong about Joelle? Could she have deceived me all along and have been playing a double game all the time? I did not want to believe this - after all they had made two attempts on her life. If she were a gang member they could be trying to kill her, and me by association, before she can spill the beans. But no,

John de Caynoth

it could not possibly be Joelle - she had fiercely denied any involvement when questioned in the enquiry and anyway, I loved her and had to believe in her.

Once I had played this awful scenario through in my mind, I tried to think of other possible alternatives.

Bernie had Joelle's diary on his desk and that surely put him in the frame: he might even have been the burglar himself. I did not want to believe this - he a nice old guy - but I pondered on this further.

Everyone on the Island knew Bernie, so Zach would certainly have recognised him, and he was certainly a most unlikely person to be involved in illegal drugs. Bernie would have known everything that was going on when I had been under surveillance, and I was aware that, when Joelle had move to the UK, he and Joelle had spoken quite frequently on the telephone and she had always kept him up to speed with what she was doing.

Another piece of circumstantial evidence was that someone had rewritten Joelle's original reports, covering the period when I was suspected of drug smuggling. Joelle had told me that she had given them to Bernie to check and send off. I think she also told me, Bernie had said he was not responsible for submitting the reports when he was questioned.

That enquiry, and the conflicting evidence between Joelle, Bernie and Tony, was one of the reasons Joelle had been suspended and investigated.

Then there was Zach's death. As far as I was aware, only Bernie had known that I was visiting Zach. Had Bernie had him silenced before he could talk to me, fearing Zach would tell me who he had seen?

The Mango Mystery

And there were Bernie's trips to Miami. He did not deny going, and told me he used to attend drug crime conventions and meetings, but when I asked Josh about that he told me, as far as he new, that there had never been any such meetings.

The more I went through events, the more convinced I became that Bernie was involved with drugs and was the mole who had kept the drug gang one step ahead throughout this whole investigation.

The question now: is Bernie acting alone or are others in the department involved and the bigger question is: what am I going to do about it without getting myself killed?

It occurred to me that the one person in the Kaetian police who could not have been involved was the Commissioner. His was a political appointment - too distant from the day-to-day running of operations to know was happening and could not therefore have passed on detailed information. This, of course, did not mean that he was not involved, but I guessed he had been appointed after the smuggling operation started. I decided I should take the risk of telling him of my suspicions, letting him handle things from now on.

The problem was that Zed was still on the Island and, I was sure, would be looking for me. I had to find a way of contacting the Commissioner without exposing myself, or where I was hiding, and all I had to help me was a mobile phone I dare not use and second mobile phone with a dying battery.

John de Caynoth

Chapter 60. The Conference Call

Joelle

After my experience last Saturday I was rather pleased to see John when he appeared at 7.30am to take me to work. I had to tell him what had happened and showed him the knife. I had not wanted to look at it since I picked it up on Saturday, carefully wrapping it in my handkerchief so I did not destroy any prints. John unfolded the material and looked at the knife.

'A flick knife with a six inch blade, and it is razor sharp' he said, as he tested the blade with the pad on his middle finger. 'This would have given you a nasty injury, and its not your average muggers weapon. I will keep this, if you don't mind.'

As we drove in John asked me how I got home on the Saturday and I explained that, when I saw the assailant on the platform, I panicked and ran. 'I think he followed me because I heard someone in the passage behind me, but I ran out of the station and took a taxi home.'

'Were you followed?' John asked.

'I don't know, I didn't see anyone obviously following the taxi - yesterday was sunny and warm with lots of people walking on the common, so it was difficult to spot anyone watching the flat.'

John looked in the rear view mirror as we drove over Westminster Bridge and as we stopped in the traffic and announced, 'there is a motor bike that has been behind us most of the way from Clapham so he is probably tailing us.'

The Mango Mystery

We got to our offices in Victoria Street without incident and John accompanied me as I walked up the stairs. Barbara Green was already in her office, so I asked if we could see her.

I explained that I had been attacked again, going home on Friday. Barbara listened without saying anything until I had finished, and then asked John where he had been. He shuffled about and tried to explain that he had needed to return home, but I butted in and told Barbara it was my fault I was alone, that I had dismissed John for the weekend. She gave us both a real dressing-down - John for allowing me to expose myself unnecessarily in a high- risk way, and me for being so stupid and putting myself at risk. In conclusion she said, 'I ought to report the pair of you for this, but just don't let it happen again.'

When we got out of Barbara's office, I asked John what he was going to do.

'I must go and report to my sergeant and tell him what happened and get yet another dressing-down,' he said ruefully, 'and then I want to get this knife examined and see if it has any history. I will be back to pick you up this afternoon.'

I went back to Barbara's office: the door was open so I knocked on the glass screen and asked her if Andrea and I could have some time with her today.

A little crossly she asked, 'what do you want now? What else have you done Joelle?'

'Nothing wrong, Ma'am, but we made some progress on Saturday and I need to bring you up to speed and then I think I need to talk with the Dutch and the Americans.'

John de Caynoth

'I am very busy at the moment, Joelle. Leave your report with me and I will try and fit you in later today.'

'I emailed the report to you yesterday, it should be in your inbox,' I explained, and I saw her checking as I thanked her and went to find Andrea.

Andrea spent the rest of the morning trawling through more newspapers on-line, and while a number of them reported the Vidnova affair, she found nothing new. I picked at the file of cases on my desk all of which needed my attention, and one caught my eye. The drug dealer, the one we had arrested when we had found the KetPil tablets in the London house raid, had skipped bail and failed to turn up at the magistrate court. Curious, I thought. I wondered if he was more than a small time drug dealer, and I thought about sending John out to look for him.

Barbara called Andrea and I into her office just after lunch. She had read the report and wanted us to explain in our own words what we had found. We took it in turns to tell Barbara, I explained that it was Tony Choizi who gave us the clue, but Andrea's idea to trawl through the newspapers. When we finished Barbara, congratulated us. She agreed that what we had found was really relevant to the case, and that my conjecture of how it all fitted together into a drug smuggling operation was plausible.

'Where is this Xavier Zedanski - has he turned up yet?' she asked. 'If we could get hold of him he could probably give enough evidence to arrest the Vidnovas and Mrs Lecarrow'.

I replied, 'Unfortunately, as far as I know, we have no idea where he is.'

The Mango Mystery

'Do we know the whereabouts of Mr Vidnova or Simeon, what ever he calls himself now?'

'Only that he lives in Miami according to the newspaper report.' Andrea told Barbara.

'Should not be difficult for the Americans to find him,' Barbara mused. Looking at me, she asked, 'you said this morning you were going to speak to the Dutch and Americans - have you done that yet?'

'No,' I replied, 'We wanted to bring you up to date first.'

Barbara dismissed us, suggesting that I go and get on with phone calls.

I asked Andrea to organise a conference call while I emailed the reports to Holland and America.

'Already done,' she told me, 'it's all set up for 4.00pm.'

Andrea and I were sitting in a conference room, promptly at four that afternoon. Barbara Green had joined us but explained that it was my show: she would only be staying for a few minutes to see who was in on the call.

Bang on time, a synthetic voice announced, 'Jan van den Leuven is joining the conference.'

'Hello Joelle, and Andrea I think,' Jan greeted us. 'I am in Amsterdam with Willam Ince, and I hear you have some interesting information for us.'

Willam said, 'Hello,' but was interrupted by the synthetic voice again, announcing that Detective Jeff Conway was joining the call.

I asked if Detective Choizi was also joining the conference.

'Uhh, well no,' Jeff Conway explained, 'he is not available at the moment.'

Van den Leuven came in and asked why Tony Choizi was not available, explaining that he understood a new lead in Florida had been found and Choizi was required.

Jeff Conway blustered, obviously embarrassed, and when Jan pushed him for an explanation he caved in saying, 'Look, I am sorry but all hell has broken loose here today. Tony has been arrested in Bermuda for possession of illegal substances, we are in the middle of an audit of the confiscated drug store, and it appears that quantities of some drugs are missing. The records of confiscations have been altered and to cap that, one of our senior officers walked out this morning when he heard Tony had been arrested and has now disappeared.'

We were all silent, stunned, and I was thinking that Douglas and his private detective have to be behind this somehow, but, far being relieved that Tony Choizi had been arrested, I was even more worried for Douglas wondering where he was and what he had done.

Jan van den Leuven was first to recover some composure and asked Jeff Conway if he was up to speed with the case. Jeff explained he had some involvement after the enquiry last year, when there had been an internal investigation to see if the leaks had originated in the Miami department, but it had been Tony's case and he had only picked it up this morning when they were told of Tony's arrest.

Jan went over recent events in Holland and Switzerland, ending with his request to Tony to ask the

The Mango Mystery

Swiss authorities for assistance in investigating Marina Vidnova.

'He obviously got them wound up as they have just contacted us asking for information and assistance.' I could imagine Jan smiling as he told us this.

Barbara took her leave and I picked up the story, running through what Andrea and I had discovered over the weekend.

It took nearly two hours for all the participants to contribute, and for everyone to feel comfortable that they understood where the investigation had got to, and then I took the lead by asking what now needed to be done.

'Jeff,' I said, 'I think you need to find this Mr Simeon and check on his company AK Transport and see what you can dig up.'

Jan chipped in, 'and we can brief the Swiss to look into this Hyluk (Europe) company, as well as the Misses Vidnova and Lecarrow.'

I had the last word, volunteering to contact Bernie to see if he could find out anything about the AK transport connection with Kaeta.

When we finished the call, John was waiting to take me back to the flat.

'I just have one last thing to do,' I told him, as I picked up the phone to ring Bernie and let him know what was going on.

When I spoke to him, he sounded old and tired, admitting that he was finding things getting harder to cope with. 'Merv does his best but he just has not got you intuition,' he sighed. I felt guilty that I was about to add to his load as I started by to tell him about the

326

John de Caynoth

Vidnovas. When I finished, Bernie was silent for quite a while.

I asked, 'Bernie are you still there?'

'Oh, yes, sorry, I was just thinking that you must be very close to making an arrest.' he answered.

I agreed, and asked if he could get Merv to check out AK Transport and their connection with Kaeta.

Bernie appeared not to hear me because he answered, 'Joelle I must say goodbye to you now. I have some urgent calls to make, but before I go I want you to know that you are the best police investigator I have ever worked with, and a credit to your father. I can't tell you how proud I was when your father asked me to be your godfather.'

We finished the call and I thought Bernie sounded as if he was loosing his grip. I decided to ring Merv myself.

The Mango Mystery

Chapter 61. The Commissioner

Douglas
I had a plan.

I spent the greater part of Sunday writing my suspicions and conclusions as a report and then copied the final document on to a compact disc.

When I first drove into Grumble, I had noticed an internet cafe, so with some trepidation, yesterday, Monday, I ventured out of the apartment to walk the short distance there, down by the marina. All the way, I was nervously looking round to spot anyone paying any undue interest in me, but as far as I could see I was in the clear, and hoped that I appeared to be just another yacht owner staying in the town.

I bought two more compact discs and I paid for time on one of the PCs and loaded my disk, making a further two copies and also printing out the report I had written. I begged a couple of Jiffy bags from the cafe owner and addressed one to the Kaeta Police for the personal attention of the Commissioner and the second to David Evans at Benson, Dodd, Sugar in London. I went across to the small supermarket, which also served as the Post Office, to send the two CDs.

I dispatched the one to London, but as I was about to post the second, to the Commissioner, I paused. What if he does not open it himself? This was highly likely, as he would have an assistant. And worse, who ever opened the post would see the postmark and would be able to guess where I was hiding. Somehow, I needed to meet the Commissioner personally to hand over my conclusions.

John de Caynoth

I went outside and sat on a wall by the marina to think. I dare not risk going to the Police Station - I was sure to be spotted and it would not take long for Zed to appear. Also, I did not want to meet the Commissioner in Grumble and give away my hiding place. There was only one solution: I had to convince the Commissioner to leave his office and meet me somewhere neutral.

I returned to the apartment. On picking up the pay-as you-go phone I saw, as I switched it on, that the battery charge monitor was now on orange. Luckily, I had the number of the Kaeta Police headquarters listed under '*Joelle Work*' and I hit the connect, button praying the battery would last.

I asked for the Commissioner and was put through his assistant, who told me the Commissioner was busy and asked what me what my call concerned. I told her I wanted to report a crime and she referred me to the front desk where they dealt with all the crime reports.

'No, I said, 'you don't understand, this crime is associated with one or more of the Commissioner's Police Officers'. She paused before informing me that she would talk to the Commissioner. After a few moments she returned, asking who was calling. I told her and she asked me to hold the line while she put the Commissioner on.

'This is most irregular Mr Jay, what can I do for you? I really think you should be speaking with Inspector Shrewd, not me.'

I asked him to please hear me out, as I had not got long before my phone died. I explained the situation as quickly as I could - that I was in personal danger from a gunman loose on the Island, and why I

The Mango Mystery

could not turn to Bernie Shrewd but had to speak with him personally. I asked him to meet me at the restaurant on Alice Hill. He started to ask me what evidence I had to back up the allegations but my phone started to bleep telling me I had only a few seconds left before it died. I said I would explain everything when I met him and needed him to agree to meet me now before my phone died. I heard him say he would meet me on his way to work, but that was it. The connection went dead.

Early on Tuesday morning, I was sitting in the Suzuki outside the restaurant hoping that the Commissioner would turn up.

He did, about half an hour later. He was not in his official car, but was driving himself in a small Toyota hatchback. He was not wearing his uniform jacket, but had replaced it with a light fleece. He got out of his car, and looked round, before walking into the restaurant. I waited to see if he was followed, before I went in to join him. He was sitting at a table with a cup of chocolate, rising to greet me I walked up to his table and shook his hand. I suggested we move outside where we would be able to talk without being overheard.

The Commissioner opened the conversation by telling me, 'you should know that the only reason I agreed to meet with you is because of your close connection with Joelle deNouvelas. I hold her in great esteem, and I am aware she has been having difficulties of her own, and I am guessing this has something to do with Joelle.'

John de Caynoth

I agreed, 'Indirectly it has,' passing him the report and starting to tell him what had been going on. The Commissioner waved to me to be silent. He read it through twice before he turned to me, and asking me for my interpretation of events.

I started with the enquiry last summer and how that threw up conflicting statements. I explained that Joelle had been suspended and then reinstated, that we had both been attacked, presumably with the intention of killing us, and that I suspected the gunman, Zed, was still on the Island looking for me. Finally I told him that it was the statement from Zach's sister, and the presence of Joelle's diary on Bernie's desk, which had led me to my suspicions about Bernie.

The Commissioner sat back, deep in thought. He asked me if he could take the report and compact disk I had given him, and said to me, 'you have handed me a big problem.'

I apologised and he continued, 'but before I do anything, I need to check what I can of your story,' and he asked me where he could find Zach's sister.

We parted at that point and I watched him drive away before I returned to the apartment, to stay hidden, with no idea of how events would play out.

The Mango Mystery

Chapter 62. Kaeta

Joelle

Douglas once said to me that one of best parts of going to the Caribbean is stepping out of the aircraft into a wall of warmth and sunlight, when only a few hours previously you stepped into the aircraft from a cold, damp and dark England. I now realised what he meant.

I descended the steps from the Airbus A330 to the runway apron and arrival hall at Kaeta International Airport. Andrea was right behind me, chattering away with excitement, and John was in front, fretting because he was not allowed to bring his gun on to the plane. I assured him the police in Kaeta do have guns and I would get him one as soon as we arrived.

Things had moved quickly since yesterday, and I was still a in a bit of a daze. I was closing down some old cases, when Barbara Green phoned me and said the Commander wished to see me. I did ask why but she just said it was urgent, and that he was in his office waiting for me.

I was surprised to see Derek Passmore in uniform today. I had not realised that he had been promoted and was now a Commander, seeming impressive, and rather frightening, as he opened the office door and invited me in. I wondered what I done, expecting some further information had come to light and that I was in trouble again. Barbara was already sitting at the conference table, smiling at me, and Derek invited me to join her.

John de Caynoth

He collected a slim file from his desk and joined us. I was puzzled: I was expecting a reprimand at the very least, but the atmosphere in the room was positive and relaxed. Derek started to explain.

'Late last night, I received a phone call from the Commissioner of Police in Kaeta. He apologised for calling me and explained that he had a very difficult situation on his hands, and needed to know to whom he should be addressing his request for assistance.'

My mind was racing. Perhaps Bernie had been taken ill - he had sounded stressed the last time we spoke. Derek Passmore consulted his file, continuing, 'I have spoken to the Deputy Commissioner and he has cleared the request from Kaeta with the Home Office and Foreign and Commonwealth Office.'

I was now intrigued, this had to be more serious than just Bernie being off sick, especially as the Commissioner of Police in Kaeta had made a request.

'There is a particularly serious situation in Kaeta, and the Commissioner there has explained that, as his own force is involved and may be culpable, he needs the assistance of a senior officer to investigate certain allegations that have been lodged with him. We understand that the allegations are connected with the drug smuggling investigation that you have been running recently.'

'Now,' Derek continued speaking directly to me, 'selecting you to lead this team may seem strange, even controversial, given you are a police officer with the Kaetian Police Force. However, currently you are also a Detective Inspector with the Metropolitan Police and I recognise there may be a conflict of interest, which you must handle. Because of your current knowledge of the

The Mango Mystery

drug investigation, combined with your experience and contacts on the Island, we believe you are the best officer we have to handle this role and to lead a team over there. Barbara is in full agreement. You will be operating in Kaeta as an Inspector of the London Metropolitan Police and will report to Chief Inspector Green here. I have spoken to the Commissioner of Police on Kaeta, who's delighted that you are to lead the investigation team, but, of course, under the circumstances, it is your decision whether or not to accept the role.'

I did not hesitate, I agreed I would like the job and asked if I would be drawing a team from the Kaetian force.

'No,' Barbara replied, 'you will take small team from the UK, and I can spare you two officers.'

'I would like to take Sergeant Andrea Spooner, and Constable John McDuff, my CPO.' I said.

'We thought you would choose them,' Barbara said, approving the selection.

Derek Passmore concluded the interview by telling me there were three seats reserved on the flight to Kaeta tomorrow morning, via St Lucia, and suggesting that I brief my team and get ready to leave.

So here we are on a warm and sunny Friday afternoon on Kaeta, with only a scant knowledge of what is expected of us.

I cleared through immigration and customs quickly, but Andrea and John, having indicated on their immigration documents that they were working on the Island, were taken aside for questioning and, when it emerged that they were police officers, the immigration officer in charge was not sure what to do. I told him to contact the Commissioner of Police if my explanation was insufficient for his purposes. He came off the phone looking very contrite and I think he wished he had accepted my explanation in the first place.

The remaining procedures were handled without further problems and we cleared arrivals to be met by the Commissioner's Official car, the Lexus I had borrowed over a year ago to drive Douglas round the Island - that brought back memories!

The driver took us to the Keata Island Hotel in Kaeta town and apologised on behalf of the Commissioner, who had to attend an official function in the evening, but told me he would pick me up the following morning when I had appointment with the Commissioner himself.

We checked into the hotel, and I felt rather strange staying there, rather than returning home. Andrea wanted to look round Kaeta to get her bearings, so we agreed to shower, change our clothes, then I would take Andrea and John for a quick tour of the town. John was not sure, he thought we should remain in the hotel as walking round the town was risky, but Andrea told him not to be an old fuddy-duddy, pointing out that no one knew we were on Kaeta so there was no risk, and anyway he needed to get his bearings also.

I took them through the town, past the Police Station and Judicial Buildings, and walked down to the market area, which delighted Andrea who immediately started foraging through the stalls. John was anxious and wanted to go back to the hotel and to dine there, but Andrea had other ideas, wanting to eat in the town

The Mango Mystery

and to "soak up the atmosphere", as she put it. It occurred to me that we could get a taxi out to my mother's restaurant, and sold the idea to Andrea by saying it was on the beach surrounded by palm trees with glorious views over the Caribbean Sea. John felt out-numbered and gave in agreeing, with a shrug of his shoulders, to do what ever we wanted.

Mary was both astonished and delighted when I walked in. We hugged for ages and eventually Mary let me go, wanting to know all about my surprise visit to the Island. I introduced Andrea and John, explaining to Mary that it was an official visit and I would be working. I asked Mary about Jasmine and she explained that she was busy studying and did not come down to the restaurant very often now.

I was still worrying about Douglas and I asked Mary if she had seen him. She told me that he had been on the island but had disappeared a few days ago. She did not where he had gone, but he had spoken to Jasmine by phone and told her he was okay, but not where he was or what he was doing. Mary paused here and looked worried and told me that since speaking with Douglas, Jasmine had been very withdrawn and quiet, but would not say why.

I had to put these worries to the back of my mind and play host to my two guests, joining in the party mood and excitement of the forthcoming job. I did promise myself to go and see Jasmine as soon as I could get away for a couple of hours. Mary served us local fish, the morning catch, and fresh vegetables from the market and both Andrea and John congratulated her, saying it was the best meal they had ever eaten. Mary was delighted and, fetching a bottle of

John de Caynoth

champagne, came to sit with us after she had finished serving. I wanted to stay sober so was only sipping at the champagne and drinking water as well, but John, who was sitting next to me had clearly decided he was off duty and was drinking and enjoying himself. Unfortunately he was also getting over familiar with me again, and at one point put his hand on my knee and whispering in my ear asked if he had been forgiven for the night in Germany. Unfortunately, Mary noticed and I could see her looking questioningly at me.

Mary and I had a lot to talk about and the three of us were the last to leave, except for one lone drinker at the bar. As we walked out I dropped back and asked Mary if she new him. 'He has been sitting there all evening, hardy drinking anything, not eating, but he has been watching us closely,' I said to her.

'I don't like that man,' Mary whispered back, 'he has been here every evening recently and he does not say anything - just sits there watching, and has a couple of glasses of beer.'

I looked at the man, who immediately turned away. I could not see his face and, in view of recent events, I wondered if he was more than a casual visitor.

I went to join the other two in the taxi, but Mary grabbed my arm and asked, 'is everything all right between you and Douglas? I could not help notice that John was paying you rather a lot of attention this evening. Is this why Douglas has disappeared?'

I could not explain to Mary who John really was and why he was travelling with me - that would really worry her - so I just told her he was a colleague. She gave me one of her knowing looks, and with an edge of

The Mango Mystery

disappointment, or perhaps disapproval, in her voice just said, 'I see.'

I joined John and Andrea in the taxi, thinking that my personal life was going from bad to worse: Jasmine in a teenage mood, Douglas disappeared and up to God knows what, and now Mary thinking I was having an affair with John.

To make it worse, when we got back to the hotel, Andrea stopped outside my bedroom door, and whispered to me, 'You know I like Douglas, he is a good man, but if you are moving on with John, I just want you know that it's none of my business what you do, and it won't upset me.' She gave me a knowing wink and walked off.

John de Caynoth

Chapter 63. The Investigation

Joelle

I had a bad night's sleep alternately thinking about the job, Jasmine, Douglas and cursing John. I realised I had made a mistake last night, I should have told John to stop, but I had not wanted to spoil the party so I had not said anything, and now I was hoping he had not seen that as encouragement.

I went down for a light breakfast before Andrea and John were up, and waited for the driver to collect me. I was amused at being driven to the Police station: I could have walked there more quickly, but when driver with the limousine arrived, he did not drive me to the Police Headquarters but took me to the Commissioner's official residence, where the Commissioner, it being Saturday, was dressed casually and waiting for me in his study.

'Come in Joelle,' he boomed, shaking my hand and offering me breakfast. I settled for just a cup of coffee and a servant brought me a flask of fresh brewed coffee, real cream and biscuits. All good meetings start with small talk, and this was no exception: after the Commissioner had asked about London and Mary's new restaurant, he got down to business.

He handed me a file marked 'Secret' and sat silently while I read it. I could not believe what I was reading, and I had to read the report again to make sure I had not misread it.

'I just can't believe this,' I said to the Commissioner, 'not Bernie, surely?'

The Mango Mystery

'I had similar feelings when I was confronted with this report,' the Commissioner sighed, 'and I checked out the allegations as best I could without arousing suspicion. I saw Zach's sister and she confirmed what is stated in the report. I also interviewed the Head of the Prison and he told me that he thought that the fight had been deliberately staged, with Zach targeted and stabbed, and that he had disagreed with Inspectors Strange's conclusion that it was an accident. Unfortunately, without raising premature suspicions, I am not in a position to check all the allegations, which is one reason why I requested assistance.'

'This report does not say if anyone else is involved,' I commented.

'No, but we can't rule that out yet,' cautioned the Commissioner.

I read the report again and said, 'from my knowledge of this whole drug investigation, I recognise that a number of the matters stated to support the allegation are accurate, but we only have the writer's word that Bernie had the original copy of my diary. That is, the evidence that the writer has sited as the key fact supports Bernie's alleged involvement, but, as the writer admits, Bernie denies this and says the diary is his. As usual in this investigation, all the other evidence is circumstantial.'

I frowned at the thought of the writer and asked the Commissioner from whom he had got the report.

'It came from a trusted source, I think, but I was asked not to reveal who,' the Commissioner told me.

'There is only one person who would have all this information and who could put this together,' I paused for thought, 'but what was he doing in Bernie's study?'

'I can see you have guessed the source of the allegation,' The Commissioner confirmed.

'Where is Douglas, is he well or is he in some kind of trouble?' I asked.

The Commissioner looked at me sympathetically and said, 'Inspector, you have to put your personal feelings aside and remember that you here to investigate the Kaetian Police force and to confirm, or not, the allegations against your colleague, Inspector Strange. If confirmed, you will have to arrest him.'

But he then added more gently, 'I met Mr Jay last Wednesday when he handed me this report and a compact disk. We met secretly up on Alice's Hill and he is physically well, but feels threatened and is hiding, presumably somewhere on the Island. He says there has been an attempt on his life and that there is someone called Zedanski on the Island who he believes to be the assailant.'

'Now,' the Commissioner became more matter of fact, 'to get down to practical matters. You obviously cannot operate out of the Police Station, so I have arranged for you to use a meeting room in the Judicial Building as your incident room. I have had phone lines and three computers, with broadband connection, installed. Anything else you need just ask my assistant, who is fully briefed, to help you. Incidentally, she, my driver, and I are the only people in the Police Department who know you are here. I have already placed all the archive files from your investigations last year, including the files marked secret, in your incident

The Mango Mystery

room. I have also left you the transcript of the Dutch enquiry into this affair, which I obtained when it was suggested that the leak came from Kaeta, and it makes interesting reading. One other thing, I have not told any of our Police Officers about these allegations yet, and I have told Inspector Strange to take a few days off to prepare for his imminent retirement, so you have some clear time before he returns.'

I asked the Commissioner about accommodation, as I had thought of returning to live at home, but the mention of Zedanski on the Island had shaken me, and I was thinking home might be too risky. The Commissioner was ahead of me here, and said he thought that living at 'Windrush' was not wise, advising us to use the hotel for the duration of the investigation.

'Is there anything else, Inspector?' he asked dismissing me.

'No sir,' I replied.

'Good,' he said, and as I walked out he called me back and gave me a set of car keys. 'I have arranged a car for you to use: it is a police vehicle that I have requisitioned for the next few days on the excuse I wish to be seen patrolling Kaeta in person.'

I walked round to the garages and found he had provided the old unmarked Suzuki, which I had always driven.

I drove myself back into town, alternately worrying what Douglas had got himself into and how I was going to tackle this investigation. Of course, I realised that this was also a test of my ability - if I messed up I would never be confirmed as an Inspector.

John de Caynoth

Chapter 64. Starting Work

Joelle

I went straight to the Judicial Building and into our incident room. It was a large, wood- panelled, meeting room with a window overlooking the buildings at the back. The table had been pushed back to one wall and two computers had been set up on it, at either end, with a printer and photocopier placed between them. A desk had been placed beneath the window, which supported a third computer. There was also a selection of notice and white boards in the room. The caretaker, who was showing me around, was grumbling that we had messed up his meeting schedule, and he did not know why we needed two meeting rooms as he showed me another much smaller room furnished simply with a table and two chairs. I assumed this was to be our interview room.

I pulled up one of the white boards and started writing up what we had to do.

Firstly, find Douglas. I was scared Zedanski may find him before I could, but his statement, and how he had arrived at his conclusions, was critical to this investigation. Next, get statements from the Prison Manager and Zach's sister. I wanted to read all the police reports going back to the beginning, starting with the Kaetian archives, and, I realised, I would also need the reports from London, and probably Amsterdam as well. I found the report from the Dutch Enquiry in the box of files left in the room and made a note to read it. I also needed to keep up to speed with the ongoing investigations in Switzerland and Florida and importantly I had to find Zedanski.

The Mango Mystery

I decided to go back to the hotel for lunch to collect Andrea and John and get to work in the afternoon. I found John in the bar with a glass of beer. 'Where is Andrea?' I asked him.

'She said she was going shopping in the market,' he replied.

I was not best pleased and told John to leave his drink and come and get some lunch as we needed to get our act together. Andrea had still not returned by the time we had finished, so I left a message at reception for to come to the Judicial Building.

I spent the afternoon with John: I showed him Douglas's report and brought him up to speed with what needed to be done. We refined my priority list and started to allocate the tasks across the three of us. It was believed Zedanski was on the Island and I mentioned that I thought we had been watched yesterday evening. John commented that this made things much more difficult and we would have to be more vigilant. He asked about arms, and I told him I would organise a pistol for him on Monday. He said we would need three pistols and that Andrea and I should be armed as well. 'We are clearly going to have to separate to cover this lot and I can't watch over you both all the time - you need your own protection.'

By five in the afternoon, I had enough and suggested we return to the hotel. To my annoyance, Andrea had still not turned up by the time we locked the room and made our way back to the hotel. John invited me to have drink with him but I declined ungraciously, telling him this was not a social relationship, and stomped off to find Andrea.

John de Caynoth

She was by the swimming pool in a bikini and drinking a cocktail. I was furious and demanded to know why she had ignored my message. Her reply was very off hand, 'I did not get back till late and, as we won't be starting until Monday, I decided to have a rest as I was tired.' I was incandescent with rage, but kept my self-control, simply saying that if she ignored me again she would be on the first plane home. I told her told her to get dressed and marched her to the Judicial building, sat her in the incident room and told her to read all the reports and be ready to start work by eight next morning.

'I assume you mean Sunday morning,' she said looking very contrite.

'Yes,' I confirmed and walked out, telling her lock up when she had finished.

Walking back to the hotel, I thought I saw the man from Mary's bar last night hanging about outside. I buzzed John in his room and told him to go down to Andrea and make sure she got back to the hotel safely.

The Mango Mystery

Chapter 65. Progress

Joelle

Both Andrea and John were waiting for me in reception when I came down at eight on Sunday morning, and we walked across to the Judicial Building together. There did not appear to be anyone watching the hotel or following us, but John was wondering if, for security reasons, it would be sensible to change hotels. I pointed out that if we were being watched, they could find easily as they knew where we were working.

John had stayed and helped Andrea last night. They had read all the reports and on one of the white boards had started cross-referencing the inconsistencies. They were both behaving very professionally today: Andrea apologised to me for her behaviour yesterday and promised it would not happen again, while John addressed me as 'Inspector' and asked me what I wanted him to do first.

I gave John a map told him to go for a walk to familiarise himself with the immediate area, check the Suzuki to see what equipment we might need, and then go for a drive and find his way around the Island.

Andrea and I continued ploughing through reports looking for inconsistencies, and support for the allegations Douglas had made. At one point, Andrea, reading the transcript from the Amsterdam Enquiry commented, 'your evidence to the enquiry matches up exactly with the Kaetian Police file covering the Coconut surveillance, but Choizi's and Bernie's statements are completely contradictory in places.'

John de Caynoth

'I know,' I replied, 'and it does not look good for Bernie because I know that some of the things he told the enquiry are not true. For example, he said I submitted all the reports to the USDEA but I know he submitted them personally.'

'We need to check the DEA reports,' Andrea told me.

'I am going to speak to Barbara tomorrow and give her list,' I assured Andrea.

A little later Andrea asked, reading Tony Choizi's statement, 'you did not really make a pass at Tony did you?'

'No, it was the other way round, he went for me on more than one occasion.'

'That sounds nearer the truth,' Andrea surmised, and carried on reading.

On Monday, I spoke to Barbara Green and asked if she could get me the reports from the Dutch and American investigations. She said she would get Commander Passmore to organise that, but she volunteered to co-ordinate the daily conference calls involving the Dutch, Americans, herself and me.

I also spoke to the Commissioner's assistant and gave her the list of items John wanted. 'Good Lord!' She looked shocked as she read that John wanted, amongst other things, four handguns, a rifle with telescopic sites, stun guns, and battering rams. 'Are you planning to start a war? I will have to get the Commissioner to approve this lot.'

Later that day, John drove me out to get statements from the Prison's Head Warden and Zack's

The Mango Mystery

sister. They both confirmed what Douglas had written, in the statement he had prepared for the Commissioner.

Andrea and I spent the next couple of days in the incident room reading and cross- referencing reports and statements. John, I dispatched round the Island to find Douglas. I told him to start at the southern end, as that was where Douglas had met the Commissioner and work his way northwards, checking in all the hotels.

On Tuesday morning, the Commissioner arrived in person, with his driver carrying a large hold-all containing a selection of arms and equipment. He apologised that he could only provide two handguns, and the only rifle he could get hold of was a 22bore, hunting rifle with a telescopic sight. I assured him that was quite okay.

While I had the Commissioner's attention, I told him I would need more manpower and asked if he could assign Merv to help us. He was a little unwilling at first, but he eventually agreed after I assured him that I was certain that no other officers had been involved with Bernie in anything illegal, and that I knew Merv to be reliable and discreet.

Later that day Merv appeared, pleased to see me and greeting me as an old friend. 'We heard you were secretly back on the Island and working on something big,' he said to me. So much for the Commissioners secrecy, I thought, as I introduced Merv to Andrea, informing him about John. I briefed Merv about Xavier Zedanski and gave him a copy of the picture I had taken of him at Gatwick Airport and asked him to check round with all his contacts and see if he could find Zed.

John de Caynoth

I also asked Merv if Bernie had done anything to investigate AK Transport's operation on Kaeta.

'No, I don't think so,' Merv replied, 'Bernie hasn't been himself since Christmas - he has been very preoccupied with something - I've no idea what.'

'Okay.' I explained the background, and asked Merv to see what he could find out about AK Transport. I left, cautioning him not to tell anyone what he was doing.

On Wednesday morning, we held the first conference call. Promptly at eight I dialled in and found Barbara and Jan waiting for me. It would be lunchtime in central Europe.

Jan explained that he had made all the Dutch reports available on a website and gave me the password.

Barbara explained that the Americans would not release their files, but were sending an officer to Kaeta to assist me. For one horrible moment I thought she meant Tony Choizi but Barbara, obviously reading my mind, assured me it would not be him, as he was still in custody. She did warn me that the US Drug Enforcement Agency was most anxious to see the alleged informer on Kaeta arrested, and were concerned that there should be no suggestion of any American involvement in the illegal disclosure of police intelligence.

We then discussed progress with the investigation. For my part, I brought Barbara and Jan up to speed with the Kaetian operation. Barbara had nothing new to add and Jan was most concerned to know if we had found Zedanski, as he viewed him as

The Mango Mystery

the key to unlocking the whole illegal drug operation. He told us that the Vidnova house had been searched by the Swiss Police, who had found the house deserted but had discovered evidence of drugs, and a small quantity of ketamine tablets. 'We think the two ladies must have been tipped off and have crossed the boarder into France,' Jan explained. 'We have put the both the French and Barbadian police on alert, as Mrs Vidnova has a villa on Barbados. We finished the call with Barbara telling me to expect a detective from the USDEA to arrive anytime soon.

On Wednesday afternoon Merv appeared with, to my relief, Detective Jeff Conway. Jeff apologised and said, not knowing where to find me, he gone to the Police Station to ask for me. Fortunately Merv had seen him and, having made sure he was heard telling Jeff I was on secondment in London, had brought Jeff across to the incident room.

Jeff pulled out of his case two slim folders. The first, he explained, contained the reports sent over from Kaeta, covering Douglas Jay's surveillance, together with Tony Choizi's statements, and the second was the report on their internal investigation following the Dutch enquiry.

I did not recognise the reports that were attributed to me. When we compared them to the Kaetian police files they were completely different, much shorter and implying Douglas's guilt. Furthermore, the later papers that I had written, as I came to believe Douglas was not involved, did not appear in the files Jeff presented at all. Jeff confirmed that these were all the reports they had received in

350

Miami and also stated that he did not think Tony Choizi could have changed the details, as all the documents sent from Kaeta had been received by a general email address in the USDEA offices and would have been opened, and filed, by an administrative assistant.

Jeff then drew my attention to the second file he had brought with him. Tony Choizi had arrested a dealer who admitted to possessing fifty-six ketamine tablets. He had told Choizi that he was selling them for good money at the moment, as there were no new supplies coming through, but that would change soon as the contact on Kaeta set up a new smuggling chain from another country.

'It is this statement that got you mixed up in this, as we knew you had moved to London,' Jeff said. 'Also, it has now got Tony into trouble as only thirty tablets were logged into the impounded drug store.'

I asked about Tony Choizi.

'He is in deep shit up to his neck,' he told me. 'He is back in Miami under arrest, while they investigate allegations of illegal drug possession and racketeering. He has been accused of running a protection racket and is also suspected of money laundering. There is also talk of rape charges - if they can find anyone willing to give evidence.'

Later that afternoon, I looked at the incident boards, which were now filling up, and the evidence pointed firmly at Bernie. I was going to have to interview him sooner rather than later, and I was not looking forward to that at all. I desperately hoped that he would have an explanation, as I did not believe he would let us all down. I secretly hoped I could discover

The Mango Mystery

he was innocent and had been working under cover, or something like that.

As I was looking at the boards, lost in thought, Jeff Conway came up beside me saying, 'It looks pretty convincing - have you searched his house yet and established how he got this diary of yours, if indeed it is your diary?'

'No,' I replied, 'we should get a search warrant,' and while this was on my mind, I rang the Commissioner's assistant to organise one.

John de Caynoth

Chapter 66. Mousey

Joelle

The next day, the Thursday morning conference call went ahead as planned, but no one had anything new to report. Jeff Conway joined me for the call, and half-way through the Commissioner walked in and sat with us, listening silently to the discussion. When the conference finished, he walked across to our evidence boards and read through what had been posted up, shaking his head. 'I just can't believe it,' he said to no one in particular, 'I have known Bernie for years and I would never have thought he would get involved in something like this.' Like me, he said he hoped Bernie would have an explanation. He left, telling me a request for a search warrant had been submitted and he expected it to be issued within the day.

John had come into the office, saying he had been to all the hotels at the southern end of the Island, and had not found any sign of Douglas. Jeff Conway offered to help him - they agreed that John would work up the Caribbean side of the Island and Jeff cover the Atlantic side, hoping to finish the search today. As they left, I warned them that I would need them tomorrow as I planned to visit Bernie and search his house.

Later that morning, I took a call from the Commissioner' assistant. 'Inspector,' she said, 'I don't know if this is important or not, but when I collected the guns you asked for from the armoury, they asked me to remind Inspector Strange to return the gun he took out. Apparently, this was the second gun he had, as the first gun fell into the sea by accident.' I thanked her and made a note on the incident board.

The Mango Mystery

At the end of the afternoon, Merv came in to update me on what he had been doing.

'I went to the airport and the docks. There is no record of either Zedanski or Douglas Jay leaving the island over the last couple of weeks. I also showed the photo of Zedanski around, but no one recognised it. What I did find though, was that Zedanski entered the Island using his own passport, claiming he was a tourist. I checked the address he gave on his immigration form, but he had never been there. I have also asked around my contacts and one of them told me that a pick-pocket they call 'Mousey' was boasting he was paid $20 a day to sit in your mother's bar and watch for a man or woman, and was given a mobile number to ring if he saw them. Anyway, this week Mousey was back in the market grumbling that the job was over. He said he seen the woman and phoned the number, and was told there was $50 for him if he found out where the woman was staying. That was easy, Mousey told my contact - he just asked the taxi driver, who told him he was booked to take three people to the Kaeta Island Hotel in the town, but when Mousy phoned the number again, a bloke with a foreign accent said he was not interested any more and the job was over. Mousey never got his $50.'

I asked Merv to find Mousey and bring him in. He replied, 'I have been looking for him all day but he seems to have disappeared and no one knows where.'

Andrea, who had been listening, came over and said, 'That's the hotel we are staying in and that sounds like Zedanski's work. He has had your mother's bar watched because he knows, sooner or later, you or

Douglas are going to turn up there if you are on the Island.'

'Yes,' I agreed, 'but why the sudden loss of interest?'

The Mango Mystery

Chapter 67. Death

Joelle

Friday morning, after the conference call, there were four of us sitting in the in the incident room - me, Andrea, John and Jeff Conway - planning how to approach Bernie and explain that we needed to search his house.

I wanted to interview Bernie myself, before any search, but John wanted us to stay put while he went in first, to check the house was safe.

He explained, 'we know Bernie is armed and, as he is the prime local suspect in this drug gang, we have no idea how he will react. Also, have you considered that Zedanski might there as well?'

We argued for a bit, Jeff siding with John and Andrea keeping quiet, but in the end I put my foot down and just said, 'No, I am going first - you lot wait in the car.'

In the end, we took two cars, John driving me in the Suzuki, and Jeff driving Andrea in his hire car. When we got to Bernie's house, we waited in the cars while he looked for anything unusual. As there seemed to be nothing out of place, he allowed me out of the car. I suggested Jeff remain in his car as he was officially here on the Island as an adviser, and told Andrea I would call her over when I needed her. Meanwhile, John had assembled the rifle and was lying on the ground, behind the Suzuki, sighting on the house. When he was satisfied, he told me I could approach the front door. 'Knock on the door and stand to one side,

John de Caynoth

so I have a clear shot at the door if needed,' he instructed me.

I knocked on the door, standing to one side as instructed, and waited.

Nothing.

I knocked again, but still there was no answer so I knocked for a third time and shouted, 'Bernie, it's Joelle, please - I need to speak with you.' I thought I heard someone move in the house so I shouted again, but got no response. I looked towards John and shrugged to indicate that I was getting no reaction, and he waved me back to the vehicles, covering me with the rifle all the way.

The four of us huddled behind the car and discussed what we should do. John gave Jeff the second pistol, and the two of them went up to reconnoitre round the outside of the house and garden. I decided to overlook that Jeff was only an adviser, and should not be involved. It was not long before they returned, reporting that the blind was down in one of the ground floor rooms and that windows were open upstairs. They had been able to look in some of the other ground floor rooms through the windows, but saw nothing unusual.

I stated the obvious conclusion that either Bernie, and his wife were not in the house or they were there and hiding, hoping we would go away, but either way, we should execute the search warrant.

John took over saying, 'This is what we are going to do. Jeff, you take the rammer and break the door open. I will cover you - if there is anyone behind the door with a gun, I will shoot. If it's clear, we go in together - me first, you covering me - and check the

The Mango Mystery

house. You two,' he looked at Andrea and me, 'stay behind the cars until we give you the all clear.

I heard John shout, 'open the door, or we will break it in!' A few moments later I saw and heard Jeff swing the ram against the door. He swung it again, harder this time, and the door flew open. They both froze momentarily before Jeff dropped the ram and held his pistol at the ready, following John into the house.

Andrea and I waited nervously straining to hear anything indicating activity. We heard nothing and it seemed ages before Jeff came to the door and waved us in.

'The house is safe, but there are two bodies in there. One is in the downstairs room, and the other in a bedroom upstairs. Be warned, the smell is bad and the body upstairs is in a bit of a state.'

We followed Jeff inside and he showed us the downstairs room. I was hit by the stench of death and then noticed a bed, a dialysis machine and various stands and drips in the room. There was the body of a woman in the bed: she looked very peaceful, asleep even, but from her colour, and the smell, I was guessing she had been dead for some days. I recognised her as Mrs Strange, Bernie's wife. I told Andrea to search the room while I followed Jeff up stairs. John was waiting outside one of the bedroom doors and stopped me before I could go in.

He warned me, 'I guess that is, was, Bernie Strange in there, but before you go in I should warn you that it is not a pretty sight. It looks as if he has put a gun in his mouth and pulled the trigger. He left the window open so the smell is not as bad as it might have been, but unfortunately the flies have got to him.'

I went into the room and gagged a bit at the stench, stealing myself as I approached walked the bed. I recognised Bernie lying there. At first glance, he did not look to bad but then I saw the pillow where his head had rested when pulled the trigger, and then the flies and maggots that had invaded his body. I rushed to the window and promptly vomited. When I had recovered, I left the room, shut the door, and went downstairs to find the others.

Andrea handed me a letter, which she had found in the study. On the envelope was written: 'To be opened on my death.' I tore it open and recognised Bernie's writing and signature at the end of the letter. I read;

'To Whom it may concern,

I can no longer live the guilt, betrayal, shame and disgrace of what I have done. I have let my colleagues down, and unwittingly placed Sergeant deNouvelas in great danger, causing much anxiety and worry. To Sergeant deNouvelas, Joelle, my colleague, friend and Godchild, I offer my deepest apologies for the grief I have caused her. I never meant for things to happen as they did.

The reason why I have committed this betrayal is that my wife was diagnosed with cancer four years ago and was told there was a new treatment for her condition being tried in America, which we could not afford. It seemed a gift from heaven when I was offered money for not looking too closely at what was going on at the Zip Line and Slave Museum on the Island. I took the money to pay for the treatment my wife needed, but I was a fool thinking it would stop there. I was paid more money to disclose security measures at the airport, and then when we got a tip off

The Mango Mystery

that the Island was on a drug smuggling route. I was offered still more money to inform the gang of the police operations. I was trapped, and threatened with exposure, and they threatened to harm my wife if I tried to stop. My wife's health deteriorated and her condition became terminal, so I used some of the money to build the treatment room for her. By this time, I had received a sizeable sum of money and we decided to move back to St Lucia where my wife was born and wished to spend her final days

This now cannot happen. I have made my last phone call and told my contact that I am finished, and to call off the hit man. I cannot live with the guilt and shame, and today I sat with my wife and helped her administer a final dose of morphine, holding her hand as she went to sleep, passing away peacefully. I must now take the final step and join her.

The only help I can give to who ever investigates this affair is that in my desk there is a mobile phone that I only used to contact my handler, whose name I never knew, but who had a Swiss telephone number.

To Joelle, my colleague, friend and Godchild, I hope one day you will find it in your heart to forgive me.

I have sorted out my affairs as best I can and left my final instructions with an attorney at Rail and Company.

With my deepest apologies,

Bernard Strange.

I had to bite back my tears, I never knew Mrs. Strange was ill - Bernie had never said a word. I thought of what he must have gone through over the last four years, silently and alone, watching his wife slowly loose her health and while he got deeper and deeper into trouble. If only he had said something, we could have worked things out and it needed not have ended this way.

John de Caynoth

I was shaking and trying not to cry. Very gently, Andrea took my arm and led me back to the car saying, 'sit there - we will finish searching the house.' I cried once I was alone.

After a while, I composed my self and went back into the house. Andrea and John had nearly finished their search and found nothing, except in the library, where Andrea showed me, sitting on the desk, the original copy of my hand written diary and notes and, in the drawer, a mobile phone.

'I guess that diary is what Douglas saw,' she said to me.

'Yes, I guess it is,' I replied. I always knew keeping a personal diary would be important, but I never guessed in this way.

The four of us stood by the cars, strangely reluctant to leave. John commented that they had found no second gun and Andrea reminded him that Bernie claimed he had lost it overboard. John thought that was unlikely and a better explanation was that he given the gun to Zedanski.

Jeff said, 'Taking you point, Joelle, that I have no authority on the Island, it might be better not to mention my part in today's exercise.'

I agreed and said I would report that he was an observer. I had a thought and turned to John asking, 'Did you find Douglas?'

'No,' he replied, 'we have checked all the hotels on the Island, all except the smaller boarding houses in Kaeta Town, and found nothing: he really has just disappeared.'

The Mango Mystery

Chapter 68. Jasmine

Joelle

We got back to the incident room in the afternoon. Jeff decided there was nothing more for him to do and he arranged to return to Miami. I asked Andrea to take a statement from him before he left.

There seemed no point in keeping our presence on the Island secret any more so went to see the Commissioner. I was surprised when John came with me but as he reminded me, 'the danger is not over yet, Zedanski is still on the Island somewhere.'

The Commissioner cut his meeting short to speak with me as soon as I arrived. I showed him Bernie's suicide note and told him what we had been doing and what we had found. I could see he was upset, but he did not say anything, he just congratulated me on closing the case quickly. I had to explain that I could not close the case finally until after a postmortem and inquest.

Also, I told him, 'I need to find Douglas - he is still hiding somewhere on the Island, and we need to find Zedanski as we believe he is still at large on the Island. There are also the other strands to this investigation: the two women, Lecarrow and Vidnova have not yet been caught, and then there is AK Transport, which needs investigation.'

The Commissioner, obviously thinking about his budgets, agreed we should stay and finalise the Bernie investigation and look for Zedanski. He told me he did not think we should spend Police resources looking for Douglas as it was his decision to go into hiding, but I pointed out he was a key witness and, at the very least,

John de Caynoth

we needed a statement from him. I offered to spare the Commissioner's budgets as we no longer needed to work in secret but could now work from Police Headquarters, and I offered to put the team up at 'Windrush' and move out of the hotel. The Commissioner was very pleased.

Before I left the Police building, I went down to the squad room and was pleasantly surprised by how pleased everyone was to see me. News of Bernie's suicide was the main topic of conversation, with words of disbelief echoing round the room.

John was waiting for me down there and was deep in conversation with Merv and one of the detective constables, so I walked across to join them. John greeted me saying, 'Merv has done an excellent job, copying your picture of Zedanski round all the possible departure points from the Island - even the private marinas - in case he tries to slip out by boat.'

It occurred to us, though, if Zed tries to leave by plane or through the port, he was clever enough to realise he couldn't use his own passport, so he would have to get another one. Merv had not picked up any clue about anyone trying to obtain a forged passport, but two passports have been reported stolen over the last week. One was a woman, and the other was an American man, in his fifties, name of Peter Black.

I asked Merv if he had anything else new. "We have just put out an alert for anyone travelling under the name Peter Black. We have also spent the last day or so going round with the pictures of Zedanski. I did ask about AK Transport though and they seem legitimate. They run a couple of old diesel powered

The Mango Mystery

cargo vessels out of Miami carrying what ever needs transporting between Miami and around Caribbean.'

I thanked Merv and told him that we would be moving our operation from the Judicial Building back to the Police station. He looked relieved and said it would be a relief to have a senior officer around again. He had done a good job as 'acting sergeant', but I think he had found it a bit stressful over the last few weeks, during the time Bernie began to loose his grip. He offered to clear a room for us to use and asked me what I wanted to do with Bernie's office. I told him we would sort it out next week.

John and I went back to the Judicial Building. Jeff had already gone, and I told Andrea that, on Monday, we would pack up this room and move to the Police Headquarters. I also told John and Andrea that we all having the weekend off and that tomorrow, Saturday morning, we would check out of the hotel and go stay at my home, 'Windrush'. I added, 'I won't be with you this evening, as I'm going to see my family, but I will come back in the morning to collect you.'

John gave me a lift to 'Windrush' in the Suzuki and, ever careful, he insisted on checking the grounds before he would leave me. Mary was down at the bar working, but I found Jasmine upstairs studying. She was delighted to see me.

'Come on - leave that for the evening. I need a bottle of wine and time with you to catch up with all the gossip.' She happily dropped her books and came down stairs with me. Jasmine prepared a snack for me while I opened a bottle of wine, and we went out onto the veranda to talk.

'You have lost weight,' I said to her.

John de Caynoth

'No I haven't,' she replied sharply, 'I am too fat.'

We sat in silence for a few moments until I changed the subject and started to tell her about London and what I had been doing. Naturally this led on to a discussion of the case and that led me into asking Jasmine what Douglas had said to her, when he phoned.

'Not much,' she replied, 'he just said he had some urgent business and had to disappear. He did say that if anyone came looking for him, to say he had gone home and to report it to Bernie. I think he was talking about the man you call Zedanski and he sounded quite frightened.'

'Did Zedanski come looking?' I asked.

'Yes, but I did not see him, Mary did and she said he was frightening, but Mary could not tell him anything and so eventually he left. I did see him in the road once, but I have not seen him for a few days now.'

I told Jasmine I was worried about Douglas, not being able to find him, or even get in touch with him. She replied that she was worried about him as well and I was shocked when I saw tears collecting in her eyes. I asked what was troubling her.

'Nothing.' She said and ran into the house. But she came back before long and said she was sorry, 'It is just that I really miss you and Douglas, and not knowing what is going on.' She looked accusingly at me and said, 'you have been away wrapped up in your police stuff and, you know, Douglas is the nearest I have had for a father since we came to this Island.'

I was taken by surprise, and shocked, She was right: I had been ignoring the family and selfishly

The Mango Mystery

thinking only of Douglas for myself, and taking him for granted, never considering how Jasmine felt, and I now I was beginning to realise what Jasmine had seen in Douglas. I saw how they had done things together, like working on the car, going shopping, helping with homework, all the things a real father should be doing. Suddenly I felt my heart breaking, I did not know whether it was for Jasmine, Douglas, or Bernie, all the people who had become most precious to me and who were now gone, or in trouble.

Jasmine broke into my sad reflections and asked, 'did you say Douglas had seen your original handwritten notes and diaries at Bernie's house?'

'Yes, that's what he told the Commissioner,' I replied.

'And you said that Bernie told everyone he was leaving Kaeta when he retired, and in his suicide note he said they had planned to move to St Lucia?'

'Yes,' I replied, 'but what of it?' not understanding where Jasmine was going.

'Really mother,' she replied exasperated, 'for a detective inspector you are a bit dim.'

Still I did not know what she was getting at.

'You told me that Douglas once said that he might move to the Island,' Jasmine prompted me. Well, don't you see?' She was really exasperated now as she spelt it out for me.

'Bernie's planning to move, so he puts his house up for sale. Douglas is thinking of moving here, so what does he do - goes house hunting and gets shown round Bernie's old house.'

John de Caynoth

The penny dropped and I realised that Jasmine had just unlocked the mystery of how to find Douglas and tomorrow, Saturday, I would go looking.

But Saturday did not go as planned.

The Mango Mystery

Chapter 69. The Arrest

Joelle

I was up early on Saturday morning. I knew that almost all the real-estate sales on the Island were handled by one firm of land agents and, if Jasmine's theory was correct, there would be a good chance that Douglas had been to see them as a prospective purchaser.

I drove my Toyota into Kaeta town and parked outside the Land Agent's offices before 9.00am, waiting for them to open. The manager arrived and unlocked the main door - I followed him in. I had to wait while he organised himself. He offered me coffee and asked me how he could help me.

'Have you had any dealings with a visitor to the Island - Mr Douglas Jay?' I asked.

'Indeed we have,' he replied, to my relief, 'Mr Jay is looking for a property on the Island, he is thinking of relocating, and we have shown him around various properties but the one he seems most interested in is one of our new apartments at the marina in Grumble.'

'Would you know where Mr Jay is at the moment?' I asked nervously.

'Yes I do. He asked to rent an apartment for a month to see if he liked the marina and the life-style down there. It's very nautical, quite different to anywhere else on the Island. Are you a friend of Mr Jay's?'

I showed him my police identity and immediately he looked worried.

'We ran what checks we could but he wanted the apartment in a hurry and, as he looked genuine, we let him take it. What has he done?'

'It is okay,' I assured him, 'he's not done anything: I am just trying to trace him as a witness.'

'Oh, thank goodness for that,' the manager said, relieved.

At that moment my mobile phone rang. It was Merv.

'Joelle, where are you?' he asked in a panic, and rushed on with his explanation, before I could answer, 'We have just taken a call from Kaeta Air, at the airport, telling us that a man called Peter Black has just bought a ticket on this morning's flight to Barbados. What shall I do?'

'What time does the flight leave?' I asked.

'Five past ten,' Merv replied.

I checked my watch - we only had forty minutes. I spoke to Merv again.

'Okay, calm down, Merv. Phone Kaeta Air and tell them to say that the aircraft has a fault of some sort and the flight is delayed. Tell them to hold all the passengers in the departure lounge and on no account to approach Peter Black, until we get there. Tell them he is dangerous and may be carrying a gun. Then pull together as many officers as you can and meet me at the airport.'

I went to run out of the shop but stopped halfway to ask the manager for the address of the apartment Douglas had rented. He gave me a slip of paper and started to give me directions. I did not wait to listen, I ran out to the car and drove to the hotel.

The Mango Mystery

I left the Toyota right outside the hotel entrance to the annoyance of the doorman, who told me I could not park there. I ignored him and rushed inside - fortunately both John and Andrea were sitting in reception, packed and ready to leave.

I explained the situation. We needed to get to the airport, meeting Merv there. John and Andrea took the Suzuki and I told John to take the lead, put the lights and siren on and get there as quickly as possible: I would follow in the Toyota. They left using the back way to the underground car park and I went out of the front door to the Toyota, but it was not there. I stared round wildly thinking, it could not have been stolen, could it? But then I saw the doorman walking towards me and I asked him where the car was.

'I have moved it to the car park for you,' he said smugly, handing me the keys.

I swore at him, and ran, heading for the vehicle ramp to the car park hoping I would catch the Suzuki before John and Andrea drove off. Luckily, John was waiting at the top of the ramp for me.

'We saw the doorman parking your car down there, Andrea is waiting beside it and I will wait here for you,' he explained.

I saw the doorman out of the corner of my eye walking towards the Suzuki and heard him shout to John, 'You can't leave that there!' I ran down the ramp so I did not hear John's reply. Andrea waved to me and I ran over to her, unlocking the car as I went. We drove out of the car park, John saw us coming and set off at speed with the siren blaring and blue light flashing with my little Toyota clinging closely to his tail.

John de Caynoth

The departure facilities at Kaeta Airport are gradually being rebuilt. The first phase, which was the construction of five new departure gates with associated security checking and X-ray equipment, had been completed but the second phase, construction of a large new departure hall with shops, bars and restaurants, was still only a shell, separated from the new departure gates by temporary screening. The old departure hall was still used and was connected to the new area by a single temporary corridor. This was relatively small, with a capacity of about two hundred people, and got very crowded especially when an International flight was due to leave.

The passenger entrance to this hall was via the emigration-control desks, passing through the security check with its single, old X-ray machine and into a central seating area. The seating was arranged in rows with each row comprising a double set of seats connected back to back. Small shops had been set up around the perimeter of the hall, further restricting the area available to passengers.

Passengers left the area through a double door, which used to be the old departure gate, but which now connected to the new corridor. There were two other access points - an emergency exit behind the toilets, and the staff door adjacent to some small offices leading through to the arrivals hall.

When we arrived at the airport, I was immediately accosted by the airport manager, demanding to know why we had locked down his airport, and how long we were going to be. He explained, 'we have two international flights leaving this today and already I have people and vehicles building up outside the

The Mango Mystery

airport. The departure hall is full, so I am holding passengers outside. It is already so crowded that soon I am going to have stop disembarkation from incoming flights, as there is no room for the passengers to get away from the airport. It is going to take all day to clear this backlog!'

I could see his point - there were people milling around outside the airport buildings trying to find out what was happening, and vehicles trying to get to the airport were already queuing on the access road, and spilling out on to the main road.

I told the manager that we would be a quick as possible, but until I gave him clearance the departure hall had to remain locked down.

Merv had spotted me and walked towards me, asking for instructions. I told him to make sure all the doors in the departure hall were locked, and to station officers at the doors to make sure they stayed shut. The four of us, Merv, John, Andrea and I, went to the CCTV room, scanning the departure hall, looking for Peter Black. The Kaeta Air agent, who had first reported Peter Black, came with us and pointed him out - he was sitting on a bench in the middle of the hall. We watched as he stood to look at the departure board, checking his watch, and then returned to his seat where he picked up a newspaper.

The last time I saw Zedanski, he had black hair, was unshaven, sporting black stubble, and always wore dark, or black clothes. He had very dark, almost black eyes, and the whole combination gave him an evil, saturnine appearance. This man was tanned, dressed in a colourful, caribbean shirt, white slacks, flip flops and was clean-shaven with a shaved head and was wearing

John de Caynoth

dark glasses, even in the relatively dim light of the departure hall.

John and I looked at him. 'That is not the Zedanski I recognize,' I said.

John agreed, but Andrea said, 'Don't be daft, anyone can change their appearance by having a shave and wearing different clothes. The give-away is the dark glasses, he is the only person in the hall wearing them and I bet that's to hide his eyes.'

'Well, whoever he is,' I said, 'he is not Peter Black, so we go in and arrest him, and I want to be the one to do it.'

'If you are going in, I am coming with you,' John said, 'but is that wise? He will recognise both of us, which might spook him - who knows what he will do.'

'Who else is going to do it?' I replied, 'Merv and the local police are in uniform and will stick out a mile as soon as they enter the hall, and Andrea can't go in on her own.'

Reluctantly, John agreed and we decided the three of us would go into the Departure Hall. Merv, and the remaining constable, would follow us but remain out of site in the security area until we had completed the arrest, but would then come forward to help us get the suspect out of the Airport.

Merv cleared the way through the crowds. When we got to the security area, he stood back to let John enter the departure hall first, followed by Andrea and I. From somewhere, I noticed John had acquired a linen jacket and had a gun in his hand, hidden under the jacket. We weaved our way through the people in the hall, making our way towards the suspect, who

The Mango Mystery

fortunately was reading his newspaper and had his back towards us. This is too easy, I thought, as John walked up behind our man. He approached the passengers, a white family of four, sitting in the seats backing Zedanski and John putting a finger to his lips gestured to them to be silent, showing them his identity card indicating they should move. Initially, the man looked as if he was going to argue so John gestured them to be quite again and showed the gun - they could not get out of the way fast enough. At the same time, Andrea moved round one end of the row of seats to approach Zedanski from the left, while I approached him from the right. As the people behind moved, Zedanski turned to look over his shoulder - oblivious to John - who moved to one side as the family vacated their seats. Zedanski returned his attention to his paper so I moved up to stand just to right of him, as John had instructed, still thinking that this was just to easy.

'Xavier Zedanski,' I said loudly, 'You are under arrest for the murder of Detective Constable Marika van Dam.' (She was the murdered, undercover police woman) and, I was going to add, the attempted murder of Detective Inspector Joelle deNouvelas, but as I spoke, Zedanski hurled at me the small ruck sack that was on his lap, throwing me off balance. Leaping to his feet, he ran towards the double doors leading to the departure gates. Passengers scattered in front him, mainly because they had seen John leap over the seats with his gun in his hand, charging after Zedanski.

Zedanski ran hard at the gates, expecting them to open, and looked stunned and shocked when they remained firmly shut. He turned, peering left and right, looking for another escape route but saw John, standing just beyond arms reach, pointing the gun at his legs.

John de Caynoth

'If you so much as twitch,' John said to him, 'I will shoot your knee caps off and you will never walk again.'

Zedanski put his hands up. John remained where he was, aiming at Zedanski's knees. Andrea and I walked up to him: I told him again he was under arrest and cautioned him, while Andrea handcuffed him. Merv and the constable had joined us by now and John, still aiming at Zedanskis knees moved to one side while Merv searched him for any weapons. Search completed, Merv did not remove Andrea's handcuffs but attached himself to Zedanski with a second set of cuffs. He, and the constable, marched Zedanski out to the waiting Police van.

The congestion by now was so bad, that there was no way I could get the Toyota out from where I left it, so I joined John and Andrea in the Suzuki. Driving along the pedestrian walk way, behind the Police van - with the blue lights flashing - we got out of the airport and followed Merv to the police headquarters building.

Zedanski was processed and put in an interview room. Andrea and I went in to question him, and John and Merv came in with us, standing at the door. It was a waste of time: Zedanski insisted he was Peter Black and refused to say anything except that he wanted a solicitor. Andrea had searched the rucksack that he threw at me, finding a passport in the name of Xavier Zedanski, but when I showed it to him he just denied it was his bag and said he did not know what we were talking about.

I could see we were not going to get anywhere, so I told Merv to charge him with murder, attempted

The Mango Mystery

murder and anything else he could think of, and lock him in the cells until Monday.

I had one last job to do before we went to 'Windrush' and suggested John and Andrea went to the hotel, checked out, collected their luggage and met me back at police headquarters.

As I walked upstairs, Merv caught me and said, 'I forgot to tell you earlier but Mousey was found yesterday. He was floating in the harbour, and had been shot in the head.'

'You can bet that was Zedanski's work,' I replied, telling him about the two bodies found in Amsterdam, 'That is Zedanski's preferred method of execution.'

Merv shrugged and said he would add it to the charge sheet.

I went up to Bernie's old office and sat at his desk. Putting my feelings of sorrow to one side, I picked the phone up to ring Jan van den Leuven in Amsterdam, using an emergency number he had given me. He answered promptly, and was delighted when I told him we had Zedanski under arrest. Of course, Jan wanted him back in Amsterdam as soon as possible. I did not think there would be a problem, but we would have to go through a judicial process before I could release him into Jan's custody. However, I did agree that Jan could send a couple of officers to Kaeta to observe the questioning, before escorting Zedanski back to Amsterdam, once we had the clearance to move him.

'Another piece of good news,' Jan announced when we had finished discussing Zedanski, 'we have found the two women - Lecarrow and Vidnova. They turned up at Vidnova's villa on Barbados and are currently under surveillance by the Barbadian Police. We are holding off arresting them until we have rounded up the whole gang, but with the evidence we are now building up - from the house search, company records, and the phone number you provided - we should be able to move soon, especially now Zedanski has been arrested.'

'That's interesting,' I told Jan, 'Barbados was where Zedanski was trying to fly to this morning.'

When we got to 'Windrush' Mary was there to welcome us, treating John and Andrea like old friends as she showed them to their bedrooms, and asking what they would like for lunch. I noticed Jasmine was more circumspect, regarding John with some suspicion, but was friendly enough for him not to notice.

The excitement of the morning had caught up with me and I was suddenly feeling very tired, so I made an excuse and took a cup of coffee out the veranda. Jasmine joined me and, in her usual blunt way, asked me if I had a 'thing' going with John. I told her I had not and explained who John was. Jasmine asked me if I had found Douglas yet. Somewhat exasperated, I explained that I had been busy all morning and not had a chance, but that I would go and look for him after lunch. Jasmine wandered off muttering something about priorities. I was cross - she was living in her own little world, with no tolerance for my pressures.

However, the conversation did remind me to look for the address I had been given. I turned out all my pockets but I did not have piece of paper with it written on. I had worn a jacket first thing against the

The Mango Mystery

early morning chill: perhaps I put the paper into one of its pockets. I went to find the jacket but remembered I had left it in the Toyota, which was stuck at the airport. The airport manager had moaned it would take all day to clear the airport and I was puzzling out how I might get to the Toyota to retrieve the address when Mary called me in for lunch.

John de Caynoth

Chapter 70. Found

Joelle

'Jasmine, will you stop pushing food round your plate and eat it,' I said to her, irritably. Mary told me to leave her alone, saying she would eat when she was hungry. I subsided into a morose silence, feeling cross with everyone.

Mary had cooked an enormous shellfish tart which she served with sweet potato chips and a green salad from the garden, which John and Andrea told her was really good. After lunch, they decided to spend the afternoon sunbathing in the garden.

Jasmine went off upstairs, on her own, and I went to see if I could get my Triumph motorcycle started. I intended to use it to get to the airport to retrieve Douglas' address. Before I left for London, I had connected one of those fancy conditioning chargers to the battery and asked Jasmine to occasionally to run the engine. Bless her, she had dutifully started it every two every two weeks, and that made me feel even more guilty for telling her off at the lunch table. I wheeled the bike out of the garage and rode it up and down the drive to check it was all working, leaving it by the front door while I went to change into my leathers.

When I came back, Andrea and John were taking a break from soaking up the sun and were looking at the Triumph. Andrea said I was mad riding that thing, but John wanted to come with me.

'Do you have a spare helmet that I could use? I could ride pillion,' he said.

The Mango Mystery

'I don't need you John, Zedanski is off the streets so there is no danger anymore.'

He pleaded with me, saying he would love a ride on the motorbike: anyway, he would like to see round the Island and would just be bored sitting around with Andrea. I was anxious to get on and certainly did not want John sitting behind me, hugging me, and hanging around when I found Douglas, so to get rid of him I told him I would be perfectly okay and, anyway, I wanted to see Douglas on my own.

The airport was still very crowded, with vehicles trying to get in and out, but with the bike I managed to get through the traffic and find the Toyota where I had left it. The jacket was in the car and I soon found the slip of paper, which I had stuffed into a pocket.

On the bike, it did not take me long to get to Grumble but the development was big: it was not that easy to find the apartment and in the end I had to ask for directions. I left the Triumph in the car park, with my helmet and leather jacket, and walked to the rear of the apartment block to which I had been directed. I knocked on the door, twice, but there was no answer. I shouted my name in case Douglas was in, but not opening the door, but still did not get any reaction. I assumed Douglas was not there, thinking I would find somewhere to wait and try again later. I walked down to the marina where there were a few shops and bars, which catered for the yachting fraternity. I walked up to bar intending to get a coffee while I waited, but sitting on his own at an outside table, tucked away behind a large leafy plant growing in a pot, was Douglas, reading a book.

John de Caynoth

'Hello Douglas, may I join you,' I said. He physically jumped in his seat and looked up, panicking.

'Joelle, you scared me death,' he said as he recovered his wits, pulling up a seat for me to join him. 'How did you find me?'

I replied, 'Actually it was Jasmine who worked it out. She remembered you once said you might move to Kaeta. Also, if you had seen my diary and notes on Bernie's desk, you must have been in his house. As Bernie had the house for sale, well, you had probably been through a real estate agent, and as there is only one of any size on the Island, it was fairly simple to get the address off them.'

'And I thought I was well hidden,' Douglas said ruefully.

'You were,' I assured him, 'we knew you must be still on the Island as we checked all the departure records, but it still took over a week to find you. Anyway, I have some good news for you.'

'That's what I wanted to hear - I have been bored stiff here and afraid to move anywhere, so I need some cheering up,' Douglas smiled at me.

'What made you hide away in the first place?' I asked him.

He explained, 'One evening, I came out of Mary's restaurant and someone took a shot at me. I was lucky: it was dark and they missed, but only by a whisker - you must have seen the damage done to your car. When I got back to 'Windrush', Jasmine told me she had seen a man hanging round. I recognised him as Zedanski, and, well, I suppose I panicked a bit, I am not used to being shot at. Anyway, I decided it was much too

The Mango Mystery

dangerous to remain at 'Windrush', and also putting Jasmine and Mary at risk, so I decided to disappear for a bit, hoping that Zedanski would give up.'

I assured Douglas he was safe to come out of hiding, 'we arrested Zedanski this morning - trying to leave the Island. He is in police custody in Kaeta town at the moment. We have also identified the two people we think are the gang leaders and they are currently under police surveillance in Bermuda, shortly to be arrested when all the evidence has been assembled.'

'And what has happened with Bernie?' Douglas paused as a thought struck him. 'What are you doing here anyway, Joelle? I thought you were in London.'

'I was, but the Commissioner here acted on the information you gave him and requested assistance from London to investigate the local police. I was seconded with Andrea and John McDuff to lead the investigation here. I am afraid that your suspicions about Bernie proved to be correct. He had been providing information to the drug gang, but on a more positive note he was working on his own and no one else in the police department was involved.'

'What has happened to Bernie - has he been arrested?' Douglas asked.

'No,' I replied, explaining that Bernie had committed suicide, feeling quite upset on telling Douglas how we had found him. He was very sympathetic, holding my hand as I related the circumstances of Bernie's death.

'Come on Douglas,' I said, not wishing to get maudlin, 'you can leave here now. Zedanski is in prison, the gang has been broken and we can get on with our lives. Come back to 'Windrush' with me.'

The Mango Mystery

Chapter 71. Something Important

Douglas

I drove my hire car back to 'Windrush' and Joelle followed me on the Triumph. She joked that, now she had found me, she did not want to let me out of her sight.

I drove along feeling very relieved that the drug investigation was over, and that Joelle had come to find me and ask me back to the house. There was only one big niggle - where did my relationship with Joelle now stand? She had seemed friendly enough, and pleased to see me, but I knew the '*something important*' was still to come.

Mary had gone to work, but Jasmine saw us arriving, rushing down to give me a big hug, welcoming me back. I felt I had to explain to Jasmine why I had disappeared: she wanted to know every detail of what I had been doing for the last few days. Eventually, Joelle saved me from regaling events by suggesting we sit in the garden with a drink, watching the sunset.

Joelle went to find a bottle of wine and I collected my case from the car, taking it upstairs to the room I used the last time I was here. To my surprise, John MacDuff was in there, changing his clothes, while swigging a beer. I apologised and retreated. I had not expected to find McDuff here, but I thought I realised what was going on. I left my case in the hall and used the downstairs toilet to change my shirt, feeling anxious - concerned that the room I had once considered mine, was now occupied by someone else.

John de Caynoth

I told myself to calm down, but still fearing Joelle's explanation, walked out to the veranda to find her.

She was sitting at a table with a glass of wine, as John, having made his way down from the bedroom, pulled up a chair to join her. Joelle saw me and invited me to sit also, 'you know John of course.'

'Yes, we just met again upstairs.' I replied feeling like the unwelcome guest in a group of three.

Joelle went to fetch me a glass, and John and I eyed each other while she was gone.

I sat silently while the two of them discussed what needed to be done next week and when they could return to London. I listened to John saying that the first thing he would do when he returned was to move his stuff out of Joelle's flat as unfortunately he would not need to be with her twenty-four-seven any more. That conversation petered out and I watched Joelle giving John meaningful looks, which he ignored until eventually Joelle said, 'John, Douglas and I have a lot to talk about - if you don't mind.'

'Oh, sorry,' he replied, 'I will push off then,' giving me a strange look as he wandered off.

Joelle and I sat silently after he left. Joelle was twiddling the wine glass in her hand and peering into it as if looking for inspiration while I waited for, what I thought would be, my dismissal.

'What is the matter Joelle?' I prompted.

She did not reply immediately, but eventually said, 'I am not sure how to tell you this: I don't want you to be upset, but I have to tell you because we can't

The Mango Mystery

have a relationship if we have secrets and don't fully trust each other.'

I heard the words 'can't have a relationship' and my heart sank as Joelle continued,'

'John and I were in Germany tracking down the Lecarrow and Vidnova women. Well, one night I had too much to drink and we slept together,' she blurted out, speaking quickly, as though to get her words out as fast as possible.

She paused, searching my face with her eyes. I felt physically winded and something very heavy landed at the pit of my stomach. Every word spoken by the woman I loved, as she told me she had slept with another man, seemed to crush every cell in my body, and I felt as if a huge pressure was squashing me into a little ball.

Joelle continued, her face strained, 'it was only the once - we never did anything like that again, but I felt so guilty - still feel guilty - and I needed to tell you. Please, Douglas believe me, I don't know what made do it, the last thing I wanted was to hurt you and I am so sorry....' Her explanation trailed off into silence as she looked at me, so sorrowfully, waiting for my reaction.

I had only really heard the words, 'we slept together,' and now I was feeling sick, trying to control a flood of emotions. All I could manage to say was, ' thank you for telling me.'

We sat looking at each other for a little longer and Joelle took my hand saying, 'Please say something, Douglas.'

I answered, 'There is nothing to say, is there - it happened, you have told me, and we have to get on

John de Caynoth

with our lives,' I squeezed her hand and she smiled at me.

We sat in silence holding hands until Joelle decided that she needed to put the Triumph away.

I walked around the garden thinking about Joelle, and John: he was in my room upstairs, he was moving his things out of her flat, and they have slept together. I wished so much it had not happened, but it had, and I wondered what more Joelle would tell me. As I stood under the trees in the front garden, Joelle did not see me but I watched her carry her leathers and helmet into the house and I could feel my heart breaking as she closed the door behind her. Almost as soon as it closed, it opened again, and she walked out followed by John. She mounted the Triumph and started the engine. John climbed on to the bike behind her and, sitting very close, put his arms around her, and they speed off down the drive, out of the gate and away.

The Mango Mystery

Chapter 72. Gone

Joelle

I could see Douglas was upset and I wanted to take him in my arms and cuddle him to make things better. With hindsight, that is probably what I should have done, but at the time I thought he wanted to be alone so I went to put the bike away, thinking that I would find him later and take him to my room where we could be on our own, and I could tell him how much I loved him.

It did not work like that, though. As I took my helmet into the house, John caught me, asking me to give him a lift to the Glass Bar, telling me he thought it would be a good idea if he kept out of the way for a bit. Anyway, he wanted to drink some beer and eat out. The Toyota was still at the airport and Mary had taken the other car, so we only had the motorbike for transport.

I dropped him at the restaurant: he asked me in for a drink but I declined, telling him I wanted to get back to Douglas. I had a feeling John was looking for crack between Douglas and me, and would not be too slow in taking advantage of it, but I was not going to give him that opportunity.

I got back to 'Windrush' to find Andrea waiting for me.

'I don't know what is the matter with Jasmine,' she told me, 'I heard a terrible wailing and rushed downstairs to find her crying her eyes out.'

'Where is she now?' I asked.

'In her room, I think,' was the reply.

John de Caynoth

I knocked on Jasmine's bedroom door, getting no answer. I gently opened the door to see her lying on her bed, crying silently into her pillows. I sat on the bed beside her and stroked her hair asking her what was wrong.

After a few moments, between tears, she sobbed, 'He has gone,' wailing, 'what did you do to him, Mother?'

I knew she had to be talking about Douglas, so asked her to calm down and tell me what had happened.

'After you rode away with John on your motorbike, Douglas came into the house. I was in the television room, and he came in, saying goodbye to me. When I asked him where he was going he said he did not know, back to England probably. When I asked him why, he said it is just better if he left now - it would be easier for everyone if he just went quickly. He wished me luck with my exams and said if I ever made it to England to look him up. And then he left.' She started crying again.

I thought, hell and damnation, why is the man so sensitive and always jumping to the wrong conclusion, sneaking off like a wounded animal without even saying anything. I had a real quandary now. I should stay with Jasmine and comfort her but equally I should go and find Douglas before it is too late.

'Jasmine,' I said, 'I need to go and find Douglas and bring him back.'

'Yes,' she replied adamantly, 'you do.'

Andrea was downstairs and asked me what was going on. I explained as I dressed in my leathers and

The Mango Mystery

went out to the Triumph, which I had not yet put away. I was banking on Douglas going back to the apartment, and I thought there was a good chance I could catch him on the road.

The apartment was dark and unoccupied. I hung around for a bit, thinking he must have taken another route, but after half-an-hour he still had not appeared. Rather dejectedly, I mounted the Triumph and sat there wondering what to do. Eventually I rode off towards Nelson's Dock: there were not that many roads on the Island, so if I rode around slowly, I must eventually spot his car. I spent an hour, doing the circuit around Nelsons Dock, Alice Hill, and the Sugar Plantation, returning to Grumble. I checked the apartment again, but it was still empty so headed off in the other direction - out to Grumble point and past Three Sisters Bay. As I rode, I remembered the last time he had walked off like this, nearly killing himself in a motorbike accident. I feared for him again, as I remembered that on that occasion he had been to Three Sisters Bay. Perhaps he had gone there again tonight?

Three Sisters Bay was where my father used to take me swimming when I was a little girl - it is one of my favourite places on the Island. It is not easily accessible, as it is some distance from the road, and approached by an unmade track. While it is possible to get a vehicle about halfway there, the last half-mile has to be on foot.

I turned off down the track and, to my relief, soon found Douglas' car. I parked the bike beside it and took the leathers off. It was a warm night and I would not need them to walk the last half-mile.

John de Caynoth

As I approached the beach, I saw what a beautiful night it was. The moon was nearly full and was glinting across the bay, casting a delicate light, which turned the white sand into glittering grains. In front of me, the small waves shone like liquid silver as they lapped gently on the beach and behind me in the trees, the tree frogs squeaked noisily as they went about their business. I stood for moment, savouring the scene. I looked along the beach and saw the silhouette of a person lying in the sand half way down.

He was silhouetted by the moonlight. He sat up as he saw me approaching - I sat down beside him.

He said nothing. 'I seem to spend a lot of time looking for you these days,' I said.

Douglas replied, 'I thought we were finished and you had found someone else.'

'Well, I have not and unless you want it that way, we are not finished. I love you and that's why I am here looking for you again, you silly man.'

'But John is living in your flat, he staying at 'Windrush' with you, you are sleeping together and went off for the evening on your bike. What did you think I was going to do, hang around until you decided to tell me to push off?' Douglas said, aggrieved.

I was impatient and cross with him for always playing the injured party, jumping to conclusions. I responded, 'You know very well he was assigned to protect me - that is why he was at the flat, and he slept alone in the living room - certainly not with me. Mary put him in that guest room at 'Windrush'. You are not a guest anymore, you belong, and you would have shared my bedroom and slept with me, if you hadn't rushed

The Mango Mystery

off. As for spending the evening with him, I took him down to Mary's. I wanted him out of the way so I could spend the evening with you and not have him lurking around us all the time. Finally,' I paused for breath, 'I told you it was a mistake sleeping with him. I did not enjoy it, in fact I spent the whole time wishing I was with you!'

All my love mingling with frustration was coming out now and I continued, 'and anyway, you slept with that Jean Handley - twice - so what is the big deal!' I subsided exhausted, but at least I got a reaction.

'Jean Handley was different.'

'Oh yes! Why so?'

'Well for a start, the first time was when you were being a police woman, checking up on me and holding me at arms length, and the second time, you and I had broken up anyway.'

'Well, that's not the point, I still loved you and felt very hurt when you told me, but I trusted you and did not walk out on you,' I said, angrily.

Douglas looked at me very seriously. I thought for a moment I had gone too far, but he said quietly, 'sorry, Joelle, I am the biggest fool in the world,' he paused, 'I really do love you.'

We kissed and lay in the sand, holding each other, but then Douglas pulled away from me. I felt a sharp pang of fear as I wondered what he was going to do.

'Will you marry me?' was what he asked.

I felt the tears of joy and relief welling up and replied, 'Only if you promise never to walk out on me again.'

John de Caynoth

Epilogue

Joelle and Douglas spent the night together on the beach, returning to 'Windrush' on Sunday morning to announce their engagement. Mary was delighted and Jasmine was overjoyed. John MacDuff, wished them well, deciding to stay in the hotel before returning early to the UK. Andrea asked if she could be a maid-of-honour. Later that day they all went down to Mary's restaurant to celebrate with Champagne.

Joelle and Andrea spent another couple of weeks on Kaeta finalising their reports, attending the post mortem on Bernie and Mrs Strange before giving their evidence. The inquest ruled that Bernie had assisted his wife's suicide and then committed suicide himself, while the balance of his mind was disturbed.

Bernie had left a will. He instructed that if any assets were left after monies acquired illegally had been confiscated, he would like them to pass to his goddaughter, Joelle deNouvelas. The disposition of his estate remains ongoing.

Jan van den Leuven came to Kaeta to observe the questioning of Zedanski. With the weight of evidence accumulating, Zedanski admitted to the murder of Marika van Dam and attempted murder of Joelle and Douglas, but said that he had been acting under instructions from Marina Vidnova.

Marina Vidnova and Mrs Lecarrow were arrested and charged with murder and various drug offences.

Tony Choizi admitted to a string of offences, concerning drugs, protection racketeering, and money-laundering, amongst other crimes, but offered to turn

The Mango Mystery

state-witness, and expose a large, organised criminal enterprise operating across the Southern States of the USA, in exchange for protection and a change of identity. The district attorney is considering this opportunity.

Jan van den Leuven escorted Zavier Zedanski back to Amsterdam to stand trial. They travelled via Heathrow, where Zedanski asked to use the toilet, a cubical, and so Jan unlocked the handcuffs, at which point Zedanski overpowered Jan van den Leuven and escaped.

After the inquest, Andrea returned to the UK but Joelle took a week's leave, to spend time with Douglas and Jasmine, before she and Douglas returned to the UK together.

On her return to the UK, Joelle reported to Scotland Yard. She was immediately summoned to a meeting with Derek Passmore and Barbara Green, who congratulated her for exposing the drug gang. She was promoted to the substantive position of Detective Inspector in the Kaetian Police Force. Derek then explained that, unfortunately, they would be losing her services in London, as the Commissioner had requested her immediate return to Kaeta to take up her new appointment.

Joelle only had a couple of days before she returned to Kaeta. Douglas remained in the UK for a little longer, to arrange their affairs before he flew out to Kaeta to join Joelle.

THE END

John de Caynoth

About the Author

Dougald Ballardie writes under the pen name, John de Caynoth. He retired following a successful business career to assist his wife running their equestrian training business and started writing to exercise his imagination and achieve an ambition.

The Mango Mystery is his second book and the second instalment of a trilogy about the turbulent and dangerous lives of the two characters Joelle and Douglas. He denies there is any similarity between himself and Douglas recognising that Douglas is much braver. He is currently completing his third book continuing the Joelle and Douglas trilogy, as well as researching his forth novel, a historical story of Protestants fleeing religious persecution in sixteenth century Europe.

John enjoys photography and his pictures of horses have been published in magazines and to illustrate the equestrian book written by Claire Lilley. His hobby is the restoration of classic cars and motorcycles and he is currently rebuilding a fifty-year old MGB and a now rare 1960's Suzuki motorcycle.

He lives with his wife Claire and their black poodle, Sammy, in a picturesque 350 year-old thatch cottage on the edge of Salisbury Plain in Wiltshire, England.

John de Caynoth February 2016
www.johndecaynoth.wordpress.co.uk

Printed in Great Britain
by Amazon